LOSS OF INNOCENCE

Center Point
Large Print

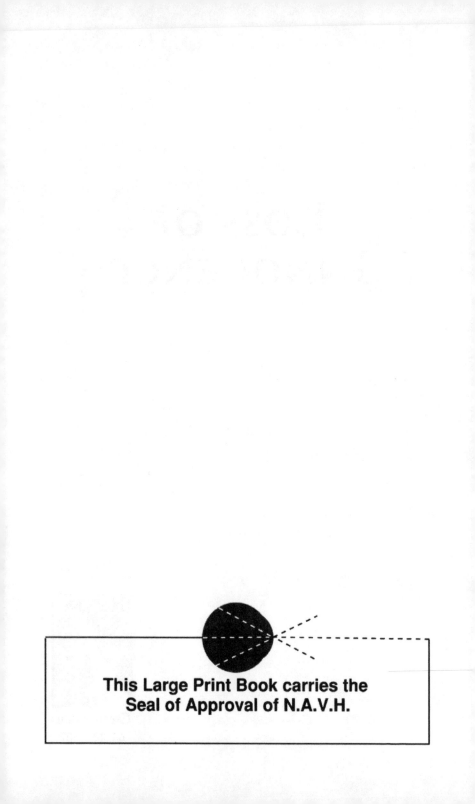

**This Large Print Book carries the
Seal of Approval of N.A.V.H.**

LOSS OF INNOCENCE

Richard North Patterson

CENTER POINT LARGE PRINT
THORNDIKE, MAINE

This Center Point Large Print edition is published
in the year 2013 by arrangement with
Quercus Publishing, Inc.

The text of this Large Print edition is unabridged.
In other aspects, this book may vary
from the original edition.
Printed in the United States of America
on permanent paper.
Set in 16-point Times New Roman type.

ISBN: 978-1-61173-944-2

Library of Congress Cataloging-in-Publication Data

Patterson, Richard North.
Loss of Innocence / Richard North Patterson.
pages cm
ISBN 978-1-61173-944-2 (library binding : alk. paper)
1. Families—Massachusetts—Fiction. 2. Young women—Fiction.
3. Family secrets—Fiction. 4. Martha's Vineyard (Mass.)—Fiction.
5. Large type books. I. Title.
PS3566.A8242L67 2013
813'.54—dc23

2013029059

For Vicki Kennedy and Phyllis Segal
and in memory of my friends
Ted Kennedy and Eli Segal

LOSS OF INNOCENCE

PROLOGUE

Two Women

Martha's Vineyard

September, 2011

Carla Pacelli and Whitney Dane had once loved the same man, one in his youth, the other in his final year, and had found their lives transformed. Now, forty-three years after Whitney's fateful summer, they sat behind the guesthouse of the summer home she had inherited from her parents, gazing out at the Atlantic, Whitney pensive, Carla pregnant with her lover's child.

Though the two women shared a quiet pleasure in the pristine August morning—a cloudless sky, light fitful breezes stirring the boughs of nearby oak trees, a thin sheen of silver-gray mist dissipating over white-capped aqua waters—Carla thought them an unlikely pair to share this history, or even this hour. A mere two years ago, Carla had been a striking presence on the screen, a lissome Italian American brunette with a carriage that radiated grace and vitality, dark intense eyes that seemed to look through whoever they turned on. Now she had the tempered beauty of a survivor, and the directness of her gaze was leavened by self-knowledge and a trace of sadness. Her parents were working class and, though she had trained her smoky voice to be more polished, it

11

retained trace elements of their Mediterranean intensity. She was not lightly educated—despite her immersion in drama, she had been an exceptional student in high school and at UCLA had a minor in psychology at which she had excelled. But because of her appearance, the impact of which obscured all else, beauty rather than intellect was what struck others at first glance, whether in person or on the screen.

Carla had been a serious actress, and her skills—which she still felt were under-appreciated—had focused her inherent ability to, as one network executive had put it, "pop through the lens into people's living rooms." But Carla now judged that woman an empty shell: the pressures of carrying a television series, and making movies during breaks, had led her to reach for the crutches of drugs and alcohol. The rabbit hole through which she had fallen—increasingly erratic behavior culminating in a sojourn at Betty Ford—had dimmed her intensity and poisoned her career. The Carla who emerged from rehab discovered that her manager, a thief himself, had parked her money with another thief, who made it disappear. With little but the determination to summon a stronger and more reflective woman capable of forging a new life, she had sought refuge on Martha's Vineyard, settling in Whitney's guesthouse through the good offices of friends.

When Carla arrived, Whitney was concluding a year in Paris, indulging her passion for French history and culture. At sixty-five, she was twice Carla's age, and while the deep-brown eyes that were her most attractive feature lent her round face an air of perception and good humor, she had never turned heads simply by entering a room. Nor was age and appearance their only difference. Whitney was a WASP, the daughter of privilege, and spoke with the flawless, slightly arid enunciation of the East Coast patrician. An accomplished novelist, she had managed at once to be well respected and widely read, not least for her grasp of the hidden recesses of human nature, which cut so close to the bone that readers might squirm in recognition, yet lacked the cruelty that might drive them away. Though Carla had not yet mentioned this, for fear of fawning, she deeply admired Whitney's writing. And she could not help but envy the older woman's air of settledness. Unlike Carla, Whitney had been disinclined to call attention to herself, preferring to let her novels speak for her. When interviewed—which she generally avoided—Whitney was tart, clear, and concise. But, again unlike Carla, her personal life remained her own.

The two women had never met. This morning, on returning from Paris, Whitney had called on Carla out of courtesy and, Carla assumed, a curiosity that was exceedingly well informed—

even in Europe, Carla's life on Martha's Vineyard had reached the tabloid media. All this because of Carla's involvement with a married novelist who was Whitney's age but twice as famous, whose life had ended in a fall under circumstances so murky that they had raised suspicions of suicide or murder. And so, once again, Carla found herself notorious, a fact that colored this encounter with considerable tension. Whitney Dane would know almost everything save the reasons for her actions, and Carla could only await her judgment and, perhaps, her expulsion from her guesthouse.

At first, the subject did not arise. Instead, the two women drank tea on the deck, the sun warming their faces. Politely enough, Whitney asked about her pregnancy, and how the guesthouse had suited her. Edgy, Carla kept waiting for the questions that never came.

Finally, she said bluntly, "I'm sorry I've become an embarrassment to you. And to say that I didn't mean to sound pathetic."

Whitney's smile, though ambiguous, was not unkind. "I understand more than you may think," she answered. "I knew him, you see."

The delphic remark puzzled Carla. "Who didn't?" she responded. "Even if you hadn't been neighbors."

Whitney's smile diminished, and her tone flattened out. "Actually, we rarely spoke. At least not for years."

Caught up short, Carla wondered what outrage of his had provoked this. That there had been one seemed certain, but given his proclivities she was reluctant to inquire. The keen look in Whitney's eyes revealed that she saw this. "No," she added, "he didn't proposition me at a cocktail party. As one look at you confirms, his esthetic standards became more rarified. The truth is that his wife and I became allergic to each other." She hesitated, then finished more softly, "A complicated story."

The change in Whitney's tone—at once bitter and rueful and valedictory—pricked Carla's curiosity. There was something this seemingly composed woman wanted to say, however reluctantly, and something else that made Carla— a stranger until now—a potential listener. "No surprise," Carla ventured. "He was a complex person."

For a moment, Whitney gazed into the distance, as if at her own past. "So were we all," she said, then turned to Carla. "Were you in love with him?"

"Yes." Intending to leave it there, Carla felt the need to explain. "Age softened him, and the cancer—facing death, really—sobered him. He could feel the window closing, that he'd leave nothing good behind him but the books he feared people would forget." She touched her rounded stomach. "We were his last hope, he told me."

"Not his wife? What an irony for them both."

This was said with what Carla took to be an unusual asperity, marbled with some deeper emotion she could not identify. Instinct told her to say nothing. "And how sad," Whitney added quietly. "The worst thing for him, I came to think, would be to face the void at the center of his all-too-eventful life. Though he concealed that awfully well."

With a sadness of her own, Carla remembered the man as she first knew him: his frame still robust; a full head of jet-black hair streaked with gray; the aggressive prow of a nose; dark, probing eyes; the sardonic, challenging smile of a movie pirate; a baritone voice; all combined with his brusque and flavorful speech to create a persona which, as he no doubt wanted, could fill a room —perhaps, as Whitney suggested, to camouflage the scars within that Carla had slowly discerned. Reading her face, Whitney shook her head in self-rebuke. "You're the party in interest here, not me. But his death seems to have shaken me more than it should. The other day, I found myself rereading my own ancient diary, written by a young woman who seems a stranger to me now. Page upon page was filled with him."

"I understand," Carla answered, unsure of what she was understanding save that it was important to Whitney. "I've come to know Adam, you see. We talked about his father quite a lot. Including the damage he caused within his own family."

Whitney's eyebrows raised. "Then Adam doesn't despise you? Despite his apparent loathing for Dad."

"No. Adam doesn't despise me."

"Nor you him, it seems."

At this, Carla looked directly into Whitney's face. "Far from it."

Whitney tilted her head, as though considering Carla anew. "So where is Adam roaming now?"

"Afghanistan. Working in agricultural assistance, he says. Not that I really believe that—there's this sense of alertness about him, like in a given circumstance he could be quite dangerous . . ."

"How like his father."

"I know. But with Adam, I think it's because he has to be, for reasons he can't reveal. Not because he wants to be."

Whitney regarded her with deep seriousness before a smile played across her lips. "I haven't seen Adam for a decade. In his twenties he seemed so like his father, ready to match himself against the world. But without the fatal product defects. Adam's the one who might be safe to care about."

Carla studied the deck. Softly, she answered, "I don't know that yet."

"But you want the chance. Even though you're carrying his brother."

The bald statement caused Carla to flinch with embarrassment. "Even so." Hoping to move past this answer, she ventured, "You said that you and Adam's father rarely spoke. But it seems you once knew him very well."

Whitney's eyes narrowed in reflection, and then she brushed away a tendril of steel gray hair. "Knew him?" she repeated. "Looking back, I barely knew myself. But there came a time when I learned a great deal about us both."

Carla watched her face. "If you don't mind, I'd like to hear about it. He changed my life, after all. But there are still so many holes and unanswered questions."

Whitney gave her a probing look. After a time, she said, "Yes, I suppose I do need to talk about him. And wouldn't he be pleased at that." She paused, adding dryly, "Under your current circumstances, I don't suppose you keep any wine around the place."

Carla smiled faintly. "No. Not a good idea for me."

Whitney sat back in her deck chair, as though trying to relax herself. "Then I suppose I can try without that."

Carla waited. Haltingly at first, then with the skill for narrative that underpinned her craft, Whitney Dane described the summer of her twenty-first year.

PART ONE

The Celebration

Martha's Vineyard

June 1968

One

In June, 1968, hours before the events that pierced her soul and scarred her generation, Whitney Dane would have said that her youth had been as blessed as her future promised to be. So as she walked the beach beneath her parents' summer home with her closest friend, Clarice Barkley—the first warming breath of spring in the air, the water of the Vineyard Sound a light, sparkling blue—this birthright informed her answer when Clarice asked curiously, "How are you feeling at this great crossroads of your life? Like the ingénue on the cover of American Bride? Or like you've been catapulted toward marriage still clutching your diploma, wondering how you got to be a grown-up?"

The tart phrasing, displaying an ironic turn of mind that Clarice tended to conceal, made Whitney smile as she considered her answer. "It's moment to moment," she confessed. "Depending on how good I am at suspending disbelief. A wife and mother is what Mom is, not me. But how can I not feel lucky? And now I've got four months with nothing to do but plan a perfect wedding on this perfect island. Unless it rains, of course."

"Even then," Clarice answered blithely, "I

imagine Peter will show up. He seems suitably besotted."

Whitney paused for a moment, a swift tug of honesty surfacing from the self-doubt at her core—she had always been the smart daughter, not the pretty one, with the pleasing but unremarkable face, and a sturdy figure which had always made her wonder at her genetic mismatch with her striking and willowy sister, their mother's ideal. "I still can't believe that someone like Peter was attracted to me," she confessed. "And now I'll have a life with him." She glanced at Clarice, adding dryly. "For one shining day in late September, hopefully sunny, Janine won't be the center of attention."

Clarice's smile at this was slightly sour. "Not that the crown princess won't try. I can imagine her using the rehearsal dinner to announce her engagement to Mick Jagger."

Her friend's jaundiced view of Janine warmed Whitney with its loyalty. "Mick Jagger?" she responded. "Dad wouldn't hear of it—you know how *he* is. And David Eisenhower is already taken."

Clarice shot her a wicked grin. "Thank God. Imagine an entire life spent in the missionary position. Not that our princess doesn't deserve it."

Startled by her friend's irreverence, Whitney laughed aloud, thinking that her luck included meeting Clarice in childhood. Among the Danes,

Clarice had become the unofficial third daughter, joining them on vacations and sharing their celebrations. On the Vineyard, the Barkleys owned the property next door, and Clarice had a standing entrée to appear at dinner unannounced. At twenty-two, she retained the careless insouciance of her class, a girl for whom the laws of gravity and commerce seemed suspended—in no rush to find a job, Clarice was spending the summer after her graduation from Wellesley on the Vineyard, sailing and swimming and playing tennis, with trips off-island to shop or see friends. At its end, she would be Whitney's Maid of Honor.

Clarice was a popular choice. Everyone seemed to like her—except, perhaps, Janine. Like Peter, Clarice was energetic, with a sense of fun, and, on the surface, disinclined to brooding or intro-spection. She had a pretty, sunny appearance, Grace Kelly with a touch of Doris Day, and people always invited her to their parties—her demeanor was cheerful, her manners impeccable, and she could be as good a listener as Whitney's own mother, a master of the art. Clarice drew boys while hardly trying; one whom Whitney had secretly liked had called Clarice "classy without being scary." Perhaps only Whitney saw the elusiveness that lay beneath. Others thought they knew her, but few really did; good grades and a well-crafted exterior concealed a subterranean wild streak and a keen sense of her social surroundings. Even for Whitney, at times it was impossible to decipher what Clarice Barkley was thinking or feeling. Her best friend, she had come to realize, was far more complicated than she seemed.

"What about you?" Whitney asked. "Is there anyone special? Or are you still searing the souls of the unwary?"

Stopping to look out at the water, Clarice dug her toes into the sand. "Why decide?" she responded delphically, then turned to her friend. "No offense, Whitney, but I'm glad that when I get married I'll have had sex with more than one man. I mean, don't you ever wonder what that would be like with someone different?"

"No offense, Clarice," Whitney replied mildly, "but I don't want to be promiscuous. I can only sleep with someone I really love."

By unspoken consent they turned to walk into the surf, feeling the cool ocean water on their ankles and calves. "Love," Clarice informed her friend archly, "is an elastic concept. There've been times when I was willing to love who I slept with, if that's what's required. I wasn't thinking about marriage.

"But after marriage sex becomes routine, and sleeping with other guys problematic. So I might as well enjoy it now, because that's not all I'm after in a husband. I'm not marrying some boy just because I like him inside me. I want a husband who's also a man." Glancing at Whitney, Clarice's eyes glinted with humor. "And please don't be shocked. These days shock is unbecoming unless you're our mothers."

"I'm not shocked," Whitney rejoined crisply. "I just don't want to be shocking."

Clarice gave a twitch of her tan, graceful shoulders. "In your position, I'd feel the same. I just hope you don't get restless, that's all. Imagining things isn't the same as doing them."

Whitney waded in up to her knees. "So maybe I'm just unimaginative," she said over her shoulder.

"You? I doubt it. So maybe having sex with Peter and imagining Paul Newman will work just fine." Clarice stepped, beside her. "So how *is* it with Peter? You never really say."

Whitney smiled a little. "Would you settle for 'sweet'?"

" 'Sweet'? That's lovely. But does the earth move? Or is it more like a mudslide?"

Folding her arms, Whitney replied with mock dignity, "I have nothing more to say, Miss Barkley. You'll have to rely on your own lurid fantasies."

To her surprise, Clarice did not respond in kind. Instead, she turned toward the sound, watching a sailboat in the distance. More seriously, she said, "I'm being kind of a pill, aren't I? Maybe I envy you a little."

"Why should you?"

Still watching the water, Clarice spoke more softly. "Your life is settled, all laid out in front of you. You have someone you love, who loves you. You don't have to wonder who he'll be, or if that man will want you, or how the two of you will live."

In faint surprise, Whitney studied Clarice's flawless profile. It was she who had always admired her friend's serene blond looks, her self-containment, her matchless ability to charm and engage others—especially men. "You can have your pick of guys," Whitney assured her. "All you have to do is choose."

"I suppose," Clarice replied in a distant tone. "But how will I know that he's the right one?"

Once again, Whitney felt her own good fortune. She, and not Clarice, was the one Peter Brooks had chosen.

Two

For the rest of her life, Whitney felt certain, she would recall the moment perfectly, and everything that followed.

They were in his dorm room at Dartmouth. It was a chill winter evening; snowflakes on the window melted into dots that blurred the darkness outside. Naked, she pulled the wool blanket up to her chin, watching Peter undress.

The weekend had followed the usual pattern. Like other women's colleges, Wheaton was a suitcase school: girls left for the weekend, or endured the consolation prize—a steak dinner on Saturday night—which exposed their datelessness. Boys seldom came to Wheaton: they were not allowed in the dorm rooms, and were less adaptable than women when it came to making conversation and fitting in with friends. Besides, alcohol was forbidden—this *was* a school for women, after all. Better to go where the guys were.

Whitney's suitemate, Payton Clarke, had their ticket to freedom—a car. So Whitney, Payton, and two other friends wrote their destination in the sign-out book and headed for Dartmouth, hopeful that, if delayed by love or folly past the Sunday evening deadline, they could sneak back through the windows of co-conspirators. Leaving the snow-covered campus, the girls had felt the elation of escape; Payton turned on the radio, and they began singing along with Aretha, the Beatles, or even dumb stuff like "Kind of a Drag" by the Buckinghams, which Jill's terrible voice made even funnier. They shared a prized invitation—Dartmouth Winter Carnival.

Not that these weekends were always a bargain. Nor was this one: as Whitney had anticipated, the huge bonfire that marked the weekend was followed by binge drinking at Peter's fraternity, during which several otherwise acceptable males devolved into buffoons with the wits of Neanderthals, an orgy of crudity which, for one guy, was capped by public retching. While Peter remained himself throughout, Whitney was happy to retreat to his room. Closing the door behind them, he left a tie on the doorknob to indicate the presence of a woman, assuring them an hour alone.

Though he undressed in front of her, a lingering modesty kept Peter from looking into her eyes; she could watch him unembarrassed, feeling a kind of wonder at their intimacy. His body was strong, yet lean, as if there were barely enough skin to cover his muscled frame. His blond curls were charmingly unruly, his blue eyes a window to what she knew to be an open heart, his smooth features engagingly complicated by a nose broken playing lacrosse. He was a boy other girls stared at. And now—at least for this time—Peter belonged to her.

She had met him the year before on a blind date. Though assured that Peter was "a doll," Whitney had approached the weekend with trepidation. He might not find her attractive; the doll might become a nightmare. In her parents' mind, attracting some Ivy League guy was a ticket to security. But in reality, you were stranded for the weekend, and guys at men's schools often treated women horribly—turning callous and trying to push them into sex. Among Whitney's friends it was known that a classmate had been raped at Princeton, triggering a nervous breakdown. This faceless Peter Brooks could become her enemy.

Whitney was nervous all the way to Dartmouth. When Peter called at the boarding house, she still felt queasy. But though he was as tall and handsome as described, instead of conceit there was a sweetness in his face. He did not seem disappointed that she was not prettier or slimmer. "I'm Peter Brooks," he said, and his easy manner and obvious sobriety filled Whitney with relief.

Throughout the weekend, he was attentive and thoughtful, always asking after her needs, what she might want to do. Though at first they struggled for conversation, his good nature made it easier, and gradually she felt comfortable with him. He took her to dinner and parties, including a smoke-filled bash where some of his fraternity brothers got stupefyingly drunk. But he kept his own drinking under control, and Whitney never felt abandoned. Though it was clear that Peter was a guy the other guys admired, he did not seem to notice. It was one of his friends, not Peter himself, who mentioned that he was a lacrosse star.

He was anyone's dream date, she realized by Sunday. So when he kissed her on the cheek, then asked if she would come back next weekend, Whitney was more than flattered. "Yes," she said simply. "I'd like that."

Now, head on his down pillow, Whitney smiled up at him. "You're beautiful."

Gently, he pulled down the comforter to look at her. "So are you."

Before, she would have been embarrassed. Peter was the only boy she had allowed to see her like this, and she vividly recalled her shame when, at Wheaton, the freshmen were marched to the gym and photographed nude to diagnose defects in their posture. Whitney's "defects" were round hips and full breasts, but she was mortified by rumors that guys from Dartmouth had stolen her class's pictures, imagining herself pinned to a corkboard while leering drunkards gave her a "D." When she had confessed this, Peter had assured her that the story was a myth. "If I'd seen your picture," he said lightly, "I'd have cut my classes and taken the bus to Wheaton."

Thinking of this, Whitney beckoned to him. "Come here," she said. "Before my nipples get cold."

Kneeling at the end of the bed, Peter kissed her stomach and breasts as he lay across her, kissing her deeply, lingeringly, before he slipped his finger inside her. "Yes," she murmured.

He filled her, moving gently at first, and then she felt the urgency in the thrust of his thighs and hips. Shutting her eyes, tried to focus on her own pleasure, urging the inside of her to tighten and find release. She was almost there when

Peter cried out, and she knew that it was done.

Whitney let her body go slack. Sometimes it worked, sometimes not. Though she had heard stories about boys who used their tongues, she could not yet bring herself to mention this. Instead, she focused on the familiar softness in his face, the warmth of knowing that her body had the power to do this.

Suddenly, he looked at her with new intentness. "Close your eyes, Whit." Complying, Whitney felt him stir, thought she heard the whisper of a drawer opening. Then she felt his lips light and playful, brushing her stomach. Her skin tingled—perhaps, this time, he would please her as she imagined.

Then Peter flicked his bedside lamp on. "You can open your eyes now."

Something small and light was resting on her stomach. She saw him smiling, then followed his gaze. A diamond ring circled her navel. To her startled eyes it looked perfect—not large or showy, but beautifully shaped, its facets sparkling.

"It's my grandmother's," he said. "Mom wanted you to have it. But you have to say you'll marry me."

Stupefied, Whitney found herself grinning until she thought she could never stop. "Are you kidding me?" she finally blurted. "I love you, and I'd love to marry you."

Hurriedly, she put on the ring, stretching out her

fingers for him to see. Suddenly they were hugging, rolling on the bed, laughing with the sheer joy of having each other. "Mrs. Peter Brooks," he murmured.

"Whitney Brooks," she amended. "I can't wait to tell Mom and Dad."

"Actually, I have. Your dad, anyhow."

For an instant, Whitney felt obscurely cheated; her father had participated in this moment before she had, a partnership of males. Just as quickly she reproved herself. Peter's father was dead; Charles Dane had lost any hope of a son after his wife's struggles in bearing Whitney. Yet her father had never betrayed any disappointment that she was not the boy he'd wanted, and it was obvious that he had liked her new guy at once. She was glad to have brought him Peter Brooks.

"How did you tell him?" she asked.

Peter grinned. "I met him for lunch at the Athletic Club over Christmas break. Then I asked him for your hand—and the rest of you, of course—just like a proper suitor should. I'm afraid I was pretty nervous. But he was so happy we killed a bottle of champagne."

Whitney imagined her father and his almost-son, enveloped in celebratory warmth. "But did he say anything, or did you just start drinking?"

"Actually, he told me that I was the son he'd never had. And that he'd done pretty well with who you'd dragged through the door." He hesitated, becoming serious. "He also said there was a job at the firm, if I wanted it."

Struggling to imagine Peter on Wall Street, Whitney was surprised, then not. "What did you say?"

"That I'd talk to you." He looked at her searchingly. "But really, it's a great opportunity. Your dad wouldn't ask if he didn't think I could do it."

Despite his confident tone, Whitney saw the uncertainty in his eyes, which she understood and shared. Though seldom harsh, Charles Dane judged younger men with a jeweler's eye—his approval once withdrawn was difficult to regain. Peter had gone through school being good at things—sailing, lacrosse, making friends, leading his teams to victory—without a clear vision of life after college. Though he applied himself to school with diligent effort, Whitney, a far better writer, had edited his papers. And the life both had led, she understood, might not breed her father's relentless drive.

"I'm sure you could do it," she temporized. "If that's what you wanted."

Peter seemed to sense her ambivalence. "But if I worked with your dad, would you be happy?"

He needed her approval, Whitney understood. "Of course," she assured him, and curled back into his arms. "So when should we get married?"

As if feeling a chill the room, he pulled the

blanket back over them both. "Pretty soon, I guess." He hesitated. "Like it or not, there's the draft to worry about."

Whitney felt a pall taint her happiness. The draft was a specter at Wheaton; it posed no danger to women. But President Johnson had ended grad school deferments—the draft calls were getting bigger, casting a shadow on their brothers and boyfriends. Whatever she thought of the war, Whitney felt it coming toward them.

"What can we do?" she asked.

"I don't really know. I've known guys who starved themselves, or said they were queer, or found some doctor to lie for them. One guy got deferred for acne—first time I ever wanted pimples. But I'm healthy as a horse, and I'm certainly not queer . . ."

"I'm glad of *that*."

He gave a perfunctory smile. "Anyhow, I talked to a draft counselor—a professor at school. Unless I go into the ministry—fat chance, huh—my best shot is the National Guard. Otherwise, I'm drafted."

"I don't want that," Whitney said, and then a simple truth struck her. "Do you know anyone who's actually gone to Vietnam?"

"No one yet. But pretty soon we will. Unless there's another baby boom. You still get a deferment for that."

It took a moment for Whitney to fathom his

meaning. "Are you saying we should have a baby?"

He shook his head, less in demurral than confusion. "Seems early, doesn't it. But I know you want kids."

They had talked about this in a casual sort of way, safely distant and abstract. Now it felt like a fist in Whitney's stomach. "I'm only twenty-one, Peter. This is all so new."

Peter took her hand. "I know. It's a lot for both of us. So first things first, okay? We can pick a date and think about kids later." He paused, then asked hastily, "How about this summer?"

"I'm going to Europe with Clarice, remember? We've been planning it since boarding school."

Thinking, Peter frowned. "Maybe your mom can put it together."

Whitney regarded him with fond exasperation. "You really are a guy, you know. You've got no clue at all what a wedding involves. Besides, it's my one and only wedding day."

"I get that, sweetheart. Honestly."

"I don't think so," she objected. "Your job is to show up and be handsome. Mine is to be frenzied from this moment until Dad gives me away, not to mention keeping my mother at bay. A wedding this summer will be like mapping out D-Day with Anne Dane hovering over my shoulder, issuing imperatives in that anxious tone of voice. And you'll be AWOL."

Peter bit his lip, failing to repress a smile. "Maybe September?" he ventured in his most contrite tone of voice.

Whitney considered this. "At least I'd have the summer," she said at length. "But what do I tell Clarice?" Feeling his glum silence, she answered her own question. "Of course, she'd be my Maid of Honor, and I'd try to spend time with her this summer. If she's still speaking to me, that is."

"Are you kidding, Whitney? She'll be thrilled."

"To miss the French Riviera? I doubt it. But she's always been a loyal friend."

Peter looked relieved. "Then it's September?"

For a moment, Whitney felt less like a newly minted bride-to-be than a wife, making practical decisions while mediating between the needs of those she loved. But the world outside this room had stopped indulging her fantasies about a perfect wedding, or even a last chance to savor freedom with her closest friend. "My parents will be thrilled," she told Peter. "And September on Martha's Vineyard is always beautiful."

Three

As Whitney and Clarice waded through the surf, the air became damper, the sunlight hazy. Over the water a stray shower fell from a wind-blown smudge of darkness amidst the filtered rays. Clarice gazed out at this with a mild distaste.

"To think," she remarked, "that this could have been the Mediterranean."

Whitney felt a wave of disappointment at their aborted plans. Turning from the water, she sat on a rock with room enough for her friend, feet resting on sand dampened by a receding tide. "What could I do? I didn't want to risk losing him before our life had even started. Starting a family, if that's what it takes, seems better than having no family at all."

Perching beside her, Clarice inquired, "Isn't that a tad melodramatic? He hasn't even got his draft notice yet. He's a long way from Vietnam."

"We can think that now. But once he's classified 1-A, the odds get a whole lot shorter." Whitney hesitated before giving voice to her fears. "I know he'd be brave and capable. But that's just it—I can see him doing something reckless to save somebody else."

"So maybe they'll stop the war?"

"Who's 'they'?" Whitney asked more sharply than she intended. "Nixon and Humphrey support it, more or less. McCarthy can't beat Humphrey, so that leaves Bobby Kennedy. The dirty secret I'm keeping from Dad is that I'm hoping Bobby wins today in California."

"My dad hates the Kennedys," Clarice said flatly. "He says their father was a bootlegger and a crook." She shrugged. "It's a class thing, I'm sure—Irish Catholics and all that. You know how they are in Boston."

"Blacks love Kennedy," Whitney replied firmly. "Chicanos, too. You can see them on TV mobbing his car, like he's all they've got left." She turned to Clarice. "Remember when they assassinated Martin Luther King?"

"I remember how upset people were at Wellesley. Most of them, anyhow."

The remark was not unkind, just dispassionate, as though Clarice were an anthropologist. But for Whitney the memory was piercing—girls crowded around the TV in Meadows South; black faces shouting or sobbing; newsmen barking updates that changed nothing. Whitney imagined the young black boy she was tutoring in Roxbury, and feared she would never see him again. "Who could black people believe in, I kept thinking. But there weren't many black girls at Wheaton, and I didn't know them well enough to talk about it."

Clarice glanced at her curiously. "So what got you into tutoring?"

"A suitemate talked me into going to an elementary school in Roxbury, so they assigned me a kid once a week." Remembering him, Whitney grew pensive. "James was nine years old and little, with this coiled hair and bright eyes. He loved to learn, and I didn't want to see those eyes go blank. So I kept showing up."

"But weren't you scared to go there?"

Whitney shook her head. "More startled. So many people were overweight, like their diets were terrible, and some were sick or missing teeth or crippled in some way. It was like I'd discovered a different species. Then I started grasping how little we see."

Clarice's brow knit. "What does Peter think about all this?"

"He's really not that political, even with the draft." Whitney smiled indulgently. "How many radical lacrosse players do you know? Anyhow, I don't think the antiwar movement has infiltrated Wall Street."

Clarice clapped her forehead in mock dismay. "How could I forget that my best friend's fiancé is now a pillar of finance?"

The jocular remark aroused Whitney's misgivings. Charles's initial comments about Peter had been provisionally approving. "He listens," Charles had said, "and asks good questions. Older men like that." But the judgment that truly mattered to Charles Dane—his own—had yet to be rendered. She dreaded the idea of Peter, found wanting, hanging on at her father's sufferance as his own confidence shriveled and died. "I don't know if this is Peter's life's work," Whitney objected. "He's barely started."

"He'll be fine," Clarice assured her. "How could he not with your dad there to guide him? Peter's lucky to have him, and so are you."

For a moment, Whitney was quiet. Not for the first time, she found herself wondering if Clarice envied Whitney her father. "I always thought our dads were a lot alike."

"In some ways," her friend replied in a clinical tone. "My dad is one of the nicest men you'd ever meet. But why wouldn't he be, when he inherited everything he has? Yours may have started at his father-in-law's firm, but he made it way more successful than it ever was, and more respected, too. Pretty admirable, I think."

Clarice was no reader of the *Wall Street Journal*, Whitney knew. This was a story told within her family—by her mother, never her father—and Clarice had heard it more than once. "I don't expect Peter to be like Dad," Whitney said. "I just hope our marriage is as happy as his and Mom's."

Perhaps she only imagined a cloud crossing Clarice's face. But what this disquiet might involve, Whitney could not tell. "I want it all, Whitney. I never wanted to get married just for the sake of being married."

Whitney chose not to hear this as a slight. "Some do," she replied good humoredly. "One girl at Wheaton got engaged her junior year, hoping to beat the rush. By that spring she'd set the wedding date for the June after graduation and planned everything out—an Episcopal Church in Vermont, caterers from New York, bride and bridesmaids' dresses from Paris, and the honeymoon in Fiji. By summer her intended groom had recoiled in horror and dumped her. And by November she'd found another guy to take his place—same date, church, caterer, bridesmaids, dresses, and tropical island. I thought her determination pretty impressive. Though I wonder if her substitute fiancé will take their wedding personally."

Clarice laughed. "There are better ways to get to Fiji. I hope *your* friends weren't so desperate."

"None 'desperate,' some marrying, others not." Whitney found she did not wish to mention the girls off on adventures—one in the Peace Corps, another moving to Australia, a third taking off for Morocco—free to do what they wanted, with not one of them looking over her shoulder. At Rosemary Hall, she had studied the literature and geography of France, imagining living there on her own or perhaps with Clarice. Instead, she was doubling down on her parents' life, trading a transient dream for a lasting one. "My friends run the gamut," she concluded. "What *I* want most, I guess, is to be a good wife and mother, more aware than Mom is. I don't think she always sees me . . ."

"Actually," Clarice put in, "she's a little obtuse about you both. She's got Janine confused with Jackie Kennedy, and you with Betty Crocker."

Whitney stood, ready to walk again. "Which makes Janine her favorite," she responded mildly.

"But Dad's a pretty great consolation prize. More important, Mom's a good and supportive wife. I want to be one, too—helping Peter socially, offering advice and encouragement and love, making a life for him and our kids."

The two friends resumed walking in a hazy mist. "And that's really *all* you want?" Clarice asked dubiously.

"Why not? I don't need to be remarkable outside our family. It is Janine who always needs attention—not just from my mother, but the world. Maybe I'm content to be the center of a family because I never felt like the center of my own."

Having said this, Whitney realized how true it was. But the troubled look in Clarice's eyes did not seem aimed at Whitney. "I'm sure families look different from the outside," she said at last. "But you've got your father, and you always knew that he'd make sure nothing ever went wrong, no matter what he had to do. Compared to that, your vain and flighty sister doesn't matter."

There was something nagging at Clarice, Whitney was suddenly sure—not envy over Peter, or regret over their lost trip—but maybe something within her own family, perhaps concerning her own father. Whatever it was, Whitney had begun to feel a watchful coolness beneath Clarice's easy manner, as though this clever girl felt the need to start looking out for herself.

"If real families were what Rockwell paints," Whitney contented herself with remarking, "there'd be no work left for psychiatrists or novelists."

Her expression still abstracted, Clarice did not respond before glancing at her watch. "We'd better change," she said abruptly, "before your dad and Peter show up. We're celebrating your engagement, remember?"

Four

That evening, the Dane family gathered at their summer home to mark the engagement of their younger daughter.

A sprawling white-frame structure from the late nineteenth century, topped by an atelier, it had been purchased in the twenties by Whitney's grandfather and renovated by her parents, who had modernized the kitchen and added a spacious sunroom and screened porch. Some of the original furnishings still remained, and the pieces Whitney's parents had added—wing chairs, couches, paintings of pastoral scenes, and carefully chosen antiques—made little concession to the more casual Vineyard style. Her father's distinctive improvements were high windows that offered a sweeping view of the grounds and ocean, and a guesthouse for the grandchildren that

Charles and Anne so fervently anticipated, to the point of promoting a jocular competition between Janine and Whitney for the honor of starting the next generation. Looking at the familiar faces as they gathered around the polished mahogany table—her family expanded by Clarice and Peter—Whitney felt the glow of knowing that she, not her sister, was the reason for this night. Then Janine—late as usual—burst into the room, seizing the attention of all.

Unlike Whitney, she had perfect posture that accented her willowy figure, an incandescent smile she could switch on and off, and a way of tossing her head back, as now, to display her perfect cheekbones and tawny mane of hair. Perhaps only Whitney and Clarice knew that Anne had purchased her daughter's perfect nose from a Park Avenue plastic surgeon, sparing Janine the curse of her father's more prominent one. After giving Peter a quick but warm kiss on the lips, which she proclaimed "sisterly," she air-kissed Clarice. With a certain lack of enthusiasm, Clarice responded, "If it isn't the 'late Miss Dane,' " before adding, "dazzling, as always."

"Oh, *you* are," Janine replied airily, "I'm so skinny I could shower in the barrel of Daddy's hunting rifle." She followed this persiflage with a glance at Whitney. "Of course the dresses I model aren't made for normal girls."

"Only for goddesses," Whitney agreed.

With a trilling laugh to acknowledge the truth of this, Janine glanced around the table. "Shouldn't we be drinking champagne?" she asked her father. "You're finally marrying one of us off, and it's my little sister. I need something to take the edge off my insecurity."

Even Whitney smiled at Janine's self-deprecation, so clearly crafted to suggest that it was nonsense. Glancing at Clarice, Whitney caught her friend coolly appraising Janine above the perfunctory play of lips. "You missed cocktail hour," Charles observed good-humoredly. "Doesn't that Tiffany watch also tell time?"

"Oh it does, Dad. Central Time."

Her father chuckled indulgently. "You're in luck, dear. As you'll note from the crystal, Mattie will be serving champagne. Now that you're here, we can all sit down."

Clarice sat across from Whitney, tan and trim in her sleeveless dress, the picture of a well-bred New Englander. Wearing a navy-blue blazer identical to her father's, Peter evoked an acolyte, taking in everything around them but, especially, Charles. To Whitney, this was a touching reminder of how young she and her fiancé were, and the role her father had come to play in Peter's life. His own father had died of a heart attack when Peter was fourteen, leaving his son well provided for, but without much guidance from a feckless mother stunned by her husband's death. Whatever her misgivings about his new employment, that Peter gravitated toward Charles was a gift to them both.

Her mother sat at the opposite end of the table, seated nearest Janine in an unspoken affinity group, her blond hair a perfectly coiffed artifice, her fine features flawed only by the slight bump in her nose, a blemish she had not permitted Janine. Anne's rationale had been that Janine was a photographer's model, occasionally appearing in magazines and more often the society pages, having developed an uncanny talent for striking a pose. But Anne's motives, Whitney perceived, went deeper than a career Janine would drop once she found a man who deserved her. Their entwinement seemed to have begun at her sister's birth, spawning Anne's current absorption in Janine's life, beneath which Whitney sensed an anxious need for Janine to epitomize the feminine role Anne embraced so completely. Whitney had once hoped to feel closer to her mother. But once Janine turned sixteen, Anne had focused on her sister's boyfriends, social life and sense of fashion, the vibrancy and allure she so often praised. Now she imagined Janine marrying someone prominent and powerful, a glamorous partner in a public life.

By contrast, Whitney had drawn her mother's attention chiefly because of her intermittent problems with weight. Nor did Whitney, who enjoyed books and literature, share her sister's and mother's interest in clothes or interior design, or in the artful arrangement of atmosphere, seating and guests that comprised the perfect dinner party. Whitney had come to accept that she would never quite gain Anne's approval, and thus might always feel a little outside the charmed circle of her parents and Janine.

At times Charles seemed to sense this. Though his tastes in books were those of a practical man—contemporary history or politics or business—he sometimes took her to readings by female writers which Whitney sensed he cared nothing about, asking her opinion so gravely that she wanted to hug him. More recently, he had come to the father-daughter dance at Wheaton, where dads dressed in tuxedos and became their daughters' dates for the weekend, a hoary tradition which excluded mothers and moved a suitemate to remark, "Paging Dr. Freud." But Whitney was proud of how pleased Charles looked, how other men deferred to him, and most of all, how attentive he was—as if, for once, no one else mattered. Instead of an odd memory, this became one of her warmest.

As Charles stood to offer a toast, Whitney gazed at him in the flickering candlelight with unalloyed affection. Beneath thick, curly chestnut hair barely flecked with gray was the countenance she had always loved, round and ruddy, featuring large brown eyes which could move from commanding to attentive to humorous at will. The planes of his face were broad, his slightly cleft chin pleasantly plump, reminding Whitney that she had always resembled her father rather too closely, her mother not at all. Were there perfect justice, she sometimes thought, she would have been his son—perhaps a business partner to be—rather than the younger, plainer daughter he praised for her stability and common sense.

These traits radiated from Charles himself, along with his self-confidence, keen mind, and the relentless ability to forge his path. To Whitney he epitomized an investment banker as she imagined the breed—a man of wisdom without illusions, cool headed and decisive, with a sense of probity that served him for the long haul. Working his way through school he had learned that time was precious, and became foresighted and proactive, never surprised or out of control. When Whitney went off to Rosemary Hall, he had told her, "Organize your time, and husband your resources. If I had to stay up the night before an exam, I'd already fallen short. It's as big a sin to be surprised by your own life as it is to let other people define it."

To Whitney's knowledge, the adult Charles Dane had never failed to control his own destiny, never allowed any obstacle to deter him. Along the way he built Padgett Brothers, her maternal grandfather's firm, into a power second to none. Charles had been born on the outside, without resources, and he was single-mindedly determined that no one in his family would ever feel as he had.

Now, as she had seen him do many times before, he looked to his right and left, silent until the others turned to him. Then he told them, "I look at this family tonight—including Peter and Clarice—and feel more fortunate than I can ever say."

His voice thickened with emotion as he gestured to indicate their surroundings. "All of this," he continued, "and whatever success I've enjoyed, would be nothing without you. Family alone is the true measure of a life." Meeting Anne's eyes, he added softly, "And of a marriage."

Across the table, Clarice watched him intently. "It all started," he went on, "with my brilliance— or sheer luck—in persuading Anne Padgett to marry me.

"When I doubted myself, she was there.

"When I was at odds with a superior, or a partner, she would seat him beside her at a dinner party, always knowing the perfect thing to say, the right time to listen, easing my way without seeming to try.

"When I worked to build the life I wanted for Janine and Whitney, Anne made certain that they were safe, secure, and healthy in mind and body."

As tears misted her mother's eyes, Whitney dismissed her own petty feelings of neglect. "By saying that life is nothing without family," Charles said emphatically, "I'm also saying that I'd be a far lesser man without Anne. For that I will be forever thankful. And so," he told Peter, "will you."

As Peter smiled, her father faced Whitney. "You have a fine mind, a great heart, and a strong character. You will be the core of a new family, true north for your sons or daughters. And if my experience is any guide, you'll work more than a few improvements on your husband." Amidst appreciative chuckles, he added dryly, "Not that you aren't perfectly adequate, Peter.

"I will admit to a few misgivings," Charles elaborated with mock sternness. "You're too tall, more than a bit too good-looking, and far too adept at snagging a lacrosse ball. By comparison I'm shorter, stouter, and have what some tart-tongued girl once called the face of an amiable peasant. Most embarrassing, you threaten to eclipse my lifetime quest to lay a golf club on a stationary ball. Whoever contrived evolution ignored the concept of simple fairness."

Whitney glanced at her mother, who smiled back in complicity. That Charles did not mean a word of this self-depreciation did not detract from its charm—as Anne often said, her husband excelled at playing Cary Grant. Then Charles addressed Peter with renewed seriousness. "Truth to tell, I'm feeling especially lucky in you. Given the qualities of my daughters, I never regretted not having a son. But now I have one— a companion in arms, and someday a partner." His tone lightened again. "Not to mention a much needed source of gender balance in a household where I've felt bound hand and foot like Gulliver among the Lilliputians. And Whitney's mother and I can hardly wait to meet the children who will be the joyous culmination of a life well lived." Extending his glass, he concluded, "On our behalf, I wish you, Peter, and you, Whitney, all the happiness we've enjoyed—and more."

As the others raised their flutes of champagne, Whitney felt a lump in her throat. "I don't know what to say," she managed. "But if we can be like you and Mom, we'll feel incredibly lucky."

As her father's eyes lowered, a sign of emotion, Clarice appraised him over the rim of her glass, reminding Whitney of the envy she sensed in her friend. Then Peter joked appreciatively, "Is it too late to ask you to be my best man?"

"*And* give away the bride?" Charles rejoined. "That would require a certain agility. Though I've always tried to make my own rules."

"You don't know how true that is," Whitney told Peter. "Best to keep him in his place."

"Don't be hasty," Charles admonished them. "I didn't want to tell you until I was sure, Peter. But the head of the Connecticut National Guard is a neighbor in Greenwich. I've spoken to him, and there seems to be a place for you. The firm will give you whatever time you need to fulfill your obligation."

Stunned, Whitney saw Peter's shoulders sagging with relief. "Thank you, sir."

"I didn't want you to worry," Charles told Whitney in a gentler voice. "Too many friends died in my own war, leaving widows and sometimes children. To see that happen to you would break my heart."

A wave of gratitude overcame Whitney. Seeing Clarice's ironic smile at her, she briefly wished she had known this before canceling their trip, then had the stray, superstitious fear that some less fortunate young man might die in Peter's place. But such thoughts were unfair to Peter, and to the father who must love her as much as she loved him. Once again, Charles had arranged life for the benefit of those within his charge. "Thank you, Dad," she echoed.

At the corner of her vision, she saw Janine pour herself a glass of wine.

Five

The dinner flowed easily, as did the cabernet, the conversation festive and light. Over the dessert wine, Charles turned to Peter, "It just occurred to me. If I can arrange it, would you enjoy meeting Richard Nixon?"

"How?"

"I've been raising a little money for him," Charles responded comfortably. "One of the venues is a private dinner in Manhattan. I'm sure there'll be room for you."

This understated her father's efforts, Whitney knew from her mother, as well as his aspirations —Charles had solicited a small fortune from friends and, though he dared not admit it, hoped for a prominent position at Treasury, perhaps even a cabinet post. "I'd like that," Peter said appreciatively, then glanced at Whitney with a droll expression. "Do you think he can win? I know at least one person who doesn't."

Charles gave his daughter a quizzical look. "Why not, Whitney?"

Whitney struggled to express her sense of a man she didn't know. "He just seems like a prisoner in his own skin, as though he has something to hide. And when he smiles, it's like someone is sending a signal to his brain, telling him to move his lips."

"That's a lot of similes for one politician," Charles responded amiably. "In that spirit, let me try one I just heard: that watching his former opponent—that dunderhead George Romney— run for president was like watching a duck try to make love to a football."

Whitney had to laugh. "All I remember is Romney saying he'd been brainwashed into supporting the Vietnam War."

"Deadly," Charles concurred. "Though in Romney's case, a light rinsing would have sufficed."

"Really," Anne told her husband. "You're being unkind. And that analogy about the sexual talents of ducks creates a rather unwelcome visual."

"Agreed," Janine said, refilling her wine glass. "Can that even be done?"

Clarice smiled at Charles. "Not easily, I imagine, and not well. But your dad is a man of wide experience."

"With ducks?" Janine inquired innocently. "Or footballs?"

"Only with ducks," Charles said reprovingly. "At feeding time in Central Park, when you were too little to speak. I'm growing more nostalgic by the minute."

"You precipitated all this," Anne pointed out.

"So I did," Charles allowed. "But my real point that the country needs a man of judgment and experience. The last four years have unleashed a terrible restiveness: antiwar demonstrations, blacks burning their own neighborhoods after that lunatic shot King, a general erosion of the standards governing our behavior. Thank God these trends don't include the young people at this table."

Whitney shot a wry look toward Clarice, who ignored it. "How do you know?" she inquired of her father. "And how is electing Richard Nixon going to stop college kids from having sex or smoking pot while they watch Ronald Reagan and a chimpanzee in Bedtime for Bonzo?"

"That's a frivolous remark," Charles responded mildly, "if an amusing one. Reagan is governor of California, after all. As for Nixon, he stands for traditional values—like respect for law—while the Democrats are hostage to forces that care about nothing but their own grievances, real or imagined." His voice gained force and authority. "Have you watched those scenes in California, mobs of Mexicans and blacks nearly tearing Kennedy's clothes off as he reaches for their hands from an open convertible? Does that seem like a president to you?"

Furtively, Whitney tried to gauge Peter's reaction. But her fiancé regarded Charles with his usual respect. Turning to Whitney, he said, "I'm with your dad on this, Whit. Stirring people up like that is the opposite of what we need. Does that really seem like a president to you?"

"Maybe he seems like one to those 'mobs of blacks and Mexicans,' " Whitney responded to both men. "Have either of you looked at their faces?"

"Yes, and it scares me," Charles rejoined, then spoke more deliberately. "I know this view isn't popular with the radical young. But blacks will get what they want, in time. Disorder only stirs up hatred."

Glancing around the table, Whitney saw the others watching her with a look of reserve. More tentative, she asked, "How long were they supposed to wait, Dad? I mean, would you want to be black?"

"I don't know, Whitney," her mother interjected. "I think of Billie, our housekeeper, for whom her work is a matter of pride. What is so wrong with being a credit to one's race, and why should that term excite derision, rather than aspiration?"

For Whitney, the mention of Billie stirred feelings she could not discuss. In her youth this practical woman had treated Whitney with watchful affection, an understanding that sometimes surpassed that of Whitney's mother. She had a wicked sense of humor leavened with empathy—during Whitney's touchy adolescence, Billie had taught her to dance, causing Whitney to imagine Billie's very different world in Harlem, from which she commuted to the cosseted white enclave of Greenwich. Billie, she came to understand, was trying to compensate for her mother's concentration on Janine. "We just don't know black people," she told Anne. "We can't sit here at this table and pretend we do."

"But when did you become so liberal?" Janine asked.

Nettled, Whitney answered, "I've just been watching, that's all. In between reading fashion magazines."

Across the table, Clarice's lips twitched before she glanced at Charles. "I don't mean to irritate you," Janine retorted. "But Dad has been watching much longer than either of us."

"A painful truth," Anne interposed. "Which also implicates me. But I agree with your father, Whitney. It's deeply unsettling to watch your generation take to the streets."

Charles nodded. "I don't mean to sound as ancient as everyone suggests. But enduring a depression and a world war taught the value of discipline and perseverance, and of ending what aggressors start. All too often I don't see these values in the young people who protest the war while our soldiers are fighting and dying."

In the guttering candlelight, Whitney looked toward Clarice. "Just this afternoon, Clarice asked if I knew someone who'd actually fought in Vietnam. Does anyone here?"

"Leave me out of this," Clarice said, raising her hands in mock surrender. "I'm a pacifist."

A shadow crossed Peter's face—guilt, Whitney felt certain, about the exit from danger that Charles had secured for him. Perhaps noting this, Charles told Whitney, "If it helps, I've told Nixon he should abolish the draft. Then all these 'idealists' who protest the war would return to their normal lives, leaving the fighting to volunteers."

To the least fortunate, Whitney wanted to retort, *and for what?* The photo of the Vietnamese president's brother-in-law shooting a Viet Cong prisoner in the temple had jarred her deeply, and the weekly body count of enemy dead on the evening news suggested to Whitney that in only a year we had dispatched an entire country. "I don't understand all this," Janine was telling her. "We're a business family, after all—we owe our existence to our grandfather's firm, that Dad made even better. I don't think any of us want that taken away."

By whom? Whitney wondered. Janine was glib, but her intellect brittle—she knew just enough about current events to slide through at a cocktail party. But she avoided serious discussion, often through strenuous, if supposedly charming, efforts to divert the conversation to herself. At bottom her political and social views were what she imagined Charles's to be. What else could a girl do, Whitney thought acidly, when her father's sizeable donation had slipped her into Vassar, commencing an education to which she had remained largely inured.

By contrast, Whitney deeply valued her four years at Wheaton. Granted, applying had been a last stab at pleasing her mother, a devoted alumna, who adored her time there and relived it through frequent reunions with classmates. But Whitney was also drawn by its pristinely New England campus, the oaks and evergreens amidst rolling lawns and red brick buildings with white pillars, the deeper sense that this was a place dedicated to educating bright young women barred from attending the all-male bastions of Harvard, Yale, Princeton, and Dartmouth. Her first day had been somewhat disheartening: she and the other new girls wore white dresses to a convocation where Wheaton's president, a bow-tied patrician named William Courtney Hamilton Prentice IV, told them that Wheaton's purpose was to educate prospective mothers, the better to raise the next generation of children. No feminist, during the holidays President Prentice sat atop a platform in the gym as he read "A Child's Christmas in Wales," to girls in robes and pajamas. But the professors were there to encourage these women to grow. Free from the scrutiny of males, Whitney had begun to think for herself. Out in the world women faced barriers, everyone knew, but the boldest believed they could, in the words of her friend Payton Clarke, be "more than the charm on the arm," a decorative helpmate. Whitney too had glimmers of a different life, encouraged by a creative writing professor who suggested that she should keep on writing short stories. Though Whitney could not quite believe it, she cherished the compliment.

"A business family?" she inquired of her sister. "What does that mean, exactly? I don't remember Mom and Dad issuing me a briefcase with my diapers."

Janine waved a hand. "You know very well what I mean."

But do you? Whitney wanted to ask. Janine's fix on the world changed from moment to moment, her account of the same people and situations oscillating wildly, depending on what she wished reality to be, or how she wished others— especially Anne—to see her. It was tiresome, Whitney thought, before catching herself. It was bad enough to disagree with her father, worse to spoil this dinner by exposing her sister's shallowness of thought. Already, Peter was fidgeting with his dessert fork.

"Janine's right," she told her father equably. "There ought to be some good in being older, including the graceful silence of a grateful daughter."

"I appreciate your passion," Charles said, his face brightening, "as well as your forbearance." He smiled at Peter. "Whitney's notions of equity developed early. When Janine was seven and Whitney was five, Anne and I paid Janine to watch her little sister while we went to a cocktail party next door. When Whitney found out we'd given Jeanine a quarter for babysitting her, she demanded a dime for having to be the baby."

Whitney was never sure whether this tale was meant to indicate her jealousy, compliment her precocity, or intimate that she retained a five-year-old's sense of justice. But everyone laughed. Squeezing her hand, Peter asked, "Is that true?"

"So I'm told," Whitney said. "In my version, I demanded a dollar for putting up with Janine."

At once, Whitney felt the others relax. "I almost forgot," Charles said, absently fishing into his coat pocket to retrieve a key chain with two keys, brass and silver. He stood, placing the keys in Peter's hand.

As the others watched, Whitney's fiancé stared at the keys with a pleased but puzzled smile. "What are they for, sir?"

Charles shook his head. "I suggest you take Whitney to the northeast corner of Madison Avenue and Sixty-fourth. If you need a clue, look for the engraved gold plate beside the door of an apartment building. The one that reads, MR. AND MRS. PETER BROOKS."

Whitney was speechless. She had imagined looking with Peter for a place in the West Village, closer to the offices of Padgett Brothers. Gazing up at Charles, Peter flushed. "I can't think of anything adequate to say."

Anne, Whitney realized, was studying her face. Following his wife's gaze, Charles said in a mollifying tone, "Perhaps I shouldn't deprive you two of the fun of house-hunting. But that's the building where Anne and I lived until Janine was two years old. We have so many happy memories."

"As well you should," Janine told her father. "But the plaque should read BIRTHPLACE OF JANINE DANE."

Clarice grinned at her across the table "Really, Janine, envy is so unbecoming."

To Whitney, this seemingly flippant barb at Janine concealed an effort to dispel the awkwardness of Whitney's silence. Catching the spirit, Janine rolled her eyes, tossing her hair in a parody of her own vanity. "Yes," she sighed, "I suppose my matchless beauty should be enough."

With this Whitney stifled her ambivalence, speaking the words she knew her father needed to hear. "It's the gift of a lifetime," she assured him. "Knowing that you and Mom started there makes it all the more special."

With obvious pleasure, Charles raised his glass. "To the marriage of a lifetime," he toasted.

Six

After dinner, Charles invited Peter to indulge in a snifter of Armagnac on the open-air porch—a 1923 Laberdolive from Gascony, which he and Anne had discovered while celebrating their twentieth anniversary in France, and so reserved for the most special occasions. Snifters in hand, he found Whitney gazing out the window of the dining room, and paused. "I don't want to stifle you," he said apologetically. "But the comfort we enjoy at our dinner table will not always be available in the social world of Peter's business. Like it or not, he won't be making his career among avatars of Bobby Kennedy."

Despite his gentle delivery, Whitney felt patronized. "I know that," she said stiffly.

"I'm sure you do," her father responded with the same paternal calm. "Nonetheless it's awkward to disagree with your husband in front of others, especially when it's a matter of first impressions. Most often you'll be the youngest woman at the table. As you and Clarice were tonight."

Still touchy, Whitney heard—or imagined—a tacit comparison. "Clarice barely said a word."

Charles smiled faintly. "A sign of her social intelligence. Including, I thought, one helpful intervention. She didn't want to attenuate any discord . . ."

"Especially when she has no opinion."

The remark was sharper than Whitney had intended. Charles regarded her closely. "As Clarice remarked to your sister, Whitney, jealousy is unbecoming—especially of your closest friend. It shouldn't threaten you to acknowledge that Clarice has considerable tact and acuity, and deserves an enviable place in the world. Even at the price of elevating some benighted male." He signed with resignation. "A somewhat thankless job, many say these days. But helping a husband's career is no small thing. I've seen unhappy women—alcoholic, neurotic, or just plain shrill—derail a spouse at crucial moments. And others whose touch with people eases the way with such grace and subtlety that no one discerns the art in it."

Suddenly, Whitney imagined herself in finishing school, learning to ease the way of men. "Like Mom."

Charles gave a slight but emphatic nod. "As I made clear, I never forget what I owe her. Nor will Peter."

Unsure of what to say, Whitney lowered her eyes. Gently, Charles kissed her forehead. "I'm very happy for you, and sorry if I upset you." He paused again, perhaps waiting for her to speak, then went off to join Peter.

Whitney faced the living room. Clarice and Janine were there, her sister sipping port and conducting what appeared to be a somewhat one-sided conversation. Feeling Anne at her side, Whitney sensed that she was the object of a parental pas de deux. Preempting this, she inquired softly, "Have you ever felt stifled, Mom?"

Anne's puzzled look contained a hint of asperity. " 'Stifled'?" she repeated. "Lord no. Your father has given me a wonderful life—love, children, and more privilege than even *I* could imagine. Never once have we disagreed about anything fundamental. Instead I was free to fill the role most natural to women." Her voice eased. "To these so-called feminists, I know, that sounds like a gilded cage. But I've had a life any generation of women in the history of the world would have envied—freedom from drudgery and enslavement, the dangers of childbirth, or the ravages of disease. Within my area of responsibility, I was autonomous, a full and equal partner. You and Janine, I devoutly hope, got the best of us both."

Beneath this statement, Whitney sensed, lay an inquiry she was not inclined to acknowledge. Instead, she asked, "But when you were supervising Billie, or seeing to our activities, didn't you ever want to be doing something else?"

"No," Anne replied firmly. "I was doing what I wished my own mother had been able to do for me. Watching over you was all I wanted, and more than I'd had."

Though Anne seldom spoke of it, Whitney understood that Elaine Padgett's death from the ravages of cancer, as the fourteen-year-old girl watched with helpless dread, was central to forming the mother she knew. Curious, Whitney asked, "Was that why you and Dad had Janine so soon?"

Perhaps because of Whitney's quiet tone, or the privacy created by candlelight and shadow, Anne seemed to relax. "This may sound odd to you, but I'd wanted children for as long as I can remember. For a woman not to, I think, betrays a terrible selfishness. And once you girls were born, I had the luxury of caring more about you and your father than myself. It felt quite liberating, really."

The remark surfaced a memory that Whitney had not parsed for years. Well short of adolescence, Janine was pushing a toy baby carriage and baby down the driveway. Watching through the kitchen window, Anne had mused to her husband, "The maternal instinct comes early, doesn't it?" Hearing this, the child Whitney had wondered when those feelings would bloom inside her, and then wondered at Janine's. Given that Janine often ridiculed or picked on her, Whitney hoped that she would be nicer to her kids.

"I had a professor," Whitney told Anne, "who

questioned all that. She argued that women aren't discontent because of some personal or psychological problem, but because of societal assumptions that put them in a straightjacket."

Her mother turned to her with eyebrows arched. "I don't know your professor, Whitney. But I once saw Betty Friedan on television. A hideous-looking woman, obviously compensating for her unhappiness through a sharp and aggressive manner. I would have felt sad for her but for all the women she'd confused in order to justify herself. I wonder if she likes men at all."

Though Anne was trying to be good-humored, Whitney heard an undercurrent of anger. "Professor Claymore wasn't like that, Mom. She has a husband, but she also has a career."

"And so do I, Whitney. But mine acknowledges that men and women are different." She paused, her manner becoming patient and tutorial. "Early on, I set out to establish my own relationship with your father's business associates. One way was to ferret out their interests, then ask questions that allowed them to reveal themselves.

"The men were often quite different, and sometimes difficult, which required me to be a bit of a chameleon. So it was better if whoever the man was never asked a single question about me, but left knowing that he'd had a fascinating conversation with an intelligent and sympathetic woman." Anne smiled reflectively. "If you know men at all, you'll be wholly unsurprised by how well that works."

"But didn't you ever want to tell them what you thought?"

"Why would I?" Anne's voice softened. "However I appear, I'm a very private person. I never really wanted people to know that much about me. If you're a woman that's easier to get by with."

"And men are different."

"Oh, yes. Your dad needed to be known, and to make a name in business. Not just because he wanted to build the firm, but because that was his essential nature. He arranges his surroundings as he wants them to be." Anne's eyes crinkled with amusement. "In his benign way, my father said that Charles was heaven-sent to keep our family's blood from thinning out. Looking at our family tonight, he's certainly done that. You girls were all the credentials I ever needed."

For an instant, Whitney chafed at the word "credentials." But what followed was an intuitive sense of her mother's loneliness, even her need for Janine as a surrogate. Without quite knowing why, she drew Anne to her, feeling her mother's instinctive resistance to closeness, perhaps fear of vulnerability, before she yielded to her daughter's embrace.

"I love you, Mom," Whitney told her.

Seven

As Whitney entered the living room, Janine turned to her, eyes alight, body tensile. "Let's go out, Whitney."

From the couch, Clarice gave her friend a wry look. "Where?" Whitney asked in her most dubious tone.

"Aren't there clubs on this island? Here there's nothing but the sound of crickets."

"Whitney likes the crickets," Clarice advised her. "This *is* her engagement we're celebrating, after all."

"So bring Peter," Janine urged her sister. "I'm sure he'd like to hear some music, maybe dance a little."

"For Peter," Whitney answered, "dancing means letting me circle him like a maypole. Anyhow, I think we're headed for a quiet evening. While we're listening to the crickets, maybe we can look up at the stars."

Janine frowned, tossing down her port before spinning on Clarice. "Come on, Clarice—let's go to Edgartown."

Clarice favored Whitney with a martyr's thin smile. With preemptive firmness, she told Janine, "Only if I drive."

Triumphant, Janine stood at once. "I'll go

freshen my makeup," she said and hurried from the room.

Watching this, Whitney murmured, "How can anyone be that restless."

"The real problem," Clarice responded glumly, "is that she can't be restless alone."

"You really don't have to do this, you know."

"And leave her to badger you and Peter? Just don't sit me next to her at the wedding. I haven't the stamina."

"You have my blood oath," Whitney pledged. "But if you really need a buffer, bring someone."

For an instant, Clarice looked oddly vulnerable, then gave a dismissive shake of her head. "At this particular moment, there's no one I can imagine running the gantlet of our parents."

"Maybe not now. But for you, four months is a lifetime."

"For me, Whitney, the next four *hours* will be a lifetime."

Brighter-eyed than before, Janine marched into the room and headed for the front door, saying over her shoulder, "Let's go, Clarice."

"Adventure calls," Clarice said to no one in particular. "I can hardly curb my excitement."

She followed Janine, each weary step miming the resignation of a death row prisoner in a thirties movie, trudging toward the electric chair. Recalling with some guilt her uncharitable remarks to Charles, Whitney reflected that her best friend deserved a better friend.

Alone with Peter in the guesthouse, Whitney described Clarice's painful sacrifice. "Maybe Clarice will meet a guy," he suggested helpfully. "To hear your mom, Janine draws them like flies."

"Does that include you?"

He lay back, head propped on his pillow, as though considering the question. "Can't see it, Whit. Your sister wears me out. There's nothing peaceful about her."

"But to look at?" Whitney persisted.

"Maybe for some other guy. But to me she looks unreal, like some girl in a perfume ad. Now if you asked me about Clarice . . ."

"She's not interested," Whitney cut in tartly. "At least not yet. She'd want to be sure you'd ripen into a titan of Wall Street. Besides, I hear she's a real taskmaster in bed."

Peter sat up, resting on his elbow. In feigned challenge, he said, "You don't think I'm up to it?"

"I don't know yet," Whitney said, and felt champagne and wine overcome her reticence. "She might want you to use your tongue."

He looked up at her in surprise, intrigued and a bit embarrassed. "You guys actually talk about that?"

It was too late to back off, Whitney realized.

Sitting beside him, she said primly, "In a scholarly sort of way."

Peter took her hand. Hesitant, he offered, "You'd like that, I guess."

Whitney felt herself flush. "I think so. After all, you're the only guy I've been with."

Peter's face softened. "I know that. But I can't do it while you're dressed."

Squeezing his hand, Whitney stood to lower the blinds and close the curtain. A single lamp cast shadows across the brass bed. She sat beside him again, wordless.

Kissing her gently, Peter reached for the zipper on the back of her dress. "I've never done this."

"I know."

Naked, they lay facing each other, Peter's lips brushed her nipples, then her stomach. Lying back, Whitney opened her legs.

Tentative, Peter moved his head. She felt his tongue flick once, withdraw, then flick again. Sensing his reluctance, Whitney tried to aid her own excitement by imagining a stranger who had no inhibitions. That she could summon no image but Peter frustrated yet comforted her.

At last, eyes shut tight, she began to feel the pleasure she had hoped for, murmuring softly. Misunderstanding, Peter stopped. For a moment, Whitney tensed in frustration. Then she stretched her limbs and then reached out for him, concealing her disappointment. They had a lifetime, after all.

Later, they lay holding hands as they gazed up into semidarkness. "Do you think I'm a coward?" he asked.

Whitney tried to decipher this. "About the draft? It's me who's the coward, sweetheart. I can't imagine losing you."

Peter rolled onto his side, looking into her face. "But what must your dad think? After all, he served in World War II."

Whitney chose not to mention how much the draft had haunted him, or that this had prompted their September wedding. "Dad loves you," she assured him. "He did this for himself as much as you." But nothing she said, Whitney knew, could change the uncertainty beneath his careless good looks and prep school air of confidence, or her unspoken reservations about Peter's attempt to follow her father's path.

Quiet, she thought about what had drawn Peter to her. When she had finally dared to ask, months after they had first met, he had said, "To start, I thought you were cute and smart—and quiet, in a nice way, not trying to show off. But pretty soon I realized how special you are." He paused, trying to find words for feelings deeper than any words he had. "Ever since I met you my life is so much better. To me, no one else could ever be like you."

For a time, Whitney had wished that Peter could conjure some magic phrase to make her specialness seem real. But she came to understand that they completed each other. It was Peter who got Whitney out of her books and into nature; he was always up for an adventure—skiing or whitewater rafting, or a hike in the wooded hills of New Hampshire. Generous and open-hearted, he allowed Whitney to see herself not as the less-favored sister, but in the mirror of a lover's eyes. In turn, Whitney helped him surface thoughts that had been hidden; coaxed him to deal with conflict rather than avoid it; showed him how to prioritize the scholastic demands that sometimes threatened to overwhelm him. Someday, Whitney had hoped, she could help Peter channel his cheerfully competitive nature into a career that was his own.

Peter understood his lack of clarity. Before taking the job at Padgett Dane, he had mused on this aloud. "I'm not sure where I'm going," he confessed. "Whenever I picture the future, I see a comfortable house, and kids and weekends on the Vineyard, golfing or walking the beach or sailing with other couples. What's harder to come up with is what I do from nine to six on weekdays. When I'm on the lacrosse field, or with friends, I know what I'm about. But pretty soon I won't."

For Whitney, this kindled a new thought. "Did you ever think about coaching?"

Peter looked perplexed. "Not really. Growing up, everyone I saw was like my dad or yours. The only coaches I knew were the ones I had."

"But you liked them, right?"

"The good ones, sure. They encouraged me in all sorts of ways."

Whitney felt the stray thought ripening. "It just feels like you, Peter. Maybe you should consider it."

But now, Whitney thought as she lay beside him, their future was resolved—free from the uncertainties against which Charles had protected them. For another wistful moment, she wished that the current of her life were not moving quite so swiftly.

"When you imagine our life," she asked him, "how do you imagine *me?*"

The question seemed to puzzle him. "As my wife," he answered. "As a mom. Helping me the way you always do. You're in every picture I come up with."

"But not at work. The Dane in that picture is my dad. So what am *I* doing between nine and six?"

Peter frowned. "I guess you're reading, or with the kids, or girlfriends. What my mom did."

"That's a role, Peter, not a person. And I'm certainly not your mom."

Peter scanned her body. "God, I hope not," he said with a quiver of feigned horror. "I've never seen Mom naked. But seriously, what do you want to do?"

Whitney hesitated. "A lot of the things you mentioned, I'm sure. But maybe I'll try to write."

"Write what?"

Uncertain, Whitney struggled to describe an image of herself so tenuous that it seemed beyond her gifts. "Stories," she confessed. "Things I just make up out of what I know or see."

"Will you have time for that?"

"Hard to imagine, isn't it? But maybe I can give up bridge club."

Peter laughed out loud. "Touché, Miss Dane. Would you like me to make an oinking sound?"

"I thought you just did."

"Nope. That was the whimper of a lapdog, saying, 'whatever you do is fine with me.' "

"Sorry I misheard," Whitney said unrepentantly. "So where do we live once I've had our triplets? Still in the city?"

"I haven't gotten that far. But maybe in Greenwich, like your folks." He hesitated, then added with youthful resolve, "At least if I do well enough. After all, look at how happy your parents are."

In her silence, Whitney recalled her father's toast, the conversation with her mother. Kissing him, she said, "They are, aren't they."

Eight

Later that night, Peter and Whitney made love, the reward for his attempt to please her. In minutes, he was asleep.

Gazing at his untroubled face, Whitney reflected on the Viking qualities of men attested to by suitemates: they could eat, drink, make love, and then fall into the deepest of sleeps in whatever bed was available—often followed by shuddering snores that disturbed their woman's slumber but not their own. Among Peter's virtues was that he seldom snored. But Whitney could not sleep here; sometime before dawn, she must steal back to the main house, observing the unspoken etiquette through which her parents pretended not to know she was having sex. As she lay besides Peter, fearing to close her eyes, she wondered if Robert Kennedy had won in California.

At length she got up and dressed, bending to kiss Peter as she left. Outside, the night was cool, the moon an oval in a sky alight with stars. Crossing the dewy grass, she saw headlights entering their driveway.

Suddenly, they dimmed, the car stopping some distance from the house. Clarice would not do this, Whitney thought. Apprehensive, she crept closer, pausing in the shadow of an oak tree.

A soft moan came from the darkness. Skin tingling, Whitney let her eyes adjust to moonlight. The vehicle was a pickup truck, and then Whitney perceived a woman with long hair bending over the hood. The dark outline of a man stood behind her, motionless but for the thrust of his hips.

"Fuck me," the woman said in a slurry voice. "Harder."

Shaken, Whitney could not look away. What unsettled her most was the resignation in the woman's primal urgings.

In the moonlight, the woman rested her face against the hood, silent as the man took her from behind. All at once, Whitney regained the power of movement. Backing away until she felt safe to turn, she scurried toward the house.

She paused at the drive, treading gingerly across the gravel before reaching the rear porch. Slipping through the screen door, she fell into a lounge chair, taking a deep swallow of cool night air. As a child, she had settled into this chair after dinner, nestled against her father as they talked or listened to the crickets chirring. Now she lay there, absorbing a fresh image she wished she could erase.

The crunch of gravel forced her to sit up. The sound became the unsteady gait of someone approaching the house. As the screen door opened, Whitney reached for the lamp on the table beside her, flicking on the switch.

Hands grasping the door frame, Janine stared at her with the dull surprise. Then she expelled a breath, body sagging. "It's only you."

Whitney felt her heart race. "Are you all right?"

Janine stood taller. "I'm fine," she said, each syllable enunciated to emulate sobriety. "Clarice and I over-celebrated, that's all."

Whitney stood. "Why don't I make you coffee, Janine? Maybe we could sit up for awhile."

To Whitney's surprise, Janine reached out to give her an awkward hug. "I'm happy for you," she said tiredly. "I always knew you'd be okay."

Returning her sister's embrace, Whitney smelled the liquor on her breath. Janine felt brittle in her arms. Abruptly, she pulled away, rushing inside the house. Whitney heard her taking the stairs with an unsteady tread, like a child learning to walk.

Burdened by unsought knowledge, Whitney sat down again, struggling to understand this fleeting moment of sweetness and all that she had seen before. In her disorientation, she reprised the familiar—the dinner, her father's toast, her interlude with Peter—touchstones of her evening before stepping through the looking glass. At last she remembered California and Robert Kennedy.

Walking to the library, she switched on the television, hoping to banish an unwelcome sense of responsibility for her sister.

The TV crackled on, its black-and-white image

casting a glow in the darkened room. Kennedy stood at a podium, looking exhausted yet smiling at the cheers that must mean victory. In his soft Boston-Irish cadence, he said, "I think we can end the divisions within the United States . . ."

He looked so young, so passionate yet vulnerable, that only a country that still believed in its own possibilities would dare choose him. It was what she had felt at dinner, but could not quite articulate. And then the speech was over, and Bobby waved to the crowd, almost shyly, and was gone.

Motionless, Whitney half-listened to the commentary that followed. Kennedy had won in California and South Dakota, eclipsing Eugene McCarthy as the primary challenger to Johnson's vice president, Hubert Humphrey, who still supported the Vietnam War. Buoyed by hope, Whitney decided to check on her sister, the least she could do.

Removing her shoes, she climbed the stairs, tiptoeing past her parents' bedroom before she cracked open Janine's door. Her sister's bed was empty. A shaft of light from the bathroom caused Whitney to peer inside.

Naked, Janine knelt over the toilet, vomiting into the bowl.

To Whitney's startled eyes, she looked much thinner than she remembered. She knelt, resting a hand on Janine's frail shoulder as she fought off the smell of nausea and sex. With a final retching shudder, Janine sagged, hair touching the rim of the bowl. She stared at her own spewings, unable to look at Whitney.

"It's okay," Whitney said softly.

Janine shook her head. "You can't tell them," she said in a dispirited whisper. "I drank too much, that's all."

That's not all, Whitney wanted to say. But pleading in her sister's eyes forced her to murmur, "I promise."

Mute, Janine tried to stand. Pulling her upright, Whitney walked her to the bed, arms around her sister's waist. "I'm okay now," Janine said wanly. "I just need to sleep."

She climbed in bed, pulling a sheet up to her chin. For a time, Whitney sat beside her as Janine stared at the ceiling. With a squeeze of her sister's hand, Whitney said, "Sleep well."

Returning to the bathroom, she flushed the toilet, using tissue paper to dab away the last traces of her sister's sickness. Then she walked softly through the bedroom, pausing to look back at Janine. Her sister lay in the same position, still staring into nothingness. Soundlessly, Whitney closed the door, heading downstairs to retrieve her shoes.

A sound came from the library. She had left on the television, Whitney realized. Entering the room, she heard a newsman's urgent cadence.

Senator Kennedy has been shot . . .

Involuntarily, Whitney cried out.

The first report is that the wound to his head may be serious . . .

Whitney stared at the screen, caught between disbelief and the sense that this felt terribly real, a tragedy materializing from deep within her subconscious. In reflexive memory, the announcement of President Kennedy's death issued from a loudspeaker at Rosemary Hall, opening a fault line between the future and a more innocent past. Her parents had never liked John Kennedy. But he was the president as Whitney ripened from adolescence toward young adulthood; unlike the ancient Eisenhower, he was a vital and articulate man, evoking the promise she hoped someday to find in herself. Then he was dead. Now Bobby might die, as King had.

No, she told herself.

She could not be alone. Briefly, she thought of Peter, then went to find the man who had always given her comfort.

Charles slept beside her mother. With gentle urgency, Whitney touched his shoulder. He shuddered, then stirred awake, his disorientation becoming puzzlement and then alarm. "What it is, Whitney?"

"They've shot Bobby Kennedy."

Her father blinked, then realized why she had come. "I'll sit up with you," he said.

Beside him, Whitney's mother stirred. Filled with dread, Whitney went back downstairs, sitting on the couch so that Charles could sit with her. The babel of voices felt like an assault.

Charles appeared in a robe, his hair matted, his face puffy with sleep. Quiet, he sat beside her, arm around her shoulder.

Senator Kennedy has been rushed to the hospital . . .

Sudden tears ran down Whitney's face. "This is what I feared," her father said in a somber voice. "The Kennedys unleash the furies."

No, Whitney wanted to say. In her unreason, she knew that believing Bobby Kennedy stirred dark and unknown forces was tantamount to wishing for his death. But she could not give voice to the fever in her brain, not to the man who had come to console her.

His face unspeakably sad, Bobby's press secretary appeared to announce that Robert Kennedy was in surgery. Beside her, Charles sagged heavily into the couch. "He can't survive this, Whitney. At least not as he was."

Still he stayed with her. Only when first light grazed the window did he say gently, "There's nothing we can do, sweetheart. You should get some rest."

"I can't."

Charles stood, kissing her forehead. Still gazing at the screen, she heard his footsteps on the stairs.

Alone, Whitney kept a vigil for Robert Kennedy.

Nine

When dawn broke, the mist and fog had vanished. Numb, Whitney remained in the library, listening to fragments of news and speculation as she prayed for Bobby to live.

Her mother appeared. Glancing toward the screen with a pained expression, she asked her daughter gently, "Have you slept?"

"No." Looking up, Whitney said, "I was up when Janine came in."

"I haven't seen her yet this morning. Did she have fun?"

"I guess so." Whitney paused, then added, "Does it seem like she's drinking more?"

"Why do you ask?"

"She was tipsy, I thought, even at dinner. I guess it worried me a little."

Anne arched her eyebrows. "She was celebrating, as were we all. No point in worrying about a girl so spirited and so sought after."

Her unwelcoming tone was a signal for Whitney to back off. But she could not shake the image of her sister being taken against a pickup truck, or bent over her own vomit, begging Whitney not to tell their mother. "If Janine's so irresistible to men," she inquired bluntly, "why don't they seem to stick around?"

Anne stood straighter. "If anything, Whitney, your sister suffers from an excess of choices. But it will take a man with considerable presence—someone like your father—not to be over-shadowed by Janine. She's much too vibrant for just anyone."

Whitney wondered about the truth of this. While Janine and their mother spent a great deal of time on the telephone, an intimacy Anne treasured, it occurred to her that Janine might alter reality to fulfill her mother's needs, or her own. "Even in adolescence," Anne continued, "Janine had a verve that created more admirers than she could cope with. It's only a matter of finding a man worthy of her. Which is why I'm so pleased for you."

"Pleased?" Whitney could not help but ask. "Or surprised?"

Anne gave her youngest daughter a look that mingled reproof and concern. "When I praise your sister, Whitney, that doesn't mean I prefer her. It's simply that   have different qualities, as any siblings do. You should concentrate on your own life—your wedding, your marriage, the family you'll soon be starting. Let your father and me worry about Janine."

Whitney understood that the intent of this veiled rebuke was to keep her at bay. For the first time, she wondered if Anne were protecting her sister, or herself. But it was not the morning to pursue this, or say anything at all.

As if unnerved by Whitney's silence, Anne turned toward the television. Listening to a surgeon describe Robert Kennedy's wounds, she said, "It's dreadful, isn't it. The world is becoming such a frightening place. In times like these, family is all the more important."

"I know, Mom. That's why I asked about Janine."

"Then just love her, Whitney. Your aunt, the college professor, and I could never manage that. She didn't care about me, or anyone in the family. Now we barely speak. I don't want that for my own two daughters."

The unspoken subtext to this, Whitney knew, was that her aunt might be a lesbian. But Anne could never acknowledge this, leaving Whitney to guess at who had rejected whom. Her mother's defenses might be more artful than Anne herself knew.

"I do love Janine," Whitney affirmed, silently asking if her mother truly did.

• • •

In the next hour, there were no definitive reports on Robert Kennedy. Whitney watched helplessly, her fears punctuated by disquiet about Janine. Then Clarice entered the room.

Surprised, Whitney said, "You've heard about Bobby Kennedy."

Clarice nodded. "Why do they let people like that have guns? It's as if we've become a shooting gallery." She looked around, then asked quietly, "I guess Janine made it home."

"Almost intact. I guess she'd been drinking a little."

"You can skip the 'a little.' I wondered what became of her, and thought you might wonder about me."

"I did," Whitney assured her. "Maybe we could go for a walk. I didn't sleep at all."

Clarice seemed to grasp Whitney's need to talk. "Fresh air beats sitting here, doesn't it? Especially on a day like this."

Stifling the childish thought that she was abandoning Robert Kennedy, Whitney changed into a light sweater and blue jeans and drove with Clarice to Lucy Vincent Beach.

A dazzling blue sky cast light on sparkling water, and there was a fresh greenness in the new grass, a harbinger of summer. To Whitney the morning was so brilliant that it mocked reality, reflecting the vast indifference of a God she could

89

never quite believe in. Taking the catwalk through the grass, the two friends kicked off their shoes and began walking at the water's edge. "So tell me about last night," Whitney asked.

"A waste of time," Clarice answered briskly. "You know the scene—a dark, smoky room jammed with islanders and college kids here for the summer. I couldn't hear a thing, and sipping Budweiser while mouthing words at strangers is my idea of misery. But Janine was drinking whiskey and swaying along with the music, sex in a low-cut dress. Pretty soon guys we'd never seen were paying for our drinks while Janine preened like a slumming princess."

Whitney put on sunglasses, cutting the brightness that hurt her eyes. "Did she pair off with anyone?"

"When I was there she wasn't playing favorites, except maybe the two guys on each side of her, each looking down her dress. The three of them drank a lot, and seemed to amuse each other in a way I couldn't fathom. When I told her I was ready to leave, Janine said one of the guys would drive her home. That was okay with me—and with them, it seemed quite clear."

"Were they good-looking?"

"They were islanders," Clarice answered in a throwaway tone. "I suppose one of them had some appeal in a scruffy, sinewy way, though it seemed best not to probe his intellect. But he certainly admired Janine—if that's what you call sniffing at her with the subtlety of a rottweiler."

It was a pity, Whitney thought, that Clarice chose not to share her powers of observation with the larger world. "So did Janine seem all right to you? Emotionally, I mean."

Clarice glanced at her curiously. "She was drunker than I've ever seen her, if that's what you're asking. Even looped she's kind of a phenomenon, and at first impression she's pretty electric. But I'd guess that she wears guys out."

"That's what Peter thinks."

"Really," Clarice said in a tone of muted surprise. "I guess it's pretty obvious."

"Not to my parents."

"They don't want to see it, Whitney." Looking at her sideways, Clarice continued, "I don't know what you're contemplating, but whatever it is, your mom won't hear of it. Questioning Janine is like attacking *her*."

With this, Whitney grasped that—however flawed his perceptions of Janine—her father understood Clarice quite well. At the core she was a careful woman, who knew when to speak and what to withhold, absorbing far more than she revealed. Though this was not a new thought, it seemed clearer now, illuminated by Charles's praise of Clarice the night before.

"I'm sure you're right," Whitney responded, and chose to say nothing more.

For minutes, the two friends walked in silence beside the lulling surf, content with each other's presence on such a terrible morning. At this hour the beach was almost empty—as if, for Whitney, the shooting of Robert Kennedy signaled the end of civilization. All she saw were three guys in faded shorts and T-shirts gazing out at the Vineyard Sound. They had brownish hair and beards in various stages of growth, and were passing around a joint with casual heedlessness. Looking vaguely up at Whitney and Clarice, the short one with glasses kept on talking.

"It's a sick country," he pronounced. But his voice was passionless, as though discussing a planet far away.

His squat friend nodded sagely. "They've taken over—the frat boys and beer drinkers and preppies with rich dads. Time to bail out, live in a world of our own invention. No point in caring about this shit."

Angry at their self-absorption, Whitney stood in front of them. "Don't you give a damn about Robert Kennedy?"

Unruffled, the boy said flatly, "Oh, he's gone—that's what those fascists do. I don't want them to kill me, that's all."

The third boy laughed harshly. "That's what Canada's for. One guy I know told the witch doctors at the draft board he loved penises, and asked to see theirs. But he had the lisp down, and walked like a ballerina. I'm not that good an actor."

"I thought you loved my penis," the first guy trilled.

"Fuck you, Steve—and that's a figure of speech, okay? Better Canada than you."

Her mood rancid with disgust, Whitney told Clarice, "Let's go back."

Clarice turned the way they had come. Indifferent to being overheard, she said, "What losers. The world really *must* be ending."

"Oh, no," Whitney corrected. "They're creating a world of their own."

"So very tempting," Clarice answered. "But maybe you should go find Peter. He'll be rising any hour now, wanting to be with you. Especially when he learns what happened to Bobby."

It was a measure of her gloom, Whitney realized, that she had not thought of her fiancé. "I should have woken him up this morning," she confessed. "But when you appeared, I was just so glad to see you."

Clarice gave her a faint but affectionate smile. "Me, too. After all, you're the first person I ever slept with. Back when we were four."

Ten

For Whitney, the hours and days that followed were a blur.

Returning to the house, she checked the television and learned that Robert Kennedy still lived. Headed to her bathroom to splash water on her face, she encountered Janine coming down the stairs.

Without makeup, her sister looked wan and tired. Giving Whitney a brief guarded look, she began chattering as though nothing had happened. Before Whitney could break in, the private phone line in Janine's bedroom started ringing. Flustered, she ran to pick it up, closing the door behind her.

Whitney paused, considering whether to confront Janine. In moments, she burst out of her room, jangling with anxious energy. "Do you know where Mom is?"

"What's wrong?"

"Nothing," Janine said with a smile that resembled a nervous tic. "They need me in Manhattan for a photo shoot, that's all."

Something in her manner evoked a lie told by a child. But Whitney had no basis for probing this, and lacked the heart to try.

"Good luck," she began, but Janine was already hurrying down the stairs.

Following, Whitney found Peter at their door. Enveloping her in a wordless hug, he held her until, in her sadness and confusion, Whitney began to cry. "It's okay," he murmured. "Everything will be okay."

For hours he watched the news with her, quiet and uncomplaining. Though not himself drawn to Bobby, he was appalled by the shooting and solicitous of the grief Whitney herself could not explain. At dinnertime he brought them trays of food, staying into the night until she encouraged him to get some sleep.

Whitney was alone when, in the early morning hours, Bobby's press secretary reappeared before the cameras, his shoulders slumped in terrible weariness. He briefly bowed his head before speaking.

Senator Robert Francis Kennedy died at 1:44 a.m. today, June 6, 1968. He was forty-two years old.

Whitney covered her face. Instinctively she recalled hearing about the death of President Kennedy, then that of Martin Luther King. She had a shamed, mordant thought—the next time someone murdered a leader she cared about, it was better to be with a crowd of friends. Then she began to cry.

In the morning Peter found her there, eyes bleary from a fitful sleep. When they returned to the guesthouse, Whitney tried to make love. But the act felt mechanical and detached, and she could find no solace in it.

She was just tired, she told him. But it was Peter who fell asleep.

Awakening to sunshine, Whitney tried to remember her own good fortune. She was surrounded by people she loved and who loved her, the touchstones of the life still awaiting. To Peter and her family, she realized, she must surely seem deranged. It was not as though she had given Bobby this much thought when he was alive.

"I understand," he reassured her. "His wife's a widow now, and all those kids don't have a father. I remember losing my dad, and wondering why. But no one had an answer."

Ashamed, Whitney realized that she had not—at least consciously—thought of this at all. Instead, she had felt that Bobby's death was something that had happened to her, which, in some indefinable way, would change the world in which they, and their own children, would live. Whatever the cause, she could not turn away from the rituals of death—images in black and white, the stoic grace that carried his surviving brother through the eulogy. Only at the end, quoting the lines Bobby had used to conclude so many speeches, did Edward Kennedy's voice crack.

Some men see things as they are, and say "why?" I dream things that never were and say "why not?"

Transfixed, Whitney watched the funeral train from New York to Arlington Cemetery, the crowds along the right-of-way paying witness to hope lost. At length Charles ventured in a kind, paternal tone, "This is a terrible thing, I grant you. But for the last few days, you've been sleepwalking through life, and all but ignoring Peter. All of us search for some meaning in the senseless, some larger force at work. But here, there isn't anything to point at." He hesitated before continuing more quietly. "Except, perhaps, that the equally senseless murder of Jack Kennedy, and the emotions Bobby evoked, made killing him the holy grail for the angry or unstable. Were I as malevolent as some acquaintances I don't particularly admire, I'd say that the hubris of Joseph Kennedy spawned an ongoing Greek tragedy that he's still watching from his wheelchair. What I *do* believe is that there's been enough—for this country and for his family."

To Whitney, this remark seemed subtly wrong, as though her father were blaming the victim for evoking passions of which he disapproved. But she had no heart to respond.

On Sunday, Charles and Peter left for Manhattan, both with a kiss from Whitney. "Thanks for understanding," she told her fiancé. "When you come back next weekend, I'll be a normal girl."

But as he climbed in the taxi with her father, Whitney suddenly felt abandoned—even by Clarice, who had called to say she was off to visit friends on the East Coast. In the glow of a candlelit dinner, Whitney allowed her mother to lead her through the menu for her wedding, oddly grateful for a quotidian distraction that so obviously pleased Anne. "It's so nice to see you becoming yourself," Anne hopefully remarked, and Whitney assured her that she was fine.

But she wasn't, quite. And so the next morning Whitney drove to Dogfish Bar.

The spot was down a mile of dirt road in an isolated section of Gay Head. A footpath through scrubby brush and sea grass led to a mile of sand and half-buried rocks, stretching toward the variegated clay promontory where the Gay Head lighthouse stood, a distant spike against the light blue sky. As often, and as she wished, Whitney was alone.

On some mornings she would swim the bracing waters of the sound, made more tranquil by a sandbar. But today she brought her journal.

This practice had started with the professor who, having discerned a talent Whitney doubted she possessed, had urged her to record her thoughts in order to discover them. Once written, he said, they were there—to be retrieved, rewritten, and polished for whatever use she chose. But he had also given her some tools. Under his tutelage, she discovered women who had become exemplary writers—Carson McCullers, Eudora Welty, Katherine Anne Porter, Mary McCarthy, and before them, Edith Wharton—as well as John O'Hara, James Gould Cozzens, and Louis Auchincloss, all of whom she admired for their ability to convey human behavior so subtly yet so well. The discipline of regular writing, her professor insisted, would develop her own gifts of illumination. Though painfully aware of her deficit in wisdom and experience, she had started keeping a diary.

Sitting with it open in her lap, she gazed out at the sound and pondered the boundaries of her life. The world in which she had grown up was comfortable and happy, one that she had never questioned. The changing manners and mores she had encountered in college were, she understood, a small repudiation of that world, in which she had gingerly participated by dressing casually, sleeping with Peter, and, more substantively, tutoring in Roxbury. But even that did not put her at odds with Charles and Anne—while they worried for her safety, they could not quarrel with her desire to help a disadvantaged boy. Torn between the rebellious fervor of those classmates who protested Vietnam or segregation, and Charles's greater knowledge and forbearance, she remained largely outside the ferment of her time in school.

This morning, however, she felt strangely transformed. No doubt this was foolish, even narcissistic. But she could not avoid sensing that the death of Robert Kennedy had caused some deeper change in her, though she did not know what it was. All that she could do was put words to whatever might emerge.

For a time she stared at the blank pages, pen in hand. At last, she began to write.

On the surface, everything is the same. I admire my father. I love my family. Clarice is still my closest friend. I'm planning my wedding, and the start of the wonderful marriage I know I can create with Peter. I have everything I could need or want, and the life ahead of me I've always imagined.

And yet.

What is happening to me? I wonder. Part of it may be Janine. She's in trouble, I'm sensing, and not just because of what I saw the night Sirhan shot Bobby Kennedy. It's more the instinct that she's at the core of some imbalance within our family, which causes us to act out certain carefully-wrought illusions, comforted but circumscribed by our own desires to see each other as we wish. That's common, I suppose, and rarely dangerous to anyone. But I've begun to worry that some difficulty may be awaiting us in the ambush of time.

Maybe that's stupid and portentous. Maybe it's just me—or Bobby's death, disturbing the chemistry of my all-too-unformed brain. Perhaps that's why I've begun to wonder why I don't speak out more often. I've started feeling a tectonic plate inside me, slipping ever so slightly, and it scares me. It's like being a child again, afraid of the dark because of whatever you may only be imagining. No doubt childish superstition is not confined to children. Still, it feels like something is about to happen to me, and I don't know what it is.

Pensive, Whitney closed her diary.

PART TWO

The Stranger

Martha's Vineyard–Manhattan

June–July 1968

One

For the next three weeks, Whitney endured the pressures of a society wedding bearing down on her. The worst of this involved sparring with Anne over each detail of her nuptial weekend. Whitney prevailed in her choice of bridal gown, as well as bridesmaids dresses, selecting pink, as her mother wished, but without the puffy sleeves Anne favored. But though Whitney chose the crystal and silverware, her preferred china—bright yellow with a modern design—was effectively vetoed by her mother, who opined that a traditional bone china with gold leaf would better withstand the vagaries of taste and fashion. The guest list was marbled with her parents' friends, often chosen less from affection than statecraft, and the Byzantine calculations through which Anne planned their seating left Whitney exasperated and amused. She came to understand too well the admonitions of older schoolmates: the wedding would not be her own. After all, it was universally acknowledged, their fathers were footing the bill.

To escape these vexations—but also to ensure that she fit into a wedding dress that left no margin for error—Whitney resolved to start each day with exercise and reflection. Every morning at dawn she took her journal to Dogfish Bar, crossing the sea grass in blue jeans so that deer ticks bearing some enervating disease did not make her a listless, sallow bride. On a bright early morning in late June, she reached the rise overlooking the ocean, and saw it glistening with sun. This was her favorite part of the day—full of promise, unsullied by whatever might follow.

Peeling off her clothes to uncover the swimsuit, she headed for the gentle, lapping waters. Though chill, after a moment they felt bearable, even bracing. Wading out to the sandbar, she plunged from there into the ocean, swimming parallel to the beach with strong determined strokes.

Pleasantly tired, she clambered back onto the sandbar. The sun was higher now; as she looked toward the beach, she saw a man gazing out at her from beside her pile of belongings. Though she could not make out his face, the leanness of his frame and an unruly thatch of jet-black hair suggested that he was roughly Whitney's age.

She hesitated, annoyed that a stranger was disrupting her special time, then headed back to where he stood. As she emerged from the water, he regarded her with his head slightly tilted, his manner suggesting he need not explain his scrutiny or his presence. Instinctively, Whitney felt self-conscious—though she had long told herself she was full-figured but not overweight, for even longer she had lived with her mother and sister. While she disliked herself for caring about a man she did not know, she could not help wondering how he would judge her.

"How's the water?" he called out.

At closer range he had a nose like a prow, a bronzed face all surfaces and angles, as though hammered out from copper. His angular frame, taller than Peter's, suggested litheness and grace even when still. The uncomfortable impact of his presence was sealed by dark eyes and an unabashed appraisal so unmannerly and direct that she wanted to look away. All in all, Whitney concluded with instinctive wariness, he resembled no one she had ever met.

"Tolerable," she answered sparely. Deciding that a trace of courtesy might make her feel less awkward, she added perfunctorily, "I'm Whitney Dane, by the way."

He extended his hand, a formal gesture which she could have sworn contained a deliberate hint of mockery. "Benjamin Blaine—Ben."

His hand was strong and rough and callused. "Here for the summer?" she asked.

"So it seems," he said tersely. "And you? I don't recall seeing anyone here this early in the day. Except fishermen, of course."

"I like this beach in the morning," Whitney replied in a cooler tone. "It's a good place to be alone."

Though a corner of his mouth twitched, his eyes

contained a hint of challenge. "And now I've spoiled it."

"Not really. It's big enough to share. How do you know it?"

"I grew up here. I used to come here at night, to fish, then camp out 'til morning."

"But not for awhile."

"No," he answered. "I left."

Though the curt response seemed intended to discourage her, it had the perverse effect of provoking her curiosity. "Have you been in college?"

"Mostly." He gave her the same unsettling scrutiny. "And you're a summer person, I'd guess. Vacationers and day-trippers never find this place, and I'd know you're not an islander even if I hadn't lived here all my life."

There was nothing soft about his face, Whitney thought, and little that suggested hesitance or self-doubt. Refusing to ask how he had pegged her, she said with a touch of pride, "I've been coming to the Vineyard since I was born."

"Of course you have," he said with sardonic amusement. "Three months in Eden every year. A hiatus from the rigors of life."

Annoyed at his tone, Whitney found that it pleased her to mention her engagement. "I'm getting married this summer, so there's planning to do. What brought *you* back here?"

"I dropped out of college."

110

Sixties fallout, she thought, feeling suddenly superior. "To do what?"

He crossed his arms, face closing, though the quick flash of his eyes suggested that her question evoked something painful. At length, he said, "I worked for Bobby Kennedy."

"You're kidding," she blurted without thinking, then realized that he was not. "What did you do in the campaign?"

"I traveled with him." He looked away, adding dismissively, "Nothing impressive. Just doing whatever he needed."

You actually knew him, she thought in real surprise, stifling the questions she was suddenly desperate to pose. Instead, she asked, "So what will you do now?"

"I don't know," he responded in an affectless tone that somehow suggested anger. "Dropping out blew my student deferment. I'm just hoping to slip by the draft board until fall, so I can finish up at Yale." His voice took on a muted bitterness. "By then maybe 'President Nixon' will unveil his secret plan to end the war. But I'm not counting on that."

Beneath his stoic veneer, Whitney detected a deep woundedness and dislocation, as though Robert Kennedy's death was like a fishhook snagged inside him. Whatever the cause, she could feel his presence on her nerve ends. "If you can get by the draft," she thought to ask, "what's next?"

111

"My ambition *was* to go to journalism school, and then become a foreign correspondent. A chance to redefine my life." The strain of irony returned. "I'm sure you go to Europe all the time, but I've never been outside the country. I'm hoping my first trip isn't to Vietnam."

But for her father's intervention, Whitney thought, Peter might share his fears. Awkwardly, she said, "At least you have friends and family here. People to spend time with."

He fixed her with the same appraising look. "Are you always this curious?"

"Not always," she answered tartly. "But you're standing right in front of me, and there's no one else to talk to."

To her surprise, he emitted a bark of laughter. "Okay, then. Yes, I have friends and family, just no one I'd care to see. Right now all I want is to sail. To answer your next question, I'm caretaking someone's house for the summer, and a sailboat comes with it. And yes, I'm acting like a jerk. I'm allowing recent events to spoil my usual sunny disposition. Not your fault."

Disconcerted once again, Whitney felt her defenses slipping. "And I really *am* sorry," she told him. "I'd say I know how you feel, but I can't."

"Maybe not." He turned toward the horizon. "After he died, there was nothing left to do. Except being on the water, and these are the waters I know. So I came home."

"*Has* it helped?"

"As much as it can. It's just me and the wind and ocean, the nearest thing to peace that I can find." His eyes narrowed, as though scouring the ocean for something he could not see. "There's nothing much good on land. The draft, this screwed up country, this heartless joke of a campaign. It hurts to watch it."

This was how she had felt, Whitney realized—at least for a time. "I liked Bobby, too," she offered, and then felt more foolish than before.

Mercifully, he did not seem to hear. She waited a moment, then began to pick up her things. "You don't need to leave," he told her. "I saw you brought a journal."

"It's nothing, really. I just keep it for myself."

"Then I'll leave you to it. Nice to meet you, Whitney Dane."

He turned abruptly, taking a few steps, then faced her again. "I don't suppose you'd like to go sailing sometime."

Startled, Whitney heard the inner voice of caution. "It sounds like sailing is better for you alone."

He shrugged this away. "At least you can swim. If you spoil it for me, I can always throw you overboard."

Whitney felt him challenging her in some indefinable way. "Maybe," she allowed. "Where are you staying?"

"Chilmark."

"That's where I am."

The hint of amusement resurfaced in his eyes. "I know. The big white house on the bluff."

With that he turned again, giving a careless wave of his hand without looking back. She watched him go, a forward tilt to his walk, moving with swift, decisive strides as though to clear a space for himself, somehow evoking her father.

I know. The big white house on the bluff.

Two

Later that week, Charles returned and, as he often did, sipped scotch while he watched Huntley and Brinkley on the evening news. Sitting with him, Whitney riffled the latest *Time* until a film clip of Resurrection City caught her attention.

A makeshift encampment on the Washington Mall, it was an attempt by the poor to dramatize their plight. "How will this change their lives," Charles inquired aloud, "and what are they teaching their children? That government has all the answers?"

But the scruffy campsite spoke to Whitney's sympathies. "If they didn't do this, maybe we wouldn't think of them at all."

Her father shook his head. "Maybe not. But if they don't want to improve themselves, what can anyone else do to help? This is just a sideshow, an excuse for the radical young to pursue their own destructive purposes."

Instinctively, Whitney thought again of Bobby Kennedy and the wounded young man she had encountered on the beach. Had her father always been this conservative? she wondered. Or had he acquired his beliefs from the moneyed classes he had joined upon marrying Anne, applying his keen intelligence until he could articulate them more clearly than his mentors? Whatever the case, it seemed that her father was passing his own views on to Peter. She wouldn't have minded if, now and then, her fiancé gently disagreed with Charles. But it was not in his nature, and she was lucky they were as fond of each other as she was of seeing them together.

"I don't think we can ignore them," she told Charles, and let the subject die.

After dinner, Whitney retreated to her bedroom, her sanctuary since childhood, listening to a rock station from the Cape, the earthy growl of Janis Joplin followed by Aretha Franklin's bluesy urgency:

I'm about to give you all my money
And all I'm askin' in return, honey
Is you give me my propers when you get
    home . . .

Whitney found the lyrics both stimulating and unsettling—was that all the black woman of the song had to look forward to? But the propulsive drive Aretha gave the lyrics pulled her in. Then her mother peeked through the door.

"What is all this gutter yowling?" she inquired dryly. "Does someone have appendicitis?"

Whitney summoned her best deadpan look. "Aretha just wants her propers when she gets home. Didn't you ever sing that to Dad?"

Her mother looked faintly amused. "I really didn't have to," she said with a certain maternal reserve. "On a tangent of that, and somewhat more pressing, I've been thinking about your wedding."

"Really, Mom? When did you start?"

Anne's perfunctory smile, a signal that she got the joke, also suggested her inability to change. "I was merely wondering if all the bridesmaids have been fitted for their dresses. As I recall, Julie hadn't."

"She has now, I'm pretty sure. That leaves only Janine."

Anne's expression became slightly more remote. "I do hope Julie doesn't gain more weight," she went on. "Sometimes I think she needs someone to take a greater interest in such things."

The remark touched a psychic nerve, causing Whitney to wonder if this were her mother's intent. "I don't think Julie's up for adoption,

Mom, and she and her mother seem to be just fine. So you'll have to make do with Janine and me. Do you happen to know if *she's* been fitted yet?"

"You know how busy she is," her mother said dismissively. "I'm sure she'll get to it soon. I just hope she's not too hurt about not being your Maid of Honor."

It was a reflex of her mother's, Whitney thought, to deflect unwelcome subjects with a witch's shaft of guilt. "Clarice is my closest friend, and Janine's had eighteen years to get used to it. What with the vibrancy of her own life, I'm sure this is merely a leaf scar."

The veiled sarcasm was delivered so blandly that Anne hesitated before saying, "As your mother, I thought it would be nice, that's all."

"Well," Whitney rejoined philosophically, "at least Clarice isn't fat. I just worry she'll look so stunning that I'll be overshadowed."

"Clarice is lovely," her mother said stiffly. "But she's hardly Janine."

Lost in their sparring was any assurance from Anne that Whitney would not be overshadowed. It was as though her mother saw Clarice as her oldest daughter's competition and, by extension, her own. But it was childish for Whitney to fault her, she chided herself: Anne had appeared at every school event, and was unfailing in her praise of Whitney's attributes and achievements. It was not her mother's fault she took such pride in Janine that her attention to Whitney felt, by comparison, like an expression of her unstinting sense of duty.

Perhaps reading her misstep in Whitney's eyes, Anne sat on the edge of her bed. "It means so much to me that you chose to marry here. It's where I spent the happiest years of my life—at least before I met your father, and had you girls. I was an innocent, of course, but life seemed perfect." Her voice filled with nostalgia and regret. "My mother was alive then. I remember getting up with her each morning, just the two of us. It was her favorite time—dew still on the grass, the greenness around us fresh with newborn sun. It was a time, she often told me, when anything was possible." Perhaps, Whitney thought, this was where she had gotten her own love of morning. With genuine feeling, she said, "I wish I could have known her."

For a moment her mother's eyes welled. "Oh, so do I. It was terrible watching her simply melt away." Her eyes briefly shut. "No, 'melt' is too benign a word. She shriveled into herself, until I had the horrifying image of her as a mummy in a museum. I can usually manage not to think of things that are so unpleasant. But not my mother's death."

Whitney wondered why this subject, so seldom touched on, had arisen once again. As she took her mother's hand, Anne told her, "You have a good heart, Whitney. Fortunately, whenever I feel like this, I can always look at her photograph— the one in the bedroom. It reminds me of how lucky I was to have her."

The photograph was so formal that Whitney could not see the warmth so vivid in Anne's memory, or have any real vision of her grand-mother other than a faint resemblance to Janine. With a stab of resentment, Whitney thought again once more that she was last in her mother's affection—behind Charles, Janine, and Anne's own mother—then recoiled from her own pettiness. "I suppose," Anne continued musing, "that's why I feel such kinship with Peter. Some grief never ends, no matter how much you wish that. All I ever wanted was for you girls to feel secure. The way I felt before I knew that my mother was going to leave me, and there was nothing I could do."

It was haunting, Whitney thought, how swiftly this memory could transform Anne into the heartsick girl she had been. "But you feel secure now," Whitney said.

"Yes," Anne responded quietly. "Thanks to your father."

A new thought struck Whitney, a connection she had not made before. "Sometimes I worry about Peter," she confessed. "He depends on Dad, as well."

"Don't worry," Anne said firmly. "Your father will look out for Peter. And if anything ever happened to him or Peter, he'll make sure you're more than comfortable."

She sounded like Clarice, Whitney thought— certain of Charles's capacities and foresight. "I know," she answered. But what she chose not to say was how vulnerable Peter seemed, and how uneasy this sense made her. For a strange moment, she envied her mother's confidence in her husband's strength of will.

They had known each other several months before Whitney fully divined the core of Peter's doubts. It was a fresh June day of the summer before; they were walking in Central Park, carefree and at ease. Then Peter stopped abruptly, gazing at the outline of a hockey rink drained since early spring, and his face took on an unwonted cast of sadness and reflection. "What is it?" Whitney asked.

Peter shoved his hands in the pockets of his jeans. "I was thinking about my dad."

"What was he like? You've never said that much."

"That hockey rink reminded me of him. He never cared for sports—like your dad, his childhood was hard, and he worked pretty much all the time. But I loved all the New York teams, especially the Rangers. Anyhow, I was maybe ten, and dying to see the Rangers play the Blackhawks. Dad was in the middle of a trial, and wouldn't have been interested even if he weren't. I got so desperate I finally said, 'But Dad—the Blackhawks have *Stan Mikita.*'

" 'Don't worry, son,' he answered. 'If the Blackhawks take penicillin I bet it'll go away.' Even I knew it was funny, and I could see the humor in his eyes. I also knew that was it—no hockey game.

"He won the trial, I recall. And the night before the Rangers next game with the Blackhawks he came home with two tickets—first-row seats, right behind the Rangers bench. I don't know where he got them, or how he even remembered. But he did." Peter smiled at the memory. "He watched the game intently, asking questions about all the players, and who I thought was good. Mikita scored a goal, and the Rangers won in overtime. It was the best night I'd ever had."

It struck Whitney that, however painful, these memories would make Peter a devoted father. "He sounds like a really nice dad."

"He was a really good *man,*" Peter affirmed. "I remember being fourteen and coming back from Taft at Christmas with mediocre grades. He was sitting in the library reading the *Sunday Times,* and I slunk in with this kind of half apology—that I knew he'd had to work while he was in school, and still nearly got straight A's, and here I was at this expensive place not doing half as well.

"My dad put down the *Times* and looked at me in this level way he had. 'It's true,' he said, 'I worked all the way through college until I got the scholarship to Columbia Law. People told me I'd developed character—I heard that quite a lot, actually. But I never had time to go to a single football game, and a lot fewer movies than I'd have liked. I came to think I'd developed more character than I could stand, and maybe more than I needed.'

" 'I don't want to spoil you, Peter, and it's true I'd like to see a little more effort. But I had too much care, too soon. It does me good to see you enjoying sports and having fun. You'll do better next time.' So I did. He died of a heart attack four months later."

The story touched Whitney, all the more because it explained Peter's affinity for Charles. Even now, she wondered if Peter should have decided to work with kids. But this was not the course he had chosen, the one taken by his surrogate father.

The next morning, Whitney took her diary to Dogfish Bar. Instead of swimming, she mused for awhile, then began to write.

It seems that my mom has tried to recreate, as best she can, the family she lost when her own mother died. But I wonder if she's almost as vulnerable as she was then. I can't imagine how devastated she would be to think that she had failed with any of us, most of all Janine.

Lately, I find myself asking if she worried less about me because she didn't need to—that she sensed something in my sister as brittle as Janine felt to me when I was hugging her that night. If so, perhaps Mom's obsession with Janine masks fears she can't admit, especially to herself.

Maybe that's jealousy couched as wishful thinking. But ever since that night I've wondered if Janine is more deserving of pity than envy and, perhaps, knows it.

She paused, watching a mist hanging over the sandbar. It was some moments before she began to write again.

It also seems clear that Janine wishes this were her wedding, not mine. But my parents worry for me, as well. Maybe by giving Peter a job and protecting him from the draft—and more than that, by serving as a second father—Dad is also assuring a solution to what Mom sees as the one area in my life, as she understands it, where I might need help. Finding the right husband.

This new thought, commingling warmth and humiliation, caused Whitney to put down her pen.

Only then did she sense someone standing behind her.

With seeming nonchalance, Benjamin Blaine said, "Hope I'm not interrupting."

Startled, she answered, "Didn't you kind of expect to?"

His eyes glinted at this. "Which means 'yes, you are, and it's annoying.' "

She put down her journal. "I've had my great thoughts for the day. So it's really not that annoying."

"Good to know. I just wanted to ask if you feel like sailing, and then I'll be on my way."

Whitney felt torn. She wouldn't mind sailing, and could not find a graceful reason to refuse. "When?" she asked, buying another moment to calculate how to avoid this stranger who kept throwing her off balance.

Perhaps he looked amused because he understood this. "Anytime," he said easily. "Ever sail to Tarpaulin Cove?"

Three

"You're sailing with whom?" Whitney's mother asked her.

"A guy named Benjamin Blaine. I met him at the beach, and it turns out he's caretaking the place next door."

"But what do you know about him?"

Stirring her coffee, Whitney tried to preempt further inquiry. "That he goes to Yale, and campaigned for Bobby Kennedy. I also assume he can sail a boat."

Her mother gave her a brief sharp look. "Have you told Peter?"

"This isn't a date," Whitney answered briskly. "Or the Dark Ages. I'm sure it's fine with Peter if I go sailing."

"Still, I wonder that you have time. The wedding gifts are piling up, and so are the thank-you notes. Best to write them now, while you can, rather than dash off hasty scribbles that sound like a form letter. Once you're married, you'll be busier than you know."

"It's three months yet, Mom. I'll catch up."

"We should also consider a wedding tent," her mother persisted, "in case of rain. A light blue canvass might not look quite so sodden."

"You really do think of everything," Whitney responded, glancing at her watch. "I'd better run. I'm supposed to be in Edgartown at nine."

Whitney felt Anne's dubious gaze follow her out the door.

Clasping her hand, Ben helped pull Whitney from the dinghy onto the deck of the sailboat, trim and perfectly maintained. "It's beautiful," Whitney said.

"It's a Cal 48, forty feet long, and built for speed.

Usually, the Shipleys race it in the July regatta—I crewed for them in high school. But they're gone this summer, and I've got no heart for racing."

As if to underscore the last remark, Ben grew silent, focused on rigging the sails. In minutes they were heading across the water toward Tarpaulin Cove with Ben at the helm. The day was bright and clear, and a headwind stirred his curly hair; absorbed in sailing, he barely seemed aware of Whitney sitting near the stern. While she did not mind the quiet, it felt as though he was playing the role of her indifferent crew. Then he finally spoke. "I wonder how many more times I'll get to do this."

"Because of the draft?"

Ben kept scanning the water. "Because of the *war,*" he said harshly. "What a pointless death *that* would be."

Uneasy, Whitney thought of Peter's safe haven in the National Guard. "You don't believe we're the firewall against Communism?"

His derisive smile came and went. "If you were some Vietnamese peasant, would you want to be ruled by a bunch of crooks and toadies? To win this war, we'd have to pave the entire country, then stay there for fifty years. And if we lose, what does that mean to us? That the Vietnamese are going to paddle thousands of miles across the Pacific to occupy San Francisco?"

Whitney had wondered, too. She chose to say nothing more.

The day grew muggy. Running before the wind, Ben headed toward Tarpaulin Cove, the shelter on an island little more than a sand spit. Hand on the tiller, he seemed more relaxed, his brain and sinews attuned to each shift in the breeze. It was not until they eased into the cove that Ben spoke to her again. "I brought an igloo filled with sandwiches and drinks. Think the two of us can swim it to the beach?"

"Sure."

Stripping down to her swimsuit, Whitney climbed down the rope ladder and began dogpaddling in the cool, invigorating water. Ben peeled off his T-shirt and dove in with the cooler, his sinewy torso glistening in the sun and water. Together, they floated it toward the shore, each paddling with one arm. At length, somewhat winded, they sat on the beach as the surf lapped at their feet. The Vineyard was barely visible; they had come a fair distance, Whitney realized, and yet the trip seemed to have swallowed time. This must be what sailing did for him.

For a time Whitney contented herself, as he did, with eating sandwiches and sipping a cool beer. Curious, she asked, "Is the war why you worked for Bobby?"

"There were several reasons, some balled up in the war. The Americans dying in Vietnam are mostly black or poor. And the Vietnamese are funny little brown people, easier to kill without thinking about them much. Do you really think we'd be napalming the French?"

"I couldn't say," Whitney responded mildly. "We did a pretty good job of firebombing Dresden."

He gave her a brief keen look. "A fair point," he said. "Except that I get letters from a high school friend who had to leave college and got stuck in Vietnam. Johnny and his buddies are scared out of their minds, some screwed up on drugs, and ended up doing some bad stuff no one talks about. Hard to blame them. But what's left is a body count of 'enemies' on the evening news."

Whitney recalled wondering how our troops could kill so many and make so little progress. "You really think you'll have to go?"

"You mean like there's a choice? Or are you talking about Canada?"

Once more, she felt discomfort at Peter's privileged status. "Canada, I guess."

"I'm an American," Ben answered with the edge of scorn. "I worked for Bobby because he cared about a lot of things—like race and poverty. That was worth the risk of dropping out. Canada is for the kids who hope McCarthy can save their lily-white asses."

Silent, Whitney watched the seagull skittering on the sand nearby, hoping for a bite of discarded sandwich. On reflection, Ben's caustic words echoed with the half-serious joke of her college friends: "If they kill all the guys we know, who'll be left to marry?" Some went to rallies; others to candlelight vigils. But their chief concerns were personal. Perhaps Charles's advice to Richard Nixon had been right. "My dad thinks that if the draft went away, the protests would, too."

Ben glanced at her with sharpened interest. "Why not? Then our ruling class can fight their wars with other people's kids. Not that I don't grasp the virtues of survival—you're a long time dead, and as near as I can tell there's no future in it. I just decided that avoiding death is not the point of living."

Whitney had no response to this. Sitting back, Ben rested on flattened palms as he squinted at the water. Covertly, Whitney studied his clean jawline and strong nose, the profile of a warrior on a coin. Unlike Peter, there seemed to be little gentleness in him. "So," Ben said abruptly, "is your fiancé going to work? Or is he sweating out the war?"

Reluctant, Whitney answered, "He's found a job on Wall Street."

"Impressive. Which firm?"

"Padgett Dane."

"As in 'Whitney Dane'?" Ben queried with a smile. "Wonder how he survived the application process. Still, isn't he worried about the draft?"

Whitney wondered how to stop this conversation. At length, she said, "He's going into the National Guard."

Ben laughed out loud. "Who arranged that, I wonder?"

"Wonder all you like," Whitney snapped. "Just tell me when it's over."

"It's over," he said amiably. "I just don't think your fiancé will be writing a supplement to *Profiles in Courage*."

Angry, Whitney stared at him. "On Dogfish Bar I could simply walk away. But on this boat you've got a captive audience. So I hope you're enjoying this conversation—if that's what this is. I'm not."

Ben raised his hands in mock surrender. "I apologize for offending you," he said in a tone so penitent it was nothing of the kind. "Far be it from me to disparage the man of your dreams."

"You really are obnoxious," she retorted coldly. "I'm sorry about your life but more than happy with mine."

"Did I say you weren't?" he said, then skipped a beat. "What kind of life, by the way? Will you be working?"

"Thanks for your interest," Whitney said, and then decided to annoy him further. "Perhaps, as my mother says, I can 'use my education in the home.' "

"On who? Your kids? Isn't that what grade school is for?"

Whitney had often asked herself the same question. "It means I can read a recipe without moving my lips. What else could a woman want?"

"Beats me," Ben said, and then regarded her with what seemed to be genuine curiosity. "What did you study in college?"

"I majored in English," Whitney said tersely, then decided to give a better account of herself. "I also tutored, and tried to write a little."

"Is that what the journal's about—writing something?"

Whitney wondered how to answer, or whether to answer at all. "Maybe," she allowed. "I took a lot of psychology courses, so perhaps I just like writing about why people are the way they are. Perhaps it's self-flattering, but I like to think that I'm not overly messed up."

"Too bad, then. Some think that's a prerequisite to a literary career—after all, Fitzgerald drank himself into oblivion, and Hemingway and Virginia Woolf killed themselves. So with all your obvious disadvantages, how did you come to writing?"

Whitney found that she enjoyed remembering. "I took a creative writing class, and my professor encouraged me to keep on. I'd always thought of writers as a wholly different species, but the diary has sort of kept the idea alive. Still, that's different from knowing how to become a writer."

"No one knows," Ben insisted. "The only way to

do it is to write. But if you need someone to share the madness, go back to school in creative writing."

Surprised, Whitney said, "Sounds like you've really thought about it."

For a moment, Ben's expression became more open, hinting at both ambition and embarrassment. "True confessions, then. Journalism is a temporary cover. My real ambition is to write the Great American Novel, which probably makes me crazier than F. Scott, Ernest, and Virginia combined. That's part of why I bothered you on the beach that morning. I saw your diary, and thought that maybe—in your words—you were a member of my species."

"I don't have a plan," Whitney demurred. "It sounds like you do."

Ben gazed out at the water. "Yup. The first part's J-school, assuming I can scare up another scholarship."

"I guess you did well at Yale."

"Well enough. But I deviated from the plan by dropping out, so now I'm a player in life's lottery. Big ambitions alone won't buy you a slot in the reserves."

Despite this jibe, Whitney sympathized with his plight. "Maybe you won't end up in Vietnam," she ventured.

With curled fingers, Ben wiped the perspiration from his dark eyelashes, staring ever more intently at the water. "Oh," he answered softly, "I think I will."

"But why?"

"Karma. I'm more afraid of being afraid than of what I'd have to face there."

For whatever reason, Whitney imagined him remembering Robert Kennedy. Pondering his fatalism in the face of the unknown, Whitney wondered what would happen to him without anyone to intervene.

Ben still scrutinized the skyline. Following his gaze, she saw a distant line of gray above the water. "We'd better get going," he told her. "I don't like the looks of that."

Four

As they sailed toward the Vineyard, Ben kept scanning the horizon. At length, Whitney asked, "What was he like? Bobby, I mean."

He let out some sail, catching the wind, seemingly intent on his task. Then he spoke without looking at her. "From the first time I met him, he surprised me. Before I knew it, he'd changed my life."

To Whitney, the phrase had a valedictory sound. "Was that when you left school?"

In the silence that followed, Whitney felt that she had probed too deeply into a wound still far too fresh. Then, slowly at first, Ben described Bobby Kennedy.

For weeks, he spent long stretches passing out leaflets or going door-to-door, still keeping a toe in college. The last days of this were in Indiana, a primary bitterly contested by Eugene McCarthy and his young volunteers. Waiting for his flight back East, Ben found himself in an argument with a clutch of McCarthy kids. Kennedy was an opportunist, they complained, jumping into the race only after McCarthy had humbled Johnson in New Hampshire. Ben responded that McCarthy was lazy, arrogant, and indifferent to minorities and the poor. Then Ben looked up, astonished to see Robert Kennedy standing between two aides, watching their exchange.

He was slighter than Ben expected, with crow's-feet of weariness that belied his youthful thatch of hair. Gazing at the McCarthy kids sitting nearest to Ben, a dark-haired boy and a pretty blond girl, Kennedy told them, "I just want to say that I admire you. You're working hard for what you believe."

The blond girl gave her head a shake. "You've got such cruddy canvassers, and you're still ahead."

In fascinated silence, Ben watched Robert Kennedy step from his imagining into life. "Well," Kennedy said mildly, "you can't blame all that on me . . ."

"I don't know what's happening," the boy interrupted. "I canvassed black neighborhoods, and no one listens."

"That's not your fault," Kennedy responded. "Why isn't Senator McCarthy more persuasive there?"

"You're a Kennedy," the girl protested. "You have the name."

Though this reference to his lineage seemed to make Kennedy even wearier, he answered without rancor. "That's a tremendous advantage, it's true. But why can't your man go into a ghetto? Why don't you see him in the poor neighborhoods? Can you tell the people there anything he's done to help them?"

The students fell silent. Finally, the boy said stubbornly, "We're sticking with him, Senator."

"You're committed," Kennedy replied with rueful admiration, "and I think that's terrific." He inclined his head toward Ben. "At least I've got one friend here."

When Kennedy faced him, Ben was struck by his eyes, gentle but intense. "You look as tired as I am. Let me buy you dinner before my plane arrives."

Stunned, Ben went with Kennedy and his aides to find a restaurant. "What's your name?" the senator asked.

"Ben Blaine."

"Wasn't very welcoming back there, was it?

Sort of like being Custer at the Battle of the Little Bighorn."

"I thought you sympathized with the Indians, sir."

Kennedy waved a hand. "Oh, I do." He stopped abruptly, facing Ben. "At any rate, you argued well. What are you doing for the next few weeks?"

"Whatever I can," Ben promised. "I want to help change the country, and you're the only one who still can."

Ben felt Kennedy go somewhere else, his gaze remote and unspeakably sad, as though he had forgotten the three men with him. Just as Ben was feeling awkward, Kennedy suddenly asked, "Think you'd like to travel with me? If you're not too busy, that is."

As he spoke, Ben's face had changed entirely. To Whitney he seemed so deeply drawn back into memory that she knew how it must feel to be twenty-two, and have a mythic figure invite you on a twisting, chaotic, and wholly uncertain ride into the unknown. Even Ben's voice was unfamiliar, melancholy commingled with pride. "After that," he told her. "I became what they call his 'bodyman'—the guy who travels with him looking after things. I did anything he needed—make phone calls, track suitcases, organize his papers—from the time he got up until he went to sleep.

"We were always rushing somewhere, surrounded by people—staffers, reporters, local politicians. But every now and then he'd ask me what I thought. One day when I brought him back a sandwich, he said, 'My brain trust tells me to cut down on campuses and ghettos—that news clips of blacks and long-haired kids will distress the middle class. What's your wisdom on the subject?'

"Somehow I knew he *needed* to see these people. 'You have to keep doing it,' I answered. 'That's who you are.'

"He was quiet for a moment, and then he shrugged. 'That's that, I guess. I'll let them know of your decision. But if I lose, I'll remember whose fault it was.'" Ben paused a moment, smiling to himself as though Whitney were not there. "Afterward, I realized I'd said what he expected me to say. Not that he ever acknowledged it. Especially after the next disaster."

You could see right away they weren't Bobby's people, Ben told Whitney—a crew-cut, unsmiling group of medical students, silent throughout his speech. When Kennedy invited questions, they were uniformly hostile. Finally, a cocky would-be doctor demanded, "So who's paying for all these programs for the poor?"

Kennedy tensed, and Ben saw that he had heard enough. "You are," he snapped, and his speech quickened with anger. "Let me say something about the tone of these questions. I look around this room and I don't see many black faces. I don't see many people coming from slums, or off Indian reservations. You're the privileged ones here. It's easy for you to sit back and say that all our problems are the fault of the federal government. But it's our society, not just our government, that spends twice as much money on pets as on fighting poverty. You sit here as white medical students, while blacks and the poor carry the burden of fighting in Vietnam . . ."

Listening to Ben describe this, Whitney felt his anger as her own. But Bobby had made a joke of it. "Now look what you've made me do," he had told Ben as they left. Then his eyes grew distant, and he added quietly, "I've had worse days, I suppose."

The clouds were closer now, Whitney saw, but she was caught up in Ben's description of a man she had never known and, equally, the way remembering Robert Kenney transformed Ben's persona. "He sounds complicated."

Ben nodded, as if appreciating her comprehension of a man she did not know. "In the course of an hour," he responded, "he could go from brooding to crisp to detached to funny. If he took a shine to you, you'd have these moments of connection. But he had no gift for small talk, and was never long on compliments. He just expected you'd do your job without a lot of bullshit or wasted time." Caught again in memory, Ben's face grew more relaxed. "Then he'd suddenly step outside the absurdities of politics in this ironic, self-mocking way. One time we landed at an airport, and there's no one there at all. Bobby sticks his head out the door, then says to the reporters behind him, 'There are fifty thousand people waiting,' and peers out to take a second look. 'Now they've seen me,' he informed them, 'and they're screaming with anticipation and delight.' Then he gets off the plane, waving to the empty tarmac, and flashes the victory sign."

For a brief moment, another faint smile of reminiscence appeared at the corner of Ben's lips. He had a writer's gift, Whitney thought; caught in his own narrative, he could capture her as well. "At other times," he went on, "you couldn't reach him at all. Like whenever he went to an Indian reservation. He'd start talking about the rates of suicide among young Indians, and come out looking ravaged.

"Once we were driving away from this ghetto, and he said, 'They should make a documentary about this place. Let some network capture the hopelessness, what it's like to think you'll never get out. Show a black teenager told to stay in school, looking at his older brother who can't find a job, or a mother staying up at night to protect her children. Then ask the rest of us to watch what it means to have no hope.' "

These were the things Whitney had wondered about since going to Roxbury, but could never articulate at her parent's dinner table. Now Robert Kennedy was dead, and she was planning her wedding. "I know this sounds stupid," she told Ben. "But once he died, I realized there was no one like him."

For a time, neither Ben nor Whitney spoke, as though briefly sharing a sort of kinship. Then he continued in a voice so muted that, to Whitney, it almost evoked a dream state. "We were headed to a black neighborhood in Indianapolis when we heard about Martin Luther King. Bobby went completely quiet—you knew he was thinking about King and his brother, maybe even what might happen to him. Then the police told him he shouldn't speak, that there'd be a riot once the word was out. He got that look, and I knew he wasn't backing off.

"The crowd hadn't heard. When someone handed him a speech he'd scribbled down, Bobby waved it away. Then he got out of the car and climbed on the back of a flatbed truck. It was dark—only the floodlights turned on Bobby, surrounded by a crowd of black people who didn't know what had happened.

" 'I have sad news for you,' he started out. 'Martin Luther King was shot and killed tonight . . .'

For a moment, Ben half closed his eyes. "There were screams and wailing—this sound of raw pain. Then Bobby said, 'Martin Luther King dedicated his life to love and justice between his fellow human beings, and he died in the cause of that effort.'

"The crowd went silent. 'For those of you who are black,' he went on, 'you can be filled with bitterness, with hatred, and a desire for revenge. Or we can make an effort, as Martin Luther King did, to replace the stain of bloodshed that has spread across this land with love and understanding.' " Pausing, Ben shook his head in wonder. "Then he quoted Aeschylus, of all people. 'Even in our sleep, pain that cannot forget falls drop by drop upon the heart. Until in our own despair, against our will, comes wisdom through the awful grace of God.'

"The crowd was completely hushed. For a minute Bobby was quiet, too, then sort of willed himself to finish. 'So I ask you to return home, to say a prayer for the family of Martin Luther King, but also for our country, a prayer for understanding and compassion. Let us dedicate ourselves to what the Greeks wrote so many years ago: to tame the savageness of man, and make gentle the life of this world.' "

What struck Whitney first was how well Ben remembered the words, as though he had read them many times since Kennedy's death. To her astonishment, tears glistened in his eyes, and for a moment she thought of Peter telling her about his father. "There were riots all over America," Ben finished. "But not in Indianapolis." Then he added in a throwaway voice, "Anyhow, it's all gone now."

Any hint of tears had vanished. But to Whitney, the weight of his loss felt tangible, as if he had lost a part of himself. "Were you there?" she could not help but ask. "In Los Angeles?"

For an instant, she caught the anguish in his eyes. Then his face closed altogether. Pointing at the horizon, he said curtly, "Let's talk about the weather. That's what matters now."

Five

In moments, Whitney heard the hiss of electricity. "What was that?"

"The first sign of a thunderstorm," Ben answered. "When the air is hot and humid like this, it combines with the cooler water to roil the weather. That's what's coming at us."

In the distance, a flash of lightning shot from darkening clouds. "Can we sail around it?"

"No chance. You can't sail in this at all." Reaching behind him, Ben switched on the auxiliary motor. "We're heading for Vineyard

Haven. Do the things we need to, and we should be okay."

A second bolt of lightning struck closer, its reflection shimmering orange on gray waters. Suddenly the skies grew even darker, and the wind vanished. "Help me get the mainsail," Ben ordered. "We'll stuff it through the hatch."

Taking down the sail, Ben began folding it tightly. In the lull, Whitney scrambled to help him. Hurriedly opening the hatch, they pushed the canvas through. When she glanced up again, the black clouds coming toward them looked like mushrooms spitting jagged light.

"It'll be here soon," Ben said tautly. "These storms are pretty scary—the winds can get up to forty knots, and it'll rain like hell. You should go down below until it's over. There's nothing you can do now, and I won't think any worse of you."

Whitney wanted to comply: framed against the vastness of the water, the skeleton of this boat without sails seemed fragile, sealing her sense of aloneness. But pride—or foolishness—forced her to say, "I'm sticking with you."

"Then sit down and stay put. We'll ride it out together."

Whitney sat. Seconds later a stinging wind lashed her face, and the first wave of rain struck the water like bullets, dulling the thud of their engine. Grasping the tiller, Ben called out, "Don't grab onto anything that's sticking up."

"Why?"

As if in answer, a lightning bolt thicker than a tree trunk cast a yellow streak near the bow. The boat began rocking sickeningly in storm-maddened waters. A hit of lightning struck beside her. Fearful, Whitney cried out. Tensed at the knees, Ben braced himself, eyes narrowing with strain.

"We'll make it through," he called out to her, and then they were enveloped in punishing winds, sheets of rain, lightning, the smell and hiss of electricity, the boat tossing crazily, lifting Whitney from her seat or jarring her from side to side. Sheets of rain flooded her eyes, near-blinded slits that barely saw the savage waves battering them from every direction. Gritting her teeth, she fought back nausea, beseeching God and Ben not to let them capsize.

He was grinning into the chaos all around them. *You don't care,* she thought in anger and despair. And then, through a crack in the darkness, she saw a sliver of blue-gray sky.

"Almost done," Ben told her over the noise and tumult.

The wind died suddenly. The darkness parted, and the wave of rain softened to a trickle. Ahead a burst of sun lit Vineyard Haven harbor, sparkling in brightness.

Whitney hunched over, arms folded, feeling her heart race. Then she saw Ben regarding her with a serious expression, as though discerning something new. "Glad you're still here," he informed her. "Losing you would have spoiled my day."

The harbormaster sent a dinghy to retrieve them. Taking her purse from the cabin below, Whitney let Ben pull her into the boat.

When they reached the dock, he said, "You look like you showered with your clothes on. Not to mention the raccoon eyes."

"It's hard being a girl. Or haven't you heard?"

"Once or twice. Why don't we sit on the dock and dry out a little?"

They found a place, legs dangling above the bright lapping water. Reaching into her purse for a Kleenex, Whitney wiped off her mascara while Ben regarded the harbor with something like contentment. "It's days like this," he said wryly, "that make life still seem worthwhile."

Whitney turned to him, curious. "How old were you the first time you sailed through this kind of storm?"

"Twenty-two. It was today, actually. I didn't want to shatter your confidence."

Whitney felt surprise become outrage. "You should have told me."

Ben laughed. "For the sake of honesty? That may have been the whitest lie I've ever told a woman. But maybe you'd have felt better drowning with Sir Lancelot."

Whitney gave him a tight smile. "I wouldn't

have minded Lancelot drowning. But going down with him would've spoiled my day."

"But we didn't, did we? If you need further consolation for surviving, I've talked to some experienced sailors who know firsthand how to ride out this kind of storm. Now I'm one of them."

In this, Whitney detected a kernel of philosophy —that challenges were to be faced, not avoided. She remembered a quote attributed to Robert Kennedy: "Man was not made for safe havens." Perhaps that, as much as principle, had had impelled Ben to follow him.

Impulsively, Whitney asked, "Can you teach me how to sail?"

He looked at her with the same surprise, Whitney realized, as she felt at her own question. "On the Cal 48? No way. Too big, too complicated."

His dismissive tone made Whitney more than a little piqued. "Fine. I'll learn from someone else."

He studied her for awhile, as though to ascertain her seriousness. Then he asked, "You're friends with Clarice Barkley, right?"

Surprised yet again, Whitney asked, "How do you know Clarice?"

"Oh, we're very close. I used to wait tables at fancy Vineyard parties. I'll never forget the night she said sweetly over her shoulder, 'More champagne, please.' " His voice lost its sardonic edge. "I *do* know her father—I crewed for him

146

one summer when he raced his Herreshoff on Menemsha Pond. It's a twelve and a half-footer, perfect to learn on, and the pond is a better place to start. If Clarice says you can borrow Daddy's boat, maybe we could give it a try."

His tone was so neutral, and his remark about Clarice so double-edged, that Whitney felt she was imposing. "I'd pay you, of course."

His face closed at once. "Don't worry about it. We can work something out." He glanced at his watch. "You'd better get going. By now your parents will have called out the Coast Guard."

His pride and resentment felt tangible now. "How did you know Clarice and I were friends? Did you see me at the parties, too?"

"The ones at your parents' place," Ben said succinctly. "Every Fourth of July."

Thoroughly discomfited, Whitney stood. "Thank you for the sail, Ben. It's one I won't forget."

He smiled a little. "That's what we strive for, Miss Dane."

Finding nothing more to say, Whitney left.

Her mother waited on the porch with a glass of wine. "I was worried," Anne advised her with a trace of asperity. "It seems I was right to. You look like a drowned rat."

"More like a raccoon, I'm told. We were caught in a storm."

Anne gave her a querying look. "Caught? It

came through here like an angry message from the Old Testament God. This young man seems more than a little reckless. You'd think he'd check the weather forecast before taking you out on the water. If your father were here, he'd be furious."

This thought had occurred to Whitney, as well. Defensively, she said, "Ben knows what he's doing."

"Fine for him," her mother answered crisply. "But he could have lost you both. Next time he plays aquatic roulette, he should do it alone."

Whitney felt herself bridle at the implicit command. "Next time, we'll be on Menemsha Pond, where it's safer. Ben's teaching me to sail."

"Really," Anne said, the single word etched with puzzlement and annoyance. "With all you have to do?"

"I've got time, Mom. And I've always wanted to learn."

Her mother appraised her closely. "I never knew that, Whitney."

Neither, Whitney realized, had she.

Six

The next morning, restless, Whitney decided to visit Peter and her sister in New York. Among her stated reasons—which deeply pleased her mother—was to accompany Janine to the fitting of her bridesmaid's dress. But beneath this was Whitney's unease about her sister's state of mind.

The fitting, Whitney's first stop after flying into LaGuardia, deepened her disquiet. Janine was fidgety and distracted; she had lost sufficient weight that the dress had to be taken in—not much, as such things went, but unsettling in a woman whom Whitney already thought too thin. At the end, however, Janine brightly suggested they use the credit card their father had just given her, and treat themselves to lunch at La Grenouille.

The gift of a credit card was no surprise to Whitney, nor was Janine's revelation, delivered with the pride of a family favorite, that Charles had begun subsidizing her new apartment. Whitney wondered if her somewhat sour reaction to this, quickly suppressed, was mere competitiveness, or the deepening sense that a twenty-five-year-old woman should have something more substantial to take pride in. But on the score of parental indulgence, Whitney could hardly claim to be different.

More unsettling was her sister's demeanor at lunch. Fidgeting, she barely tasted the side salad, which was all she ordered, and her desultory remarks roamed from subject to subject. Finally, Whitney steered the conversation to Janine's life in Manhattan. "So who do you see for fun?"

Absently, Janine stabbed a radish with her fork.

"It's hit or miss. What with working and dating, I get pretty strung out. Every so often I'll go out with girls I know from modeling, or friends from Vassar."

Whitney made her voice bright with interest. "Anyone I know? I really liked your suitemates senior year."

The seemingly innocuous question caused Janine to draw in her shoulders, as though Whitney had cornered her. "There's Laura Hamilton. You remember Laura."

"Of course. What's she doing now?"

"She's got this great job at *Vogue*, editorial assistant to someone important. But she's so busy that it's hard to get together."

To Whitney, this last had the sound of evasion; for whatever reason, her sister was guarding the details of her days and nights like a miser hoarding gold. "Would you like to share a dessert?" Whitney asked. "You haven't had that much to eat."

Janine gave her sister a quick once-over. "Not for me, thanks. I have to watch my figure."

Whitney glanced around the elegant room—the soft colors, the crisp white tablecloths, the expensively turned out men and women in twosomes and foursomes defined by gender—affording herself time to ignore Janine's jibe. "You look great," she assured Janine. "You don't need to lose a single ounce."

"Still, I have two photo shoots coming up. You know how it is—a model can't be too careful, or she'll be out of a job. Besides," she finished with sisterly warmth, "I have to look good for your wedding. Have you and Mom sorted out the details?"

"She's certainly sorted *me* out," Whitney said dryly. "I've begun to feel like a project instead of a bride."

Janine flicked back her hair. "You know who she is, Whitney. You just have to roll with it. Has she at least told you where the ceremony will be?"

"The back lawn, with a view of the water. Exactly where I always imagined it."

A brief shadow crossed her sister's face. "So did I, actually—on my wedding day. But what if it rains?"

"It won't," Whitney said firmly. "Did *you* ever imagine it raining?"

Janine smiled a little. "For my wedding, it's always sunny. I'm just worried about yours. It would be absolutely miserable if a storm blew in off the water."

Did Janine secretly hope for this, Whitney wondered, preserving her hopes of being the first sister with a pristine outdoor wedding? "Mom's ordered a tent," Whitney said equably, "and space heaters. It's her way of ensuring perfect weather. But if it's miserable, at least the bridesmaids won't freeze."

Janine toyed with her fork again, then laid it atop the limp remains of lettuce. "So who are the groomsmen? Anyone who'd catch my interest?"

For an instant, recalling the startling image of Janine being taken over the hood of a pickup truck, Whitney was tempted to say, *I hope not.* But the image lent her sister's inquiry a tinge of desperation. "They're all from Dartmouth—athletes mostly, and pretty cute, though none as handsome as Peter. There is one guy, Carter, who looks a little like Warren Beatty when he smiles . . ."

"Not bad."

"No kidding. But they're all Peter's age, so they may look like tadpoles to you."

"I can always winnow them out," Janine said with the exaggerated carelessness of a queen, "and take who strikes me as amusing."

Smiling, Whitney asked with seeming innocence. "So I guess you're not seeing anyone special?"

The guarded look resurfaced in her sister's eyes. "Maybe," she said, then hastily added, "I really don't know. So don't say anything to Mom."

"Why would I? Besides, don't you talk to her pretty much very day?"

Janine touched her glass of tomato juice, fingers circling the rim. "She needs that, Whitney. I mean, Dad's great, but sometimes she gets lonely. I understand her."

The tenor of this answer, protective and

proprietary, reminded Whitney of her mother's defensiveness about Janine. Perhaps this was their mutual conceit: that as women gifted with poise and beauty, as well as mother and daughter, Anne and Janine shared a special bond. "Consider me a sphinx," Whitney assured Janine. "No point in overstimulating Mom's febrile imagination. But if there's a guy on your horizon, I wouldn't mind a preview."

Janine looked down, briefly shaking her head. "Too soon. I don't want to jinx it."

Something about whatever this situation was, Whitney felt sure, made her sister anxious. "The wedding is almost three months away," she said in an encouraging tone. "Maybe by then you'll have no room for groomsmen who look like Warren Beatty."

Janine's smile seemed to question, rather than reflect, a belief in her own happiness. "I hope so," she said, and reached for her fork again.

Perhaps Whitney only imagined that her hand trembled briefly before she put it down. Then it occurred to her that, contrary to her usual custom, Janine had not ordered a glass of wine —perhaps from worry about her weight, or a concern about what Whitney might say to their mother. "Why don't we go out tonight," Whitney proposed. "Peter and Dad have a dinner, so maybe we can catch Bobby Short at the Carlyle. You always liked him, I remember."

Janine bit her lip. "Thanks. But I may have plans. So I'd better leave it open."

Who was it? Whitney wondered. "Call if you change your mind," she suggested, knowing as she said this that Janine would not.

Arriving at their building, Whitney used her key to the outside door, introduced herself to the doorman, and took the elevator to the fourth-floor apartment she would soon be sharing with Peter.

Though her parents had lived there with the toddler Janine, Whitney had never seen it. Now she stood in the atrium, imagining it as her own. Though not unduly spacious, it was bright and clean, with a remodeled kitchen and a freshly lacquered parquet floor. The sparse furnishings were gifts from her parents—a couch and coffee table in the living room, a double bed with end tables, a small table in the kitchen where Peter could eat. As to the rest, Whitney had insisted the newlyweds would furnish it gradually, defining the space for themselves. Opening the refrigerator, she was amused to see one space Peter had already defined—not enough food, too much milk, and a leftover sandwich that might, in few days' time, resemble a science experiment.

She returned to the living room. Sunlight from the window above Madison Avenue cast a square on the parquet floor, reminding Whitney of her mother's memory that Janine had liked to play there, feeling the warmth of the sun on her round, pretty face. Whitney resolved to cover it with an armchair.

Proceeding to the bedroom, she made the bed Peter had left in collegiate disarray, then lay down to riffle a copy of *House & Garden*. Gradually, her thoughts drifted from décor to her sister. By six o'clock, having heard nothing from Janine, Whitney picked up the phone on the nightstand and asked for the number of *Vogue magazine*.

When Whitney arrived at the King Cole Bar, Laura Hamilton was already at a table. She was dark and pretty, as Whitney had remembered, and though Laura greeted her pleasantly, she seemed a little harried. After ordering cocktails— an Old Fashioned for Laura; a Manhattan for Whitney—the older girl offered some chit-chat about Manhattan. But beneath this, Laura seemed puzzled and a little wary.

Finally, Laura said briskly, "On the phone, you told me there was something you wanted to ask. If it's about a job, I wish I knew of one. But I can put you in touch with some girl who might."

Feeling intrusive and a little embarrassed, Whitney hesitated. "I may need that sometime. But this is about Janine."

Eyebrows slightly raised, Laura looked at her steadily, saying nothing. "I'm not trying to spy on her," Whitney added hurriedly. "But at lunch today, she seemed jumpy and preoccupied. I mean, she's always been kinetic . . ." She cut herself off. "I just wondered if you've seen her lately."

"Not really," Laura answered matter-of-factly. "I've tried a couple of times, but it's been difficult to connect. You know how she is, always changing plans." Pausing, she gave Whitney a cautious, curious look. "At lunch today, did she say anything about the agency?"

"Just that she had a couple of shoots."

"Nothing else?"

"No."

For a moment, Laura stared at her in silence, then rested her chin on folded hands. "Maybe I shouldn't tell you this, Whitney—Janine clearly didn't want to. But I've been calling her because another girl heard she'd been fired."

Whitney felt a twitch in her stomach. "For what?"

"She missed a couple of jobs, apparently. I've been wondering what that means."

"What do *you* think it means?"

Sipping her Manhattan, Laura did not answer. Finally, she said, "We were roommates for a year, so I have a fairly good sense of her. In many ways, Janine's pretty transparent, and very sweet. All that surface energy can create a sense of fun. But your sister has a secretive side—she keeps secrets from friends, and even from herself. Sometimes she'll flat out lie to preserve appearances.

"If there is a problem, she won't want you to know it, the better to tell herself and others that there *is* no problem." Frowning, Laura put down her drink. "Even if I see her, I'm not sure I'll learn a lot. But you're her sister. Maybe in time you'll figure out if there's really something wrong."

"I hope so, Laura. I worry about her."

"So do I," Laura affirmed. "In the meanwhile, you didn't hear any of this from me, okay? But if you find out she's in trouble, and I can help, please let me know."

Whitney promised that she would.

Returning to the apartment, Whitney called a pizza place recommended by the doorman. When the pizza arrived still hot, its crust appropriately thin, she wrote down the number for evenings when she and Peter felt lazy. Then she picked up the phone to call Janine. But this and several other calls, the last at ten o'clock, went unanswered.

At length, Whitney fished the diary from her suitcase. After a moment, her thoughts—confused as they were—flowed easily.

Who is Janine? I ask myself over and over. Am I the only one in our family who suspects that her "glamour," as our mother puts it, conceals a lonely and unstable girl? Or am I dwelling on the petty resentments of a very privileged life, hiding the need to prove myself superior beneath a veneer of sisterly concern? And, if so, am I weaving odd scraps of her behavior into an imaginary plight that answers my own needs?

Am I really that bad? I ask myself in the next moment. I've always believed I was the invisible one, it's true. But I'm becoming more certain that none of us knows Janine—and that, knowing this, she's desperate to maintain our illusions. If this is right, and no one else cares to see it, what is my responsibility? And to whom?

For a moment, she stopped writing. Her last words came much more slowly.

I feel alone in this. But not as alone as I imagine Janine. Whether my version of Janine is real, or the psychic revenge of an envious sister, this may be the first time I've truly loved her. God help me if I'm wrong.

Seven

The next morning, Peter and Whitney had coffee and French toast—Peter in a robe, Whitney in one of his shirts, a pleasant foreshadowing of their married life together. It was their first real time to talk; when he had come in late the night before, she was already asleep. Now she saw that his hair was cut much shorter, taming the blond curls she had always loved, and that his sideburns had vanished altogether. "Why the new haircut?" she inquired. "Not that you don't look nice."

He smiled a little sheepishly. "Camouflage. This may come as a surprise, but the counterculture doesn't exist at Padgett Dane."

Though it was foolish, Whitney felt a sense of loss, as though another piece of her youth was being swallowed by adulthood. "Here we are," she said wryly. "Just like Mom and Dad. So tell me, dear, how was your dinner last night? Did all you masterful men decide the fate of the Western World?"

"Just the fate of America," Peter amended, sounding pleased despite his best efforts. "It was Richard Nixon and a dozen heavy hitters from Wall Street exchanging ideas, with me as a fly on the wall. Your dad was the one who pulled it all together."

Despite her reservations about Nixon, Whitney felt a certain pride; now and then she was reminded of the respect her father commanded in realms beyond his own. "What did you think of Nixon?" she asked curiously.

Peter sipped his coffee. "I was really impressed. Like Charles says, he's not flashy or a charmer, but he's sharp and really knowledgeable, and you can see him taking everything in. I could tell he's really impressed with your dad. If Nixon's elected, I think he may be in line for secretary of the Treasury."

Whitney could imagine her father's quiet satisfaction at how far he had come. "Was anything said about that?"

"More that Nixon kept asking Charles about the economy. Each time, he was able to answer right away, with Nixon just listening and nodding." Peter's voice softened in admiration. "Your dad is really an amazing guy, you know."

They were quiet for a time, united in their mutual affection for Charles and, in Whitney's case, her renewed happiness that Peter had found a man to replace—as much as such things were possible—the father he had lost too soon, just as Charles had found a would-be son to mentor in his chosen world. Taking a sip of coffee, Peter asked, "So how was Janine?"

Whitney felt the innocent query reviving her anxiety. "There's something wrong," she said at once, relieved to unburden herself. "At lunch she was distracted and evasive, and later on I found out she's been fired."

Peter's eyes narrowed slightly. "Found out? Not from Janine, I guess."

"From Laura Hamilton, one of her college friends. After I saw Janine, I called her."

"Out of the blue?"

"Not really. Janine mentioned that she saw her now and then, and I thought Laura might know if something was going on. Obviously, there is."

Peter held up a hand. "Please back up a minute. So Janine told Laura but not your mom?"

"No," Whitney replied somewhat testily. "Laura heard it from another girl at the modeling agency. Anyhow, what difference does it make?"

"Quite a bit." Peter puffed his cheeks, exhaling slowly. "If it's true, Janine clearly doesn't want your family to know. You can't even be sure it *is* true."

"I think it is."

"Maybe so. But remember boarding school, the way rumors went flying around? Like hearing my senior year that I'd had sex with a girl I'd never even touched. She was cute, so at first I didn't mind too much. But once I saw how hurt she was, I felt worse than if we'd done it." Pouring them both more coffee, Peter concluded firmly, "Even supposing that the agency canned her, it seems like Janine wants to deal with it herself. If she

161

cared to involve her family, she would have."

Whitney crossed her arms. "Obviously. But the fact that Janine conceals things doesn't make it a good idea. What if she's in trouble?"

"But what kind of trouble?" he persisted. "Was she drinking at lunch?"

"Not a drop."

"Then maybe there *is* no problem." Peter reached for her hand. "Look, I know you don't feel that close to her . . ."

"Which must be *my* problem," Whitney cut in.

Peter looked at her intently. "That's not what I'm saying at all. Just that she makes it easier for you to imagine the worst."

Whitney felt her temper snap. "Then try this, Peter. The night of our engagement dinner, she let some guy she didn't know screw her up against his pickup truck. I *saw* them, okay, so don't ask me how I know . . ."

"Jesus, Whitney . . ."

"She was so drunk she went upstairs and vomited her insides out. When I put her to bed, you know what she said to me? 'Don't tell Mom.' So I didn't. Now she's gotten fired from her job and is turning into a skeleton. Do you want me to wait until she jumps off a bridge?"

"I sure as hell hope you're wrong about the bridge." Peter paused, rubbing his eyes. "Look, I'm not big on keeping secrets unless I have to. But can you imagine telling your parents—

especially your mom—that Janine's gotten fired and screws guys she doesn't know? Then what? And what about your own relationship to Janine? Sometimes staying quiet is the best of two bad choices."

He said this with such feeling that Whitney stopped to study him. "Would you keep secrets from me?"

For a moment, Peter looked confused as to how to answer. "Of course not," he assured her. "At least not about anything you needed to know."

"How do you define *that?*"

"Anything that's about me or you—the two of us. But until right now, you didn't tell me that you saw Janine doing this guy. You must have had a reason."

For a moment, Whitney gazed out the window at the buildings across Madison Avenue, their façades brightening with early sunlight. "I guess so," she acknowledged. "Maybe I didn't want to embarrass my sister, or have you think any less of her."

Peter nodded. "Also, you didn't *need* to tell me. And I'm a whole lot safer than your parents."

"But that's just it," Whitney insisted. "Janine is their daughter. The more I've thought about it, the more I think she's captive to their whole idea of themselves. She was the first member of my dad's family to go to prep school, which delighted him no end. When it came time for college, he wanted her to go to one of the Seven Sisters, so he pulled strings to get her into Vassar. When she came out as a debutante, my mother was wound so tight with anticipation and anxiety that I swore I'd never do it . . ."

"But you did, right?"

"And mostly hated it. I kept imagining Mom comparing us . . ."

Hearing herself, Whitney stopped abruptly. With a renewed calm, Peter said, "I think you're playing with dynamite, Whitney. In eleven weeks, we're getting married. It's not a very good moment to create a family crisis. There'll be plenty of time for that later on."

The timing could not be worse, Whitney knew. "I just worry that there's something else—that getting fired means she's spiraling downward. Do you know how she got into modeling in the first place? It wasn't her idea at all."

"Whose was it?"

"Mom's. The summer she turned fourteen, Mom thought Janine seemed depressed and pretty down on herself. So she got Janine into teen modeling to 'give her confidence a boost.' Ever since then, Janine's been all about her looks. I'm not so sure that Mom did her any favors."

Absently, Peter ran a hand across his formerly unruly crown of hair. "Janine's a little squirrelly," he conceded. "But first she has to believe she has a real problem that needs fixing. Or else it's you against the three of them, the snoopy sister saying terrible things out of jealousy or spite. The last thing I want is for you to hurt yourself." His smile was tentative. "Remember that history paper about Lord Melbourne you helped me write?"

"All I remember is that it was brilliant."

"A-minus, thanks to you. I've already forgotten most of it. But Melbourne said something about government that stuck with me: 'That which is not necessary to do, is necessary not to do.' Maybe that applies to families, too. At least for now."

Peter was no scholar, Whitney reflected, but he had a sense of people—much like Charles or Clarice. Perhaps she worried too much about his future. "Part of success," she had heard her father tell him, "is figuring out what people want before you speak or act. Always keep your own counsel until you know the consequences."

"So," she inquired, "what would Lord Melbourne do now?"

"Right now? He'd realize there was still an hour before work, and find out what you were wearing under that shirt."

Whitney smiled a little. "Do you think that really qualifies as 'necessary'?"

"Indispensable," Peter responded with great assurance, and led her to the bedroom.

For the rest of the day, Whitney looked at furniture for the apartment, writing down places to which she and Peter might return. Intermittently, she called Janine from pay phones without result, deepening her anxiety. If Janine was still working, as she claimed, wouldn't she want to be near the phone? But perhaps she was working—photo shoots could last all day. Of course, not finding her was in some ways a relief; Peter's misgivings enhanced her sense that she was thrashing about in a pitch-black room, more likely to break the china than find a wall switch. When Peter appeared with tickets to see George C. Scott and Maureen Stapleton in Plaza Suite—a surprise gift from her father—Whitney resolved to put her worries aside. And on her return to Martha's Vineyard, when Anne asked about her trip, Whitney temporized by starting with Peter and the play.

"I love Neil Simon," Anne enthused. "What I wouldn't give to be that clever." Arranging fresh cut roses in a vase, she inquired casually, "How was Janine?"

Whitney paused to compose her answer. "The fitting went fine. But when I asked her what was new, she acted a little edgy. She seemed more interested in discussing the bona fides of Peter's groomsmen."

Her mother gave a tight-lipped smile. "Sounds normal enough to me. Sometimes, though, I think Janine breaks hearts just for practice. Looking as she does is an asset, but it carries with it a certain responsibility to be kind."

A terrible burden, Whitney thought but did not say. "I just wondered if she'd mentioned anything about her work."

"Only that she's busy. Why do you ask?"

"For one thing," Whitney said carefully, "she seemed too nervous about gaining weight, when that's not her problem at all. Sometimes I wonder if depending on her looks for a career is good for her. Like that's all she has to offer."

Anne looked at her askance. In her flattest tone, she responded, "I don't know what you're saying, Whitney. Janine's not insecure in the least."

Once again, Whitney felt the barrier between them. It was as if Anne was defending herself against a threat posed by her younger daughter, perhaps even a betrayal. Not for the first time, Whitney felt like an alien presence within the family—the people who, with Peter and Clarice, she loved more than anyone. Whatever their imperfections, and her own.

"Anyhow," Whitney assured her mother, "it was good to see her."

Eight

"So," Clarice said, "this guy you picked up on the beach is teaching you how to sail."

Whitney sat beside her on the promontory behind the Barkley house, watching the sun set over the water while Clarice sneaked a cigarette.

167

"This particular guy," Whitney rejoined, "crewed for your dad in summer races. So I guess he qualifies as a sailing instructor."

Clarice gave her a droll look. "If you were interested, he might instruct you in several areas of life."

Whitney ignored this. "Do you know him?"

"I've *seen* him. He used to help cater my parents' parties. You don't forget someone who looks like that." Exhaling smoke, Clarice added carelessly, "Anyhow, my dad is willing to trust him with his precious boat. I'll look forward to a full report."

Whitney resolved not to let Clarice tease her into a defensiveness she did not feel. In her most innocent voice, she replied, "Thank you, Clarice. Have I ever withheld anything from you?"

The Barkley's Herreshoff was moored about one hundred feet off a catwalk on Quitsa Pond. When they arrived, Clarice was standing on the catwalk, one hand on her hip, another leaning on a post, her pose—which Whitney thought it was—casual yet proprietary. Extending her hand, Clarice gave Ben an amused appraising look. "I'm Clarice Barkley."

"I know you are."

"Do *you* have a name?"

"Pretty much everyone does. But I think you already know mine."

Clarice's look of amusement resurfaced. "Hi, Ben."

"Hi, Clarice. How's your summer going? No tragedies, I hope."

"None at all. Actually, Whitney is providing the high point. I'm playing an indispensable role in shepherding her into matrimony."

"I'll bet. Are you getting married, too? Or will you have to find a job?"

Standing to the side, Whitney felt like a spectator. Though Clarice and Ben were virtual strangers, there seemed to be a contest between them, taking place in some undefined place between aversion and flirtation—flirtation on her part, perhaps dislike on his. "I've considered employment," she said in airy self-satire. "Let's just say that it's under advisement."

Folding his arms, he glanced at the sailboat, a gesture clearly meant to signal his impatience. "I wouldn't rush things. Someone has to keep the 'idle' in 'idle rich.' "

Clarice gave him a measuring look. "Lassitude is such a burden. But at least it keeps me busy." Glancing at her watch, she added, "In fact, I'm late for a tennis lesson."

"Nice to meet you," Ben said dismissively. "Formally, at least. I never spilled wine on your dress, did I?"

"Not that I recall." Turning to Whitney, she said, "Call you tomorrow," and left without another word to Ben. Nor did he mention Clarice.

They rowed out to the sailboat in a dinghy. Mooring it, they climbed onto the trim wooden boat. "It's beautiful," Whitney said. "I don't think I've ever seen one."

"It's from the early part of the twentieth century, made as a sporting boat for the wealthy. They call it a Herreshoff twelve and a half—its length on the waterline." He gestured at one of two benches opposite each other. "Sit over there, and we'll talk about what we're doing."

Whitney complied. "The whole point of the exercise," he began, "is good seamanship, safety, and enjoyment. This is a great boat to learn on—comfortable, responsive, simple in design, and, most of all, beautiful under sail. They don't make them like this now."

The usual irony in his voice had vanished altogether, replaced by an unalloyed appreciation of the craft and its abilities. Infected by his mood, Whitney asked, "When do we start?"

"Not today. It's essential to know a boat before you sail it." The sardonic note returned. "Sailing a Herreshoff isn't like driving a Fiat."

The glancing reference to Clarice pricked Whitney's curiosity. "Can I ask what the Bogart and Bacall routine was all about?"

"Is that what you thought it was? She isn't Bacall, and I'm certainly not Bogart—I wasn't having enough fun." His manner became brisk. "Back to why we're here, each part of this boat has a function, and a name. Before you learn how to sail, you have to master the language. So let's start."

Ben pointed at the sails. "The largest is its mainsail," he told her, "the smaller the jib. The two lines controlling them are the main and jib sheets. Watch, and I'll show you how to hoist them."

As he did, Ben pointed out the arrow atop the mast that showed the direction of the wind, then started naming other parts of the boat. For Whitney, terms like "bow," "tack," "gaff," and "head" were as bewildering as a foreign tongue. "I'll never remember all this," she protested.

"Don't need to." He took some folded papers from the pocket of his jeans. "I drew you up some diagrams with everything labeled. The artistry isn't great, but they're good enough to help you pass the exam."

"What exam?"

"The one you're taking before you sail the boat."

Whitney felt herself bridle. "This isn't first grade, Ben."

"Just the functional equivalent. I want you to know this boat as well as I did before I sailed it. When George Barkley let me take the tiller, it was one of the biggest privileges of my life."

The reverence in his tone surprised her. "Did you ever race it yourself?"

"I did." He spoke softly, gazing at the sailboat. "Someday I mean to own a boat just like it. Perhaps even this one."

"I don't know if Mr. Barkley would ever sell it."

"You never know. I can't see your friend bothering with it, and as near as I can make out, she's an only child. She certainly acts like one." He handed her the drawings. "Anyhow, take a look at these, and compare them to the real thing. It'll be easier to remember than you think."

Whitney began. Leaning back, Ben gazed out at Quitsa Pond in the bright sun of early afternoon, the woods and meadows on the gently sloping hills surrounding it half-concealing the houses—some old, some very new—which had a charmed perspective on the pond. With the sun on his face, Ben seemed to relax, his expression softening. After awhile, Whitney looked up at him again. "You must love this place," she said. "What was it like growing up here?"

"It had its moments. A life lived outdoors is bound to. You learn things other people don't."

He still had not mentioned his family, Whitney realized. "Did your dad teach you how to sail?"

Without looking at her, Ben gave a quick explosive laugh. "My father was a lobsterman. All he taught me was to set lobster pots, like his father taught him. My brother and I learned to sail by begging our way onto rich men's boats."

Whitney hesitated, then let her curiosity take over. "Are your parents still living?"

"If you can call it that. As far as I know, Dad's still *breathing*. Long ago I learned to my sorrow that being dead drunk isn't the same as being dead. My solution is not to deal with my father *or* my poor pathetic mother. Unless Jack ratted me out, they don't even know I'm back."

If anything, his emotionless monotone made the words more corrosive. Groping for a response, Whitney said, "I'm sorry."

"Don't be. Early on I learned a valuable lesson—that family can be a snake pit, with all the Rockwellian archetypes of love and warmth rubbing salt into the gaping wounds of reality. It's the setting in life where the gap between reality and myth is the widest and most damaging, all the more so because family claims us at birth and never lets go. Hobbes disguised as Santa Claus."

Thinking of Janine, Whitney wondered at the protective instinct that made her say, "Maybe I'm lucky, but my family isn't like that."

Removing his sunglasses, Ben gave her a long, skeptical look. "Fitzgerald said to Hemingway that 'the rich are different.' No doubt your parents are well educated and well mannered—as Hemingway retorted, 'they have more money.' But Yale gave me a window into the pretenses of the privileged. Affluent families can be even more lethal because their lies are more seductive, their methods of entrapment more subtle and sophisticated. Maybe when your father is a vicious, ill-educated drunk, and your mother timid and weak-willed, they're harder to sentimentalize. But don't you ever stand outside your family and question it?"

"Of course," Whitney said at once. "But that's different than being trapped in a lunatic asylum. Which is how you make it sound."

"Which is how it felt," Ben said, his tone matter-of-fact. "For islanders, they say, this is the poorest place in Massachusetts, with the richest life. For some that's no doubt true. Most people here farm or hunt or fish or grow things—they learn how to cope and how to share. A lot of them have extended families to help out. But my father was an only child—a drunk, an isolate, and mean as a snake. So we were on our own.

"The only relief came at night, after he'd passed out. On summer evenings I'd lie in the bedroom with Jack, listening in the dark to the Red Sox games, the announcers' voices and the sound of the crowd barely audible through the static, and try to imagine I was there in Fenway Park. I didn't want Jack to say a word, shatter the illusion. After a while I forgot our dad sleeping in his chair, or our mom praying he didn't wake up and hit her, and imagined that Ted Williams was my father—not just the greatest hitter who ever lived, but a fighter pilot in two wars, an ace, who gave up five of the best years of his career rather than be a coward. And I swore I'd become like him."

Surprised by this moment of self-revelation, with its undertone of melancholy and desperate hope, Whitney thought of her first memory of baseball. Her father was a fan of the Yankees, the Red Sox's hated rivals; the Yankees' president, a neighbor in Greenwich, had given her a baseball cap and a ball signed by Mickey Mantle, Whitey Ford, and their housekeeper Billie's favorite, Elston Howard. But none of these heroes held the totemic power Ted Williams did for Ben. Perhaps he needed to identify with Williams—or Robert Kennedy—in order to reinvent himself; compared to fighting in two wars, or running for president, dropping out of Yale was a mere down payment on courage. Then Whitney remembered interviewing her own father for a school project on family history. In contrast to his usual indulgence of her, Charles had been terse—his only interest was in the present, he told her, and the future. Instinctively, she sensed that he did not like to remember himself without money or advantages; it was as though he might become that person again, the solid ground of his achievements collapsing beneath him unless he were able to control his surroundings. But Ben had not yet left himself behind, Whitney saw—his scars were too fresh, and any hope of success lay in the future.

Aware of her own silence, she said, "How did that affect your brother?"

"Jack?" Ben repeated with veiled scorn. "It shrunk him. I'd watch my father beat my mother, then turn to Jack—two years older—praying he'd do something. He never did." Ben stared out at the pond, and Whitney could feel the rage trapped inside him escaping in words her presence had somehow catalyzed. "That's the reason I won't go to prison to avoid Vietnam, anymore than I'd run off to Canada. It was prison enough watching Jack placate our father, or tell our mother not to provoke him. Only cowards turn petty tyrants into gods." He paused, then spoke more deliberately. "When I was fifteen, I realized that it was going to be one of us—my father, or me. So I decided to take control for good."

The iron in his tone left Whitney caught between dread and curiosity. "How?" she asked.

Still Ben did not look at her. "I studied a book on boxing. Then I hung up a heavy bag in a neighbor's barn and tore into it everyday after school. Not to let the anger out, but to train, until the stuffing bled through the canvas. A sign from God, I thought.

"That night, at dinner, my father slapped my mother—there was something about the stew he didn't like. She was cowering in a corner with that same look of incomprehension, a small animal petrified of a big one. I got up from the table and grabbed him by the wrist. 'You're a pussy,' I told him. 'Good only for beating up women and small boys. You're just smart enough to know I've gotten way too big for that. But way too stupid to know what that means.' "

Whitney felt her stomach clench. "The bastard's eyes get big," Ben continued. "Suddenly he takes a swing at me. I duck, like I've taught myself, and Jack tries to step between us. 'Get out of my way,' I shout at him, 'or you'll come next.' " Ben's speech quickened. "Jack backs up a step. Before my father can move I pivot sideways and hit him in the gut with everything I've got. He doubles over, groaning. As he struggles to look up at me, I break his nose with a right cross." Ben's voice was thick now. "His blood spurts on the floor. I'm breathing hard, years of hatred welling up. 'Remember hitting me?' I manage to say, and send a left to his mouth that knocks out his front teeth.

"My father starts blubbering, and he looks like Halloween. I pull him up by the throat and press my thumbs on his larynx 'til his eyes bulge. 'I run this house now,' I told him. 'You just live here. Hit her again, and I'll cut your balls off with a butter knife.' "

Whitney felt herself recoil. Suddenly Ben stopped himself, as though sensing her reaction. He breathed once, then turned to her, eyes filled with shame and fierceness, his mouth twisted in a smile of self-contempt. "Listen to me," he said in a chastened voice, "awash in self-pity masked as heroics. I never talk to anyone like this. God knows why I inflicted myself on you."

"People talk to me, Ben. They always have. As strange as that may seem to you."

Ben looked at her intently. "Not so strange," he said more softly. "Anyhow, I've kept you here long enough."

Whitney did not protest. On the trip home, Ben said almost nothing. He stopped at the foot of her driveway, well short of the house. To her surprise, he got out of the truck as she did.

Once more his tone was expressionless, his face closed. "I'm sorry, Whitney. You didn't need any of that. I'm not quite right yet, and I've spent too much time alone."

"I didn't mind listening, really. A lot has happened to you."

The smile he gave her was more like a grimace. "If you want to, we can try this again in a few days. Without the family portrait."

"I'd like that," Whitney told him, unsure of whether she would. As if perceiving this, he turned abruptly, got back in the truck, and drove away.

She watched him go, trying to imagine how it felt to be Benjamin Blaine. Then she heard footsteps on the gravel.

Turning, she saw Peter, freshly arrived on the Vineyard, still wearing a suit from work. "Who was that?" he asked.

"Just a guy I met—the caretaker next door. He's teaching me how to sail."

Peter's usually guileless eyes were questioning. "Looked to me like you were pretty caught up in him."

"Hope so. Mom always taught me to look at whoever was speaking to me." Before he could answer, she kissed him, pressing her body against his. "Only two days, and I've missed you already."

Mollified, Peter took her hand. "Not as much as I've missed you. Why don't we get a gin and tonic? Pretending to be a grown-up is hard work."

The next morning, Whitney drove to Dogfish Bar alone. Instead of swimming first, she opened her journal, wanting to write but unsure of where to start. Finally, she began.

I've never met anyone like him. Maybe this is melodramatic, but somehow I think he'll end up famous—or dead. There's something brilliant about him, and something terribly damaged. If I truly believed in prayer, he's someone who I'd pray for.

She stopped, thinking about his family, feeling lucky in her own. Then honesty caught up with her, and she picked up the pen again.

I've done nothing about Janine.

Nine

Sitting beside Whitney on a beach towel, Clarice languidly spread suntan oil on her slender, perfect legs. The sky was clear; the air, cut by a fitful breeze, was temperate and dry. On the transistor radio beside them Grace Slick was belting out "White Rabbit." Casually, Clarice said, "Sorry if I barged in on you yesterday."

Lying back, Whitney put on her sunglasses. "It's your boat, after all. Anyhow, I thought you and Ben really hit it off."

"If he's not careful," Clarice responded with a laugh, "that chip on his shoulder will turn him into a hunchback. But I'll admit to being intrigued. Especially since your dad called mine to ask about him."

Surprised, Whitney turned on her elbow. "Did your dad say why?"

"Obviously, your parents are curious about who you're spending time with. I just thought you should know."

Angered, Whitney wondered if Charles had also spoken with Peter. "That's pretty irritating—it's like I'm two years old. What did your father tell him?"

"I guess Dad allowed that Ben was a pretty good sailor. He did ask me what *I* knew about him.

'Next to nothing,' I told him, and decided to see for myself."

Whitney felt on edge. "Please tell me that you're not reporting back to your dad. Who's reporting back to mine."

"Of course not," Clarice protested. "I love both our dads, but you're my best friend. Besides, a certain level of obliviousness is good for parents. Sometimes cluelessness really *is* bliss."

"I guess I'll bite, then," Whitney found herself saying. "What *did* you think of Ben?"

Gazing up at a skittering cirrus cloud, Clarice considered her answer. "He's sex on a sailboat— and knows it. But there's something dangerous about him. You can almost feel it on your skin."

As usual, Whitney thought, Clarice was able to put her own instincts into words. "And here I thought it was poison ivy."

"You know what I mean. He seems like a guy who knows what he wants and how to get it." A quizzical look crossed Clarice's face, as though she had just surprised herself. "In a funny way, he reminds me of your dad."

Whitney turned on her elbow. "What drugs are you taking? I can't even imagine them in the same room."

"You're talking about politics, Whit, or maybe class. This is about who they are. Your dad's the best, but would *you* want to cross him?"

"How do you mean?"

Clarice gave her a shrewd look. "He's your father, I know, and for you he's charm incarnate. But if you back up and watch, you can sense a very cool brain at work, constantly alert to whatever might affect his interests." Her tone became mollifying. "I'm not comparing them as people—Ben's got an edge that is all his own. I'm just saying that he looks like someone hell-bent on having his way in the world."

Whitney eyed her friend. "You seem to have gotten a lot from those five magical minutes."

"I did, actually," Clarice responded with serene assurance. "I hope it doesn't irritate you to talk about Ben Blaine."

"It doesn't. I just wonder why it's worth our time. It's not like I'm going to sleep with him."

Clarice pushed her sunglasses down her nose, scrutinizing Whitney over the rim. "That's a funny thing to say. Especially for someone who's getting married."

A Frisbee landed at Whitney's feet. Waiting for a lanky guy and his terrier to retrieve it, Whitney composed her response. "What I'm trying to suggest, Clarice, is that it should be unremarkable for men and women to spend time together. The way we were brought up is antiquated: guys are the people you marry, and women the ones you get for friends—segregation by function. All because our genitals are different."

"But they *are* different," Clarice responded with

the patience of a teacher whose student is a bit dull-witted. "And we're different. Since time began we've played different roles in the world."

Whitney scanned the crowded beach—men and women and families clustered together, some under bright umbrellas, one mother reading as her husband built a sand castle with a small girl and smaller boy. "Maybe that made sense when we lived in caves—I'm pretty sure Peter would eclipse me in killing saber-toothed tigers. But my dad uses his brain, and there's no inherent reason I couldn't work with him just as well as Peter does."

Clarice gave her a thin smile. "Start expressing these uncomfortable truths aloud, Whitney, and people will think you're a feminist." To ward off Whitney's retort, Clarice hastily continued, "I'm not trying to put you down—honestly. But men are competitive and less nurturing. They start wars; we have babies. They get erections from looking at pictures of naked women. We don't look at pictures of naked guys with erections. Just be glad that most of them don't get erections looking at pictures of other guys with erections. Imagine the implications of that." As Whitney began laughing, Clarice concluded with mock profundity, "You and I wouldn't exist, and the world as we know it would end. Which is why *Playboy* is part of God's plan."

This explication of the world according to

Clarice piqued Whitney's curiosity. "*Is* there a God, Professor Barkley?"

"Seriously? We won't know until we die, will we—the ones who die before us don't give exit interviews. So it's just easier for people to say they *do* know." Pausing, Clarice asked pointedly, "Aren't you and Peter having an Episcopalian priest perform the wedding ceremony?"

"Of course."

"Then expect to hear more about God than you and Peter. And nobody there will ask if God exists, or why He isn't a woman. I certainly won't—some things aren't worth the trouble of upsetting anyone. In our circles, at least, most people don't like thinking about things they've already decided are decided. If that makes sense."

Once again, Whitney was impressed by the cynical wisdom concealed by her friend's sunny façade. "It does, actually."

Encouraged, Clarice went breezily on. "Once the honeymoon starts, God will return to His proper place, and you'll be back in the world of men. One man, particularly, who'll want you to go down on him every so often. In that way, Venice will look a lot like Dartmouth. Assuming Peter likes that, though I never met a man who didn't. Sometimes my vagina just can't compete . . ."

Amused and appalled, Whitney interjected, "Good God, Clarice . . ."

"God has nothing to do with that one," Clarice

persisted blithely. "Funny how that's when they gasp the loudest."

Covering her face in mock horror, Whitney remembered her mother's one remark on oral sex: "Thank God your father never insisted on it, let alone the other thing. When I think of homosexuals, it's hard to imagine an entire relationship based on that." Between her fingers, she murmured, "This conversation would simply horrify my mom."

"What a surprise. Mine would sooner turn communist than utter the words 'blow job.' But moms aren't exactly our target audience."

"Put it this way," Whitney acknowledged, "I don't think Peter minds a lot."

"You're a truly keen observer, Whitney." Lying back, Clarice stretched out her body to take full advantage of the sun, reminding Whitney of a cat lying beneath the window. "Speaking of which, do *you* think young Mr. Blaine is sexy?"

"At the risk of disappointing you, I've never thought about it."

"Come off it, Whit—it's just how people are. I'm sure *he's* thought about it, not to suggest that he's obsessed with you. I bet he even wondered about me—he'd probably wonder about your mother, if he ever met her. According to a highly scientific survey I read in *Cosmopolitan*, if you only think about sex every fifteen minutes, you're probably dead."

"I think part of him is dead," Whitney retorted. "Or at least in a coma."

Turning her head, Clarice looked at her with renewed curiosity. "What do you mean by *that?*"

"Until a month ago he was traveling with Bobby Kennedy. It sounds like Ben knew him pretty well—for sure he believed in him enough to drop out of Yale. The assassination has made him really bitter."

Clarice took this in, her expression changing from surprised to sympathetic. "I'm sure it must have," she allowed. "Look how it upset you, and even me. But people outlive grief, and so will he."

"Maybe so. But Ben had a pretty rough time before that. Bad family, no money. All his life he's been pretty much on his own."

"You seem to know a lot about him."

"He talks, I listen. Right now he needs that, and maybe it's better with someone he's not close to."

A skeptical look surfaced in Clarice's cornflower-blue eyes. "So maybe you're his therapist. But while he's pouring out his heart, he's still thinking about sex. If you're human, there's no escaping human nature."

It was time, Whitney decided, to divert the conversation from herself. "So what did *you* think when you were looking at Ben?"

Clarice emitted a theatrical sigh. "I always have to be the brave one, don't I? Okay, Whit. Ben's no boy. If he ever got around to it, a girl would know. You wouldn't have to teach him anything." She regarded Whitney seriously. "He has a certain fascination, I'll admit—danger always does. But you see a brooding, lonely guy. I see a hungry and ambitious guy with trouble written all over him, who's had more women than I've got fingers and toes."

"I'll be sure to ask him about that," Whitney replied sarcastically, and decided to change the subject altogether. Ben meant little to her; she wasn't even sure she wanted to see him. But talking about him like this felt invasive and uncomfortable, just like her father's questions. For reasons Whitney could not name, she sensed no good would come of it.

Ten

Half-teasing, half-curious, Whitney said, "Just between us, Clarice, how many guys have *you* slept with?"

"More than you have," Clarice answered briskly, "which wouldn't be hard. But please don't play the innocent, Whitney. Both of us broke sexual barriers."

"Me? How did I manage that?"

"By sleeping with Peter. We've already rejected this ridiculous notion of being virgins until we marry, turning our honeymoon into the Amateur

Hour. Because of the Pill, we can have the freedom men do. The difference being we still have to pretend we're different."

"I thought you just said we *are* different."

"Women have more self-control, for sure—we've had to. But for the longest time I thought we were another species, because that's what our mothers said. They raised us in the cult of virginity, to be sacrificed on the altar of marriage in exchange for eternal love. What nonsense."

Whitney smiled in recognition. "After we were engaged, my mom said, 'Peter will be gentle, I'm sure. But if it hurts, tell him.' I couldn't figure out whether she really believed I was still a virgin, or just wanted to preserve the myth."

"Such a trap," Clarice said ruefully. "Sleeping with my first guy was really a big deal. So I tried to believe I loved him. Then I realized I didn't have to marry him just because I'd opened up my legs. And if *that* made no sense, neither had saving it for marriage."

"And you didn't regret it?"

Clarice shook her head. "I was free to do what I wanted. Don't you ever want to have sex just because you feel like it?"

"Sure," Whitney conceded. "That's when I remember my suitemate's paper on masturbation. Required reading among our friends."

"Sometimes you have to be your own best friend," Clarice concurred with a smile. "But the

Pill has given us choices—no pregnancy, no risky abortions, and all we have to worry about is getting some disease. We can sleep with whomever."

Whitney paused to scan the beach: in the warm mid-afternoon sun, kids scampered in the surf, and a few fishermen with fly rods had begun casting into the waters. Pensive, Clarice pulled out a pack of Chesterfield filters and lit one, another small act of rebellion indulged out of her parents' sight. In her friend's contemplative silence, Whitney reflected on how Clarice's commentary echoed in her own life—anxieties about missed periods, the silence between girls and their mothers. Though it occasionally unnerved her, Whitney valued Clarice's candor.

Still, she sometimes wondered about her friend. The more reckless of her college acquaintances had picked up guys at Charlie's, the townie bar, and one had even bragged about sleeping with Wilt Chamberlain before she contracted herpes. For Whitney, she became the cautionary tale that confirmed Anne Dane's advice—if you sleep around, bad things will follow, and your reputation will be ruined. Ostensibly, Clarice's code was different: she could sleep with who she wanted as long as she was discreet. But in an odd way, Whitney realized, both Clarice and Anne arrived at the same place—reputation was perception.

Stubbing out her cigarette, Clarice interrupted

Whitney's musing, "On the subject of Peter, let me pose a hypothetical. If you hadn't decided to sleep with him, would you be getting married now?"

Whitney recalled the pressure she had felt to yield: though Peter's desire had been sweetly pressed, she was overcome by the fear of losing the first boy who had ever loved her. "I don't know," she answered honestly. "But I'm glad I did."

"You should be," Clarice said firmly. "Men care even more about sex than they do about baseball. It's only a fraction of the time they spend with us, and their orgasm is over in ten seconds. But they think about it for hours, which keeps them coming back. Though they don't know it, their penises empower us. And when we lose our figures, or our looks, the power goes away. We can only hope that our husbands sentimentalize us when we're old. Unless, of course, they're much older than we are."

Clarice said this so clinically that Whitney felt the chill of loneliness. "I wonder how much power Janine has."

"Very little," Clarice responded with a phlegmatic shrug. "She's way too anxious to have any sense of strategy."

"But you do."

"I'd like to think so. God knows women should have one. Men like our fathers make the world, allowing others to live in it. The difference is that your dad could eat mine alive." Clarice's expression became serious. "Your grandfather Padgett was smart—your mother too. They needed a man to preserve their place in business, and picked out Charles Dane. Now your family goes on as it should. Maybe that's what I meant about Ben resembling your father—someone who can take life by the throat."

It was revealing, Whitney thought, that Clarice had doubled back to Ben and her father. "Do you mind me asking, Clarice, if something's worrying you?"

Clarice frowned at this, as though begrudging an answer. "My mom worries."

"Should she?"

"I've got no way of telling, and no interest in Dad's business. All I know is that we made our money three generations back. My father runs the company because he's the only son, not because he's good at it." Clarice gazed off in the distance. "Lately, I've thought he'd rather be painting landscapes. Which would be fine, except that it concerns my mother. Which has started me wondering if there's trouble."

Through other friends, Whitney had seen fathers who had frittered away a family business or squandered an inheritance, trading affluence for struggle, respect for pity. But she had never imagined this threatening Clarice. "If it came to that," she assured her friend, "I'm sure my dad would help."

Clarice smiled a little. "I guess he could, couldn't he?"

The next morning, Whitney returned to Dogfish Bar.

This time she brought a book to read, chosen over *The Confessions of Nat Turner* by her parents' friend, Bill Styron—John Updike's *Couples*, a novel of adultery among the upwardly mobile residents of a New England suburb. But though the first few chapters were seductive enough to intrigue her, she turned back to her diary.

Today, she found, her subject was Clarice.

Clarice has always competed with me, lightly, for my dad's attention. I've never thought about it much; when it comes to jealousy, Janine had all my attention. But now I realize more clearly that my father symbolizes the dominant male who can protect the only life Clarice has known. Which would explain the instinctive rejection/attraction I think she feels for Ben, for all their differences in class. Perhaps because my father, too, came from nothing.

Pausing, Whitney gazed out at the calm blue horizon, waiting for fresh thoughts to surface. But the one that did stirred discontent with herself.

I just caught myself wondering if Clarice was jealous of me. How foolish—Janine is one thing; Clarice another. Perhaps I need to imagine that more attractive women—my sister, my best friend, even my mother—secretly envy me for reasons I can't even name. Worse than projection, such fantasies are pathetic; worse yet, they make no sense. Believing that other people wish they were you is the first step toward the insane asylum.

Putting down the journal, she headed for the water, resolved to exorcise her toxins through a vigorous swim.

Eleven

Mid-morning sun cast a glow on the ocean, warmer in early July. Whitney waded out until the lapping waters reached her waist, then dove in, swimming with strong, sure strokes toward the sandbar. Then something struck her leg with a sudden stinging lash.

A searing pain shot through her. With animal incomprehension, she flailed ahead in panic, desperate to escape her attacker. With the next thrashing stroke, her head struck a rock, jolting her neck and spine. Darkness surrounded her; stunned, she was conscious only of salt water flooding her lungs. As the darkness thickened to a surreal black, her consciousness began slipping away.

Something grasped her waist. In a feeble reflex, her legs kicked. But she could not escape. Then she was pulled from the water and thrown down, rough hands pushing on her chest, an insistent mouth forcing hers to open.

"Breathe out, dammit."

His palms pressed harder into her thorax. Whitney coughed, body wracking, water spewing from her mouth. Her eyes half opened. In mute recognition she saw Ben's face inches from hers, eyes intent, his breathing ragged. Words escaped her raw throat in a croak. "What happened?"

Relief flashed in his eyes. "I saw you thrashing around and realized you weren't doing the butterfly." His gaze ran down her body. "From the welt on your leg, I'd guess a Portuguese man-of-war whipped you pretty hard. But you'll live. This shouldn't spoil your wedding."

Whitney felt a wave of nausea. They were on the sandbar, she realized, the sun warming her clammy face. Then she was drifting away. Closing her eyes, she murmured, "I need to lie here."

"No one to stop you," she heard him say, and then heard nothing at all.

When her eyes fluttered open, she had lost all sense of time. Ben watched her intently. "Was I asleep?"

"More like shock. You barely snored at all."

She hoped this was a joke. "I never thanked you, did I?

"No manners, I guess. Try to sit up."

Using her elbows, Whitney looked around her. The world was as before, only brighter. "I could have died."

Sitting back on his knees, Ben smiled a little. "It's hard to drown in five feet of water. Though it did look like you were trying."

His T-shirt and shorts were damp, she thought in foolish surprise. "I didn't see you."

"When I got here, you were headed out for a swim. I decided to wait."

She did not ask him why. Taking another deep breath, she examined the raised red welt that felt like it had poisoned her. "I still don't feel so great."

"You won't for awhile. The first thing is to get you home. Think you can stand?"

Using her hands, Whitney tried to push herself up on her good leg. Ben clasped her hips, helping. "Better lean on me."

She did that, feeling her imbalance. "How do we get to shore?"

"I'll prop you up so you can hobble on one leg. Let's try."

Together, she and Ben started laboring through the waist deep water, Ben's arms around her waist. The salt water stung her leg.

Stoic, Whitney bit back cries of pain. They forged on together, silent, until they reached the sand. She stopped there, inhaling the fresh salty air. "Terra firma," Ben said. "Kind of. One good hurricane and this beach ends up at your place."

With Ben at her elbow, Whitney hobbled back to her blanket. Kneeling, he picked up her clothes and journal. "I'll drive you home."

"My car's here."

"No kidding? I thought you flew." He glanced at her impatiently. "Only a moron would let you drive. Someone can pick up the car."

Whitney hobbled with him to his beat-up truck, leg throbbing. In the truck bed was a fly rod, tackle box, spools of test line, and a half-finished bottle of whisky she supposed he sipped while fishing on a cool, windy night. Ben opened the door to help her, then began driving down the bumpy dirt road. "I'd play music to distract you," he said, "but the radio's busted."

"How long have you had this truck?"

"Since sophomore year in high school. Those catering jobs paid for it."

Whitney thought again about how little he had, how much she took for granted. She wondered if he thought her a spoiled rich girl, like Clarice, then was certain that he did. She sat back, closing her eyes until they entered her driveway.

Parking, Ben got out and opened her door. "I'll

walk you to the house," he informed her brusquely. "I don't want you passing out on your parents' doorstep or throwing up on their lawn. Just lean against me, okay?"

Without awaiting her answer, he put his arm around her waist and began helping her to the porch.

Sitting in a chaise longue, Anne put down her magazine, giving her daughter a look of puzzlement and alarm. Then she hurried to open the screen door. "What happened to you?" she asked quickly.

Still propped against Ben, Whitney stood straighter. "I'm okay now. But a stingray swiped me while I was swimming, and I guess my head hit a rock. If it weren't for Ben, I might have drowned."

Anne glanced at him, taking Whitney's hand. "Please come in," she told Ben.

He followed them in, standing to the side of the chaise. Whitney saw him peer into the living room, taking in the Persian rugs and antique furnishings, the decorative vases Anne had added with such care. Settling Whitney onto a chair, her mother looked up at him. "Thank you," she said with quiet politeness. "I can't express how grateful I am."

He shrugged his shoulders. "A freak accident, Mrs. Dane. One in a million."

"That's how I feel about my daughter." Anne

hesitated, then added, "May I get you a cup of coffee?"

"No, thanks," Ben responded with a smile. "I'm too wet to sit on the furniture. Anyhow, I need to get going. Work to do, and all that." Turning to Whitney, he told her, "Your leg's going to hurt for a couple of days. Keep off of it, and try to keep from drowning in the bathtub."

Both nettled and amused, Whitney retorted, "That was pretty condescending."

"It was, wasn't it?" Facing her mother, Ben inquired, "Have any meat tenderizer around?"

"I'm sure not. We never use it."

A corner of Ben's mouth twitched. "They sell it at the Chilmark Store. It also acts as an antidote to this kind of sting. Put it on her, and it'll cut down the pain and swelling."

"What about sailing," Whitney said to him. "You don't have to stand on a sailboat."

Ben gave her a long, dubious look. "Study those drawings?"

"No," Whitney admitted. "Not yet."

"Maybe you'll have time now. You certainly won't be playing tennis."

At the corner of her eye, Whitney saw her mother watching their exchange. As though sensing this, Ben said, "Nice to meet you, Mrs. Dane," and turned to leave, stepping off the porch with a careless wave over his shoulder.

"So that's the boy," Anne said. "Or the man, I

198

suppose." Pausing to gaze after his retreating figure, she added, "What was he doing on the beach, one wonders."

"Minding his own business, I expect. At least until I started drowning."

Anne regarded her closely. In her most careful voice, she said, "I don't suppose you arranged to meet him."

The not-so-subtle insinuation reminded Whitney of her father's quiet inquiry to George Barkley. "Why would I?" she answered sharply.

Anne kept studying her face. "Yes," she said at length. "Why should you. Let's get you out of that swimsuit and into bed."

PART THREE

Adversaries

Martha's Vineyard

July–August 1968

One

Two mornings later, limping slightly, Whitney went to find Ben.

He was at the mooring behind the house he tended, ripping away rotted boards and hammering new ones into place. Standing at the end of the catwalk, Whitney waited for him to notice her.

At last he did, turning as he rested on his knees. "How you doing?"

"Much better. I just came over to thank you."

Ben wiped the sweat from his eyes. "No need. You already did."

Whitney paused, weighing whether to express her feelings. "I guess so. But I wasn't sure we were adequately effusive."

Ben shot her a sideways grin. "Your mom wasn't exactly thrilled to see me, was she? At least I didn't track seaweed on the Persian rugs."

"She was just startled." There was no point in saying more about her mother, Whitney realized. "Speaking for myself, I'm happy to be alive."

Ben put down his hammer, regarding her with an indecipherable expression. "Speaking for yourself, want to cook some lobster on the beach tonight? I haven't done that in years."

Stuck between gratitude and ambivalence, Whitney hesitated. "Where should I meet you?"

He gave her a knowing smile. "Here's fine. Bring some wine, if you have it."

When she left the house that night, she told Anne she was going out with Clarice, chagrined that Ben had read daughter and mother so well.

They drove to Menemsha a little before seven. The fishing village felt quaint and peaceful—the trawlers were in, the last soft putter of an outboard motor echoed in the harbor, and the sun slipped toward the ocean in a pastel sky. All that was open was the fish market. Ben and Whitney ordered two lobsters and drove to Dogfish Bar.

In the bed of Ben's truck was a lobster pot and a cooler containing ice, shrimp, and a container of green salad, to which Whitney contributed a bottle of Chassagne-Montrachet from her parents' spare refrigerator. As they reached the rise sheltering the beach, the half disk of a setting sun cast a shimmering glow on the water, backlighting the line of clouds bright orange. "It's what I love about this place," Ben told her.

Gathering driftwood and dried seaweed, they dug a pit with their hands. Within minutes Ben had a fire crackling beneath the pot, and they were sipping wine from paper cups. Then Whitney heard the still-living crustaceans rattling around in their cardboard container. "It feels weird to boil them alive."

"That's why I didn't name them," Ben said

laconically. "That way you don't become attached." He took another sip of wine. "Do you folks always drink nectar like this?"

"Always."

The last traces of sunlight faded in a cobalt sky. As Ben tossed the wriggling lobsters into the pot, Whitney reflected on her meager cooking skills. All her life, various people had provided her meals: Billie or her mother at home; her father at restaurants; cooks at summer camps, boarding school, and college. There was a metaphor here, she supposed—others had always taken care of her needs. Now it would be Peter and, she admitted, her father. Little wonder that Clarice worried about her own father, or that Whitney had been more grateful than rebellious. Little wonder Ben felt so much older.

"How did you get into Yale?" she asked.

Ben started stirring butter into a skillet. "I was always smart enough. But I didn't know what to do. Fortunately, I had an English teacher and a coach who helped me win a scholarship." His voice softened. "When I got in, I damn near wept. Neither of my parents had gotten past eighth grade. Now I was going somewhere I'd never dreamed of, all because two other people cared enough to tell me I could."

Whitney could feel Ben's wonder at his own deliverance. "You must have felt really grateful to them."

"Not felt—feel, and not just to them. A lot of my classmates were the sons of rich alumni. For them, going to Yale was as natural as breathing. But I'd never have gotten there without people who funded scholarships like mine." Taking lobster tongs from a grocery bag, Ben continued in the same quiet tone. "Same for Yale's president—even though some alumni hated it, he pushed to admit more Jews and blacks and public school kids. Without Kingman Brewster, I don't get to Yale."

Though Whitney did not say so, her family knew the Brewsters. They had a summer place on West Chop; the Brewsters and the Danes interacted socially, and Janine and Whitney knew their kids. That the Brewster children might be viewed as somewhat aimless served, in her father's view, to confirm what befalls the offspring of wealthy liberals. But Whitney admired Kingman Brewster for his principles. "What was Yale like for you?" she asked.

"A mixed bag." Ben deposited the lobsters on paper plates. "It opened me up to a larger world—not just ideas, but possibilities. It also stripped the varnish off our pretenses about equality. My closest friends were like me—without connections to the clubby world of the East Coast establishment, the network of influence that protects each new generation of the lucky sperm club. Some of our smugger classmates called us 'blips'—accidents in the life of Yale. They're the ones who have jobs waiting for them, and will never see Vietnam except on television."

This last sentence, clearly referring to Peter, was delivered so casually that it took a moment for Whitney to react. "Up to this moment," she said sharply, "I was enjoying myself. But you just can't stifle your resentments, can you?"

The look he gave her contained a glimmer of regret. "No," he acknowledged. "I can't. But can you say I'm wrong?"

Whitney weighed her answer. "Yes, if you're calling Peter smug. He's one of the kindest people I know."

Ben poured them both more wine. "And generous enough to let somebody else get drafted in his place. But Peter aside, I don't hear a rousing defense of privilege."

"I won't defend Peter or myself," Whitney said evenly, "or a world we didn't make. All I can do is try to become a halfway decent human being. But whatever I am, I'm not accountable to you."

To her surprise, Ben smiled at this. "Fair enough, Whitney. I don't want to spoil your lobster."

Using a nutcracker and small fork, he separated the tail and meat from shell, placing them on her plate. Then he served her salad and put a cup of drawn butter between them. They ate in the glow of the fire, its warmth cutting the chill of descending night. Content, Whitney watched the stars appear in the darkness over the water, listened to the faint susurrus of waves splashing on the sand.

After a while, Ben told her, "What I should have said is that I won't turn into one more guy who pulls the ladder up after me, forgetting who lent me a hand. Too many people still don't get the chance that I had."

"I agree, Ben. That's what you should have said."

He held up his hand. "That was a semi-apology, okay? So let me ask a simple question—how many blacks and Jews came to your parents' home? Except for those favorite mealtime companions, Uncle Ben and Aunt Jemima."

Whitney gave him an arid smile. "Are you trying to prove that you're incorrigible? As I'm sure you know, blacks don't live in Greenwich, and there weren't many at Rosemary Hall or Wheaton. I did have a Jewish friend in college, if you're still keeping score."

Whitney paused there, remembering a class-mate saying indulgently about her friend, "Lisa doesn't seem that Jewish to me." Lisa had later confessed to Whitney that she worried about being stereotyped. Though Whitney had reassured her, Lisa had been right to worry; her subsequent engagement to a guy from Brown raised a stink within his family, culminating in their stiffly worded request that any children be raised as Episcopalians. Whitney had been dismayed; though there were no Jews among their closer family friends, she had never heard a trace of anti-Semitism from either of her parents. "Actually," she continued, "Lisa encouraged me to tutor in Roxbury. Maybe that seems like naïve do-gooding to you, two white girls spending a couple of hours in the ghetto before returning to the cloistered halls. But at least we did something."

Ben's expression changed, becoming thoughtful and even conciliatory. "You're right, Whitney. No one's responsible for where they're born, only for what they do. For myself, I'd have happily traded places with you or your fiancé. Feel free to call me on it."

The surprising concession softened Whitney's defenses. "And vice-versa, Ben. But without taking shots at a guy I love, who you don't even know."

Ben batted away a stray cinder. "A last question, then. Did Peter applaud your forays into Roxbury?"

Once again, Whitney considered her answer. "If it matters to you, Peter respects me enough to support anything I do."

From the glint in his eyes, Ben caught her syntactical evasion. "But has he ever asked what *you* want, or taken an interest in your writing? Or does he assume that all you need from life is to be married?"

Whitney did not know what stung her more—Ben's assumption that he knew the answers, or the questions themselves. "I don't want to talk about Peter," she said stiffly. "I don't know why you do."

"How quickly I've fallen from grace," Ben said in mock dismay. "All I'm really wondering is what you want for yourself."

At first Whitney did not answer. The final stanza of the Wheaton Hymn sounded in her mind:

A hundred years pass like a dream
Yet early founders still are we
Whose works are greater than they seem
Because of what we yet shall be
In the bright noon of other days
Mid other men and other ways.

The future was open, the hopeful words had said to her, Whitney's to write for herself. But perhaps her future was already written. "I don't know yet," she admitted.

In the light of the fire, Ben studied her. "You've still got time," he said, and left it there.

That night, unable to sleep, Whitney took *Couples* to the library, and began reading in the light of a standing lamp. To her surprise, Charles emerged from the bedroom in robe and slippers, headed for the kitchen before he spotted Whitney.

"Hi, Dad. When did you get home?"

"A few hours ago. I decided to start the weekend early."

He did not say why, and Whitney recognized the abstracted look he wore when there was something on his mind. Instead, he asked, "What do you think of the book?"

"Too soon to tell, except that Updike's a wonderful stylist. I stop to reread a sentence, and wonder if I could ever write anything that perfect."

Charles gave her a veiled look. "The language is fine, I'm sure. But I understand that the story is elegant smut—one act of adultery after another. You might have chosen something a little bit more uplifting."

What was this about, Whitney wondered. "It's just a novel, Dad."

"No doubt I'm a bit musty in my tastes. This is a free country, after all, where adults can read what they like." Her father sat across from her. "Still, I've often thought that people's lives are defined by the thoughts they choose to entertain. But I wonder if books like this cause people to consider doing things they otherwise wouldn't."

Watching his face, Whitney sensed a second, wordless conversation lurking beneath the first. Mildly, she said, "I hope you're not including me."

Solemn, Charles appraised her. "Of course not,

Whitney. You've always had a sturdy character, as well as a fine mind. It's just that a society is defined by what the more educated deem acceptable, whether in art or film or—in this case—a novel that elevates infidelity."

Whitney gave him a deflective smile. "I won't know if I've become wanton until I finish the book. Then I'll tell you how I turned out."

His smile in return was measured. "Please don't, Whitney. I like you too much as you are."

Without saying more, Charles proceeded to the kitchen.

Whitney put down the book, pondering the recesses of her father's mind. Did his core philosophy, focused on predictability and order, exist to suppress something in human nature that he deeply feared—whether personified by demonstrators, leftists, or a novelist who dared to write so explicitly about adultery and despair? But there was no one to whom she could express those thoughts. Except, perhaps, for Benjamin Blaine, and that would feel like a betrayal of her family and, even worse, of Peter.

Two

The next day dawned warm and clear. Whitney got up eager to test her leg in a tennis match with Clarice. It was good to be young, she thought; somehow this reminded her to wonder about her sister. Checking her watch, she called Janine.

The phone rang for a long time. Whitney was about to hang up when her sister answered, "Who is it?"

Her tone sounded off, groggy yet anxious. "It's Whitney, Janine. Are you feeling okay?"

"Whitney," Janine repeated, and her voice became lifeless. "I had an all-day photo shoot, then I stayed out late. Call me some other time."

"Okay," Whitney began, and heard the click of her sister hanging up.

She found her mother sitting on the porch, sipping coffee as she gazed out at the dewy grass and, beyond it, the swath of ocean visible through the trees. It was Anne's favorite time, with the house still quiet, the day untouched by the disorder of normal life, when she could lose herself in unspoken reveries and, Whitney was sure, remembrances of her mother and a childhood that, in the filter of time, had become flawlessly secure. Whitney sat beside her, saying hesitantly, "I haven't heard anything from Janine lately. Have you?"

"Of course."

"I was just wondering why we haven't seen her more."

Putting down her cup, Anne kept gazing toward the water. "I miss her, too. But she's busy with photo shoots, and her social calendar sounds fuller than ever. That doesn't leave her much time to visit."

This cool recital, Whitney sensed, was designed to close the subject. "Think there's anyone special?" she asked.

"Not that I know of, Whitney. It's more that so many men keep asking her out. Her usual problem of traffic control."

That this sounded like a catechism enhanced Whitney's concern for Janine. "Just wondering," she said. "I should go change for tennis."

Breeze rippling her blond hair, Clarice drove them to West Chop with the top down on her Fiat convertible, radio tuned to Janis Joplin singing "Me and Bobby McGee."

"There's something wrong with Janine," Whitney told her. "When I called her this morning, she could barely speak. It was like she'd fallen down a mine shaft."

Clarice turned down the main street of Vineyard

Haven, still sleepy at this hour of the morning. "Had she been drinking?"

"Her voice was slurry enough. But to me she sounded more anxious and depressed. All she said was I'd woken her up."

"At nine o'clock in the morning? What a shock. This *is* Janine we're talking about, Whitney."

"I think she's in trouble," Whitney insisted. "But no one else does. More and more it seems like my mother's world depends on airbrushing unpleasant thoughts. Even my dad's. Last night he found me reading *Couples*, and gave a lecture on how books about adultery destroy the social fabric. Like if I read about it, I'll do it."

Clarice glanced at her. "What do you suppose *that's* about?"

Whitney thought she knew. But she did not want to say so; perhaps she was more like her mother than she wished. "I don't know, really. Except that it upset him."

Clarice gave her a second, more narrow-eyed glance, then shrugged. "So read it in your bedroom," she advised.

Passing the lighthouse, they arrived in West Chop. Shaded and well maintained, the tennis court was surrounded by the large and venerable houses of families like the Brewsters who, for generations, had gazed out at the water from their private enclave. Reflecting on her conversation with Ben, Whitney realized that everyone she knew there was Protestant and privileged. "Out of curiosity," Whitney asked, "do you know any Jews who live here?"

Clarice gave her a querying, amused look. "I'm not a demographer, Whitney. But are you sure that's even allowed?"

Without awaiting an answer, she took her place on the court.

They rallied for awhile, allowing Whitney to determine that she ran well enough to play. Once it began, their match was competitive as always— whereas Clarice was swift and graceful, Whitney was dogged and more consistent, scrambling to return the ball until Clarice hit some stylish but erratic stroke just out of bounds or into the net. Within forty minutes, Whitney had won the first set six to four.

"I wouldn't call that pretty," Clarice groused mildly. "But you're amazingly persistent. Some days it feels like I'm playing against a backboard."

More pleased than she should be, Whitney chose not to mention her throbbing leg. "Why don't we rest up, Clarice. I know this can't be easy for you."

They sat on a shaded bench, two young girls in white tennis dresses on a fresh summer morning, content in each other's company. "So," Clarice asked, "is the wedding falling into place?"

"Pretty much. It's more afterward that I'm

wondering about. I've been thinking about some sort of career."

"What does Peter say?"

"Not much. He wants my parents' life—kids, a place in Greenwich, weekends at the club or on the Vineyard, trips to Europe in the summer, the occasional dinner and play in Manhattan . . ."

Listening to herself, Whitney started laughing as Clarice did. "What drudgery, Whitney. Putting one foot in front of the other until you die, with children tugging at your Chanel ensemble who'll be even cuter and smarter than you and Peter." She placed a hand on Whitney's shoulder. "There's only one solution, dear. Get yourself sterilized, then take a job in some office, working in a cubicle beneath a bank of fluorescent lights as you await the unpredictable thrill of being fondled by the moron you have to work for. Not to mention spending time with the real people you'll meet in the subway, many of whom won't mug you. Let me help you with your résumé."

Whitney laughed again. "You've thought about this, I can see."

"I've had to," Clarice said glumly. "My parents are insisting on it."

"So what about using your brain?"

Clarice gave her an incredulous look. "Outside of academia? How many places do *you* know where women get paid to think? All I'm saying to you, Whitney, is that the charm of all too many jobs depends on not having done them. At Wellesley, I went to a lecture by Betty Friedan, quite possibly the most shrill and unpleasant woman I've ever seen . . ."

"So my mother claims," Whitney interjected. "She says Friedan's a feminist because she's ugly."

"I'm not sure about that one. But she's certainly not getting by on her looks."

"Is Janine?"

Clarice shot her a curious look. "Back to her again? You don't have to be ugly to be a mess, though it probably helps. Personally, I think that women should be allowed to try whatever they like. It's just that you can't repeal human nature. Women like Friedan are going to liberate the rest of us to work like dogs, plus do all the things we already do until we're gobbling uppers just to keep ourselves going. Do you really think men are going to start raising kids, as opposed to coaching Little League on weekends? Good luck."

"Maybe you're right," Whitney allowed. "But I keep thinking about Karen Claymore, my psych professor at Wheaton. She insisted that sexual predestination was more a matter of conditioning, and that society shapes girls from birth to believe that it's our inherent nature to tend to men and kids. Professor Claymore wasn't against marriage —she just argued that what kind of marriage you have is a choice like any other, but that we'd been raised not to think we had one."

Clarice's gaze turned skeptical. "That's hardly novel," she said crisply. "So give me credit for having thought about this one, too. Maybe some women will have great careers and be blissfully happy—far be it from me to get in their way, and it would be nice if men didn't either. But I think the only way most career women won't get stuck doing two jobs is not to have kids.

"Most men want them. So what you'd get in the end is a lot of single, unhappy women with plenty of time to consider their regrets. Compare that to where we are now. We've been 'stuck' with a role that, by and large, is a better deal than men have. Or haven't you noticed that they're the ones who keel over from heart attacks after too many years spent as 'man, the hunter,' earning the money that allows their widows to mourn them without having to work?"

"Didn't turn out so well for Peter's mom, did it? She's pretty unhappy."

"That's still better than how it turned out for Peter's dad. He's pretty dead." Clarice sat back, clearly pleased with her argument. "Most women's biggest job is to find a guy who's reasonably attractive, hell at work, and pleasant enough at home, who's also an adequate lover and doesn't get sloppy drunk in public. *You,* Whitney Dane, don't ever need to worry about *that* much. You and Peter have your dad to catch you before you fall."

Clarice was no visionary, Whitney thought, but

she was a sharp observer, and dead practical. "You should write your own book, Clarice. *The Anti-Feminist Mystique*."

"Oh, I prefer to keep my wisdom to myself. It preserves my guise of innocent wonder when some guy is explaining to me how the world works."

The remark, Whitney realized, evoked her mother's advice about concealing her own opinions behind attentive listening. "I'll remember that," she said. "Speaking of male wisdom, did you read where the Pope condemned every form of birth control except the rhythm method?"

Clarice rolled her eyes. "Thank God we're not Catholic. What's that old song, 'I've got rhythm, I've got my girl, who could ask for anything more'? But what can you expect from a middle-aged virgin who looks like an accountant."

"Not much," Whitney agreed. "As my dad would say, 'if you don't play the game, don't make the rules.' But I wonder if this Pope thinks God wants thousands of kids in Africa or Latin America starving to death."

Turning sideways, Clarice studied her friend. "You're becoming very serious, I have to say."

"Am I? Most of this stuff doesn't touch us, I know. But it hasn't been that great a year, has it?"

"So far it has for you." Clarice paused again. "Forgive me, but I'm wondering if some of this comes from Ben. You've been spending enough time with him."

Nettled, Whitney retorted, "Now you're sounding like my dad. Expose me to a different thought, and I'm a different person. Incapable as I am of thinking for myself."

"Oh, I'm sure it's just coincidence," Clarice said with a dubious smile. "But have you mentioned any of these thoughts to Peter?"

This time it was Whitney who paused. "Not really, no."

"Then maybe you should, Whitney. He's the one you're marrying, after all." Clarice stood, shortcutting the conversation. "Let's finish out the set, best friend. I plan on running you 'til that leg of yours screams for mercy."

Later that afternoon, Peter flew out for the weekend.

After dinner, he lay beside her in the chaise longue, tie unknotted, his air of fatigue underscored by the weariness beneath his eyes. Kissing him, Whitney murmured, "You look tired."

"I just need some sleep," he acknowledged. "I worked late the last two nights. There's still so much to learn."

Whitney imagined the pressures he felt—as Charles's future son-in-law, his presumed security in the eyes of others could only nourish his own self-doubt. "Just for the fun of it, Peter, can I ask you to imagine something?"

"Chapter Ten of the Kama Sutra?"

"A little less acrobatic. I've been thinking more about how much you liked your coaches. Could you ever see yourself at a boarding school like Exeter?"

"Away from New York?"

"Uh-huh. I can imagine living in a quiet place, teaching and maybe writing."

Peter turned his face to hers, his expression puzzled and surprised. "I don't know, Whitney. That's a whole different life, way more modest than you're used to. My teachers didn't even own the houses they lived in—the school provided them. I'm sure it was the same for your teachers at Rosemary Hall."

"It was. But they didn't seem miserable to me. Did your lacrosse coach?"

"No. I just never imagined being him."

"But can you?"

Peter's gaze became more probing. "Are you worried I won't make it at Padgett Dane?"

"Of course not," Whitney assured him. "It's not the only thing you can do, that's all. I don't want you to feel stuck."

Frowning, he sat up. "I can't let your dad down, Whitney—not after everything he's done. Besides, I don't know of any teaching jobs."

"Not yet. But you could always look. If not now, maybe in a year."

"I just joined the firm, all right? Let me try it without thinking about a whole other life.

Besides, do you really want to work? Who'd take care of the kids when they're babies?"

He looked so young, Whitney thought, to be imagining his life as a father. "We both could—our hours would be flexible, and there must be a way of arranging care when we're both working. It's really no different than Billie watching after me so Mom could see her friends."

Peter grimaced at this. "Maybe it seems like that to you. But I don't want strangers raising our kids so we can work, at least when they're small. I'd like them to know we're always there."

This was about losing his father, Whitney surmised. But though she sympathized, she could not quell her own misgivings. In the life Peter imagined for her, she would have several roles—wife, mother, helpmate—but none unique to her. Instead, those roles had awaited her since birth, as they had for countless women of all kinds. But there was no way she could articulate this to him, at least right now, without eroding his self-confidence. He felt too vulnerable in his new identity not to read his own doubts into hers.

"I understand," she told him. "We can talk about it later."

Exhausted, Peter turned in early. Climbing into bed, Whitney took *Couples* with her. She read for over an hour, then put it down again.

It was beautifully written. At times, she

confessed to herself, the sexuality of Updike's characters had spoken to her own, the desire to lose herself so completely that sex felt like transcendence. But she found his cycle of adultery between linked couples ultimately depressing, a march through meaninglessness toward death, undertaken less from lust than from fear of one, the other, or both. She could understand her father's aversion: his life was too purposeful, in business and at home, his convictions about marriage and family too central to his idea of himself. Nor could she imagine living with and yet betraying Peter in such a casual way—or, she amended, any way at all.

She put aside the book, unsure that she wished to finish it.

Three

On an afternoon in late July—warm and cloudless, with a light breeze on Quitsa Pond—Whitney and Ben rowed the dinghy to the Barkley's Herreshoff. She had passed the test, naming each component of the boat. Now it was time for her to sail.

Sitting behind him, Whitney said, "I guess you saw that the Senate killed the gun control bill. Republicans, mostly."

Ben turned to her, a bitter light in his eyes.

"Surprise, Whitney. Nixon needs the NRA. A few nuts with guns kill people every day, so why should one more dead guy make a difference—especially Bobby Kennedy." He started rowing again, speaking over his shoulder in a low, angry voice. "But it wasn't just the Republicans. That pompous prick Gene McCarthy said we shouldn't pass it under 'panic conditions.' His last chance to piss on Bobby's grave."

He lapsed into silence, rowing fiercely. Whitney regretted saying anything at all.

Reaching the mooring, they tied up the dinghy and climbed into the sailboat. Under Ben's tutelage, Whitney helped him rig the sails, his concentration on their task leveling his mood. Manning the tiller, he pointed to a passage between Quitsa and Menemsha Pond. "I'll get us through the narrows. After that, you'll take over."

Propelled by a southeast wind, they headed toward the passage. "It's called Chaukers," Ben explained. "It's shallow there, easy to run aground. To thread the needle requires tacking with each wind shift, consistently moving the mainsail. You'll have to keep ducking or the boom will take your head off."

As they headed toward the opening, Ben started tacking with the wind, fighting the tide from Menemsha Pond. Caught by each shift, the mainsail swept across the boat, Whitney ducking beneath the heavy wooden boom. Atop the mast, the arrow that showed wind direction kept veering. Taut and intent, Ben tacked again as the banks of Chaukers closed around them. Thirty feet of width, then twenty. "Notice where the water's brown," Ben said between his teeth. "That's where it's shallow enough to run aground."

Swiftly tacking, he guided the Herreshoff along a ribbon of blue between the smudged brown nearer the banks. A gust of wind carried them into Menemsha Pond. "One of my favorite places on the Vineyard," he told her. "About a mile across and over a hundred feet deep, left by a glacier millions of years ago. God's gift to sailors."

Ben still held the tiller, allowing Whitney to take in the expanse of blue water, the direction of the wind. "Now it's coming from the side of us," he pointed out to her. "We're sailing sixty degrees off the wind—a full reach, the perfect tack to be on."

All at once they were moving faster. As they cut through the water, Whitney felt her spirits lift. "I wish you could see us," Ben told her. "There's nothing prettier than a Herreshoff under sail."

Gaining speed, they headed toward the soft green banks of Herring Creek. "Closer to land, Whitney, the wind will change direction. If you know where and when that happens, it can help you win a race."

He was different now, she thought—fully

absorbed in a task that seemed to touch the deepest part of him, happy in a primal way that perhaps only sailing could create. For a moment it was as if she were not there. Then he turned the boat in a semicircle, away from land. "Your turn, Whitney."

She sat sideways to the tiller, Ben beside her. As he handed her the mainsheet, she felt the mainsail tugging on it. "Can you tell where the wind's coming from?" he asked.

"Right at us."

Looking up at the arrow, Ben nodded. "You can't sail into a headwind. So you tack off starboard, or port, depending on where you want to go. Pick a direction."

Whitney pointed toward the far bank. "See the white house? The one peeking through the trees?"

"Head for it, then. Move the tiller toward you, and the boat will go in the opposite direction. Same thing when you move it away. It may seem counterintuitive, but you'll catch on."

Unsure of herself, Whitney gripped the tiller tightly. "No white knuckles," Ben said in the same even tone. "Just keep three fingers on it, with a light touch. Don't worry that you've never done this. You're not going to break this boat, and you've got me to help you."

He was different than on land, Whitney thought —calm and reassuring. Her grip lightening, she moved the tiller toward her, and saw the mainsail fill with wind. In a half minute, she had them gliding along the water, experimenting with the feel of a boat responding to her hand. Suddenly, she felt the exhilaration of being in control—that she, the wind, and the sailboat were working together. It took Ben's chuckle to make her realize that she was grinning from sheer pleasure.

"I love this feeling, Ben."

"I know. I want to do this all my life, sail everywhere there is to sail. I hope I get the chance."

Hearing the softness in his voice, Whitney felt she knew him in a different way. For a brief moment, she was aware of how close they were sitting. Then a powerboat rocked the sailboat sideways, and left them foundering in its wake. "These boats don't capsize," Ben assured her. "Check the wind, then get us back on course."

Glancing at the arrow, she saw that the wind was shifting and angled the mainsail to catch it. Instantly, they were skimming along the water again. Pointing ahead, Ben told her, "You'll want to miss that lobster pot."

Moving the tiller away from her, she cleared the pot. "The wind's behind us now, Whitney. Use it."

Within seconds they were racing so close to the wind that the water sped by. In a fresh burst of elation, Whitney thought that she was doing something no one in her family ever had, something all her own. She loved this new sense of mastery—now nothing mattered but the boat, the water, and her. "Want to take us back through Chaukers?" Ben asked.

"Sure."

"Turn it around, then. You'll have to be patient, and you'll be fighting the wind. But I can help you tack."

As the boat circled, sailing became work again. With Ben's guidance, she tacked back and forth for endless minutes as the sailboat struggled closer to the passage. Whitney felt herself tense, unsure of where the shallows were. She tacked again, then again.

Abruptly, the boat lurched, stuck in mud she could not see. "Damn," she muttered.

"Happens all the time," Ben said with a shrug. "Hard to see these shallows in the afternoon light."

Peeling off his shirt, he lowered himself into the waist-deep water and began pushing the boat off the mud. As he pulled himself back in, Whitney saw again how lean and muscular he was, the line of dark hair down the center of his chest. For a moment, she imagined herself as Clarice.

Taking the tiller, Ben worked them through the narrows. "Did you ever swim here?" she asked.

"Sure. When I was sixteen, I swam across the pond."

"The whole mile?"

"Uh-huh. It was a point of pride for me, because my father never learned to swim. That's a common superstition among fishermen—they take learning to swim as an admission they might drown. So Dad didn't, cementing his chance of drowning. One of the many reasons I don't use him as a role model."

With a final tack, they made it through the narrows. Then Ben let her sail them to the mooring.

Together, they took down the sails. This time, Whitney felt different—his partner as well as his student. "Thank you," she said. "That was even better than I'd imagined."

Ben nodded. "I think you have a feel for this, Whitney. Not everyone does."

His approval warmed her. "You made it easy for me, really. You're very patient on the water."

Ben started folding canvas. "As opposed to on land, you mean? Another reverse lesson from Dad. On the lobster boat he would shout and curse—the worst way to teach anyone. The trick is to never make a beginner feel intimidated by the water. That makes it easier to learn, as does this boat."

Whitney thought again of her friend. "I should thank Clarice for both of us."

Ben shrugged. "The boat means nothing to her. She knows just enough to know that I won't sink it."

Whitney looked up at him. "You don't like her much, do you?

"To the contrary, I admire her clarity of purpose. As I perceive it, she's a girl who knows exactly what she wants—which is what she already has. What's most intriguing about Clarice is the steely quality she tries so hard to conceal." He smiled. "To all outward appearances, she has no ambition but to keep on living the life she was born to, killing her allotted time on earth as pleasurably as she can."

To Whitney's surprise, his assessment had an uncomfortable ring of truth. "You could say at least some of that about me."

Ben gave her a thin smile. "I could. But I won't. Though you may not think so, you're different."

Whitney stared at him. "Why do you say that?"

"At the risk of being presumptuous, you've been living your life on autopilot, sleepwalking toward eternity. The challenge presented by Clarice is her relentless self-interest, and whether anyone could ever penetrate that. But unlike Miss Barkley, you ask questions, and you're curious. I also think you're questioning yourself." He shot her a quick grin. "A dangerous tendency, Whitney. Trust me about that."

Whitney felt the remark jangle her nerve ends. There was something uncanny about him, she thought, that made her want to hide. "I think you're imagining things."

"Am I? Would you mind if I read your diary?"

"Actually, I would," she said stiffly. "It's private."

"Obviously." Pausing, he regarded her with surprising seriousness. "You're more like me than you think—a loner. Except that you're surrounded by other people."

Whitney shook her head, resistant. "I certainly don't feel alone."

"I think you are," Ben retorted calmly. "You want to write, but I'd guess no one urges you on. You taught black kids, but I'd give odds that everyone in your family—and certainly your intended—saw it as an experiment in idealism, from which you managed to escape without being gang-raped by a pack of subliterate schoolyard basketball players . . ."

"That's not fair," Whitney snapped.

"Isn't it? Has your fiancé ever encouraged you to do anything other than get married?"

Whitney sat straighter. "I have to say that you wear better under sail. Here on land, it's my dim understanding married people grow together . . ."

"Actually, mine shriveled."

"Maybe so," Whitney retorted sharply. "But most men don't beat their wives."

"Most men don't have to. Would you say that your mother has grown in her marriage?"

Whitney gave herself a moment to speak more calmly. "You're in no position to ask that question, let alone to answer it. My mother raised us, and helped my Dad in every way she could. That's how she wanted to spend her life, and there's a lot of good in that for everyone. In spite of your jibes about Clarice."

Ben smiled at this. "I certainly didn't call Clarice a fool. I'm quite sure that beneath her very pretty and vivacious surface she's coolly determined to find a husband capable of protecting her many prerogatives in life."

Once again, the accuracy of his perceptions unsettled Whitney. "So was my mother," she told him. "At least if you mean that it's easier to stay in love with a man you admire and respect, rather than to some guy you have to prop up every minute. Even if he has money."

"Didn't your father?"

"Hardly. Despite your seemingly unshakable prejudices, my dad came from nowhere. In fact, oddly enough, Clarice gave you a bigger compliment than you deserve. She said you reminded her of him."

Surprise bled the irony from Ben's expression. "Interesting coming from Clarice, who I take to be a keen judge of men. At least the ones she knows well. But it's odd she should pick your father as my soul mate. From what I can gather, we're nothing alike."

Whitney gave him a wintry smile. "True. Dad's far more generous of spirit."

The trace of humor reappeared in his eyes. "A pretty low bar, I guess. But have you ever defied him, or known anyone who has? Not your fiancé, certainly. Seems like Dad's arranged life precisely the way he wants it."

Once again, Whitney felt herself bridle at his presumption. "Let's talk about something else. You can pick the topic."

Ben smiled again. "But they're narrowing so quickly. First Peter, then Clarice, and now your father."

"Then choose one you know something about, like sailing. I thought you were here to teach me."

A new and unreadable emotion moved through his eyes, then vanished. "I am," he said simply.

Four

On a warm, humid evening in early August, the Danes and Barkleys attended a charity dinner to support the purchase of land for nature preserves. It took place on the lawn of a rambling summer home overlooking Quitsa Pond, evoking for Whitney her last sail with Ben. The men wore blazers—often navy-blue like Charles's and Peter's—the women bright summer dresses. Whitney's dress was pink, cut slightly above the knee, while Clarice's yellow miniskirt revealed the tan, slender legs that were her pride. Waiters in black bow ties and white cloth jackets dipped in and out among the guests, serving canapés and drinks on silver trays. To Whitney it seemed much like other such evenings—pleasant enough but ultimately boring, a gathering of lemmings whose chatter was as bland as the hors d'oeuvres. Deciding that a glass of wine might improve her perspective, she drifted away from Peter and her parents, and realized the waiter approaching with a drink tray was Benjamin Blaine.

Despite his lack of expression, she sensed an awkwardness that matched her own. Recalling that Ben and his brother had catered parties in high school, she wondered how this felt to him after his years at Yale and the murder of his candidate-hero. As he held out the tray, she mustered her warmest smile. "Hi, Ben. It's nice to see you."

"And you, Lady Dane."

Whitney took a glass of white wine. "Lady Dane? Didn't the Rolling Stones record that?"

Ben had the grace to laugh. "I preferred 'Under My Thumb.' Enjoy the party, Whitney."

As he started to leave, she said swiftly, "So when are we sailing again? It was a nice day, I thought. At least mostly."

He stopped briefly, glancing at her sideways. "I don't have my appointment book with me. But you know where I live." Then he was off again, circulating among the guests.

Gazing after him, Whitney sensed someone at her shoulder. "Isn't that your friend?" Peter said. "The outfit looks good on him."

To Whitney, this attempt at bluff humor carried a trace of belligerence. Before coming, Peter had enjoyed a cocktail or two with her father, who insisted on at least one glass of single malt scotch before Vineyard charity events—the spirits would be paltry, he groused, the wine second tier. But while a tumbler of Macallan reliably elevated Charles's disposition, it seemed to have left Peter a little fuzzy of tongue.

"Friend is overstating it," she told him. "We're friendly, that's all."

Still looking toward Ben, Peter said nothing. Whitney sensed that his brain had slowed a little, calibrating his reactions with less facility than was usual for the easy, openhearted young man everyone liked so much. "Why don't we find our table," she suggested. "These new pumps are hurting my feet."

There were seven people at the table for eight—to her mother's distress, Janine had chosen not to come for the weekend, pleading fatigue from days of photo shoots. Clarice sat between her parents, a genetic mixture of them both. While George Barkley's sandy hair, blue eyes, and fine features were the prototype for his daughter's good looks, Clarice's vitality came from her energetic if somewhat fidgety mother Jane, a diminutive brunette whose quick tongue never quite concealed the insecurity that had caused Clarice to dub her "Our Lady of Perpetual Anxiety." Tonight her worries were no doubt exacerbated by the fear that her husband stood on fiscal quicksand. As often, Whitney was grateful for her father, sitting between her and Anne with his accustomed air of tranquil authority. But Peter made her edgy; he was drinking more wine than normal, and a flush stained his cheeks and forehead. Across the table, Clarice's gaze moved from Peter to Whitney, her eyebrows slightly raised, before flickering toward someone standing behind them.

Turning, Whitney saw Ben passing with dinner plates in both hands. As he paused to give her a fleeting glance, Peter held out his wine glass. "Fill this for me," he demanded.

Ben stopped where he was, regarding Peter with a long, cool glance, silence his only response. Peter thrust out the glass toward him. "Wine," he demanded.

Still, Ben took his time to respond. "I'm serving dinner now. That explains the plates I'm holding. But someone will be over soon enough."

"I'm asking you," Peter insisted with rising belligerence.

Ben's smile, a brief movement of his lips, suggested his disdain. "Yeah, I got that. But maybe you should ask for coffee."

Embarrassed, Whitney glanced at Clarice. She was studying Charles, who, to Whitney's surprise, was watching Ben with the utter lack of expression she saw only when all his faculties were trained on assessing another male. The others were not as self-possessed: George Barkley looked away; his wife rediscovered her wine glass; and Whitney's mother shot Peter a surreptitious look of worry.

Before Peter could respond, Ben left him holding his glass aloft. "Can you believe that?" Peter asked, his voice louder in their silence.

Ignoring this, Charles still watched Ben walk away. To her relief, Whitney noticed a tall, solemn-looking waiter approaching their table. He gave her a faint but reassuring smile, then addressed Peter. "May I get you something?" he asked politely.

Unlike Ben, he had an inherent gentleness of manner. Mollified, Peter said, "A glass of red wine, thank you."

"Of course." Filling Peter's glass, the young man glanced briefly at Clarice. "Would anyone else care for wine?"

"A final glass for me," Charles said, which Whitney took as a tacit directive to Peter. Then the moment passed, allowing Whitney's mother to remark on Clarice's hemline.

Upon their return home, Peter and Whitney remained on the lawn. Even in the moonlight, his chagrin was apparent. "You were pretty quiet tonight, Whit."

"Was I?"

His shoulders hunched. "Didn't handle that very well, did I?"

"You treated him like a menial, Peter. It's not like you."

"Ever meet someone who makes your hair stand up? There's something about this guy. You saw how insolent he was."

"Only after I saw how insulting *you* were. Can I ask what brought that on? Other than scotch, that is."

He shifted his weight. "I guess I don't like you hanging out with him."

"We're not 'hanging out' . . ."

"He's going after you, Whitney. Maybe you don't think so, but he is."

Was he? she wondered. She found this hard to imagine: in the hours they had spent together, Ben had done little to suggest that she was other than a mildly diverting specimen of her class in his interregnum of loneliness and uncertainty. "He knows I'm getting married," she said firmly. "He's no more interested in me than I am in him . . ."

"Then why were you upset?"

"I wasn't upset. I was embarrassed, and I felt badly for you. This wasn't about him at all."

Peter shoved his hands in his pockets. "I don't want you apologizing for me, Whitney. I don't want him thinking he's that important."

"I won't, and he doesn't. So please let it go, all right?"

At length, Peter sighed in apology. "So tell me we'll be fine tomorrow."

Rising on her tiptoes, Whitney gave him a kiss. "We're fine now," she assured him. "And you'll be fine tomorrow if you take some aspirin."

Peter smiled ruefully. "I hope so. Good night, Whit."

Pensive, she watched him walk slowly toward the guesthouse. When she went inside, her father was sitting in the living room. "Can we talk a minute?" he asked.

Tense, Whitney sat across from him. "I guess this is about Peter."

Charles nodded. "He didn't handle that well, it's true. But your mother and I felt for him, and his behavior should give you pause for thought."

The remark, calm but faintly accusatory, aroused Whitney's stubbornness. "It did, actually. I was thinking you should cut back on cocktail hour. I'm not the one who primed him with scotch, after all."

Her unaccustomed sharpness caused Charles to flush. "And I'm not the one who struck up a random friendship with another man." His voice rose. "Every instinct I possess tells me that *this* man is a human stick of dynamite, whose mere presence in your life could blow it up. *You* may think nothing of spending time with him, but others will. Especially Peter. No man wants people believing him a fool, and no man wants to be one."

"What are you implying, Dad?"

"About your intentions, nothing. I'm simply suggesting that you act with the care appropriate to a woman about to marry a fine young man."

"I'm not a child," Whitney objected, "and Peter has no reason to be jealous. I can't shun someone just because of what other people may think." She softened her voice, hoping to persuade him. "I don't want to treat Ben as poorly as Peter did. He's had a tough time all his life, and a worse one lately. He got himself into Yale on a scholarship, then dropped out to campaign with Bobby Kennedy. He's devastated by what happened, and now the draft may get him."

Charles put curled fingers to his lips. "You seem to know a lot about this boy."

"I've always been a decent listener, haven't I? Actually, he's pretty annoying, though I admire his determination to succeed. In fact, Clarice says he reminds her of you."

Charles's eyes narrowed slightly. In a cooler tone, he said, "Really."

"I don't see it," Whitney consoled him. "Except that you're both overly opinionated, and better at arguing than listening, you're nothing alike."

Charles allowed himself a smile of self-recognition. "I'm the soul of tolerance, Whitney."

"Of course you are. If it weren't for Ben's politics, I'm certain you'd adore him."

Charles regarded her in contemplative silence. "You do make him sound interesting," he responded in a more suitable tone. "Certainly the part about resembling me. Perhaps you should invite him to dinner. That might relieve whatever awkwardness you feel, and put your mother and me more at ease. It's even remotely conceivable that I've been a bit too harsh."

Whitney felt a stab of apprehension: the image of Ben with her family filled her with misgivings. "I don't think that's necessary, Dad. Let's drop it."

"Suit yourself," her father said easily. "But he did fish you out of the water, and we've always welcomed your friends. Once Peter returns to Manhattan, why don't you see what Ben thinks."

After a moment, Whitney nodded, resolved to do nothing of the kind.

Five

The next morning, Whitney went looking for Ben.

He was not at the guesthouse, nor anywhere on the grounds. When she tried the catwalk, the waiter who had intervened the night before was caulking a powerboat. "I'm trying to find Ben Blaine," she told him.

Looking up from the boat, he said, "Ben's not here today. I'm his brother, Jack."

They could not be less alike, Whitney thought. Jack's demeanor was solemn and gentle, his long face was somewhere between handsome and homely, and his air of watchfulness reminded Whitney that he had grown up in a violent home. Within the family, Ben had told her, Jack had been the peacemaker. "I'm Whitney Dane," she said. "Thank you for last night. My fiancé wasn't at his best."

Jack nodded, watching her with perceptive eyes. "So that's what it was."

To Whitney, the ambiguous remark implied an impression she wanted to dispel. "It was a misunderstanding. Afterward, Peter felt terrible."

His expression, briefly skeptical, reverted to modesty. "I saw what happened, that's all. It seemed like I could help."

"You did." Whitney hesitated, then asked, "Is Ben out sailing today?"

Jack climbed from the boat. "Good guess," he responded with a trace of humor. "My brother had urgent business on the water."

"Do you know when he'll be back?"

Standing in front of her, Jack gave Whitney a curious look. "After noon, I'd suppose. Should I pass on a message?"

"Not really. I just wanted to see him for a moment. I feel badly about last night."

The faint smile at the corners of Jack's mouth did not reach his eyes. "I guess the 'misunderstanding' was about you."

"It was about boys, not me. Peter had a little too much wine, and forgot his manners."

"A bad idea. My brother can be touchy."

For Whitney, the admonition evoked an image of Ben ruining his father's face and teeth. "Ben has a certain idea of himself," Jack continued more easily, "and he wants what he wants. He takes it hard when other people fool with that. I'd give him a day or two. If not a year or two."

There were multiple ways of interpreting this, Whitney thought—a concern for Peter; a warning to her; or the resentment of a gentler, less ambitious man for the younger brother who seemed to scorn him. Whatever the case, Jack was not as dispassionate about Ben as he might prefer to seem. "Then I'm glad you were there," she told him. "With all that testosterone flying around, I wanted to duck for cover."

A brief smile creased Jack's face. "Story of my life," he said dryly. "The voice of reason. I appreciate this moment of recognition."

Whitney detected more truth in the words than their tone implied. It struck her that she had asked nothing about Jack himself, and knew very little from Ben. "What do you do when you're not protecting people from Ben?"

"I'm a woodworker. Chairs, desks, armoires,

dining room tables, even doors and mailboxes. Whatever people need, as well as I can make it."

"Sounds like you enjoy it."

"I do." Jack's voice became more animated. "When I finish a piece—a desk, say—it's something that never existed before, unique to me, that becomes a part of other people's lives. When I used to paint, or sculpt, sometimes they'd just sit there. Now I put my craft into furnishings people use."

While Ben aspired to be a writer, Whitney reflected, Jack was already an artist. Though the reasons surely lay deep in childhood—and in their opposing reactions to a violent father—their distance from each other seemed regrettable. "Is there a place that sells your pieces?" she asked.

"I've got a shop in Vineyard Haven. Come in sometime, and I can show you how they're made." He hesitated. "If you like, you can bring your friend Clarice."

"Do you know her?"

"Only from catering. But you two always sit together."

With some embarrassment, Whitney realized that she had never noticed him before, and guessed this was also true of Clarice. "I'm sure she'd like that," she heard herself saying. "What time is good for you?"

A new warmth surfaced in Jack's eyes. "Any afternoon," he assured her. "I'll look forward to it."

Whitney thanked him and left, wondering if Ben had gone sailing to avoid her.

That night, Whitney's parents watched NBC cover the eve of the Republican convention. Joining them, Whitney heard a commentator note that George Wallace, the independent who had made his name as a segregationist, was polling at fifteen percent, even higher in the South. *The danger for Republicans,* he explained, *is that Wallace will peel away crucial votes among Southerners and blue-collar voters leery of the civil rights movement and the supposed breakdown in law and order. . . .*

"Wallace is a carnival barker," Charles groused. "He's running as the last firewall between the barbarians and civilization. But all he can really do is deliver the election to Humphrey and all the people he excoriates. If he were serious, he'd get out of Nixon's way."

"What about black voters?" Anne asked him.

"Hopeless," Charles said gloomily. "Unfortunately, they're in thrall to the Democrats. To win we need the Wallace people."

The unspoken subtext, Whitney supposed, was that Nixon could appeal to their fears without the crassness with which Wallace discomfited more genteel whites. Then the cheerful visage of Ronald Reagan appeared, speaking to a bank of microphones. "Of course I'd like a crack at the

Presidency," he said. "I don't want people thinking I'm some pebble-pushing actor."

The moment conjured Whitney's sense of the surreal. From childhood, she remembered him as the host of GE Theater, pitching appliances and half-hour melodramas with the same unvarying enthusiasm. Even as governor of California, Reagan seemed to her more like an entertainer than a potential president, combining breeziness with a folksy demeanor exhumed from some bygone era of vaudeville. "He's a coming man," her father told Anne. "But he has to wait his turn."

To Whitney, the remark had a familiar, faintly proprietary note, as though Reagan were a promising salesman who, with the right patronage and seasoning, might aspire to greater things. Then she thought of Ben's evocation of Robert Kennedy in Indiana, telling a crowd of grieving blacks that their most hopeful leader had been shot and killed. "I think I'll go for a walk," she told her parents.

Ben's light was on in the guesthouse. When Whitney knocked, he opened the door, beer in hand. At a glance, she saw that his television was turned to the same coverage her parents watched, now focused on a crowd of Republican delegates. Following her gaze, he remarked, "That's the whitest bunch of people I've seen since yesterday evening."

Whitney ignored this. "I'm sorry," she said.

"For what? You didn't do anything. And if you'd wanted to apologize, you could have done that last night."

Whitney flushed. "That would've only made things worse. Peter saw us together, and misunderstood."

"I don't know why Peter should worry. He's the one holding a royal flush. Though he seems to have forgotten that your father dealt it to him."

"He's really not like that," Whitney insisted. "Last night was completely out of character."

"Does he have any?" Ben inquired in an indifferent tone. "Then why did I notice an inverse relationship between your fiancé's accomplishments and his sense of entitlement? When Robert Kennedy told me to do something, there was a reason for it, and he was never rude. Of course he wasn't some empty sport coat out of *Love Story*. Good luck with him, Whitney."

Whitney crossed her arms. "You really *are* angry, aren't you? Or else you wouldn't try so hard to be insulting. Before, it just came naturally."

"You're right," Ben snapped. "On a better day I'd have mentioned that your beau ideal is marrying you to get out of the draft. Only a moron couldn't see there are better reasons to marry you than *that*. Too bad you and your father can't see it, either."

Whitney felt the words cut to her core. "You have no idea why Peter's marrying me," she said angrily, "and never will." Abruptly, she stopped herself. "Please tell me what we're doing, Ben. I'm lost."

Ben stared at her, and then she saw him expel a breath. "The ersatz Ryan O'Neal struck a nerve. A shame you had to be there. But that's what you get for maintaining an acquaintanceship no one wants you to have." His voice softened. "I'm sorry, Whitney. If it helps, you can take my diatribe as a compliment. I think one slipped in somewhere."

Whitney shook her head. "You know what's so sad to me? I look at all of us—Peter, and my family, and you—and what I see is good people with the faults life gave them. I met your brother today, and thought the same thing. But you're so hurt and angry all you can see is black and white."

Ben raised a hand, a glint of humor in his eyes. "Stop, Whitney, please. It's way too late for group therapy, and I don't know the words to 'Kumbaya.' I'm not taking your boyfriend sailing, or renting a tuxedo for the wedding. You'll have to settle for a punch bowl from Tiffany's."

"I don't need one," she retorted, then felt Ben's jibe ignite an impulsive thought. "And you needn't wait for the wedding. My dad's inviting you to dinner."

He studied her, angling his head. "Tell me you're joking."

"Not really." Caught in her own trap, Whitney forged on. "He feels awkward about the other night, and grateful you bothered to pull me out of the ocean. I also told him that if you two were civil about politics, you might even like each other. He didn't grow up with a trust fund, either."

For once, Ben's expression was devoid of irony or humor. "I'm not sure this is a good idea, Whitney."

She had said as much to her father. But, whether from hope or incaution, she had gone too far. "Not if you're determined to see him as the great class enemy, and my mother as the lady of the manor. But if you keep an open mind, you might find each other interesting."

The glint reappeared in his eyes. "Are some black kids from Roxbury coming too?"

"We asked them, of course," Whitney said tartly. "But they're tied up playing basketball."

Silent, Ben studied her face. More quietly, he asked, "So what do you want me to do, Whitney?"

Despite herself, Whitney realized that she wanted her parents to like him. "To show up for dinner. More or less on time."

"Not fashionably late?" Ben said in an ironic tone tinged with resignation. "That's what *my* parents always taught me."

Six

When she heard Ben knock on the door, Whitney hurried to open it.

To her surprise, he looked different—his hair was damp from the shower, and combed into a semblance of discipline; he wore a blue sport coat and khakis that seemed slightly worn; and, most incongruous to her, carried a vase of freshly cut flowers. Despite his insouciant smile, Whitney could feel his discomfort—entering the Dane's home ground, he seemed less self-assured.

"Here goes the neighborhood," he murmured, and followed her inside.

Charles waited in the living room with Anne, a scotch already in his hand. He put the tumbler down on a mahogany drink coaster, and stood to meet their guest. "Hello, Ben," he said, extending a firm handshake and a smile that perhaps only Whitney saw as short of fully welcoming. "I'm Charles Dane."

"Nice to meet you, Mr. Dane," Ben responded a trifle stiffly. He turned to Anne, holding out the vase of flowers. "I brought these for you, Mrs. Dane."

"How lovely," Anne said with a smile of her own. "Where did you find them?"

Ben shifted his weight. "I picked these while I

was weeding the Dunmores' garden. Seeing how they're in Europe this summer, I thought you might enjoy them."

Anne's smile diminished. "The Dunmores' loss is our gain," she responded, and put the vase on the coffee table, sliding a magazine beneath it so that nothing got on the wood. A brief but awkward silence was interrupted by a sharp rap on the rear door.

"It's Clarice," Whitney told Ben. "I invited her to join us."

The glint in his eye suggested he fully grasped her reason—Clarice could serve as a social buffer, helping to make this a dinner for young people rather than a simulacrum of parents meeting a new boyfriend in front of their captive daughter. When Whitney answered the door, Clarice whispered, "Is he already here?"

Nodding, Whitney said under her breath. "I can't believe I did this."

"So let's make the best of it," Clarice said with a mischievous smile. "Charlotte Brontë meets Edith Wharton. Personally, I see Ben as Heathcliff."

Briskly, Clarice entered the living room with a minuet of courtesy, embracing Anne without smudging her makeup, giving Charles a bright smile followed by an decorous daughterly kiss on the cheek, and according Ben a casual, "Hi, Ben," suited to his age and standing. Charles offered the women white wine, then turned to his guest. "What's your pleasure, Ben? We have every-thing."

"Whiskey, thanks. No ice."

Reaching into the liquor cabinet, Charles poured him a generous measure of Maker's Mark. Then everyone sat, Whitney's parents in two wing chairs, Ben and Whitney on the couch with their duenna, Clarice, between them. Charles raised a glass to Ben. "This is my first chance to thank you for saving Whitney from drowning."

"My pleasure, sir. As I told Mrs. Dane, it was sheer luck—Whitney swims off my favorite place on the island."

"Tell us about yourself," Anne requested pleasantly. "The four of us know everything about each other. But none of us knows what it's like to really live here."

Ben took a hasty sip of whisky. "I don't have much to compare it to. My family came here a long time ago. Whaling, to start, then fishing, then lobstering."

"The whaling industry must have been interesting. Were they sea captains?"

"I doubt it," Ben answered with a smile. "I expect they went along for the ride and whatever they could make from a year at sea. But nobody thought to keep track of it. All I can know is that the headstones on Abel's Hill go back to the early 1800's."

"That *is* a long time," Anne agreed, "Where on the island do your parents live now?"

"In Menemsha, near the harbor."

"Is that the family home?"

Ben smiled fractionally. "In the sense that my family lives there. It's not new, but I couldn't say when it was built—nothing about it would tell you, and neither of my parents is big on family history. For them history begins every morning when my father gets up before dawn, and ends with him falling asleep in his chair."

Ben said this courteously enough, and Whitney was grateful that he had airbrushed the violence that had distorted his youth. But the laconic words underscored the chasm between his life and that of the Danes, leaving Whitney to wonder whether her mother had intended to adduce this, or simply had always been too affluent to imagine a much harsher existence. From beneath lowered eyelids, Clarice seemed to be watching Ben intently. "So you grew up on the island," Charles said. "Seems like a nice place to do that."

"In some ways," Ben allowed. "I guess you've never been here in February."

"I haven't. We close down the house every fall."

"Good idea. We don't get the picture-postcard winter people associate with New England. The Vineyard is cold and gray and barren, and the days end so quickly that darkness feels like it's closing in around you. By February it's so raw and bleak it seeps into your bones. That's when you know you're on a rock in the middle of the Atlantic. It changes people, and not for the better."

Ben's tone was not complaining; instead, it had the reportorial neutrality of someone describing an experience to others who have never had it. "When you say it changes people . . ." Charles inquired.

"They start to look hunched, like they're cooped up in a cage. I've come to think there's a kind of cruelty in having summers so beautiful and yet so short, followed by this claustrophobic winter you'd swear will never end. It makes for too much drinking, too many fathers beating their wives and kids. Sometimes worse."

"What could be worse?" Anne asked with muted horror.

Ben took a sip of whisky, considering his answer. "Lines get crossed. Ever notice how many deaf people there are on the island?"

Anne's brow knit. "I suppose so. There are a couple of businesses that employ them, aren't there?"

Nodding, Ben continued in the same dispassionate tone. "In the last century, when the menfolk got shut in for months, some of them got tired of turning to their wives. After a few decades of pregnant daughters, some of the babies started getting born deaf. But that's not the kind of family history people put in books."

Discomfited, Whitney saw Anne's expression of shock, and Charles shaking his head before saying, "That's a terrible story."

"It is," Ben agreed. "Fortunately for me, everyone in my family can hear just fine. At least when they're listening." As though feeling Whitney's unease, he continued, "You're right, though—there's a lot about growing up here I wouldn't change. In the summer, I couldn't imagine being anywhere else, especially when I was on the water." He glanced briefly at Clarice. "In fact, I used to crew for Clarice's dad."

"So George tells me," Charles responded. "He says you're quite the seaman."

"It's in the blood, I guess. If I'd had some other life, I'd never have set foot on Mr. Barkley's boat. I've learned to appreciate when I'm lucky."

Charles nodded his approval. But to Whitney, even this pleasant exchange carried an unspoken subtext: that Charles had called George Barkley to inquire about Ben; that Ben felt the Danes took their good fortune for granted. "And the schools here must be excellent," Anne was saying. "Whitney says you're going to Yale."

"I was. College is where I got lucky in a couple of respects. Yale had started looking for more public school kids. Then some teachers helped me get a scholarship, so I could actually go."

Charles smiled to indicate that this aspect of Ben's story was familiar. "I was a scholarship boy, too, at Columbia. Every day I told myself to make the most of it."

Ben glanced at their surroundings with a respectfully appreciative gaze. "Seems like you have, Mr. Dane. I hope that I can, too."

It was good, Whitney supposed, that Ben did not know that the house had belonged to Anne's father—or that Charles, like Peter, had married into the firm. Aware of her silence, she told her parents, "Ben's interested in writing."

"Really?" Charles said to Ben. "What kind?"

"Journalism, to start."

"Then I imagine you plan on journalism school."

Ben grimaced. "I was. But I dropped out of Yale to campaign for Robert Kennedy. One of the unfortunate by-products is that I lost my draft deferment."

Her father must have forgotten this, Whitney thought. His expression somber, Charles said, "That was a shame, Ben—all around. So what will you do now?"

"As I told Whitney, I hope to get back to Yale at the end of summer, finish up before the draft board snags me. Right now they're looking for bodies, anyone without a deferment. Until September, that's me."

Feeling Clarice's glance, Whitney wished that her father had not steered the conversation so close to the escape he had obtained for Peter.

"I'm sure you're worried," Charles said. "But I'd think there'd be enough candidates so that you could get by for another month or so."

Ben's face turned blank. "Hope so. But that particular kind of luck may depend on where you're from."

"How do you mean?"

Ben finished his drink. "Seems like the local draft board has fewer prospects than some do. About a year ago, a friend from high school ran short of money and had to drop out of UMass. Within two months, they'd reclassified Johnny 1-A and called him in for a physical. The way he told the story, he stripped down to his underwear and tramped around with a bunch of other guys, while Army doctors in white coats certified they were still alive. Johnny thought that breathing was pretty much the baseline qualification—unless you'd found your own doctor to say you had some debilitating disease."

Having finished a substantial glass of whiskey, Ben was sounding more like himself. Whitney did not find this reassuring; nor was she happy, when her father poured another inch or two in his tumbler, reminding her that Charles's over-generosity with liquor had led to Peter's gracelessness. "I *do* know some guys who got out," Clarice offered encouragingly. "Quite a few, actually."

"No doubt," Ben said in a slightly ironic tone.

"At the end of the physical, Johnny told me, they asked the next fifteen guys in line if they had a disability that would exempt them. Thirteen of them were white, like Johnny—except they were graduate students from the mainland who'd already slipped into a reserve unit." Ben took another swallow of whisky. "Strangely, all thirteen had doctor's letters explaining why they couldn't serve. Even though all they had to do was show up for drill a few weeks every year, and their only chance of dying would be to fall on their own bayonets."

To Whitney, the parallel to Peter had become far too exact. From the cool look in his eyes, Charles saw it, too. But Ben went on in the pleasant manner of anyone narrating a story. "Most of the white guys got out. Without a letter, Johnny was doomed. But you know what he thought even funnier? The black guy turned out to have one leg an inch shorter than the other. When they rejected him, he was actually let down. Turned out he couldn't find a job, and was hoping to make the Army a career."

"I think that's admirable," Anne said firmly. "Someone using military service to better himself."

Ben nodded, an indecipherable expression on his face. "Hopefully he's found a job by now. A safer one."

Whitney saw Clarice watching him with

renewed attentiveness. Quietly, she asked, "What happened to your friend?"

For a moment, Ben started into the bottom of his empty glass. "Oh," he said softly, "Johnny's dead. He stepped on a landmine in Vietnam, less than a week ago. At least that's what his mom told me when I dropped by this morning."

A deep silence descended, no one looking at anyone else. "A terrible thing," Charles said gravely, and then the housekeeper announced dinner.

Seven

On the way to the dining room, Clarice touched Ben's arm, murmuring words of consolation. Her gesture made Whitney feel chastened yet strangely proprietary; she alone was aware of how furious Ben must be at the waste of his friend's life. But whether from good manners, or because his feelings went too deep, he seemed to have willed himself past anger. When Anne seated them, Whitney found herself facing Ben and Clarice, with her parents at opposite ends of the table. As though to compensate for the pall he had cast, Ben told Anne, "This is a beautiful place, Mrs. Dane. When I was a kid, I used to look up at it from the water, and wonder who lived here."

He had chosen not to mention catering parties

at the house, Whitney noted. "We're very lucky," her mother replied. "My father bought it years ago, before people from New York realized how wonderful the Vineyard is." Smiling, she corrected herself. "At least in the summer."

Turning to Clarice, Ben asked, "So this is where you and Whitney met?"

Clarice glanced at her friend fondly. "When we were four, and my parents brought me over to play with the shy but precocious girl next door. Since that day, we've been best friends, one of the few parental fix-ups that ever worked."

"If we could have stolen Clarice from her family," Charles put in comfortably, "we would have. One of my specialties is mergers and acquisitions."

Ben gave Whitney a quick, ironic glance; at once, she knew he was thinking about her father's role in Peter's life. In an interested tone, he asked Charles, "How *is* your business, Mr. Dane? I really don't know much about it."

As the housekeeper served the first course—a fish stew accompanied by a chilled Meursault—Charles answered, "No reason why you should, Ben—most people don't. Actually, it's a little bumpy right now. With all this unrest and political uncertainty, investors are somewhat skittish."

Ben took a sip of wine. "Do you mean about the election?"

"At the risk of boring you, politics is part of it,"

Charles replied. "But if our country settles down, investors will settle down as well. Where else will people put their money but America? We certainly need them to—they're the people who create jobs for everyone else." His voice became animated, "Take your father, for example. He makes his living because other people with decent jobs can afford to order lobster tails at restaurants. Why? Because capital creates business, which creates employment. So there's a direct correlation between my clients' investments and your father's livelihood."

Ben gave him an inscrutable look. "I don't think Dad has thought about it that much."

Charles smiled indulgently. "He would if Americans stopped eating lobsters. The economy is a seamless web, the pattern of which can't be rent without damaging many millions of people outside the so-called investor class. No doubt your father has more immediate concerns. But I'd argue that he has a direct interest in policies that encourage capital formation and leave free enterprise to work its will."

Ben gave him a wry look in return. "I'll mention that to him, sir. Before he becomes a Keynesian."

Whitney found herself smiling—whatever his private thoughts, and however much alcohol he'd consumed, Ben retained enough self-control not to set off conversational landmines. "Speaking of politics," Charles went on, "and given the tragedy that befell Senator Kennedy, who is your alternative choice for president?"

Ben's face clouded. "No one."

Watching him, Whitney hoped her father would leave it there. Instead, Charles asked with the same politeness, "At this point, isn't Hubert Humphrey your party's best hope of winning?"

Ben took a deeper swallow of wine. "Winning what?" he inquired softly. "When he signed on with LBJ, Humphrey put his manhood in a blind trust. Now he's using hair dye and rouge to play at being young, which makes him look like he belongs in a coffin. The only sign of life is that he can't stop talking." Contempt seeped into his voice. "If there are two sides to every question, Humphrey will find three. Assuming you can locate a thought in that army of words searching vainly for an idea."

At the end of the table, Anne's eyebrows raised, a signal that the conversation was stretching the bounds of politesse. But Whitney perceived that Ben no longer cared; instead of impairing his power of speech, liquor appeared to unleash it. "A fairly scathing dismissal," Charles said pointedly.

Quickly, Whitney interposed, "Ben was very committed to Bobby."

"That must have been terribly hard," her father acknowledged. "I'm sure it's still painful. But the world keeps on spinning, and you young people have more at stake than anyone. I gather you oppose the war, Ben."

"Yes," Ben answered tersely.

"Then what about Eugene McCarthy? Like you and Robert Kennedy, he favors withdrawal from Vietnam."

Stop, Whitney silently implored her father. Across the table, Ben drew a breath. "McCarthy," he said with a cool precision, "is the candidate of draft dodgers—the comfortable white kids who discovered their idealism the day LBJ abolished draft deferments, and they suddenly imagined getting blown to pieces like Johnny did. Their reasons for caring aren't mine."

As Charles stiffened, Whitney felt herself cringe—intentionally or not, Ben's statement implicated Peter. Clarice watched Ben fixedly now, less with approval or disapproval than in seeming fascination with observing a new and unusual species of male. With the same incisive swiftness, Ben continued, "McCarthy was too lazy and self-satisfied. When did he ever stand up for minorities or the poor?" Glancing at Clarice and Whitney, he asked, "Can either of you think of any black kids or Latinos for McCarthy?"

Assuming that you know any, he did not have to add. When Clarice hesitated, Whitney softly answered, "No."

"To play devil's advocate," Charles said to Ben, "maybe your man knew where the voters are. Hispanics helped him win California . . ."

"Bobby also visited illiterate blacks in the South, migrant workers in California, and Indians on reservations. Where are the votes in that, Mr. Dane? McCarthy's so-called crusade was to keep white kids from showering in some cruddy barracks with the people Kennedy fought for. If the war keeps going, half those patriots will be showering in Canada, or weaseling out some other way."

Charles fixed him with a gelid stare. "I grant you your idealism, Ben, if not your opinion of others. But was Kennedy really such an idealist? For all your scorn of McCarthy, he's the one who chose to take on Lyndon Johnson. Bobby didn't jump in the race until McCarthy showed him it was safe."

Ben met his eyes. With a terrible quiet, he said, "Wasn't all that safe, was it?"

Anne seemed to flinch. "Perhaps . . ."

"I should answer your husband's question, Mrs. Dane." Ben paused, reining in his emotions with visible effort. "For an egotist like McCarthy, piggybacking on the antiwar movement was his only chance to become a national figure. But it was Kennedy who drove Johnson from the race . . ."

"So you don't think he was ruthless?" Charles persisted. "Even though in the 1950s he kept company with the other McCarthy, Joe, whom liberals despised as a red-baiter?"

"Not for long," Ben shot back. "And Joe McCarthy had company. Richard Nixon for example, who made his career by smearing liberals as communists."

Clammy with tension, Whitney regretted withholding from Ben her father's relationship with Nixon. But neither she nor Clarice had seen anyone—much less a young person—challenge Charles Dane in such a sustained and relentless way. Leaning forward, Charles said in a louder voice, "You don't think Nixon grew? To many, he's a seasoned man who'll restore sound judgment to the White House."

Ben took a last swallow of wine. "To many others," he countered succinctly, "he's a morally bankrupt striver . . ."

"Then why," Charles cut in, "has he risen from the political dead to attract such broad support?"

"Because he's a tool of the rich. If he didn't exist, our ruling class would have to invent him, just like they have with Ronald Reagan."

Biting off his words, Charles retorted, "The rich, as you call them, are a tiny minority of Americans. Someone else has to vote for him."

"True enough. That's why Nixon is pandering to racists who hate the civil rights laws and people like my father who blame 'welfare queens' for how their life has gone. The rich who back Nixon don't care." Ben paused, then seemed unable to stop himself. "After all, what's a poor black woman to someone who spends more on one dinner at a fancy restaurant in Manhattan than she has to feed and clothe her kids for a month? Nothing. Because to those people it isn't about what they owe the country, but what the country owes them. The privilege to be even more like themselves."

Even in her dismay, this struck a chord in Whitney. Desperate to divert her father, she said, "Ben has a point, Dad. The only way I learned how people in Roxbury lived was to go there. A lot of my friends still don't have a clue."

Charles hesitated, plainly nettled, yet given pause by Whitney's intrusion. "Well," he said to Ben, "at least we both can hope that if Nixon wins, he'll find a way to conclude the war. Better than nothing, yes?"

"Yes," Ben said simply. "But Nixon won't end the war until affluent kids can't find enough safe havens to keep them from getting shot at. Then maybe Nixon will start paying the underclass to fight our wars, and the better-off can resume their life as armchair warriors, supporting the troops over cocktails."

Charles's face darkened. "The soup is getting cold," Anne said pleasantly but firmly, "and the main course is on its way. So the political discussion will have to end." Glancing at Ben, she added, "Though I must say the commentary has been interesting."

Ben smiled at her. "I hope so," he said with equal politeness. "Isn't that what you invited me for?"

The rest of the evening was strained but uneventful, with Anne and Clarice drawing the others into clever and mildly diverting conversation about the wedding, memories of other summers, and a favorite subject of Charles's— the fortunes of the New York Yankees—in which Clarice feigned a credible interest. Perhaps Whitney only imagined that her friend was playing to Ben as well as her father.

At the dinner's conclusion, Ben thanked Whitney's parents graciously enough, leaving without Charles's usual offer of a postprandial snifter of Armagnac. Whitney walked him to the door, hoping for a quiet word. "Well," he said with sardonic resignation, "I certainly helped your father make his point, didn't I?"

Whitney looked at him intently. "Not the way he wanted. He never should have mentioned Bobby."

Ben shrugged. "Again, not your fault. I could have avoided it by keeping my mouth shut. But maybe he knew I wouldn't." He paused. "You're also apologizing for another man in private, yet again. Someday, Whitney, you'll have to figure out who you are."

Turning, Ben left her there.

Eight

Whitney stood there, absorbing the sting of Ben's last words. Then Clarice emerged from the house. "It was time for a tasteful good-bye," she told Whitney.

Whitney nodded. "That was awful, wasn't it?"

Clarice smiled a little. "But interesting to watch, don't you think? When the fallout disperses, call me."

With a squeeze of Whitney's arm, Clarice headed for her car.

Alone, Whitney struggled to sort through her emotions. When she went back inside, her mother had vanished, and Charles was sitting in a wing chair with his snifter of brandy. For an instant, they regarded each other in silence.

"Well?" Charles said.

Whitney felt a constriction in her throat. "You set out to bait him. With his friend's death, it didn't take that much."

"No, it didn't," Charles agreed calmly. "But not just because of his friend."

Whitney remained standing. "You're the one who brought up Bobby Kennedy. Ben's twenty-two, not forty—once you got him started, he was going to say his piece. What was the point?"

"You tell me, Whitney."

271

"I can't."

"Can't you? I saw you watching him—as was Clarice. What did you see?"

"Someone with ideals."

"And I, of course, have none." Charles gestured toward a chair. "Sit down, please. Can I get you something?"

Whitney sat in the opposite chair. "No," she answered coldly. "Thank you."

"All right, then," Charles commenced. "To start, Ben Blaine is no idealist. Beneath the class rhetoric—and not far beneath, at that—he's a very angry young man who knows whom he dislikes most: 'the privileged.' But his supposed sympathy for blacks or Hispanics or Indians? They're just convenient weapons to throw in our face, the better to rationalize his hatred as something more noble . . ."

"You don't even know him . . ."

"Don't I?" Her father's eyes bored into hers. "When Clarice compared us, she got one thing right. I *do* know him, far better than anyone at that table. I remember all too well how it feels to want things you may never have—to believe you may never get the chance other people were born with. But I turned that into ambition, not pointless rage."

"Whatever Ben feels, he'll make something of it, too."

"As a journalist? You may be right. It's an

outsider's profession, he's a born outsider. He's more than self-possessed—he's arrogant and self-absorbed. He'll chew up everyone around him."

"He's not self-absorbed," Whitney protested. "Of all the people I know, Ben's the one who's most curious about who I am and what I think."

Charles managed to look both skeptical and astonished. "More than your mother and me?" he inquired.

"Much more," Whitney found herself saying. "You've known me for so long you think there's nothing left to know."

"For God's sakes, you're our daughter. Of course we know you . . ."

"Just like you know Janine?"

"What's *that* supposed to mean?" Her father's voice hardened. "You're younger than I thought, Whitney. Why do you think Benjamin Blaine has taken such an interest in you?"

Stung, Whitney replied, "Maybe because we can talk."

Charles eyed his daughter with a knowingness that made her bridle. "It's because he wants something from you. That's how he's made, and that's what concerns me most. I think Peter has the instinctive good judgment to be bothered by it, too. But he doesn't have this young man's weapons—he can't play the romantic rebel, and he lacks Ben's insolence and guile. One problem with goodness and predictability is that they have a certain sameness."

Whitney felt the sting of tears in her eyes. "Are you saying I don't appreciate Peter?"

"No. I'm asking you to stop and think—including about why Ben is such a presence in your life that he's become a subject within our family."

"Because *you* can't stand him," Whitney burst out. "You say he's arrogant. But you took over grandfather's firm as soon as you were able, and since then you've dominated every room you've ever been in. Except for tonight. *That's* why Ben made the hair stand up on the back of your neck."

"So which of us doesn't know the other?" Charles said tightly. "Do you really think this boy is that important to me personally? What do you take me for?"

All at once, Whitney felt sick inside—guilty about Peter, devastated at quarrelling with the man she had always loved most. But a last spurt of honesty made her say, "I don't think this is about politics, or me, or even about Ben. It's about you." She stood, voice tremulous. "I can't do this anymore, Dad. I love you, and I don't want to fight with you. I just need to be alone."

She turned and walked quickly to her bedroom, closing the door behind her.

For hours Whitney thrashed in bed until she fell into a broken slumber. When she awoke, exhausted, she lingered there, reluctant to face anyone. Upbraiding herself for cowardice, she put on her robe and went looking for her father.

Her mother was in the sunroom with her coffee, riffling a copy of the *New Yorker*. Seeing her, Anne said gravely, "Good morning, Whitney."

"Is Dad up?"

"Yes. And gone back to New York."

"Why?" Whitney asked in surprise. "He didn't tell me he was leaving."

Anne set side her magazine. "I gather you fought last night. It seems some memorable things were said."

"There were," Whitney admitted. "Most of them by me."

"I gathered as much," her mother said, not unkindly. "Nevertheless, your father regrets it, too. This morning, for once in his life, he didn't quite know what to do."

Whitney sat in the chair beside her. "I'm sorry, Mom. But he's making way too much of my relationship with Ben."

For a moment, Anne studied the greenery outside, dappled with new sunlight. "Is he?" she inquired. "Speaking for myself, I'm mystified by whatever appeal this boy holds for you. He's from an entirely different background—a family of alcoholics, according to Clarice's mother. I don't mean to sound Victorian. But class still matters, if only because it creates a common understanding."

"You understood Dad well enough."

"Your father was different," Anne insisted. "He found where he belonged. So what *did* you say to him, exactly?"

Whitney hesitated. "That he didn't like being challenged."

Anne shook her head in dismay. "Oh, Whitney—what man does? Not your father, not Peter, and certainly not Ben. It's been that way since they were chasing dinosaurs and fighting over women with clubs."

"But why should Dad always be the voice of authority? We arrange our life around him."

"Of course we do—to all of our benefit. Your father takes care of us. Please don't make our family a cauldron of unpleasantness."

Whitney drew a breath. "Is he really that fragile?"

"He's the strongest male I know. But even cavemen must have had their vulnerabilities." Anne paused, then added softly, "Because he loves you, last night hurt him more than he'll ever admit."

Whitney felt her sense of guilt resurfacing. "I know how much you love him, Mom. But do you really need to protect him like this?"

"I do," her mother replied. "He's under pressure

at work, and doing a lot for Richard Nixon—far more than you know, and with high hopes for a cabinet appointment, making Ben's comments last night all the more unfortunate. Your father has enough on his mind already." Anne's brow knit, an expression Whitney knew as doubt and worry, "Usually he spends whole weeks here. But this summer he's been running back and forth. After twenty-seven years of marriage, I still miss him when he's gone. I want this to be a refuge for him, not a scene of familial strife."

"You're putting a lot on me, aren't you?"

Anne considered her. "Perhaps I am," she said with a trace of humor. "A serene summer, culminating in a lovely wedding. Far too much for a mother to expect."

Suddenly Whitney thought of Janine, her mother's favorite. "Is anything else bothering you?"

Anne shook her head, as though to banish the suggestion. "No, nothing. Just do me a favor, and call your dad this afternoon. You don't have to apologize. Just say that you miss him, and hope he'll be back soon."

It was little enough to ask, Whitney thought. "All right."

Anne's face softened with relief. "As to Peter, when he comes back, give him the attention he deserves. That should end any lingering worries he may have about Benjamin Blaine."

Once again, Whitney thought of Peter's kindness and good humor, the boyish sweetness she loved, the way her heart leapt when her handsome fiancé had first whispered, *I love you.* "Of course I will," she assured her mother. "At the end of the summer, I'll be married. Like you love Dad, I'll love Peter all my life."

Gently, Anne touched her daughter's wrist. "Then perhaps it's also time to end your friendship with Ben. That would put all this to rest."

After a moment, Whitney nodded.

Instead of calling Clarice, Whitney took her journal to Dogfish Bar.

As she expected, no one was there. At first she felt the tug of disappointment—without seeking Ben out, she could have explained how things must be. But what followed was relief; she did not feel ready to do this, or know what she might say.

Opening her journal, she found her thoughts drifting to her mother. Did some deeper anxiety remain unspoken, perhaps about Janine? But when she began writing, it was about a morning spent on the golf course with Peter and Charles.

The summer my father took up golf, I was twelve. He had never played when he was young; his life was too serious then, and he had no time. Now he got up every day at 5:30, playing nine holes with a professional he paid to instruct him. No one else was there. He would never golf with friends or associates, my mother said, until he was ready to beat them. By the end of the summer, he was telling self-deprecating jokes about his skill at a game he had already mastered.

The first time he played with Peter, I went along to watch. Peter is an athlete, easily Dad's superior in strength and coordination. His drives went farther, and he took a pleasure in his own gifts that seemed close to innocence. But my father is no innocent, and he knew the refinements of the game.

After seventeen holes, their match was even. But by then I'd perceived that my father's swing was the same every time, precise as a machine. And I knew, before the near-perfect chip that stole the match from Peter, that my father would never let him win.

"Just lucky," Dad said lightly.

Putting down her pen, Whitney felt a nagging worry she could not label. Not for Peter, whom her father loved, but for Ben.

Nine

Whitney's father returned on Thursday, good humor restored. They said nothing about their quarrel. For the sake of amity, Whitney joined her parents in watching the final evening of the Republican convention.

Richard Nixon had won the nomination. But Charles was concerned about his vice-presidential choice, an obscure governor from Maryland named Spiro Agnew. "One of Nixon's strategists called me about this," he told Anne and Whitney. "I asked him how this man would help us win. I still don't know."

Whitney heard her father's worry—victory might slip away and, with it, his chance at public eminence. But the scores of white faces attending the convention listened raptly to Nixon's acceptance speech, as though convinced that he alone could deliver them from the chaos and confusion of this terrible year. "As we look at America," Nixon told them in his deep, portentous voice, "we see cities enveloped in smoke and flame. We hear sirens in the night. We see Americans dying on distant battlefields abroad. We see Americans hating each other, fighting each other, killing each other at home. Did we come all this way for this? Die in Normandy and Korea and Valley Forge for this?"

With an odd detachment, Whitney wondered how this man could seem so disingenuous, yet come so far; why the delegates, so respectable in dress and mild in appearance, could be so intense in their devotion. Then it struck her—Nixon was speaking for them. "Listen to the answers," he continued. "The quiet voice in the tumult and the shouting. The voice of the great majority of Americans, the forgotten Americans. The non-shouters, the non-demonstrators. They give drive to the spirit of America, lift to the American dream, steel to the backbone of America. Good people, decent people, who work and pay their taxes . . ."

Charles nodded his approval. *This is how to do it,* Whitney imagined him thinking. Then Nixon's peroration brought her up short.

"The time has come for us to leave the valley of despair and climb to the top of the mountain . . ."

I have been to the top of the mountain, she recalled Martin Luther King proclaiming, *and I've seen the promised land.* Hours later he was dead, the speech a tragic premonition.

"To the top of the mountain," Nixon repeated, "so that we may see the glory of a new day for America, a new dawn for peace and freedom in the world . . ."

And then he was done, and cages filled with

balloons opened from the rafters, floating above the white, upturned faces of the delegates.

The next morning, Clarice returned from forty-eight hours in New York City—pleased with the alterations on her maid-of-honor dress—and suggested lunch and a movie.

They ate at a crowded outdoor restaurant above the Edgartown harbor. It was surrounded by white wooden houses, many in the style of a sea captain's home, in the town where most old line families made their summer residence. "So," Clarice asked, "what was the aftermath of Ben's dinner at the Danes?"

"Not good. I accused my father of going after him, and Dad expressed his loathing for Ben and everything he stood for. It escalated from there. When I got up the next morning, Dad was gone, and Mom intimated ever so politely that I'd driven him back to Manhattan."

Setting aside her shrimp cocktail, Clarice gave Whitney a curious look. "That's a funny thing to say. He does work there, after all."

"More, these days. Apparently that's now my fault."

"Do you imagine that's even possible?"

"No. But I wonder if Mom's more insecure than I've realized."

Clarice dabbed at her lips with a paper napkin. "About anything in particular?"

"I'm not sure. Maybe about Janine; maybe something else. Her great reason for being is to make Dad happy."

Frowning, Clarice contemplated the harbor, its blue waters crowded with yachts and sailboats at mooring. "You don't think there's trouble in their marriage, do you?"

The thought had never occurred to Whitney. "Of course not. But any controversy within the family upsets her. Mom believes that the appearance of serenity creates its own reality."

Clarice steepled her fingers, reflective. "Tell me more about what your dad said."

Perhaps she was like her mother, Whitney reflected; thinking about this still depressed her. "He was pretty caustic. To Dad, Ben's a self-centered boy whose politics camouflage a seething class resentment, and whose relationship with me serves some hidden agenda. I stood up for him, at least to a point. So now Dad's worried about what that means."

"What do you think it means?"

"That my father has a hyperactive imagination."

Clarice turned to look Whitney in the face. "I've known you all your life, Whitney—in some ways better than your parents. The other night, sitting across the table, I saw you watching Ben. You barely took your eyes off him."

Whitney felt herself redden. "Dad says you didn't either."

To her surprise, Clarice looked disconcerted. "The scene had a certain fascination, I'll admit. But after awhile I just wanted to disappear."

"So you don't find Ben attractive?"

"I find him interesting," Clarice parried. "But I'm not the one spending time with him, or defending him to my father . . ."

"I just don't think he's the person Dad describes."

"And you don't want him to be that person, do you?"

"What are you getting at?" Whitney demanded. "You're sounding a bit like Dad."

Clarice placed a hand on Whitney's arm. "This is *me*—Clarice Barkley. I'm asking you to be honest with me, so we can actually talk about whatever this is. So let me try again: are you attracted to Benjamin Blaine?"

He was only a friend, Whitney wanted to protest, and not always friendly at that. But then she remembered Ben walking away from her, and felt the same knot in her stomach. Briefly closing her eyes, she conceded, "Maybe there's something . . ."

Clarice's expression commingled sympathy with satisfaction. "Don't be embarrassed, okay? Even women who love their husbands experience that."

Stubbornly, Whitney said, "I don't think my mom does."

"If that's true," Clarice retorted, "maybe it's because she doesn't like sex all that much."

Whitney felt another sliver of unease, the sense of a buried truth made more uncomfortable because it concerned the sexuality of a parent. "I wouldn't know."

"But you do know about yourself. Sex is something you like, and you may not always get what you need." Clarice paused. "Still, as committed to monogamy as you are, it might be best to avoid Ben altogether."

"I mean to. Anyhow, in five weeks, he'll be back at Yale."

Clarice eyed her curiously. "Don't you think it funny that you've counted the weeks?"

"Anyone can do that, Clarice. Even a college graduate."

"True. So you've got only thirty-five days to get through without yielding to some terrible impulse."

Caught between irritation and amusement, Whitney objected, "You'd think I was sex-crazed."

Clarice glanced at the other diners, ensuring they would not be overheard. "Just a little restless. But that's what masturbation is for. So look at the upside—you've got five weeks to polish your technique for those nights when Peter's out with clients."

Whitney shook her head with mock amazement. "You really *are* a cynic, Clarice. But here's the real upside—you've got Ben all to yourself."

Clarice gave her an enigmatic smile. "I'll wait to see how he turns out. In the meanwhile, why should I play with matches for no reason? I can hardly bring him to your wedding."

"Is there anyone right now?"

Shrugging, Clarice turned back to the harbor. "Nothing I'm ready to talk about."

A veil seemed to fall across her eyes. Glancing at her watch, Clarice said, "About time for the movie," then added, "I've got the check. As far as I know, the Barkley fortune is still intact."

The film was The Thomas Crown Affair. Steve McQueen was a patrician art thief, the quarry of an insurance investigator, Faye Dunaway; the main point seemed to be how much erotic heat they could generate before one bested the other. When their cat-and-mouse game became, quite literally, a chess match, Dunaway began fondling the chess pieces. Leaning closer to Whitney, Clarice struggled to repress laughter. "This gives foreplay a whole new meaning," she whispered.

"I think the rook is getting taller," Whitney whispered back. But despite herself, she was aroused by the crossing of boundaries, the dance of sexual desire between a man and woman intended to be adversaries.

• • •

Once at home, Whitney showered. Emerging from the bathroom, she stood naked in front of the mirror.

With a critical eye, she studied herself, imagining how a man might see her. Full breasts, round hips, a ripeness to her. Touching her nipples, she felt them raise, then a stirring between her legs. She closed her eyes, trying to empty her mind of sensuality. After all, she told herself with a certain irony, there were thank-you notes to write.

Stationing herself at the dinner table, Whitney consulted her list of gifts, then started composing on the embossed gold-leaf stationery Anne had bought her for this purpose. Hearing voices, she saw her father emerge from the library with three golfing companions—a Boston lawyer, the head of an insurance company, and a somewhat florid local merchant who, Whitney recalled, was also an elected official.

The four did not see her. "It's only the one house," the insurance man said to Charles. "But termite infestations start small."

His acidic tone aroused Whitney's social antennae. "I wouldn't call the Wallaces and Buchwalds termites," Charles temporized. "Their neighbors in Vineyard Haven don't seem to mind their presence."

The red-faced merchant pursed his lips. "Are

you going to help us, Charles? It's your business associate who's selling, after all."

"Still, he's not my ward. Ted has other concerns—a costly divorce, to be specific. Or he wouldn't be selling at all."

"You know him," his interlocutor persisted. "So please emphasize that he shouldn't be responsible for turning West Chop into Brooklyn." He placed a hand on Charles's shoulder, a gesture of intimacy. "As we discussed on the phone, you and I can help each other."

"I understand," Charles replied, and graciously shepherded them out the door.

Heading for the kitchen, he saw Whitney. "Writing thank-you notes? At last your mother can sleep at night."

Instead of answering, Whitney asked, "What was *that* about, Dad?"

Her father hesitated, then answered dismissively, "A molehill aspiring to be a mountain. Far more important to them than me."

"Don't a lot of Jews live in Brooklyn?" she persisted.

"True enough," Charles conceded glumly. "A man I know in West Chop proposes to sell to a Jewish family from Boston. Some of the residents, my visitors included, seem to feel it would change the character of the place."

"In other words," Whitney said sharply, "they're anti-Semitic."

"They don't see it that way, Whitney, and I'm certainly not. In my business, one deals with Jews all the time, many of whom I respect and even admire. But these men fear that this sale will disturb a communal understanding."

"So West Chop is like our country club in Greenwich—no Jews allowed?"

"Not indefinitely," Charles said in the same patient tone. "But these things take time. Just last year the club began admitting Catholics—one of whom I sponsored—and no one said much of anything."

"Nice of them," Whitney said with quiet sarcasm. "Given that seven years ago we elected one president of the United States. But I guess our club is more selective."

Charles managed a smile. "A matter of pride, for some. I don't argue they're not foolish . . ."

"So what did you tell those men?" Whitney persisted. "That they were foolish to worry about Jews 'infesting' West Chop?"

Charles crossed his arms. "That would have been pointless. They're not going to change, and sooner or later someone in West Chop will sell to a Jew. Whenever that happens, I'll be able to help ease the way, in part because I didn't dismiss these men as bigots. Sometimes you have to change things from the inside. If I hadn't learned that, the O'Connors of Greenwich would still be waiting for admission."

Quiet, Whitney considered the man she had not merely loved, but admired. "Just promise me that you won't persuade this man not to sell."

"Don't worry," Charles assured her. "That's beyond my powers."

At length Whitney nodded, less from belief than the desire to be done with this. But after her father left the room, she had the brief but unsettling wish that she could talk with Ben.

Ten

For several days, Whitney avoided the Dunmores' property, or even walking in that direction. But this did nothing to drive him from her thoughts. Aware of her tangled motives, she visited Jack Blaine's woodworking shop.

It was a plain wooden building on the edge of Vineyard Haven, cut into sections for artisans and artists. The day was overcast, and the illumination came from a skylight and several bare bulbs hanging above a work table where Jack, in an oilskin apron, stood surrounded by lathes, a sander, several handsaws, and bottles of oil, varnish, paint, and shellac. The place smelled of sawdust and something like turpentine. Jack looked up in surprise, and then a wry, lopsided smile softened his usual gravity.

"Welcome," he said. "I guess Clarice isn't with you."

Whitney shook her head. "I was in the neighborhood, and decided to drop in."

Somehow, she sensed, Jack knew that this was not quite true. "Anyhow, it's a good time. Let me show you what I'm working on."

Laid out in front of him were rounded knobs for a chest of drawers. Jack pointed out the drawers themselves, standing among a captain's chair, a desk, and a newly stained parson's table. Each appeared to be crafted and joined with exquisite care, as close to pieces of art as Jack's hands could make them. Touching the chair, Whitney asked, "How long will this take you?"

"Weeks."

"Then you must hate to part with them."

"I do. But not as much as I enjoy placing a piece in someone's home—knowing that their kids and grandkids may find a place for it long after they, and I, are dead. A strange thing to think about, I know. But given that life is finite, there's something consoling in that."

Even his speech and manner of speaking struck Whitney as those of an artist. It was hard for her to believe that Jack was the son of a lobsterman, let alone the angry and stunted primitive Ben had described. "How did you learn to do this?"

Eying the chest, Jack opened a drawer, as though to assure that it fit precisely. "By apprenticing over the summers, and catering to compensate for not getting paid. After high school I spent two years at Pratt Institute in New York. But my scholarship didn't come close to covering expenses, and I was piling up debt I couldn't handle. By that time I'd learned a fair amount about furniture design. So I came back here."

This brief account—delivered without discernable bitterness—captured a narrowing of opportunity foreign to Whitney's life. But she could not help but think that, in Jack's place, Ben would have found a way. "And if you'd been able to finish?" she asked.

He gave a fatalistic shrug. "I don't think about it much. There's a lot I love about this island—the ocean, the ponds, the quiet, the wildlife, so much nature left unspoiled. The people, too. Like me, they stay because they've become committed to the place as it is. So we do whatever we can to make it work for us—shucking scallops, making jewelry, waitressing." The hint of a smile moved through Jack's brown, expressive eyes. "Then we hope that people from the mainland confine their visits to the summer, leaving behind enough money to get us to the next one. No offense, of course."

"None taken."

"It's just that what we have here is rare. This island exists in a time warp—like more places must have been before the Second World War. As a kid I could just walk into a friend's house if no one was home, raid the refrigerator or watch the Red Sox on TV. No one has a lot. But most people are generous and straightforward, and we share a sense of freedom that's hard to find."

"Does Ben feel like that?" Whitney inquired. "I've never heard him say so."

A smile crossed Jack's lips without reaching his eyes. "You won't. Ben would say I lack ambition. But he has too much for the island to hold."

"He wants to be a writer, I know."

"Not just any writer. I remember us catering a party at Bill and Rose Styron's. After we came home, the two of us were lying in bed. For a time Ben was so quiet I thought he was sleeping. Then his voice came from the darkness. 'Someday I'm going to walk down the street, anywhere in America, and hear a man or woman tell their kid, "That's Benjamin Blaine, the greatest writer of our time." ' " Jack paused, as though bemused by the memory. "It's like he was making himself a promise I happened to overhear. Ben confides in no one."

Sometimes he confides in me, Whitney wanted to say. "That sounds a little like the way Ben imagined Ted Williams, when he was listening to those games."

"He told you about that?"

"Yes."

Leaning back against the work table, Jack said

quietly, "You've started to care about him, haven't you?"

"Only as a friend," she said firmly. "In six weeks, I'll be married."

Still watching her eyes, Jack nodded. "Just as well."

"Why do you say that?"

He gazed at the floor, as if considering how to answer. "When he wants to, Ben's got all that charm. People fall in line for him, women most of all. But I've never known a woman who Ben respected. Our mother wasn't much use to us, and he remembers that too well."

Whitney wondered how far to venture into a past so intimate and painful. But the pull of hearing more proved irresistible. "He told me your father beat her."

Briefly, Jack looked discomfited. "I'm surprised by that, seeing how ashamed he is of our family. But I guess that makes him Mom's heroic protector."

"That's not how he told it. It was more that he couldn't stand your father ruling the space he lived in. So he put an end to it."

"Because I was such a coward, right? That's the other part of the story."

The cauldron of family had scarred them in different ways, she thought, turning brothers into adversaries. At length, she said, "It's your father Ben despises, not you."

"He seems to have shared a lot with you. But I guess you're safe enough." Jack jammed his thumbs in his belt loops. "So do you think he's going after Clarice?"

Surprised, Whitney forced a smile. "I don't even think he likes her."

Jack gave her a skeptical look. "Maybe not. But he certainly noticed her. He seemed to make a point of catering parties where she was likely to show up."

Was this true? Whitney wondered. "Not the best way to meet girls," she objected.

"Especially wealthy ones," Jack responded pointedly. "Something about wearing an ill-fitting white jacket and skinny bow tie while balancing drinks on a tray."

Hearing the distaste in his voice, Whitney realized that he, too, felt resentful. "My brother has his pride," Jack continued. "No doubt that's why he bridled when your fiancé ordered him around in front of Clarice Barkley. I haven't seen that look in Ben's eyes since he beat our old man to a pulp."

For Whitney, this put a humbling new slant on that volatile evening, making Clarice—not her—the catalyst in a tragicomedy of errors in which Peter utterly misread Ben's motives. "A bad night," she said.

"Ben can bring out the worst in people, and your fiancé couldn't have known about Clarice." Jack paused, then said with synthetic casualness, "Does she have a boyfriend? It looked like she wasn't with anyone."

"Not as far as I know. I can tell you it's not Ben."

He cocked his head. "Maybe. But summer people *do* end up with islanders, you know. Usually summer girls and island guys."

Whitney summoned a wry smile. "So who is it that likes Clarice? I'm losing track."

Grudgingly, Jack returned her smile, as though to acknowledge his own foolishness. "I don't really know her. So maybe I just imagine that she also needs protecting. Another reason I can't see her with Ben."

Whitney found herself hoping that Jack was projecting his own feelings onto Ben, his superior in force and boldness. "Don't worry about Clarice," she assured him. "She's pretty good at protecting herself. Next time, I'll bring her around, and you can judge for yourself."

The next day, Whitney and Clarice returned to Lucy Vincent Beach. It was more crowded in August, and Clarice began looking for people they knew. Then she became still, gazing fixedly in one direction before murmuring, "Don't stare. But see the dark-haired guy to our left, talking to his friends? I'm sure it's Dustin Hoffman."

Surreptitiously, Whitney conducted her own reconnaissance. The guy in sunglasses looked short, older than on the screen. But then she flashed on his first scene with Katharine Ross, playing Ben Braddock in shades. "You're right."

Sitting up, Clarice steeled herself. "I'm going over there."

Whitney was taken aback by her friend's nerve. "What will you say to him? 'Plastics'?"

"I'll ask him who he wants—Mrs. Robinson, or Elaine. I can play either part."

Clarice walked over to the actor and his friends, kneeling close to Dustin. Though Hoffman looked bemused, he began smiling as she spoke. He said something; she said much more. At length she retreated, casting a sharp grin at him over her shoulder. "And . . . ?" Whitney asked.

"Pretty shy, not that much to say. But the last smile I gave him did it. He'll wake up tomorrow, and realize he's in love."

"Poor man." Whitney took out suntan lotion from her handbag. "On a seemingly unrelated subject, I visited Jack Blaine at his workshop."

"Ben's brother?" Clarice gave her a knowing look. "You didn't go looking for Ben, did you?"

"No," Whitney said tartly. "I was looking for a dining table. Ben and Jack aren't exactly close."

"A keen observation, Sherlock. So how did you meet him?"

"He was patching up a boat at the Dunmores' catwalk. But he gave me the impression you knew him a little better."

Clarice nodded, unsurprised. "When he was waiting tables, we spoke a couple of times."

"What did you make of him?"

Pondering the question, Clarice took longer than Whitney had expected. "He seems like he'd make a nice friend—the kind of guy who sticks to things. If all you had to worry about was finding a man who wouldn't let you down, he'd be one to go for."

Lying back, Clarice shut her eyes, her further thoughts about Jack—or Ben—unavailable to her curious friend.

The next morning, Ben was not at Dogfish Bar.

Opening her diary, Whitney reflected on her conversation with Clarice, then began to write.

Clarice is a surprising girl. Among the surprises is that she has clearly thought about a guy—Jack—who she barely knows and can't matter to her much. Still, I think she caught something true about him—a steadiness and loyalty. But the Jack I imagine also wrestles with a deep anger, the repression of which allows him to deny his kinship with Ben. As so often, it seems, family both defines and distorts.

Pausing, Whitney thought about Clarice. As she pondered their time together, she began to re-imagine her friend as a character in a novel—a complex, even mysterious woman concealed beneath the sunny, mischievous girl Whitney had known for eighteen years. Perhaps both personas were Whitney's own creation, the question being which was truer to the Clarice Barkley she knew now. But what perplexed her, she realized, went beyond her closest friend.

There's something strange about this summer. Even the people I know best have begun seeming like quicksilver, as difficult to grasp as I'm finding myself. I wish that Peter could come here and stay.

Eleven

As days passed, and Whitney did not see Ben at Dogfish Bar, she began to feel childish and cowardly. After yet another solitary morning at the beach, Whitney got tired of herself, and went to find him.

He was sitting on the deck of the guesthouse, a steaming cup of coffee in his hand, a folded letter on the table in front of him. He looked up at her without expression, as though her absence, and now her presence, was unremarkable.

"How are you?" she asked.

"I've been better," he said, and handed her the letter.

It was headed "Order to Report for Armed Forces Physical Examination." Shaken, Whitney absorbed the contents—in one week, Ben was to be given a draft physical on the Cape. In a muted tone, she asked, "What are you going to do?"

"Not much I *can* do," he said in a dispirited tone. "I called one of my professors, a guy who counsels kids about draft problems. One week's notice is no time at all—he's never seen a draft board move this fast." His voice became bitter. "When Jack dropped out of Pratt, it took them nearly a year to call him in."

"Why didn't he go?"

"Asthma," Ben said with palpable disdain. "They classified him 4-F, and then he returned to the womb of Martha's Vineyard. Hard for a man to do any less with such good fortune. But now I'm on the fast track. If they re-classify me 1-A, I can't get back to Yale. Instead I'm in the Army."

Whitney felt shock morph into anguish for him, and then a second fear she had only felt for Peter. "I'm so sorry, Ben."

He gave her a long, appraising look. "I guess you've been avoiding me. Or is planning a wedding more stifling than I imagined?"

Whitney had no good answer. "I've been wondering how you are."

After a moment, Ben smiled a little. "Now that you know, feel brave enough to risk going with me to a beach party?"

"When?" she asked in surprise.

"Tonight—in Gay Head, near Dogfish Bar. A couple of guys I know from high school are doing something with a crew of kids from off-island—the usual mix of music and pharmacology. The way things are, this may be my last experience with the counterculture before they shave my hair off. So I'm going as an observer."

"And you want company?"

"I asked, didn't I? A draftee's last request."

Whitney hesitated, then had the superstitious fear that he would vanish—not just from her life, but from life itself. "Okay, then."

He gave her a sideways look. "How are you going to explain this to your parents?"

Whitney did not know. Shamed by her worry, she said, "Leave that to me."

Closing the door to her bedroom, Whitney called Clarice. "I need your help," she began.

She could hear the tension in her own voice. "Sounds serious," her friend responded. "You're not pregnant, are you?"

"Worse than pregnant. I've decided to go with Ben to a beach party." Hastily, she added, "He's been ordered to report for a draft physical, and I feel terrible for him. But I can't imagine Mom feeling all that sympathetic."

"So you'd like to say you're with me."

"In a word, yes."

Clarice hesitated. "You're really putting me on the spot, Whitney. I'm not sure a best friend should help you sneak around your parents with this particular guy, five weeks before you're getting married."

"This isn't about betraying Peter," Whitney said defensively. "It's just something I need to do. You've said it yourself—parents don't need to know everything."

Clarice sighed audibly. "No matter what you say, I feel something bad coming on. But yeah, okay. My parents are off-island, so you can meet him here."

The Barkley's home was a rambling white-frame structure not dissimilar to the Danes', with roses and a festive garden, the assiduous work of Clarice's mother and grandmother. When Ben arrived, she and Whitney were waiting on the porch. Clarice gave his beat-up truck a jaundiced once-over, then regarded him with a small, appraising smile. Seeing his expression, her smile vanished quickly.

"I'm sorry about the draft, Ben."

"Yeah," he said curtly. "A shame, isn't it?"

Remembering Jack's comments, Whitney watched his face for signs of interest in Clarice. Instead he turned to her. "Let's go," he said, and opened the passenger door.

Embarrassed by his rudeness, Whitney

murmured, "Thank you," to her friend, and got inside the truck. As they drove off, Clarice gave them a demure wave of benediction.

Ben's face clouded. "So Clarice is your beard."

"It seemed better than fighting with my parents over nothing." To change the subject, Whitney added, "I guess you know that your brother's attracted to her."

Ben turned down South Road toward Gay Head. "Where did you get this insight?" he asked.

"From Jack. I visited his shop the other day."

He looked surprised, and then laughed softly. "Jack was born to spend his life on the sidelines. Why expend emotional energy on a girl who's that entitled? He might as well decide to become a cosmonaut."

Whitney wondered if this remark was also directed at Ben himself. "What if you were the one who liked her, and not Jack?"

Ben shrugged. "I didn't ask her to the beach party, did I?"

Considering this remark, Whitney found several possible implications. She let the subject drop.

In the failing light, the beach had the dusky softness of an impressionist painting—the sea grass was darker, the sand dung-colored, the clouds wispy and indistinct in a blue-gray sky. Young people in twos or threes were gathered around a sputtering bonfire—the women with long flowing hair, most of the guys sporting beards or mustaches. A few passed around joints as a yipping dog sniffed at a couple of small, towheaded children, a boy and a girl, playing with plastic pails and shovels near a metal keg of beer. Ben and Whitney sat at the edge of the group, greeting no one. "Who are they?" she asked.

"Rich kids, mostly—they don't invite too many locals. What you've got is one of your parents' summer parties through the looking glass."

"I don't see anyone I know."

"Maybe you won't. A lot of these kids are trust fund babies who figure it doesn't matter if they screw up. So now they're dropouts and druggies —still your class, but not your type." Taking a bottle of wine from his knapsack, he continued in the same dispassionate tone. "Some of them play at being hippies. But instead of living off the land, they're living off Mom and Dad. A make-believe Eden I could never quite buy into even as an escape."

Whitney looked around. Nearer the sea grass she saw sleeping bags, some occupied; a few more couples under blankets; a lone man strumming his guitar so lightly that it made no sound. "Aren't they worried about the draft?"

"I doubt it." Pouring Whitney some Chianti in a plastic cup, he nodded to indicate a stringy guy limping toward the keg of beer. "I know him from high school, and what you're seeing is a war wound. He chopped off his toe to avoid the army."

Whitney winced. "All of them can't be maimed."

"A primitive method, the last recourse of the underclass. I'm sure most of these people found an easier way out." He glanced around, then stopped to stare at something. "See that couple screwing in the sleeping bag? For the purposes of draft, I'd expect the guy's probably gay."

Embarrassed, Whitney laughed uneasily. Then she recalled Ben was here not as participant but observer, recording his impressions of a slice of life before he lost the freedom to do so. "I hope you don't have to go," she said quietly.

Ben gave her an oblique glance. "I know you do."

To Whitney's relief, his tone was free of sarcasm. They settled into companionable silence, sipping wine as night closed around them. The fire cast flickering light on the group closest to it. Some of the women were topless now; two more, naked, danced in vague association to the beat of an invisible drum. Others swam in the moonlight, their heads bobbing shadows. At the edge of the sea grass, a couple made love, the woman on top of the man, long hair rippling as she moved. Whitney's first instinct was to look away. Instead, she took a deep swallow of wine. "Not much like Winter Carnival at Dartmouth. At least people closed the door first."

Ben nodded. "At Yale, too. Another bourgeois hang-up."

Nearby someone turned on a transistor radio, its sound thinning as it reached them. "WBCN," he told her. "Used to be a classical station in Boston, and then one day it went rock—Joplin, the Airplane, the Dead, the Stones, even political stuff like Phil Ochs. Used to listen to it all the time."

From the darkness came Joni Mitchell's distinct voice. Straining to hear, Whitney caught a song about a woman who leaves one relationship after another to avoid being consumed by men.

And her heart is full and hollow
Like a cactus tree
While she's so busy being free
Like a cactus tree
Being free

"You know that song?" Whitney asked.

Ben nodded. "It's either an anthem for female liberation or an ironic warning. Maybe both."

Backlit by the fire, a tall, lanky guy came up to them, squinting in the darkness. "Ben?"

"None other. How are you, Huck?"

Huck looked from Whitney to Ben. He was squinting, she guessed, because he was high on something. "Good, man. You were at some Ivy League place, right?"

"Yale. But the Army may have other plans."

"Shit. How'd that happen?"

"Bad karma, I guess."

Huck shook his head in commiseration. "You heard what happened to Johnny, right? Got wasted in Vietnam."

A coolness entered Ben's face and voice. "Yeah. I heard."

"Bad times," Huck said sententiously. "At least out there in the world."

"Hardly a new development. So what about you, Huck? You look like a fighting man to me."

"No fucking way, man—I've got a *serious* hiatal hernia." Huck jerked his thumb in the direction of the fire. "Some of the others and me are starting a commune on some farmland in West Tisbury. We'll grow our own food, do something more creative than being cannon fodder or working for the man—writing or painting or photography. Me, I'm finally going to have time for my music."

Ben nodded solemnly. "Good to see you slowing down a little, Huck. I envy you the creative freedom."

Whitney repressed a smile. Though she knew Ben well enough to detect his utter disbelief that this man would accomplish anything, Huck heard only approval. "We're going to change the world," he said with ponderous certainty. "End wars, legalize pot, save the earth, make abortion free for everyone, liberate women, and demand equal rights for all people of color."

"Impressive," Ben said. "I can't even memorize all that. Must be terrific weed you're smoking."

Huck laughed a little. "The best." Belatedly acknowledging Whitney, he asked, "You guys together?"

Ben shook his head. "More like a one-night stand. Whitney's into sport-fucking."

Huck gave them both a dubious look. "Cool," he murmured, and wandered off.

Whitney felt amusement tugging at her indignation. "Thanks," she said to Ben. "You just ruined my reputation."

"Here? That would be impossible. Anyhow, in a couple of hours Huck's synapses and dendrites will start misfiring, and he won't even remember meeting you."

"Too bad. It felt like we really connected."

"Oh, well," Ben responded philosophically, "You can always invite him to the wedding."

Near the fire, Whitney saw a short, ponytailed guy reeling spastically, struggling to stay upright. "What's wrong with him?" she asked.

"Mescaline, I'd guess. Your limbs start feeling like spaghetti, except twitchier. Colors get more vivid, and start combining with other colors. The last time I did that I was listening to Dylan's 'Highway 61 Revisited,' and every note and lyric was a revelation."

Laughing, the guy pointed at a dog trying to shit near the fire. Suddenly, he folded up, falling to the sand, his eyes staring and unfocused. "He looks catatonic," Whitney said.

"He's passed through the elation stage. All in all, mescaline is a bad idea." His voice turned sober. "I had a roommate who thought he'd use that stuff to 'break through to the other side.' The other side turned out to be driving a taxi. I hope I'm wrong, but I don't think Jim is ever coming back. So all I do anymore is pot."

"When I was younger," Whitney confessed, "my mom told me it was the gateway drug to heroin. Later there was the honor code at Wheaton—no alcohol or drugs. So I've never even tried it."

"No harm in it. In fact, the Surgeon General has certified that pot is good for you. Told me so himself, the last time I smoked some." Reaching into his windbreaker, Ben took out a perfectly rolled joint. "Up to you, Whitney. But I'm driving, and I know my limits. If you want to experiment, you'll be safe with me."

Though he did not seem to be pushing her, Whitney felt embarrassed by her lack of sophistication. "Maybe a puff."

Ben lit the joint, taking a deep drag before exhaling. "That's how you do it," he told her, and passed the joint.

Taking it between her fingers, Whitney tried to remember smoking a surreptitious cigarette with Clarice when they were both sixteen. Then she took a hasty puff. "A little deeper," Ben advised. "Just not too much."

With the second puff, the hot, acrid smoke made Whitney cough. Determinedly, she took another, holding it in as Ben had. Taking the joint from her hand, Ben said, "I admire your commitment to research."

For awhile, they passed it back and forth, quiet. Whitney's sensations began merging—the bonfire, the strumming of a guitar, the lapping of surf, the riot of stars in a black sky, the cool, gentle breeze on her face. Everything else—her family, Peter, the wedding—felt very far away.

She was floating, Whitney thought. Mute, she took Ben's hand. He did not seem to notice. Hours passed, or maybe minutes. Ben appeared lost in his own thoughts.

Then someone was touching her shoulder. "Time to go," he told her gently. "Before you turn back into a pumpkin."

Whitney wished she could stay.

As Ben drove, Whitney laid her head back against the seat. "Still stoned?" he asked.

"I'm just wondering where I was. No one seemed connected to what's going on."

Ben glanced at her with a look of interest. "That's the point. To escape what's really happening and achieve a state of Nirvana at odds with human nature. Then their lives will all be different, and they'll create a whole new world where everything is heartfelt and lovely. Why did Bobby bother to run, I wonder, when there's Huck to liberate 'all people of color.' "

Whitney angled her head to look at him. "You don't like them much, do you?"

"Let's just say I don't respect them. Because they don't really care about anything but their own lives. It will be interesting to see them at our parents' age."

"What do *you* think they'll be like?"

Scanning the road, Ben flicked on his brights. "Some will hang on at the margins. Others will become their parents, only with a liberal gloss. Others won't even bother to pretend. And a very few will dedicate their lives to making the world a better place, in the face of a lot of selfishness and inertia."

Whitney thought of Robert Kennedy's assassination, a dead weight on his soul. "You're becoming a cynic."

Ben shook his head. "Scratch a cynic, someone said, and you'll find a bruised idealist. So I'm trying to be a realist. Still, I mean to live life like it matters." Driving carefully, he braked to negotiate a curve. "Including my career. A lot of these people have bought a ticket to nowhere. The notion that creativity comes from being drunk or stoned or moonstruck is infantile. Art comes from engagement and hard work."

"You're sounding strangely like my dad," Whitney observed.

Ben's eyes narrowed. "Only in the sense that he didn't succeed by medicating himself into oblivion. I mean to be a writer, and the romantic myth of the drunken writer is nonsense. Fitzgerald proved that by burning out without ever growing up."

But he did sound like her father, Whitney thought—older than his age, fixed in his identity. There was a core to him, a wall against extremes, that kept him from believing that any other person or way of being could take him where he wanted. For the rest of the drive, she pondered that, while preparing to lie to her mother.

Ben stopped at the foot of the driveway. Briefly, Whitney thought of the stranger who had parked there, having sex with Janine as she lay over the hood of his truck. "You all right?" Ben asked.

"I think so."

"Then let me see you walk."

He got out, watching her slide from the passenger seat, turning in a pirouette to imitate a ballerina. "I'm pretty sure I can make it."

Looking into her face, Ben smiled a little. "I hope so, Whitney."

She gazed back at him. He was her friend, after all; he had wanted nothing more than her company after an event which, were he unlucky, might spell the end of his life before it truly began.

A friend who she could trust, who knew that she was bound to Peter. "Thank you," she said, almost bashfully, and headed for the house.

Her mother was up late, reading in the living room. Putting down her book, she gave Whitney a long, quiet gaze. She must still be a little stoned, Whitney thought—it felt like she was looking at someone in a mask through the wrong end of the telescope. "How is Clarice?" her mother asked politely.

"Fine," Whitney said. "But I'm really tired."

She went to bed, falling asleep on top of her covers. When morning came, the night before felt like a dream, its fragments half-remembered. Her clearest image was of Ben, standing close to her in the driveway yet not touching her at all, the war a shadow behind him.

Twelve

The next days passed uneventfully, with Whitney and her mother putting the final touches on her wedding—floral arrangements, tablecloths, reviewing the guest list to arrange the seating for dinner. With the major questions resolved, there was less friction with Anne—neither mentioned Ben, and sharing these last details created a companionship that, Whitney knew, both pleased and calmed her mother. Clarice was off-island,

and difficult to find. But Whitney spoke with the other bridesmaids frequently, grateful for their anticipation of her day, and Payton Clarke gave her a bridal shower in Boston, a lively reunion with classmates who, in a matter of weeks, had come to view their years in college as a precious, irretrievable time. Some were getting married; others had their first purchase on a tentative career; still others would be teaching in the fall. But they pledged to spend a weekend together every summer, no matter where they were. Caught up in the forward pull of life, Whitney thought less about Janine or Ben—save for her fears about his draft physical, and his seeming inability to avoid whatever fate awaited him. Despite the tug of conscience, this made her all the more grateful that her father had secured Peter's safety, and with it, the future life that would begin in four weeks' time.

On another lazy morning, awakening to shafts of sunlight at the edge of her curtained window, Whitney turned on her bedside radio. Expecting rock music, she was surprised by a newsman's solemn voice, reading a report from Radio Prague:

Yesterday, on August 20, at about eleven p.m., troops of the Soviet Union, the Polish People's Republic, the Hungarian People's Republic, the German Democratic People's Republic, and the Bulgarian People's Republic crossed the frontiers of the Czechoslovak Socialist Republic . . .

Whitney sat up. In a distant way, she had followed the stirrings of hope that, despite its dominance by the Soviet Union, Czechoslovakia could grope its way toward freedom. But the Russians had moved to snuff this out with overwhelming force. Listening, she was moved by the reports of young people marching into the center of Prague, surrounding Russian tanks to protest the gray subservience enveloping them once more. Picking up her phone, she called Peter at work.

He, too, had heard the reports. "There's nothing for it," he opined soberly. "Like your dad says, it's the nature of that system. All we can do is resist them where we can, like in Vietnam, or else they'll take advantage somewhere else."

He was partly right, Whitney knew—the Czechs were on their own. "All our talk about freedom," she said, "and yet we're completely helpless. Whatever we do in Vietnam doesn't help these people at all."

"I know." Peter hesitated. "Why don't I ask your dad if I can fly over tomorrow evening. I can't change the world, but maybe I can brighten yours a little."

"I'd like that," Whitney told him, and resumed following the news.

Throughout the day, her mood darkened—the tragedy in Eastern Europe had ripped her cocoon. For whatever reason, Anne suddenly seemed distracted, disinterested in the fate of Czechoslovakia or Whitney's wedding. Intermittently, she retreated to her bedroom, the usual locus of calls to Janine or Charles, suggesting to Whitney that she was trying and failing to reach her older daughter. At dinner, Anne drank more wine than usual, remarking not on the Soviet invasion but on feminists protesting the Miss America Pageant. "You'd think that being attractive and well-spoken was a sin," she observed. "Sometimes I think those women don't like being women."

"Maybe they just don't like women parading in swimsuits and high heels," Whitney responded mildly. "I'm more concerned about the Czechs."

"You're right, of course," Anne said with ironic weariness. "The world can be a depressing place. Some days I'm very grateful not to live in it."

The sense of isolation stealing over Whitney surprised her with its force. It was then she thought to wonder about Ben. "I'm going for a walk," she told her mother. "The days are getting shorter now."

She found him at the end of the dock, sipping from a whisky bottle and gazing up at the stars as they appeared in the darkening sky. "Are you okay?" she asked.

He did not look up at her. "More than okay, I'm peachy. In fact, you could say I'm 1-A. I passed the physical, of course. Thanks to the fates or whatever, I'll be protecting you and your husband when the Vietnamese invade Greenwich, Connecticut."

She sat beside him, gripped by sadness and foreboding. "I'm so sorry, Ben."

"I suppose you have that luxury. Courtesy of Dad, you won't be getting Peter back in a body bag . . ."

"That's not fair."

Ben took a deep swallow of whisky. "Fair?" he repeated. "What's 'fair' about me getting on the conveyor belt to Vietnam while Peter comes home to your very safe bed?"

He was drunk, Whitney realized, or at least well on his way. In a tentative voice, she said, "I wish I could help you."

"But you can't, can you?" Suddenly, Ben turned, gesturing at the Dunmores' spacious grounds. "Can you get me *this*, Whitney? God knows I want it. All of it. The money, the space, the freedom—whatever it takes to erase these feelings . . ."

"What feelings?"

"Not being able to stand even thinking about my life—all the months and years I spent in that house, believing I was powerless, that I'd never escape." He looked at her fixedly, his face so close that Whitney smelled the liquor on his breath. "For all I despise your family's smugness, you have no idea how much I envy you—the entitlement, the lack of that sharp-toothed rat gnawing at your insides like the ones who gnawed the food in our pantry." His voice lowered. "I thought I'd escaped. But now they've got me again. And there's nothing I can do."

There was a part of him she could not reach, Whitney sensed, a hunger no thing or person could ever slake. "But why complain," he went on. "Here I am, singing sad songs for myself, and these poor bastards in Prague can't get out either. I'm sick of seeing shit like this, and feeling so fucking helpless. They're having this joke of a convention in Chicago next week, Humphrey's coronation, and Daley's cops are planning to pen up protesters in camps just like they're the fucking Russians. So what does McCarthy say? That antiwar protesters should stay away to avoid a 'tragedy.' A tragedy is Bobby getting shot. A tragedy is what's happening in Czechoslovakia or Vietnam—or here. And now McCarthy tells us to be quiet so that pig Daley can put on his sham convention. Fuck them all."

He stopped abruptly, staring at the dark sky above the darker ocean. Apprehensive, Whitney said, "You're not thinking of going, are you?"

"Why not? What the hell do *I* have to lose?"

"I've been reading up on this, Ben. There's

going to be trouble in Chicago. Some of the radicals want that, and maybe Daley does, too—you could get thrown in jail, or get your head bashed in. For what? You're not a radical Weatherman, or someone who campaigned for McCarthy. Like it or not, Bobby's dead. Why get beaten up for someone else's benefit?"

Ben shrugged. "Who the fuck cares?"

Whitney hesitated. "I do," she said quietly.

He turned, looking into her face, his smile somewhere between puzzled and derisive. "So what are you offering, Whitney?"

"Free advice," she snapped. "I'm sorry you're getting drafted, all right? But that's no excuse for being reckless."

Ben's face darkened. "I'm not a coward," he said stubbornly.

Frustrated, Whitney grasped his shoulders. "You don't have to prove that anymore—to me, or to yourself. All that's left is to prove you're not a fool."

Ben looked into her eyes. Wordless, they stared at each other, their faces inches apart. "Whitney?" someone called from the darkness.

She recognized his voice just before she caught the unfamiliar tone, angry and proprietary. Pulling back from Ben, she stood.

Peter strode quickly toward them, footsteps thudding on the dock. Stunned, Whitney realized that he had come a day early, no doubt with her father's blessing. Ben sat there, remaining quite still, regarding Peter intently.

Stopping two feet from them, Peter looked from Ben to Whitney. "What's going on here?" he demanded.

Slowly, Ben stood. "We're talking about world affairs. If you have any thoughts, feel free to join in."

Peter took two steps forward, standing close to Ben. "You want trouble, smartass? You just found it."

"I wasn't looking."

"Bullshit. You're after Whitney, and now it's going to stop."

"You're right," Ben replied, glancing at Whitney. "I'm leaving." Angling sideways, he slid past Peter, then looked back over his shoulder. "Your problem isn't with me or Whitney. It's with yourself."

With two quick steps, Peter grabbed Ben, turning him around.

"Watch it . . ." Ben warned, and then Peter swung wildly.

"No," Whitney cried out.

The closed fist struck Ben's mouth with a cracking sound, knocking him off balance. He stared up at Peter, blood trickling from his lip. Rushing to Peter, Whitney pressed against his back, enveloping him as tightly as she could. "Don't," she said. "Please."

Ben stood, wiping the blood off his mouth. With surprising softness he said, "I don't want to fight you, Lord Fauntleroy. And you damn well don't want to fight me, you *really* don't . . ."

Peter swung again.

This time, Ben ducked, backing up a step while circling to Peter's right. "No more punches, Peter. Then I'll let this go, for Whitney's sake."

To Whitney, Ben seemed suddenly, lethally sober. Confusion appeared in Peter's eyes, followed by anger and humiliation. Crouching at the knees, he launched a right at Ben's jaw.

With a slight movement of the head, Ben avoided his fist, pivoting so suddenly that Whitney barely saw his vicious but compact blow to Peter's solar plexus. As Peter slumped, a sick, stunned look on his face, Ben hit him with a straight punch to the nose.

Blood spewing from his nostrils, Peter staggered backwards. He had no chance, Whitney knew: Ben's ferocity, even hatred, was all the more frightening because of his controlled and brutally efficient application of force. "No," she shouted as Ben hit Peter with a left hook to the jaw, lifting him up before he fell to the dock and crumpled on his side.

Desperate, Whitney stepped between them. "That's enough," she implored Ben shakily. "Please."

Facing her, he took a deep ragged breath. In a

tired voice, he said, "He'll be all right, Whitney. The only lasting damage I did is to his self-image. And he has way better reasons to doubt himself than losing a fight he was too stupid to avoid."

Abruptly, he turned and stalked off, as though in a hurry to leave them both behind.

Kneeling beside him, Whitney looked into Peter's stunned eyes, as guileless as a child's at something beyond his comprehension. Kissing his forehead, she murmured, "I'm so sorry. I love you, Peter, and I'm sorry."

Thirteen

When Peter could stand, Whitney led him to the guesthouse.

Penitent, she sat beside him on the bed, holding a damp cloth to his nose until it stopped bleeding, then wiping the blood off his face. "I'm all right," he said stiffly.

Whitney shook her head. "I know what you're thinking, Peter. But he's just someone I've gotten to know. He passed his physical today—he's going to be drafted. He doesn't want to go, but he has to. We both know what it's like to worry about that." She hesitated, then finished gently, "This was the wrong night to pick a fight with him, and you're the wrong person. The one who's safe."

Peter's lips compressed in a stubborn line. "This

wouldn't have happened if you'd stayed away from him. But you didn't. Or maybe you didn't want to."

"I will now," Whitney promised firmly. "I don't want you to worry, or wonder. But I can't say I'll never speak to him again. He's going away soon, and so will we—him to the Army, us to an apartment in New York City. I can't just treat him like dirt on my shoe."

"What about how *I* feel?" Peter demanded. "What's more important to you—me, or this guy you say isn't even a friend?"

"You are." Whitney removed the cloth, looking him in the face. "If you didn't know that before, tonight should make it clear."

"Then why were you hanging out with him?"

"Because he's in a bad place, and I've got some pride, too." She paused, groping for words that could help him comprehend her. "I wasn't there because I'm attracted to him. It's more how I feel about myself, as a person. That's different than how my parents feel about me, or even how you feel. Can you understand that?"

Peter wore the same unyielding expression. "I'm not sure I should even try. Not when we're talking about my fiancée and this conceited prick who set out to humiliate me in front of her."

"Not until you swung at him . . ."

"He *wanted* me to," Peter insisted. "I know when someone hates me. That sonofobitch does."

323

He was right about this, Whitney knew. "I understand," she assured him. "If I were you, maybe I'd have swung at him, too."

Mollified, Peter touched his nose. "He sure picked the right guy, didn't he? I hated you seeing that, Whitney."

Feeling his shame and vulnerability, Whitney took his hand. "Believe me, so did I. But only for your sake."

Peter grimaced. "I don't want your parents to know, okay?"

"They don't have to—we can tell them you bumped into something. And I don't think any less of you for losing a fistfight. I'm not marrying Muhammad Ali."

"That's for sure," Peter replied with a rueful smile. "He damn near knocked me into tomorrow."

Relieved at this glimmer of good nature, Whitney kissed him gently on the mouth. "So does that hurt?"

"Not at all."

Kissing him more deeply, she felt him respond. "I am marrying you for your body, though. Any interest in reminding me why? Or do you need rest and rehabilitation, supervised by Florence Nightingale?"

Peter managed a genuine smile. "Depends on what she's wearing. A nurse's outfit, or something less."

"Sounds like I've got choices. Why don't you

lie down on the bed, and see what happens."

Peter complied, his head propped on the pillow. "Okay, Whitney. So what now?"

Standing at the end of the bed, Whitney pulled the sweater over her head. She saw his eyes move to her breasts, swelling from the thin black bra he always liked to see her in. "Keep watching," she instructed.

Slowly, Whitney slid out of her blue jeans, letting them drop to the floor. Suddenly, bashful at what she was about to do, she wondered if some deep sensual impulse had seized her, or whether she needed to salve his pride, put this night behind them before they faced her parents. She had never stripped for him before.

Closing her eyes, she slipped one strap of her bra from her shoulder, then the other, bending forward to expose the tops of her breasts. Then she reached behind her back, unsnapping her bra, letting them free.

"Yes," she heard him say from deep in his throat.

She turned from him, slowly sliding her black silk panties down to show him more, and then turned again, facing him, exposing the dark triangle of hair between her legs.

"Jesus, Whit."

Her skin tingled now, feeling his arousal. She dropped her panties to the floor. "Take off your clothes," she ordered in a husky voice.

He stripped in haste, his gaze rapt. Sliding onto the bed, she took his penis into her mouth. He gasped with pleasure while her mouth and hand worked on his hard shaft. As Peter tensed, she withdrew her mouth, sliding her breasts across his chest as she whispered into his ear. "I want you to fuck me, Peter."

"I will," he whispered back, even as she wondered at the woman who had said this.

"Then stand at the end of the bed. I'll show you where to go."

Hurriedly, he did, staring down at her with his shaft in his hand, his face contorted with desire. Looking into his eyes, Whitney slowly opened her legs to show him everything, then slid one finger inside her. "There," she told him. "Right there."

As he gazed down at her, she touched herself with the tip of her finger, moving it gently until she felt the blood rush of stimulation and desire. For an instant she imagined herself as Clarice. "Do you want to fuck me?" she asked. "Or just watch me?"

"I want to fuck you," he answered in a thick voice.

He knelt on the bed, hastily kissing her mouth before he slid inside her, tentative at first, then thrusting harder, Whitney pushing her hips against him, filled with a desperate need to drive away any thought but this, the muscles inside her tightening with a primal urgency she had never felt before, crying out, "Please, fuck me harder," dazed and lightheaded now, her world going black, as though all the life in her had moved to the place of release until she tightened irrevocably, her body shuddering in an agony of pleasure, and her mind suddenly filled with the shocking image of Benjamin Blaine on top of her, feeling the warmth of his release inside her as his face replaced Peter's and Ben's name caught in her throat.

Peter slumped on top of her. "My God . . ."

Whitney's eyes filled with tears. "That was beautiful," she whispered.

For the next three days they kept busy as Whitney, contented on the surface, struggled to isolate one startling discordant moment. Each night, alone, she wished she could describe it to Clarice, so that her friend could put this in some safe category of the human and expected. During the day, she and Peter did the things that young people do. They went to the Agricultural Fair in West Tisbury, where livestock vied with the attractions of a traveling carnival, riding the Ferris wheel and eating pink cotton candy. Peter threw a baseball through a hole in the middle of a target, winning Whitney a stuffed bear. "My hero," she told him. Giving her a crooked smile, Peter touched his tender nose. "Oh, yeah . . ."

Later they went out to see Franco Zeffirelli's

Romeo and Juliet. Despite the liberties it took with Shakespeare, Whitney found herself caught up in the hunger of two young people, rebels against family and a social order that had no room for them. "A sexy movie," Peter judged afterward. "But we have a better ending, don't we?"

"Do you mean tonight?" Whitney asked. "Or later?"

They went home to make love, Peter pleased at her new ardor. But Whitney felt herself holding back, afraid to pierce the wall between her conscious thoughts and the outlaw image that threatened her peace of mind.

The next evening featured fireworks in Oak Bluffs. Peter and Whitney took blankets and a bottle of wine to Ocean Park, watching a glorious display that framed a moon glimmering through a thin layer of fog. "Remember the scene in To Catch a Thief? he asked.

Through the warm glow of wine, Whitney tried to recall this. "I'm not sure."

"It's where Cary Grant and Grace Kelly are lying on the couch, and the camera pans to fireworks in his hotel window. That's when you know they're making love."

As though on cue, Whitney said, "Then let's go make our own movie."

Their days and nights together passed like that, Peter wanting her again and again, the elixir of male confidence refreshed, Whitney bent on pleasing him while being good company to her parents, who were disappointed that Janine had canceled yet another trip to see them. Though Clarice dropped by to visit, Whitney found no time with her alone. Instead, she was deeply attentive to Peter, still shadowed by the fear that the sudden release of her sexuality, the erotic jolt of a single night, came from a desire she must erase. At times she felt like a stranger to herself and those around her, her greatest solace the belief that, as with any strong but vagrant impulse, time would banish this as quickly as it had come.

When Peter had to leave, Whitney kissed him at the airport with a fervor that made him grin. "Sooner than you realize," she told him, "I'll be Mrs. Peter Brooks."

He smiled at the sound of this. "All the unborn little Brookses are looking forward to that."

"Let's just practice for awhile," Whitney replied. "Now that you're in the reserves, you don't have to be an instant dad."

As he walked to the plane, blond curls glistening in the late afternoon sun, he turned to smile and wave, everything forgotten, it seemed, but Whitney herself. The swell of affection in her heart felt pleasurable and reassuring.

Less than four weeks, she told herself again.

PART FOUR

Betrayals

Martha's Vineyard–
New York City
August–September 1968

One

Returning from the airport, Whitney decided to watch the eve of the Chicago convention on NBC, worried that the confrontation of protestors and police would—as Eugene McCarthy had predicted —explode into violence.

The first film clip seemed peaceable enough, a crowd of McCarthy backers greeting their candidate as he arrived at Midway Airport. Though they looked subtly different from the Nixon delegates, they had this much in common—all were white. Watching their restrained enthusiasm, a reflection of McCarthy's own, Whitney recalled Ben saying, "All someone has to do is abolish the draft, and they'll go back to screwing and driving Volkswagens and watching films with subtitles. Their 'crusade' won't have been about much of anything, and they'll disappear like ether." She was about to switch channels when the coverage changed to Grant Park.

Shaken, Whitney sat. The scenes unfolding on the screen were wholly unlike the America she knew—police beating a crowd of demonstrators with clubs to keep them from marching on the convention center. From their midst someone thrust a sign aloft—WELCOME TO PRAGUE! Then, amoeba-like, the throng shrunk back from a wave of tear gas, police with gas masks and billy clubs flailing at long-haired youths. Transfixed, Whitney belatedly realized that Charles was standing beside her.

Silent, they watched fresh images of conflict filling the screen—kids burning draft cards in front of cops; radicals stoning police cars; protesters bloodied from beatings, or incapacitated by tear gas. Softly, Charles said, "So this is how it ends, where dissent becomes contempt for law, the prelude to social disintegration. It's why we need Richard Nixon."

"Nixon," Whitney repeated with instinctive disdain.

He looked at her closely, then continued with weary certainty. "I know that, to some, all this upheaval seems terribly romantic—youth in rebellion, throwing off the shackles to remake the world in your own deeply admired self-image, convinced that no other generations' experiences have any value. But eventually, these people will have to find jobs.

"After that they can begin the quiet but equally destructive work of the self-indulgent: changing partners at will, spending money without regard to their children's futures, reading books that assure them that they—the sacred individual—is the person they should love first and best. They won't build anything, because they don't think they owe anything to anyone else. I pity their children and grandchildren." He turned to Whitney. "I don't mean you and Peter, or Janine. But I'm afraid your peer group will make mine look far better than it should. And God knows there's a lot of you."

In some ways, Whitney realized, he sounded like Ben commenting on the beach party. "And that's reason enough for the cops to beat them? These people hate the war, but have no power to stop it. Protest is the only way that they can be seen or heard . . ."

"It's *not* the only way," her father objected. "They're like blacks who 'protest' by destroying their own neighborhoods. Now the police are giving them what they want—a bloody shirt to wave."

"And Nixon will step in to save us?"

Charles shook his head. "Let's not quarrel, Whitney. I've said my piece, and you've indulged me. It's probably good I'm going back to New York tomorrow morning."

Touching her gently on the shoulder, Charles left.

Suddenly Whitney felt alone. She went to her bedroom and called Clarice.

"She's gone to Boston," Jane Barkley reported dryly, "or so I understand. It seems she has important business—seeing friends from college, certainly. Perhaps even finding a job."

"Wherever she is," Whitney responded, "have her call me."

"Of course," Jane promised. "As soon as we reestablish contact."

Returning to the living room, Whitney watched new images of violence, hoping that Ben was not in Chicago but safe, at least for the moment, a few hundred yards away.

For the next three nights, Whitney watched the convention. Her mother refused to join her, drinking a little more wine at dinner, then retreating to her bedroom to call Janine or Charles whenever she could find them. But she said nothing about Janine, and Whitney wondered again at her sister's elusiveness. More often she thought of Ben, wishing that Ted Kennedy—the last hope to defeat Humphrey—would allow his name to be placed in nomination, yet fearing what could happen if he did.

Instead, each night brought its own repellent images and stunted hopes. After Mayor Daley proclaimed to the delegates on Monday that "as long as I'm mayor in this city, there's going to be law and order in Chicago," police moved on a throng of demonstrators in Lincoln Park, and a few rogue cops pulled black residents off their own porches to beat them with leather truncheons. On Tuesday, as more police in combat gear cleared out Lincoln Park, Edward Kennedy, still devastated by his brother's assassination, asked his supporters to cease trying to draft him. Wednesday brought a police riot.

Bent on marching to the convention hall, the protestors regrouped in front of the Chicago Hilton and were confronted by another phalanx in uniform. Blindly, the cops flailed at the demonstrators closest to them, trapping some against the wall of the hotel. Sickened, Whitney watched the jumbled film clips—protestors crashing through first-floor windows amidst shards of glass; bloodied men and women desperately pushing into the lobby; blue-helmeted police beating others fallen to the concrete; demonstrators trampling their comrades as they retreated in terror to a cacophony of sounds—clubs striking bone, police shouting, victims crying out, the screech of police sirens. In the convention hall, Senator Abe Ribicoff decried "Gestapo tactics in the streets of Chicago"; Richard Daley's supporters rose in derisive outrage, shaking their fists, and the screen filled with Daley's face as he mouthed obscenities at the speaker. On the first ballot, the delegates nominated Hubert Humphrey. Whitney felt like the world had gone insane.

On Thursday morning, she took her journal to Dogfish Bar, struggling to find words for what she felt.

She could write little. Closing the leather volume, she lingered in the hope that Ben would appear, relieving her of the vow she had taken—

for Peter and herself—to avoid him. She saw no one.

That night she turned on the television yet again. An ominous climax was building—the triumphant appearance of Humphrey as protestors marched on the convention. When the police confronted them with a shower of tear gas, Whitney went to call Peter. "Are you watching this?" she asked.

"The convention? No. It all seems so stupid and pointless—I don't know what these people think that they're accomplishing."

"They're getting maimed and teargassed, Peter."

"It's bad, okay? I know that. But this is what they wanted." His voice softened. "So how are *you,* sweetheart? Is everything okay over there?"

Whitney thought of her mother: in the last few hours, she had repeatedly called Janine, clearly agitated that she could not find her. "Fine," Whitney said reflexively, and realized that this is what Anne would say. "So how is work?"

"Really good," Peter said. "We've got a new underwriting, a public offering for a big chain of nursing homes. After we get back from the honeymoon, your dad's putting me on the due diligence team."

This was a plum assignment, Whitney knew. Facilitating sale of stock to the public was a lucrative part of Padgett Dane's business, and an inquiry into a company's prospects was an indispensable prerequisite. "That's great," she heard herself saying. "I'm proud of you."

"Thanks, Whitney. So don't worry too much, okay? The country will straighten itself out."

Returning to the living room, Whitney felt lonelier than before.

It was not Peter's fault, she reminded herself: he was striving to succeed in her father's world, a few scant weeks from the only world they had ever known—where everyone was their age, and what absorbed them most was classes and activities and dating and late night conversations about the quandaries of life in this halfway house between adolescence and adulthood. She felt for him now, compelled to become a man on the great conveyor belt of life, which had a schedule all its own.

On the screen, Robert Kennedy appeared.

It was a convention film offered to pacify all those who loved him. But even on celluloid Bobby seemed more real than anyone else at the convention—alive again, passionate and wry and funny and melancholy. Whitney wondered if Ben, too, watched alone, painfully reliving his time with the man for whom he had sacrificed so much. Or whether he was among the demonstrators, choking on tear gas and despair.

Unable to stop herself, she stepped outside, pausing but briefly, then hurried to Ben's place, dreading yet hoping to find him.

Two

Approaching the guesthouse, Whitney saw a light inside and, through a window, the silver glow of a television. Relieved yet unnerved, she hesitated, then knocked on the door.

In the silence that followed, Whitney sensed him deciding whether to answer. Then his rough voice came through another window cracked open to admit the cool night air. "Let yourself in."

He was sitting in the dark, a bottle of whiskey beside him, staring at clips of Robert Kennedy moving inexorably toward his death. "I came to watch with you," she said.

He shrugged, still fixated on the screen. Whitney sat on the couch, as far from him as she could, until the film was over.

Instead of placating the dissidents, it unleashed a wave of mass emotion—delegates standing on chairs and holding signs proclaiming BOBBY, WE MISS YOU. When the chairman of the convention tried to gavel them down, they responded with repeated stanzas of "The Battle Hymn of the Republic," voices rising in a mutiny that showed no sign of stopping. Ten minutes passed, then ten more, fueling a pulsating outcry of defiance against Humphrey, Daley, the police, and all the forces determined to control the city and send them home with nothing. The hall seemed like a tinderbox.

Quietly, Whitney said, "I'm glad you didn't go."

"I couldn't. I didn't have the heart for it."

On the screen the Kennedy delegates were singing, chanting, stomping on the floor, their caged energy building. Trying to drown them out, the mayor's forces began shouting from the gallery, "We love Daley, we love Daley, we love Daley . . ."

As if on signal, their shouting stopped. A black man appeared on the podium, asking for a moment of silence in memory of Martin Luther King. There was a murmur of confusion until, from respect for another murdered leader, the demonstration of love for Robert Kennedy dwindled like the slow leak of a tire.

"I guess King still has his uses," Ben said bitterly, then continued in a softer voice, "From the day he was shot, I started watching the crowds, wondering who'd come for Bobby. A few days later we entered a one-story town in Indiana, and saw police snipers on the rooftops over-looking the square where Bobby spoke. When I asked a cop if there'd been some kind of threat, all he said was, 'We just want to make sure he leaves here the same way he came in.' Bobby felt it, too—you could see it in his eyes. But he kept on riding in open convertibles, letting people see him.

"That last week in California was like a fever dream—the crowds, the screaming, the desperation of whites and blacks and Hispanics reaching out for him. In Los Angeles, someone put a kid in his arms as we passed, this pretty black girl of maybe five. There's this craziness all around us and she's just sitting in Bobby's lap, holding a stuffed rabbit while he whispers in her ear, like nothing matters to him except what's going on with this kid. Finally, he gets her to remember her phone number and address, tells the driver to stop, and asks me to find a cop to make sure she gets home safely. When the car started moving, he was still looking back at her. It was the last time I ever rode with him."

"Were you there?" Whitney asked hesitantly. "When it happened, I mean."

Still staring at the screen, Ben nodded mutely. "After his victory speech," he said at last, "I expected him to wade through the crowd, like he always did. Instead someone told him to take a rear passageway out of the hotel. So Bobby and his bodyguards go down a hallway past a serving kitchen, with me trailing behind him." In profile, Ben's eyes moistened almost imperceptibly. "I see him stop to shake hands with a dishwasher, then hear a sound like dry wood snapping. Suddenly I can't find him, and there's chaos and screaming all around where Bobby was standing. When I get there, Ethel's kneeling over him. For an instant I can see the look in his eyes, aware but unsurprised, like he was thinking, 'so this is it.' Then his bodyguards closed around, and they took him away. It was the last time I prayed for anyone, or ever will."

Her throat constricted, Whitney found nothing to say.

Reaching for the bottle, Ben resumed staring at the convention's heartless pageantry, the cameras trained on Daley as he scanned the floor with the satisfaction of an oligarch certain of his power. At last, Hubert Humphrey came to the podium, looking as happy as anyone could manage amidst the violence in the streets, the thwarted longing for Robert Kennedy inside the hall.

"Are you sure you want to watch this?" Whitney asked.

"It's the new reality," he answered.

"Rioting, burning, sniping, muggings, traffic in narcotics, and disregard for the law," Humphrey was declaiming in his pipe organ voice, "are the advance guard of anarchy, and they must and will be stopped . . ."

Daley's galleries released a full-throated roar, drawing from their nominee an incongruous look of delight. Then he launched into what sounded, at least to Whitney, like some nightmare amalgam of hackneyed Fourth of July speeches.

"Once again, we give our testimonial to America. Each and every one of us in our own way should reaffirm for ourselves and our posterity that we love this nation, we love America." Invoking Democratic presidents like a litany of saints, he concluded with Lyndon Johnson. "And tonight, Mr. President, I say thank you. Thank you, Mr. President . . ."

"For making me a eunuch," Ben muttered with bottomless disdain.

But Humphrey's pieties continued unabated. "We are, and we must be, one nation, united by liberty and justice for all, one nation, under God, indivisible, with liberty and justice for all . . ."

"And Wonder Bread," Ben added, "which builds strong bodies twelve ways."

"With the help of that vast, unfrightened, dedicated, faithful majority of Americans," Humphrey effused, "I say to this great convention tonight, to this great nation of ours, I am ready to lead America . . ."

He was in a bubble, Whitney thought, more otherworldly and horrific for the violence outside. She could not easily imagine how Ben felt.

The telephone rang. Abruptly, he got up to answer, listening intently before murmuring, "Jesus Christ . . ."

For the next few moments, Ben said little. Hanging up, he stood there, arms folded tightly, staring at the floor.

"What is it?"

At first, he did not answer. "That was a friend, a

346

Kennedy guy who went to Chicago. While Humphrey was bloviating there was another riot at the Hilton, worse than last night. Seth got caught between the cops and the hotel."

"Is he all right?"

"Except for a split lip and two missing teeth. Some guy from the McCarthy campaign pulled him into the lobby, still puking from the tear gas, then took him up to a hotel room fifteen floors up. From there he could see everything. A man carrying a woman with her skull cracked open until the cops pummeled them to the ground; people begging for mercy as police beat them to a pulp; more cops clubbing anyone with a camera; waves of cops in blue helmets trampling helpless kids. Even that far up Seth could hear clubs cracking skulls and smell the mace and tear gas. He says the floor of the hotel room was like a MASH unit, people lying there bleeding onto the carpet." He stopped, then finished with acidic quotation of Hubert Humphrey's speech, " 'Once again, we give our testament to America . . .' "

Whitney stood, walking toward him. "I'm sorry."

For the first time Ben looked into her eyes. "For what?"

"That it ended this way for you." She hesitated. "For all of us."

Wordless, he stared at her. "Oh, well," he responded tonelessly. "Life will go on for you."

Rebuffed, Whitney turned away. "I'd better go . . ."

"Damn you," he said under his breath. "Damn you, Whitney Dane."

Startled, she looked up at him, shaken by the intensity in his eyes. Placing his hand behind her neck, Ben pulled her face to his.

In her confusion, Whitney did not pull away. She felt the warmth of his lips, her blood rushing, the world closing down. Instinctively, she shut her eyes.

She was kissing him back now, she realized, their tongues touching, bodies pressed against each other's. A last protest from deep in her core caused Whitney to pull back.

"My God, Ben—what am I doing?"

He gazed at her, breathing hard, hands clasping her waist. "What you want to do."

"I can't . . ."

Tearing herself away, Whitney hurried through the door.

Blindly, she rushed toward home, the air chilling the flush on her skin, tears of shock stinging her eyes. She felt as though the earth had opened up beneath her.

Her mother had left the porch light on. She headed toward it, legs still weak from panic and desire. She forced herself to slow, fighting to compose herself, then entered the house.

Her mother was in the living room, dressed in a

chiffon robe. "Where have you been?" she asked in a tight voice. "When I knocked on your bedroom door, you weren't there."

Whitney had no answer to give. "Sorry if I worried you."

Anne gazed up at her. More quietly, she said, "You look a mess, Whitney. Is there anything we should discuss?"

"No. Nothing."

Without awaiting an answer, Whitney went to her room.

Undressing, she lay in the dark, a stranger to herself, bereft in her solitude, yet grateful for it.

Who am I? she wondered. But all that came to her was the warmth of Ben's lips, the press of his body.

Instinctively, Whitney touched herself.

Ben came to her, as he had with Peter inside her. She felt her body tighten, seeking him again. The climax came in waves, leaving her limbs slack, the warmth of her release commingling with shame.

Please, she told herself, *don't do this to yourself. Don't do this to Peter.*

She had to see him. She did not know what she would say or do. But she could not stay here, or something irrevocable would happen. Perhaps it already had, for Whitney no longer knew herself.

Three

The next morning, Whitney found her mother in the sunroom. "I've decided to visit Peter this weekend," she informed her. "I've already booked the ten o'clock flight. I'd like to do some grocery shopping and surprise him when he gets home."

"What a nice idea," Anne remarked with evident relief. "When we were living in that same apartment, your dad always loved it when I had his scotch and a good dinner waiting for him. No matter how late the hour."

Whitney caught a wistful note. "I'll try to remember that."

Though Anne smiled, a glimmer of uncertainty surfaced in her eyes. "Perhaps you can also drop in on Janine. In the last few days I've had trouble reaching her."

At last, Whitney sensed, the worries she had expressed for her sister were, though unacknowledged, germinating in their mother's mind. But she had deeper worries of her own.

"I'll try," she promised vaguely.

In the taxi to the airport, Whitney felt anxious and confused. Issuing from the radio, the new Beatles anthem, "Revolution," became the ironic soundtrack for her own disorientation, jumbled images of the violence in Chicago merging with her desire for Ben. Perhaps she should tell Peter the truth, confessing her fault, and seek his help in sorting through her emotions. But she could not easily imagine hurting him this way—or her own hurt if she lost the only boy she had ever loved.

Had she done enough to deserve that, really? She had broken away from Ben, unfaithful only in her imaginings. In another week or two, he might be gone to the army; a short time after that, she and Peter would be safely married. As Clarice often told her, sometimes it was best to conceal what could only create harm. It would become Whitney's mission to make up for her behavior without seeking absolution.

She mulled these thoughts over and over as the half-empty plane rose from the tarmac and headed out over the Atlantic. After a few moments of choppy air, the flight settled into a smooth trajectory, the only sound the whirring of propellers on the wing visible through her window. An hour later, as they descended toward LaGuardia, a few cirrus clouds hovered over New York City. But it was warm and sunny when she fetched her luggage, hailed a Yellow Cab, and headed for midtown Manhattan.

Crossing the Triborough Bridge, she felt the familiar surge of excitement at the sight of the Empire State Building jutting from the skyline. She and Peter would be lucky to live here before they retreated to the green tranquility of Greenwich, the hush of sweeping grounds and secluded homes. And she was anxious to see the apartment again, to contemplate its spaces at leisure and in solitude, picturing what furniture or pieces of art might go where, so that later she could share her thoughts without straining Peter's limited patience with such things. Imagining this, she felt an inexpressible relief to have left Martha's Vineyard and Benjamin Blaine behind— for once, Manhattan seemed the simpler place, a refuge that also held her future.

In this mood, even the gridlock, the horns blaring as her cab made its fitful progress from block to block of the East Side, felt less annoying than enveloping. Instead of counting the minutes, she scanned the streets for restaurants or galleries that she and Peter might frequent on crisp fall days, envisioning leisurely mornings and afternoons of unearthing finds for the apartment or visiting museums before stopping at an outdoor café. She felt lucky beyond words to have been granted such a life.

At last the cab stopped in front of their apartment building. In a philanthropic mood, she tipped the cabbie generously, then toted her suitcase to the door. The doorman seemed to be missing. Reaching inside her purse for the keys that Charles had given her, she unlocked the glass-and-wrought-iron door and carried her suitcase across the polished marble floor of the lobby to the bank of elevators that, by the look of them, had been in service since her parents' time. Pressing a button, she heard the whine of cables before the elevator settled with a metallic clank, its steel mesh creaking as it parted to admit her. She stepped inside, the mesh closing around her, and the elevator lurched upward before its ascent ended with a slightly jarring abruptness.

Savoring the eccentricities that lent the building character, Whitney went down the hallway and stopped at the wooden door, marked 9-E, with the brass knocker beneath the eyehole. She put down her suitcase, and opened it. Pausing in the doorway, she surveyed their apartment, smiling to herself, then stifled a sharp, sudden intake of breath.

A woman's leather purse, its style familiar, lay on the breakfast table. Whitney stepped inside.

The bedroom door was ajar. Through it she heard footsteps on the wooden floor of what had been her parents' sanctuary and now was Peter's. The sounds made by a light, bare foot.

With agonizing softness, Whitney closed the door behind her.

Instinctively, she stepped out of her pumps, inching sideways to peer through the door. "I know what you want," a woman's voice teased.

Heart racing, Whitney saw her blond hair and slender, perfect form—the tip of a pert breast, the tan, slender legs and firm bottom as she glided toward the bed. "I enjoy it, too," Clarice assured him softly. "But maybe I'll torture you a little."

Her tone was serene, that of a woman confident in her allure for the man who watched her. Then the sliver of Clarice's body vanished like a flickering frame of film.

There was a rustling of sheets, a muffled male sigh. Whitney closed her eyes. She could not bear seeing or hearing them, searing this terrible moment into her memory until she died. Numb, she knelt to pick up her shoes, her backward footsteps silent, the only sound in the apartment the quiet stirring of the two lovers in her bedroom.

Careful to make no sound, Whitney closed the door as she left, then rested her face against it, tears running down her cheeks.

She stayed there like that, with no desire to move until, at last, she willed herself to take her purse and suitcase and, dabbing at her eyes, tried to reclaim some semblance of the woman who had come here.

Like an automaton, she pressed the button to the elevator, hand trembling with the shock of Peter's betrayal, the toxic selfishness of her closest friend. No wonder Clarice spent time away, and what a fool they must think her to be. But what shriveled her soul was the callousness hidden beneath Peter's guileless persona, his enjoyment of Clarice's sexual insouciance despite all of Whitney's efforts to please him, shattering her belief that she was capable of knowing anyone at all.

The elevator came to a stop, its passage yawning open. Stepping inside, Whitney allowed it to take her down. When it opened again, she stood there, suspended in misery, before stepping back into the lobby.

The uniformed doorman had returned, a stocky Italian with a seamed face. Though Whitney had encountered him before, he gave her a slightly puzzled smile. In her dream-state, she thought he must not recognize her then realized the doorman must have known, long before her, who was visiting 9-E, and for what purpose. Humiliated, she passed him without speaking and walked to the door, not acknowledging that he held it open for her.

Outside, the sun of early afternoon felt pitiless, and the humid, sooty air stung her eyes. In a dull fever, Whitney crossed the street, heedless of the cab that skidded short of her with a sharp blare of its horn, reaching the other side before she turned back toward the apartment building, still clutching her suitcase, a refugee from her own life. All she could manage was to lean against the rough bark of the nearest tree, its shade a barely noticed mercy in the searing heat.

What could she do now?

She had come to Peter ashamed of her betrayal,

only to learn she had been betrayed by the two people who, outside her family, she loved most— her closest friend and the man to whom she had entrusted her heart. The full measure of her friend's duplicity struck her hard, less as a surprise in itself—Clarice was candid enough about that much—but that she would turn it on Whitney, claiming the right to toy with Peter without respecting him as a man, all the while condescending to Whitney in her pitiable innocence. And so had Peter, counseling her to conceal her sister's secrets, all too conscious of his own.

A belated fury seeped through Whitney's shock. Suddenly all she wanted was to unleash her rage on whoever left the apartment, one or both, indifferent to what might follow the moment of feral satisfaction when her startled quarry saw her coming toward them.

Taking a deep breath, she struggled to calm herself and wait.

She passed an hour against the tree, its shelter overcome by heat that dampened her forehead and the back of her dress. She tried to empty her mind, blocking out the cars and pedestrians and delivery trucks—the urban life all around her— intent only on watching the door. She must not think of the future she no longer had.

The door opened.

As Whitney tensed, a gray-haired woman

emerged, smiling at the doorman as her cocker spaniel strained at its leash. Reflexively, Whitney slid behind the tree, head lowered, a tremor of trapped emotion causing her chest to rise and fall. When she looked up, the door was opening again.

A soft cry escaped her throat.

Charles Dane strode into the sunlight, turning his head sharply to spot a cab, his air as commanding as though he were moving from one business meeting to the next, expecting this one, too, to go as he willed. The sight of him was like a punch to the stomach—she felt nauseated, helpless to fight the searing image of her own father mounting his surrogate daughter. If Charles looked across the street, he would see her.

She waited for this to happen, overcome by the enormity of what this moment would mean, now and for the rest of their lives. Then a taxi cruised to a stop in obeisance to his careless, peremptory wave, and the man she had loved more than anyone on earth ducked inside and vanished.

It was a moment before Whitney felt the fresh tears flowing down her face.

Paralyzed, she fought to absorb the sequence of lies irreparably destroying the foundation of her life. The bonds of loyalty Clarice had invoked to mask her own duplicity. Her father's profession of love for his wife, the cover for a corrosive hypocrisy that now poisoned their family and all of Whitney's memories; his primal need to dominate the world he had created for himself, where the needs of others were secondary to his own wants. With sickening suddenness, she perceived the second layer of betrayal. She had believed Peter to be unfaithful; instead, he was her father's accomplice in the betrayal of Whitney's mother. Then another realization caused her to slump in anguish—that Clarice had fueled her father's loathing for Benjamin Blaine by revealing Whitney's confidences.

Whitney had no one—not for this. Not her father or Clarice or Peter—or, without destroying their ultimate victim, her mother. Though Whitney did not know what she would, or could, tell her, all she had left was the slimmest of reeds. Her sister.

Four

Janine, too, lived on the East Side, in an apartment on East Seventy-fifth paid for by their father. In the muddled hope of finding solace, or at least a hiding place where no one else could see her fall apart, Whitney carried her suitcase for blocks and, moist and bedraggled, pressed the buzzer outside the entrance.

No answer. Maybe Janine was asleep, Whitney thought—her sister's hours seemed increasingly erratic. She pushed the button once more, then again, her vision of asylum slowly ebbing. As she stood there, utterly lost, her sister's voice echoed through the speaker, sounding narcotized yet anxious.

"Who is it?"

"Me. Whitney."

A moment's 7silence followed. "What are you doing here?"

"Please," Whitney pleaded, "can I come up?"

"Now?" her sister asked. But the uncertainty in her voice suggested that Whitney's tone of entreaty had punctured her resistance. "Did Mom send you?"

"No," Whitney insisted desperately. "Why would she?"

Again Janine was silent. Then the buzzer sounded, allowing Whitney to enter.

Taking the elevator, she longed for the innocence with which she had entered another building, a scant two hours before, marking the fault line that separated her past, now a dream state, from the black hole of her future. What could she say, she wondered, having discovered that their family was an illusion? A mirage like Janine herself, Whitney thought, unsure of how to approach a woman whose charmed existence was yet another myth. When she knocked on the door, knowing only that she wanted to sit somewhere cooler and darker, seconds dragged by before her sister peered through the crack in the door, its chain strained tight.

Her face was drained of blood, and there were dark smudges beneath her eyes. She looked years older than she had at the celebration of Whitney's engagement, like a female Dorian Gray ensnared by the ravages of time. Though Janine's eyes were dull, she seemed to register Whitney's expression. She looked down, as though ashamed at her exposure, then unlatched the door, backing to the side.

What she saw in the small, shadowed space jarred Whitney even more. On the coffee table was a near-empty bottle of vodka, a carton of orange juice, and a large glass with a residue of pulp at the bottom. Turning toward the couch, Janine stumbled, knocking a plastic bottle off the table and spilling pills across the carpet. Righting herself, she sat there, her expression miserable and trapped.

For a moment, Whitney could not speak. She smelled, then saw, a pool of vomit on the carpet. Picking up the bottle, she read the word *Valium*. All she could think to do was head to the bathroom for a glass of water and a washcloth to cool her sister's clammy, pallid face.

Entering the bedroom, she paused again. Her sister's bed was disheveled, a bloody towel strewn across its tangled sheets. Whitney forced herself to continue to the bathroom, filling a glass and dampening a washcloth, overcome by her own confusion and inadequacy. When she returned to the living room, Janine's gaze held a shame that made it seem more lucid.

Whitney sat beside her, holding out the glass of water. "Drink this," she instructed.

Shakily, Janine complied. Asking her to lie back, Whitney placed the damp cloth to her sister's face. In a strained voice, she asked, "How many pills did you take?"

Janine closed her eyes. "I don't remember. They level me out, so I'm not so anxious . . ."

"When did you take the last ones?"

As though compelled by Whitney's urgency, Janine mustered the will to respond. "A few hours ago, I guess—I was sleeping for awhile." Though her eyes remained shut, Whitney saw tears on her lashes. "I hoped I wouldn't wake up, that everything would just go dark."

Whitney steeled herself. "I have to call emergency . . ."

"No," Janine protested. "I don't want them to know. Please, just stay with me."

Irresolute, Whitney felt her sister's pulse, light but steady enough. "I saw that towel in the bedroom, like you're having a really awful period. Tell me what's happening—please."

Though she did not speak, Janine's eyes welled again. With a new foreboding, Whitney pressed, "What was it, Janine?"

Janine's throat worked. "I had an abortion. This morning."

Whitney felt shock, then fear. "We should get you to a hospital. With all that blood, there could be something wrong inside."

"I think I'll be okay," Janine said wanly. "A doctor did it—David arranged for everything." Her voice faltered. "I threw our baby away, like it was trash. Because he wanted me to."

Whitney struggled to drain her speech of judgment. "Tell me about David."

"He's a photographer. I met him on a job."

"Why isn't he with you now?"

Janine curled sideways. "He's married."

Absorbing this, Whitney saw the pattern of Janine's behavior. "When did you find out?" she asked.

"I always knew." Janine paused, inhaling. "When he asked me to dinner, he was so completely charming I said yes. Later, I said yes to the rest of it."

"Why, Janine?"

"You should have seen the way he looked at me." Janine hesitated again, her remembered excitement descending into hollowness. "He told me I was different—that I made his world brighter, his enjoyment of everything more complete. That he'd never heard the longing in Sinatra's voice until he listened with me."

Janine spoke in a child's voice, made more

heartbreaking by how deluded she sounded. Whitney felt a fresh, pulsing anger at both her mother and father. "I guess he promised to leave his wife."

Janine nodded. "Then I got pregnant," she added huskily. "David got so upset. He said if I loved him, I'd get rid of it. So I did. Now he's gone, and so is our baby."

Whitney grasped her hand. After a time, she asked, "When did you lose your job?"

Her sister showed no surprise, as though Whitney had cracked open the door to her life, and become omniscient. "When David couldn't see me, I got lonely and depressed. So I started taking the pills he gave me. After awhile, I was missing work. So David gave me money, and Dad . . ."

"Did *he* know?"

"Of course not." Janine's voice filled with a weary, dispirited irony. "Mom helped, too. I told her I needed new clothes, and she sent a check from her own account. Her note said I deserved to feel as beautiful as I am."

Reflexively, Whitney responded, "You *are* beautiful, Janine. I always wanted to look like you."

Hearing herself, Whitney realized that this was all she had to offer. "Beautiful," Janine repeated in an ashen voice. "I'm like an empty glass they filled with all these brightly colored stones, and imagined the stones were diamonds. But the stones are worthless, and the glass is, too."

Suddenly, Whitney felt the burden of a psychic devastation too complete for her to shoulder. Her parents alone had the resources and authority to repair what they had created. "We're going to the Vineyard, all right? Our parents have to know what happened."

"No," Janine exclaimed with renewed vehemence. "They can't."

"Why?" Whitney asked fiercely. "So you and they can go on inventing a daughter who doesn't exist? If they don't help you now, they'll destroy you." She paused, softening her voice. "I love you, Janine. I don't want you dead, or wishing you were. I won't let them take you with them . . ."

"What do you mean? The two of them are so happy . . ."

"Are they?" Whitney cut in, and stopped herself. "Then they're strong enough to deal with this. It's not your job to prop up our mother anymore. You can't fill the holes in her heart by letting her play dress-up with you as the doll."

Facing Whitney, Janine opened her eyes. Dully, she said, "What holes?"

"Oh, she has them. And I think you've always known it. In your own way, you're been trying to take care of her for years. I won't let that happen anymore."

To Whitney's surprise, her sister did not protest.

Finding a telephone in the kitchen, Whitney called the airlines, then booked a taxi.

In the hour before they left, Whitney packed Janine's clothes, then washed the sheets clean. It bothered her that this seemed like something Anne would do.

When she reappeared in the living room, Janine regarded her with a new curiosity. Without preface, she asked tiredly, "What's going on with you and Mom and Dad?"

Startled at her sister's question, Whitney resolved to protect her from the truth. "I don't know what you mean."

"Is it something about Peter?" Janine persisted. "Or another guy?"

Tensing, Whitney sat beside her. "Who told you that?"

"No one, exactly." Janine bit her lip. "It was something I overheard . . ."

"Where?"

"At Dad's office, when I went to ask him for money."

She stopped abruptly. "Tell me," Whitney persisted. "I need to know."

Slowly, Janine nodded. "His door was ajar, so I just stepped in. Dad was on the phone. But he was facing the window, so he didn't see me. I just stood there, not wanting to interrupt. Then he said something like, 'Thank you, Commissioner. The army needs able young men, and I need this particular young man out of my daughter's life.' When he turned and saw me, he had this funny look, like he'd been caught at something."

Staring at the carpet, Whitney felt short of breath. Then she remembered the last piece in the mosaic of events—her father speaking with a local politician, the man who wanted to keep a Jewish family from buying a home in West Chop. "As we discussed on the phone," the man had said, "you and I can help each other."

By whatever sleight of hand, Whitney knew, Charles had thwarted the sale to ensure that Ben was drafted. He had put his finger on the scales of Ben's life, in order to direct the course of Whitney's, and in the process, eliminate a discordant element from his own—a young man who, whatever his lack of resources, had challenged Charles's dominance without realizing what the older man could do. Her father would sooner cause Ben's death than be bothered with him.

"You bastard," she said in a low voice.

Janine stared at her. "What is it, Whitney? *Is* there someone else?"

Choking on her own guilt, Whitney felt a loathing so profound that Janine, watching her face, asked nothing more. Nor could Whitney speak. She despised herself, but not as much as she hated Charles Dane.

Five

Pale as china, Janine endured their check-in at LaGuardia, wearing a spectral, otherworldly expression, then sat near the gate while Whitney found a pay phone to call their mother.

"Janine's pretty much broken down," she said tersely. "I'm bringing her home. Lock up the liquor cabinet and any pills in her bathroom . . ."

"What happened?" Anne broke in. "Is she all right?"

"She probably won't die, Mom. But, no, she's not all right and hasn't been for years. It's time for you and Dad to face the truth."

She hung up without permitting her mother to answer. As she returned to the gate area, her sister regarded her with fatalistic blankness. "What did she say?"

"Not much. I didn't give her a chance."

Janine slumped back, eyelids half-closed, for once oblivious to how she looked. Whitney sat beside her, trying to imagine their homecoming.

Mercifully, no one they knew was on the plane. Once it took off, Janine curled up and fell asleep. Staring out the window as dusk enveloped the fading light, Whitney thought of how she had spoken to her mother. Perhaps this was her act of revenge, dragging her damaged sister home the way a cat deposits a dead bird at the front door.

See this?

The last few hours came crashing down on her—the falsity of those she had loved, the loss of her own identity as their masks slipped away. Who was she if not solid and sensible Whitney Dane, daughter of a loving couple—the wise, masterful father and poised, contented mother; the fiancée of Peter Brooks, her honorable and open partner for life; the best friend of Clarice Barkley, her loyal confidante since childhood; the younger sister to a stunning model who, whatever her flaws, was far too good at pretending to have become the listless, defeated woman who slept beside her now. A life built on deceptions and delusions, the life she was to emulate with Peter and now saw as a charade. Though she despised her father, Clarice had betrayed her almost as cruelly—sleeping with Charles, spurring him to ruin Ben by revealing Whitney's secrets. As Clarice's friend, she had thought she was in on the joke. But the most heartless joke was on her: she had never anticipated that Clarice's elusive nature, the protective coloring she deployed against men and adults, could be turned on her as well.

She had no one to believe in. How could she even believe in herself when she no longer knew who she was, or what she wanted? With a mix of empathy and dispassion she regarded her sister anew.

Janine was still asleep, her streaked blond hair falling across her face. "If I have only one life," the ad proclaimed, "let me live it as a blonde." Janine had certainly done that, Whitney thought— she was exhausted by the effort to look like something, rather than be someone. If only by comparison, Whitney supposed, she was the fortunate daughter. But she and Janine had more in common than either had known—both were their parents' inventions.

Interrupting her thoughts, the plane swooped in a vertiginous descent. As they landed, Whitney found herself in a familiar place she no longer knew.

Startled awake, Janine blinked, the remembrance of reality clouding her eyes. She walked haltingly down the stairs to the tarmac, waiting for Whitney as if she were a girl waiting for her mother. They did not speak on the cab ride home, punctuated by oncoming headlights that illuminated Janine's waxen profile.

The cabbie stopped at the house and carried their suitcases to the door. Anne opened it before Whitney could finish paying him, shooing Janine inside with an impatient glance at her second daughter, as though preparing to seal the family from the outside world. When Whitney followed them into the alcove, her mother was addressing Janine in an anxious, peremptory tone. "What happened to you, Janine?"

Janine glanced at her sister. "Alcohol and pills," Whitney told their mother flatly. "We're lucky they didn't kill her, and right now she needs rest."

Her tone induced in Anne a stung, confused expression. Reasserting herself, Anne told Janine, "I'll take you to your room."

"No," Whitney snapped. "I will."

Stunned, Anne looked from Whitney to Janine. "It's all right, Mom," Janine said tiredly. "I'm too wiped out to talk."

Without awaiting Anne's response, Whitney picked up Janine's suitcase and, lightly touching her arm, led her up the stairs. Turning on the bedroom lights, she went to the bathroom for a glass of water and placed it on the nightstand. Watching her sister undress, she was appalled by the thinness of her body. In a feeble voice, Janine asked, "What will you tell her?"

Everything, Whitney wanted to say, imagining the savage pleasure of shredding her mother's fantasies before recoiling from her own thoughts. "I don't know," she answered tiredly. "All I'm sure of is you can't go on like this." Quiet for a moment, she regarded this new creature who was still her sister. "I love you," she added gently. "I just want you to be all right."

Kissing Janine on the forehead, she went to confront their mother, softly closing the door behind her.

Anne waited in the living room, her expression

in the thin electric light composed in a semblance of calm. But her tone was brittle and demanding. "Tell me what happened, Whitney. I need to know."

Still standing, Whitney regarded her in silence, angry yet irresolute.

"I'm her mother, dammit."

Whitney felt the desperation in Anne's voice cut through her own desire to lash out, replacing it with a strange, sad resolve. Anger had no place now; what she had to say felt cruel enough. "You certainly are, Mom. That's a big part of Janine's problem."

"Just what do you mean by that?"

"I went to see her without calling ahead. It took awhile for her to answer, and she looked like walking death. Her apartment was like the inside of a madwoman's brain. She'd drunk nearly a fifth of vodka and had taken pills on top of that. If I hadn't showed up, she might have kept on going."

Anne stiffened in protest. "What would make a girl so vibrant . . ."

"Kill herself? Because no one in this family knows her, you least of all. Do you know why she didn't want me to tell you what she'd done? Because it would hurt you too much." Whitney's tone hardened. "You've built a myth of beauty and drama with Janine as your surrogate, filling the empty spaces in your own life . . ."

Her mother sprang up, face contracted, hand raised to slap her daughter—less out of rage, Whitney sensed, than the visceral need to silence her. Whitney grasped her wrist in midair, their faces close. "Do you think shutting me up will erase all the damage to Janine? Then go ahead—hit me."

Whitney released her mother's wrist. Slowly, the fury in Anne's eyes was replaced by shame; as though by its own volition, her hand fell to her side. Heart racing, Whitney told her, "She's become a walking Barbie doll, with no one home inside, who lives to be who you imagine because she's got nothing else but her looks and your approval and the desperate need for a man to complete her. But it hasn't quite worked for you, Mother, and Janine isn't half as strong as you are. She's not 'too strong' for men; she's pathetically needy and insecure, and once they see past that electric first impression they use her for awhile and then run from her like the plague . . ."

"How can you know this?"

"How can you not? Anyone could read the pattern who wasn't invested in a fantasy of their own creation." Whitney paused, considering her next words. "The human wreckage I found was the result of an affair with a man who treated her like garbage. You don't need to know the details —for once, please don't pump Janine. She can tell you what she wants, and it's not important now.

"What matters is that you and Dad accept the truth: she's not your society-page ingénue, but a fragile, damaged woman who depends on alcohol, drugs, and falsehoods to keep her going. You need to send her somewhere where she can get help, away from this family and the world she's been drowning in. Then you can start trying to love whoever you get back."

Listening, Anne recovered a semblance of poise. "So suddenly our twenty-one-year-old daughter is the head of our family, the great authority on all our faults."

Having said so much, Whitney felt too exhausted to defend herself. "I just want you to be a real family for Janine. All I've got left is to tell you what I see. Whether Janine destroys herself is up to you."

All at once, her mother seemed deflated. "Your father is flying in tomorrow morning with Peter. He'll know what to do."

The thought of seeing Charles, or Peter, was more than Whitney could bear—she had already passed the moment, with her mother, which had been as far ahead as she could see. Then she remembered Ben and wondered if the light was on in his guesthouse. But she could not run to him, let alone imagine what she would say if she did.

"Get some sleep," she told her mother. "I'll stay with Janine." She paused, then added in a reflex of politeness, "Good night, Mom."

Janine slept in the darkened bedroom, her breathing shallow but even. Whitney settled in an overstuffed chair, uncertain of whose needs she was serving, her sister's or her own. Like Janine, part of her wished to fall asleep and never wake up or, if she must, to awaken to the life she had before, still innocent.

Six

The next morning, Whitney prepared herself to meet Charles and Peter at the airport.

Dressed in a sweater and jeans, she watched the plane taxi to a stop, her nerves jangling from the coffee she had gulped to fight against exhaustion. Her father and her fiancé climbed down the metal stairs in the sunlight of a bright morning, the air heavy with what promised to be a hot, humid day. Edgy and apprehensive, she did not kiss either man, hoping that they would think her distracted by worry about Janine. As they hurried to the car, Charles asked, "How is she?"

"Still sleeping. I guess Mom told you how I found her."

"Hungover, apparently. To be honest, your mother wondered if you were being a tad melodramatic."

Whitney felt her jaw tense. She climbed into the driver's seat, waiting for the two men to slide into the car. Driving from the parking lot, she told her father, "Before you see either one of them, we need to talk."

Charles turned to her with a look of irritation. "Don't you think that can wait?"

"No."

Glancing in the rear view mirror, Whitney saw Peter's worried expression, as though he sensed a danger he could not identify. "I'll drop Peter at the house," she told her father.

The quiet command in her voice, an attempt to conceal her nervousness, so resembled Charles's at such moments that it startled her. He scrutinized her more closely, choosing to say nothing.

Reaching the house, she stopped at the head of the driveway, silent, until Peter took his cue to get out. She turned the car around and headed toward the Lucy Vincent Beach.

"Let's hear it," Charles demanded.

Irresolute, Whitney struggled to arrange her thoughts. "Let's wait until we get there," she temporized.

The parking lot was near-empty. Still quiet, they took the catwalk through the sea grass to the beach, white-capped waves spilling onto pristine white sand. Near the water the air was a little cooler, the last mist of morning dissipating over sparkling blue ocean. A few fly fishermen had waded out into the surf, and an early scattering of sunbathers had arranged themselves over several hundred feet of sand and driftwood, watching the sea like sentinels. Hands shoved into the pockets of his blue sport coat, Charles walked beside his youngest daughter, regarding the scene with narrowed eyes before he turned to her.

"And so?"

She stopped to face him, digging her tennis shoes into the sand. "I told Mom how I found her," she finally said. "I didn't say Janine had just gone through an abortion, after an affair with a married guy who dumped her once she got pregnant . . ."

"Who *is* this man?"

"Forget him. The important thing is that she could have died. If Janine hadn't become his victim, she'd be someone else's. I think men have started using her for sex. What I know for sure is that she was fired by her agency because she's addicted to alcohol and pills." Whitney felt a rising anger strengthen her resolve. "I've seen it for awhile—take away her bright, frenetic manner and she looks like a cadaver. But Mom kept clinging to her false image of Janine, trying to compensate for what's missing in her own life. You've sacrificed Janine to pacify her, so you could go on living as you pleased."

To Whitney's surprise, her father looked less angry than startled. "They've always been close," he protested. "They're mother and daughter, who share things men can't really understand . . ."

"Are women really that mysterious? Doesn't a string of failed relationships tell you anything about your own daughter? What about how jittery she is or how much she drinks? Did you really think she was just 'vivacious'?" Whitney's speech quickened. "Suppose she'd killed herself yesterday. What would you have told yourself and all your friends? Not the truth, I'm pretty sure. Any more than you've told the truth about your marriage—even to each other."

Her father's blue eyes turned hard. "Meaning?"

Whitney steeled herself. Voice trembling, she said, "I know about Clarice."

Charles folded his arms, regarding her with a fair show of calm. "What is it that you think you know?"

"I came to the apartment yesterday." Drawing a breath, she quoted her closest friend. " 'I enjoy it, too. But maybe I'll torture you a little.' "

Astonishment moved through her father's eyes, quickly followed by comprehension. A stain of red appeared on his face, unleashing Whitney's rage. "She was my best friend, Dad. You took us to the beach when we were little. I still remember the day you spent hours helping us build a sand castle, and all the dinners at our house when Clarice and I were growing up together, you with your indulgent smile for me and your quasi-daughter." She paused, then added with quiet fury, "That special dinner to celebrate my engagement, with her watching while you went on and on about your wonderful marriage and how you wished the same for Peter and me. The errand boy who loaned you and Clarice our bed . . ."

"That's not fair," Charles cut in angrily.

"To whom? The three of you knew, and Mom and I sat there like fools. How could you do that to us—to her?"

Charles grimaced. In a lower voice, he said. "It hadn't started with Clarice."

Whitney gave him a look of contempt. "So when did you find each other, Dad?"

"Early in July." Charles turned away. "We went to lunch, as we often did when she was in New York. But this time . . ."

"She seduced you," Whitney said scornfully.

"I'm not saying that, Whitney. I'll spare you the details . . ."

Whitney laughed harshly. "A little late, I'd say. But thank you."

Charles gazed past her, his eyes filling with shame. "I'd never imagined Clarice felt that way, or ever could."

Silent, Whitney reprised Clarice's admiration for Charles; her questions about the Danes' marriage and Anne's insecurity; her worries about her own father's finances. More quietly, she said, "Don't flatter yourself, Dad. Clarice is worried that her father's going broke, so now she's hoping you'll secure her future. And you couldn't resist a twenty-two-year-old who was crazy with desire for you."

Charles winced, then spoke in a quieter voice, as though repeating what he had told himself. "Whatever you think, I love your mother. This was the first time I've been unfaithful. But I was never really young. Your generation has all this freedom to do whatever you want. My life was duty, going from one rung to the next— school, the war, succeeding at your grandfather's firm. Doing everything I needed . . ."

"So Mom should pay for all this virtue you've been practicing and preaching."

"Not at all. But in this brave new spirit of honesty, there's one more 'truth' about our marriage. Your mother lost interest in intimacy with her change of life—not that she had much before." Her father's tone became insistent. "Of all the things she told you about womanhood or marriage, did she ever suggest that making love was a good thing for its own sake? Or did she present it as a marital obligation?"

The sound of her father's excuses reignited Whitney's loathing. "I don't care what happened with you and Mom. You asked my fiancé to cover for you, and you slept with my closest friend. That's more than selfish. You need to dominate everyone around you." She stopped, then continued in a calm, bitter voice. "You want full credit for making others who they are, so you can look at them and see yourself. I don't think we're even real to you . . ."

"You've always been real to me," Charles broke in. "I knew that you envied your sister. I knew you wanted Peter, and how much happier and more confident you were since he came into your life. I could see how much you wanted to have that feeling forever. So I did my damnedest to help you . . ."

"Then how could you use him like this, and how could he let you?"

Charles shook his head. "Peter didn't know . . ."

"I don't believe you," Whitney snapped. "You were afraid of being seen at a hotel. But you needed to know we wouldn't be there when you met Clarice, so Peter needed to know when you *would* be."

She stared at him until he finally nodded. "All I told him, Whitney, is that I needed the apartment from time to time. I never told him why."

Whitney felt a wave of sadness overtake her. "You didn't have to. This was a manly arrangement between men, though certainly not equals." Her voice filled with disdain and pity. "Poor Peter. What could he do, after all? You'd given him a job and kept him out of the draft. All he had to do in return is keep your secrets and marry your daughter."

Her father shook his head. "I was unfair to him, I admit that. But you shouldn't be. He loves you and, more than that, respects you. The two of you are an excellent match."

Whitney's voice turned cold. "And you won't let *anyone* get in the way of that, will you."

Charles stared at her. With a kind of fascination, she watched him decide that it was better not to speak. "The subject now is Ben. You pulled strings to have him drafted, in return for keeping a Jewish family out of West Chop."

Charles looked stunned. He exercised power so reflexively, she thought, that he had forgotten what Janine might have overheard. Hastily, he answered, "I thought that he'd ruin your life. You're my daughter, and I was looking out for you. When you're defending your child, you'll kill to protect her happiness."

"Maybe you have," Whitney said with lethal softness. "If Ben dies in Vietnam, I'll never speak to you again . . ."

"You can't mean that."

"I do, believe me." Her voice lowered. "Get him out, Dad. You got him in, so get him out."

"It doesn't work that way, Whitney. All I did was have them move Ben Blaine to the top of the pile. Now he's caught in the machinery and there's nothing I can do . . ."

"I despise you," Whitney burst out.

Charles turned from her, gazing at the water. "Are you going to marry Clarice?" she asked.

"Of course not."

"No, of course not. You have bigger plans—a cabinet position." Pausing, Whitney faltered, struggling against the instinct to give in to this man, the central figure in her life since her first conscious thought. "So you'll have to cut her off. As for me, I'll never speak to Clarice Barkley again."

"How will you explain that to your mother?"

"That's your problem, isn't it?" Pausing, Whitney groped for a tenuous calm. "One last thing. If Clarice's father's business is failing, and she comes to you for help, you're going to refuse her."

Turning, Charles looked into her face, his eyes probing. "I don't believe you'd tell your mother about Clarice. You could never be that cruel."

Whitney felt a lump in her throat—if he chose to disbelieve her, she did not know if she could persist. "How do you define cruel?" she willed herself to ask. "Is it me telling Mom the truth? Or helping you deceive her about a marriage that she's begun to sense is empty? Because if I stay quiet, that's what I'll be doing. Just like Peter."

"Use your head," Charles admonished harshly. "Beneath the surface, your mother's very fragile."

"I agree. But not as fragile as Janine, who you've let Mom swallow whole. So tell me how you're going to help my sister."

Charles's face became a rigid mask. "Is this your final demand, Whitney?"

"Yes."

Facing the water again, her father frowned in thought. Tense, Whitney watched him consider his choices. "There's a place called McLean," he said at length, "near Boston. One of my partners sent his daughter there when she got too deeply into drugs. I gather they're careful to protect a family's privacy . . ."

"Maybe they'll even help Janine," Whitney interjected caustically. "So don't let Mom interfere. You want to run your family's lives, so do some good with it for once. And keep Peter in his job. God knows he's earned it."

Charles shot her a look of doubt and curiosity. "What do you mean to say to him?"

"That's between the two of us. I don't want you telling him anything about this. We're none of your business, for once."

Turning from him abruptly, she walked back to the car, afraid that he might see her crumble.

They returned to the house in silence. Drained and weary, Whitney felt years older, an alien to herself.

Seven

Whitney found Peter in the guesthouse, unpacking his clothes with the distracted air of someone at loose ends. He looked up from his suitcase, his appraisal of Whitney cautious, then sat on the bed with his hands folded, looking, for once, less like an athlete than someone who felt awkward in his own body—or, she amended sadly, in his life.

"What's happening, Whit?"

She sat across from him, underscoring the distance she felt. "I know about the apartment," she told him, "and what you've let my father use it for. How could you do that to us, Peter?"

Peter's gaze was shamed but steady. "Because he asked me." He paused, touching the bridge of his nose. "I didn't like knowing, and it didn't feel good to see him differently. But it was something he trusted me with."

Whitney felt comprehension overtaking her. "Like a father trusts a son."

Briefly, his gaze flickered. "I wouldn't have wanted to know that about my own dad. But, yeah, maybe a little." He paused, looking at her directly. "I still believe he loves your mom. I just had to accept that he isn't perfect, and that there were things I couldn't understand."

"But what about *me,* Peter? And us?"

"I *did* think about you," he said with a trace of anger. "A lot. But what was I supposed to tell you, Whitney? Do you feel better knowing that your dad has been cheating on your mom?"

Heartsick, Whitney considered his question. "I don't know," she finally answered. "But I wish you'd told him 'no.' For my sake, *and* yours."

Peter's throat worked, "I couldn't, Whit. I wanted to, and I couldn't."

The weight of this sounded crushing. It was beyond Whitney to be angry when she felt so sad for them both. "I don't even know who she was," he said. "Do you?"

"Yes." Feeling her own solitude, Whitney wished she could reach out to him. "My father and I will never be the same, Peter. None of us will."

For a moment, he looked like he wanted to stand, closing the distance between them. Watching her face, he stayed where he was, gazing at her pleadingly. "What about us, Whitney? I still love you, and I don't want to live my life without you. I'll find a teaching job, if that's what you want. Anything."

Whitney felt her throat constrict. "But what do *you* want, Peter?"

"You, Whitney." He got up, kneeling by her chair to take her hand in his. "A life with you. Nothing means more to me."

Whitney gazed into his face, guileless and

sincere, and felt love commingled with sadness. "But what kind of life? We're still the miniature bride and groom on the wedding cake my parents bought, with no idea of what to do except follow an example we know to be a lie. All I'm sure of now is that I don't want to be my mother."

A hint of desperation stole into his eyes. "You wouldn't be."

Whitney struggled to believe this. But she could not even envision herself the day after tomorrow. "Oh, sweetheart," she said softly, a mist in her eyes. "For the longest time, I thought I wasn't worthy of you. Now I think we're not worthy of getting married. How can we be, when all we know is to imitate our parents?" She paused, then said in a clearer voice, "I can't marry you, Peter. At least not in three weeks, marching toward the altar like windup dolls, oblivious to everything but what other people expect from us."

He slumped, hurt graven on his face. "Because I didn't tell your dad to stuff it?"

Still dazed at what she had said, Whitney slowly shook her head. "It's because we're all tangled up with him, and I've got no idea of who we are anymore. Or who I am . . ."

"Is this about that guy?" he said accusingly.

She owed him the truth, Whitney thought miserably—whatever that was. But knowing the truth was beyond her. "It's so much more," she answered. "It's true that I started feeling something for him—a kind of fascination, I guess. I didn't know what it meant, and never would have let myself find out . . ."

His face hardened. "And now you will."

"This really isn't about that. But I've watched Ben tell my father to 'stuff it,' as you put it. After yesterday, I have to admire him for it."

Pride made Peter remove his hand. "You'll never see me the same, will you?"

Amidst her own sadness, Whitney searched for an honest answer. "You're a wonderful person, Peter—in so many ways. But however desperately I want to erase everything that's happened, I can't."

Peter stood at once. "I think I'd better leave," he said stiffly. "I need to clear out the apartment, find a place of my own."

At once, Whitney felt a terrible loss—once they had been innocent, two young people in love, with a life ahead untainted by her family. Now all that was gone. "I guess that's best," she told him softly. "There's a lot for me to face here."

"Then don't bother to drive me," he snapped. "I'll take a cab."

Despite everything, his sudden withdrawal deepened her misery. With a fixed expression, Peter took his grandmother's ring off her finger and put it in his pocket. To Whitney, the act had a strange formality, a ritual of relinquishment and loss.

Seeing the tears in her eyes, his face softened. "I'm sorry, Whit."

"Me, too," she answered in a husky voice. "For both of us."

She did not trust herself to say anything else. Standing, she kissed him on the cheek, then walked quickly to the door before yielding to her impulse to look back at him. He held his head higher, trying to smile as she left, like a proud athlete facing defeat.

When Whitney returned to the house, Janine was closeted with their parents.

For a long time she lay in the window seat, her thoughts jumbled. She heard, rather than saw, the taxi stopping in the driveway. As the car door opened and shut, tears stung her eyes again, she could not bear to look out the window.

At last her mother came downstairs, ashen beneath the perfect hair and makeup, her last defense against events she could not control.

"How's Janine doing?" Whitney asked.

"Not well. Your father insists on taking her to a clinic near Boston that supposedly exists to help people involved with drugs and alcohol."

Whitney felt relief overwhelm her sense of tact. "Good. She needs that."

"She's *my* daughter," Anne said tightly. "Or was. It seems that you and your father have taken over."

It was sadly predictable, Whitney supposed, that Anne perceived a conspiracy to wrest away her striking and confident daughter, the one people always remembered. She could not help but hear a subtext—*I hope you're happy now.* "I'm sorry, Mom. But if you'd seen her yesterday, you'd know how much she needs this."

For a time her mother said nothing. Seemingly bewildered, she looked around her, as though in search of reassurance. "Where's Peter?"

"Gone. I've broken our engagement."

Anne's face froze, accenting the hurt in her eyes. "Now? With all that's happening, how can you do this?"

"To Peter? Or to you?"

"To yourself, Whitney. To all of us."

"All of you aren't involved in this."

"Are we not?" her mother cried out. "The wedding is less than three weeks away. What will your father and I say about this?"

A strange calm came over Whitney. "Anything you like. I really don't care, as long as it's not embarrassing to Peter."

"How can it not be," her mother said grimly. "I suppose this is about that boy."

"Ben, you mean? Funny that you can't speak his name aloud." Whitney's voice softened. "I wish it were that simple, Mom. Then I'd know what I'm doing tomorrow, and the day after that."

A sense of Whitney's disorientation seemed to

penetrate her mother's outrage. Shaking her head, Anne said in a broken voice, "I'm sorry, Whitney. It just feels like everything is falling apart."

"I know, Mom. For me, too."

Anne sat down beside her, gazing out at nothing. "I've tried so hard. All I ever wanted for my daughters is that you have the life that I've had."

Whitney felt a kind of chill. "I guess we'll have to find our own way," she replied. "But there's something else I need you to accept. About Clarice."

"Clarice?"

"We've had a falling out, Mom. She won't be coming here anymore."

"But she's like a member of our family," Anne protested. "Why are you turning all of our lives upside down?"

"This is about *my* life," Whitney insisted. "What happened with Clarice is personal. So please try to focus on Janine. She *is* a member of our family, and she needs for all of us to help her."

Mute, Anne shook her head. Instinctively, Whitney took her in her arms, conscious of how fragile her mother felt.

"We'll be all right," the new keeper of her father's secrets murmured, doubting this would ever be so.

That afternoon, Whitney fell into a deep sleep, her roiled mind shutting down from sheer exhaustion.

When she awoke, it was morning again, and her parents were preparing to drive with Janine to the ferry, the first leg of their journey to McLean.

No one asked her to come, and she did not want to. In the driveway, Janine stiffly kissed Whitney goodbye, her face still pale, her manner remote and a little resentful. Then she got in the backseat with her mother.

Alone with Charles, Whitney said, "I may not be here when you get back."

Her father's lips compressed. "For God's sake, why? Your mother is going to need you more than ever."

"I've done what I can for her, Dad. Now it's your turn." She paused, then told him firmly, "It's time for me to deal with my own life. I'm going to see Ben, to tell him the truth. I owe him that, don't you think?"

"No," her father snapped, "I don't." But for once there was nothing he could do.

Eight

In early evening, filled with doubt, Whitney knocked on Ben's door.

He opened it, seemingly surprised, then mustered a smile that did not conceal his wariness. "I thought you'd run away."

"I had to," she said simply.

"So what are you doing here?"

Where to start, she wondered. But all she could think to say was, "I've broken my engagement."

His expression changed, doubt and curiosity warring in his eyes. "That can't have gone over very well."

"It didn't. Can I come in?"

He held the door open. As she entered, she saw some official-looking papers on his kitchen table. Following her gaze, he said, "Not a good weekend for me, either. I got them the day after you took off."

She went to the table, and picked them up. The first document was headed, "Order to Report for Induction." Whitney stared at it, the small print swimming in front of her, then saw the date and time of his induction: *September 21, 1968, at 7 a.m.* "Seems like they're in a hurry," Ben remarked. "I must be very desirable."

Whitney sat down at the table, feeling queasy, though she made herself look up at him. "My father did this, Ben."

His expression darkened. "How?"

"He used his influence to move you up the list, so you couldn't get back to Yale." She bit her lip, then added baldly, "To make sure nothing happened with us."

Ben's face closed. "I should have guessed. Truth to tell, I wondered once or twice. He's the kind of man who safeguards his possessions."

Whitney shook her head. "He doesn't own me anymore. No one does."

He sat across from her. Staring at the draft notice, he said softly, "All this because we spent time together. What a mistake it was to meet him."

"That was my fault. I can't tell you how terrible I feel."

"Oh, I can—and then some. Amazing how easy it is for him to play with other peoples' lives. Whether I live or die is less important than some waiter screwing up his drink order." His voice quickened with repressed anger. "It's not even callousness—that takes too much thought. It's the carelessness of privilege. Lesser humans like me are stick figures on the periphery of your lives."

"I know how you feel about my father. But that's not fair to me."

The cast of his face became a shade less adamantine. "Maybe not. But some days it's hard to make these fine distinctions."

Whitney did not answer. "Is there anything you can do now?" she asked.

"My draft advisor doesn't think so. If I were married, he tells me, maybe I'd have a chance. But I'm single, healthy, poor, and dropped out of college to campaign for a liberal. Perfect raw material for the American Imperium." His voice took on a sarcastic fatalism. "During the Civil War, the sons of wealth paid boys with no prospects to join the army in their place. Now men like your father can arrange for pawns like me to substitute for guys like Peter Brooks. He didn't even need to open his wallet."

There was nothing Whitney could say to this. For a painfully long time, Ben watched her, his hatred for her father replaced by a neutral curiosity. "So now you've explained my fate, Whitney. Is there anything else?"

To her surprise, she found his dispassion more devastating than anger. "It doesn't matter now. I just came to tell you the truth, and to say goodbye."

He cocked his head. "Are you going somewhere? Or am I the only one?"

Whitney hesitated. "Actually, I don't know where I'm going."

"Literally? Or figuratively?"

"Both," she said, and realized how much she wanted his understanding. "How can I know where I'm going, Ben, when I don't know who I am?"

"But you *do* know. You're Whitney Dane, daughter of a wealthy family, with all the resources and time in the world to find out what you want, and a swarm of people—your parents' friends—to help you on the way. All you have to do is tell them what you've decided to become."

"You really don't get it. Everything has changed for me—especially how I see my parents. I may not know who I am, but I know who I never want to be."

His puzzled smile was not unkind. "Poor little rich girl. You really *are* lost, aren't you?"

She did not need to answer this, and to try would only seem foolish. "That night, why did you kiss me?"

The grin he shot her contained a dose of real amusement. "You're kidding, right?"

Whitney felt belittled. "Because I was there, I guess. Sort of like Mt. Everest."

He shook his head, the grin becoming a smile that played across his lips. "With all respect, I'm hardly Sir Edmund Hillary, and even you're not voluptuous enough for comparison to Mt. Everest. Climbing you would not require heroism."

Whitney flushed. "I guess you hadn't been with anyone for awhile."

His face closed again. "With all that's gone on with me lately, I haven't been counting the weeks. But if the mood struck me, why not go for Clarice? She's not engaged to anyone."

The startling image of Clarice naked before her father left Whitney speechless. There was so much she wanted to tell him; so little, for her mother's sake, that she could say—especially to someone so filled with hatred for her family. "This is hopeless," she said. "I should have stopped with an apology."

"Talk about hopeless," Ben retorted with quiet

vehemence. "For such a smart woman, you're a complete idiot. I spent hours and days talking with you—a girl who's engaged to be married and out of my reach even if she weren't, telling you things I don't tell anyone, and all you can do with that is wonder why I kissed you. Maybe you should ask Clarice. She might actually be able to tell you."

Whitney stared at him. For once his eyes seemed naked, his desire for her so startling that she looked away. "I didn't know," she said softly.

"You didn't want to. So now you do, and there's not Peter anymore. Or is there?"

Thinking of Peter, she felt a renewed sadness. "No. There's not."

"So what do you want with me, Whitney Dane?"

Her next words, whatever they were, felt so consequential that the answer caught in her throat. The doubt in her eyes made him reach across the table, gripping her arm in a way that felt proprietary. "At least I know what I want," he told her. "And who."

He drew her up, face close to his. Whitney found herself unable to move, or turn from him. Ben's mouth met hers, kissing her hard. Reflexively, her lips opened to receive his tongue as she pressed against him, not asking herself why or what she should do. Drawing back, he started kissing her neck with surprising tenderness. "God," he murmured. "I want you."

An answering murmur came from deep within her throat, the sound of assent. He began unbuttoning her blouse.

It was dusk now, and the unlit room was shadowy and dim, a mercy to Whitney in her shyness. Unsure of what to do, she let Ben undress her, lingering on each part of her with his hands and mouth, now on her nipples, then her stomach, then the lushness of the fur between her legs. Then he was standing again, gently kissing her as he undressed, leading her to the bed, her heart beating, skin tingling with uncertainty and anticipation, knowing only that she wished to be swept through this moment to another not governed by her conscious mind. She lay back, and felt his lips repeating the downward journey until his tongue was inside her with an avidity so unlike Peter that, writhing against him, Whitney prayed he wanted this as much as she. She moaned her pleasure, worried that he might pull away. But the insistent probing of his tongue, an end in itself, kept on until the blood rushed to the center of her, and her shuddering cry of anguish and rapture muffled his quiet laugh of pleasure in her release. And then, kissing her tenderly on the mouth, he slid on top of her.

Whitney opened her legs to receive him. Slowly, he slipped inside her, filling her with his hardness, moving slowly and gently as he spoke her name. She felt herself again swelling with desire, whispering "more," wrapping her legs around him as if to pull him in deeper, their movements losing all sense of reason except their need for each other. The world turned black. Whitney cried out with pleasure, nipping at his neck as she felt him quake with his own release, becoming for this moment hers. And then he was lying beside her, fingers tangled in the tendrils of her thick brown hair. But the ebbing of desire, she discovered, left her feeling lost.

"Let me turn on the light," he told her. "I want to see you."

She writhed with embarrassment. With shaky humor she said, "Don't you think that's pushing things a little, Mr. Blaine? I barely know you."

"If it helps, Whitney, you can close your eyes."

He moved away, flicking on the bedside lamp. She blinked, her eyes adjusting to the light, and saw Ben smiling as he gazed at her. "You're beautiful . . ."

"Please, stop . . ."

"I've never heard a more halfhearted protest. You look as good as you feel—full and generous in all the ways I imagined. And I imagined you quite a lot."

Whitney covered her face. "I can't believe this."

"You should, Whitney. You remind me of Tim Hardin's song: *You look like love forever—too good to last, too lovely not to try.* You still don't grasp your power as a woman. Just like I'm guessing you sell your abilities as a writer way too short."

She felt a mix of pleasure and confusion. "That's very nice of you, Ben. Now please turn off the lights."

He kissed her. "Only if you'll stay the night."

For a moment, she was quiet. "Yes," she answered. "Where else would I go, after all?"

Nine

That night a thunderstorm struck the island, awakening Whitney with a start.

Outside, the wind whistled and moaned, rattling windows and branches, driving pellets of rain like bullets as streaks of lightning illuminated the pitch-black night, pursued by explosions of thunder so close that they felt like the judgment of an angry god. Sitting up, Ben turned on the bedside light. A bolt of yellow struck near the guesthouse, knocking out the electricity and causing the lamp to sizzle before it went out in a flash. The sheer violence of the storm had an awesome grandeur, making Whitney feel smaller, unmoored from all she had known. Ben held her until the storm passed, and she fell into a fitful, broken sleep.

At dawn, Whitney stirred awake, fleetingly startled by her surroundings before remembering where she was. Ben was making coffee at the gas stove, dressed only in cutoff jeans. The look he gave her combined humor and uncertainty.

"Well," he said, "do you still respect me in the morning?"

Whitney fought back her own disorientation. "You, yes. Me, I'm not so sure about. It's like I've fallen down a rabbit hole, and there's nothing to grab onto."

Ben studied her. "I'm real enough," he said, then inquired matter-of-factly, "What do you take in your coffee?"

"A splash of milk, thanks. If you have it."

Ben brought her the coffee in bed. She sat up, trying to cover her breasts with a sheet, then giving up. The sensuality yet domesticity of the moment felt strange, even embarrassing, but not entirely unpleasant. "You're also beautiful this morning," he assured her. "If that's what you're wondering about."

She shook her head. "I can't even say what I'm thinking. There's been too much."

He sat in a chair with his coffee cupped in both hands, legs stretched out in front of him. "Do you want to stay for awhile?"

The sense of all that awaited came crashing down on her. "Truth to tell, I'd like to pull the covers over my head until everything goes away. But my parents are coming home again, and there's a lot for me to face up to."

Alone, she did not need to add. His expression became guarded. "Will I see you again?"

The question surprised her, suggesting that he might be as confused as she. "After last night? I'd hope that's something we both want."

He got up, sitting beside her on the bed, then reached for her hand. "Did you think I was just killing time?"

"I didn't know. I still don't, really."

"I'm not," he said flatly. "Thanks to your father, all I've got is the next three weeks. You can decide how much of that belongs to us."

Three weeks from now, Whitney thought, she was to have been married. She drank the coffee in silence, not letting go of his hand, gazing out at the sunlight brightening a newly cleansed world. Asking nothing, Ben let her be, her companion in limbo—his time foreshortened, her future unfathomable, neither able to help the other. After awhile she dressed as he watched her, then gave him a chaste kiss before she went back to her empty house, showered, dressed, and drove to Dogfish Bar.

For a long time Whitney watched the blue of the sea and sky deepen with mid-morning, unable to write a word. Her journal felt like an artifact from another life, a narrative of doubts and observations recorded by a stranger whose life was bounded by certainties—the goodness of her family, the loyalty of her best friend, her love for Peter Brooks, her own children waiting some-where beyond her wedding day. The young woman who had upended her own world, separated from her former self by the chasm of a single weekend, had yet to write a line.

All that seemed real to her was Benjamin Blaine—if only more real, she amended, than she did to herself. But how do you describe a void? she wondered. The touchstones of the life she had believed in until now had spawned questions she could record, then ponder, in safety. Her writing was part of all she had lost; stripped of certainties, she had nothing to doubt, or even to say. She felt empty, and achingly alone.

Except for Ben.

There were times she came alive with him. Alive as a sexual being; alive as a woman who discovered thoughts and feelings in his presence she might not have found on her own. It was not just when he was inside her that Ben filled her heart and mind.

She went to find him again, pulsing with anticipation and confusion.

He was working beside the catwalk, sitting cross-legged inside the dinghy as he replaced the frayed rope of its outboard motor. He looked up at her, his dark eyes questioning, his lean body unnaturally still. "So I came back," she said.

The weight of these words hung there in the silence. "For what?" he asked.

"Whatever happens."

There was nothing more either wanted to say. Reaching out for her, he helped her into the dinghy. Kneeling between his outstretched legs, she looked into his face, reaching beneath his T-shirt to clasp his shoulder blades. He kissed back hungrily, both of them knowing that this was not enough. Neither seemed to care who saw them.

Hurriedly, she peeled off her sweatshirt, bra, and jeans, as he struggled out of his clothes. They fell together to the floorboard, Ben on his back, Whitney taking him in her mouth. She felt him swell, tasting his saltiness, heard him say in a low, fierce tone, "I want all of you"—the only words she needed from him.

Whitney sat up, arching her back. She was already wet when he slipped a probing finger inside her. His eyes smiling into hers, he moved so that she could slide down on his shaft, his hands cradling her breasts as he flicked the tips of her nipples with his fingers, sending currents of desire racing through her body which merged with the sun on her skin, the cool whisper of breeze against her face. His hips thrust upward, eyes locking hers as though he never wanted to look away. Moving with him, she forced her eyes to shut, willing herself to experience only the tightening of her body before it broke with a deep, ecstatic shudder that drew a long cry from lips tightened to suppress it. As her spasms died, she heard him call her name from the distant place she had sent him until, at last, his body went slack as hers.

Her eyes opened, blinking at the sunlight as if she had just emerged from a darkened room. Ben gently touched her face with curled fingers. "Hope no one saw us, Whitney. Bad for your reputation."

"What about yours?"

"Nothing to lose. Not on this island, or any-where else."

Against her will, his faintly sardonic inflection made her imagine other women—a chastening reminder of how Clarice Barkley had read him, perhaps sensing the kinship of two sexual adventurers. Then she remembered what his brother had said: *People fall in line for him, women most of all. But I've never known a woman who Ben respected.*

Was this an adventure for him? Whitney wondered? However little she understood about herself, whatever she had chosen to precipitate, she knew that she was not that way. She lay down beside him, looking for answers, and found only an answering curiosity.

"I can see your mind working," he told her. "Already. It's not very flattering."

Whitney found she could not question him—at least not yet. "Wasn't what we just finished flattering enough?"

He did not smile, instead giving her the narrow-eyed look she had begun to associate with wanting to peer inside her. Softly, he said, "I guess it'll do." He paused, then added in an even voice, "Actually, there *is* another way you can prove your love."

"You're certainly demanding," Whitney said with mock vexation. "I didn't know there was anything left."

"At least one thing," he casually responded. "I'd like to read your journal."

Surprised, she leaned on her elbow, looking down at him. "Why?"

"Weeks ago, I made a guess about you. I need to know if I'm right."

Whitney felt herself withdraw. "It's personal to me, Ben."

He smiled at this. "More personal than sex?"

"Different. I've never shown it to anyone. Including Peter."

This caused a glint in his eyes. "I'm not 'anyone,'" he retorted. "And I'm sure as hell not Peter. Writing is something I care about—yours, especially. You can pick any pages you like."

Whitney frowned, fearing, yet stimulated by, the thought of exposing herself in this way, cracking open the protective wall she had built around this hidden part of her. "It's that important to you?"

"Yes."

She felt the warmth of their lovemaking slip away, an instinctive reluctance to cross one more boundary, leaving another piece of her in someone else's hands. Yet she cared deeply about what he thought, she suddenly realized. As strange and unsettling as this was, perhaps if he read what she had written she would feel less alone, be comprehended as more than another woman who wanted him.

"It's in the car," she said simply.

Ten

When she returned, Ben was leaning against the inside of the dinghy, still shirtless. He looked up at her, expectant. Whitney hesitated, then handed him the journal with two pages dog-eared. "You can read what I've marked," she told him.

He nodded, opening the journal. She stepped away, willing herself to trust him, gazing in the opposite direction so that all she saw was the endless water.

The entry she had chosen contained her musings about Clarice, the distillation of elusive thoughts that, in some morning of intuitive dis-quiet, had anticipated her friend's betrayal. She remembered its final passages almost perfectly.

Clarice lives in compartments. Presenting one face to her parents; another to mine; still another to the men she chooses as lovers, preserving for those she does not want the image of an unattainable woman. Then there is the Clarice who goes on about her days, optimistic and spirited, an uncomplicated girl who savors the life she has been given, and accepts others for who they are. Beneath all those is my friend and confidante, filled with clear-eyed realism, a cool knowingness and practicality, who views all the other Clarices, and the audiences she conjures them for, with a clinical detachment that verges on the ruthless.

I've always felt close to her, able to say anything without being seen too harshly. But which one of all the people who know Clarice is indispensable to her, the person she feels so bound to by a love and loyalty she could not do without? Before this summer, I would have said it was me; more often than not, I still think that. But at stray but strangely lucid moments, I wonder if there's anyone at all.

Those moments come more often now. I've begun to think there is something about Clarice that is unknowable, perhaps even to herself. It's always been easy to imagine her finding a happy life. But she could also have a lonely one, forever distant from herself and others, deepening the loneliness of those around her.

She heard Ben climb up out of the boat, standing beside her on the mooring before he placed the journal in her hand. "You certainly nailed her," he remarked. "Is that what you wanted me to see?"

Whitney did not look at him. "That's not what mattered to me most."

He fell silent until she faced him and, when she did, his eyes held a new intensity. "You can write, Whitney—and you can see things. That was the bet I'd made with myself. Whatever else you do, don't let that go."

Whitney felt a surge of relief, swiftly overwhelmed by self-doubt that washed away his words as though written in sand. "It feels like I have nothing left to say."

Ben's voice became sharp and almost angry. "Because of a rift with your parents and their presumptive Mr. Right? Give me a break, Whitney—or better yet, give yourself one. Your talent didn't come from them, and it will surface on the page again, bet on it. One of my professors once told me, 'writers write. To them, it's like breathing—what they're meant to do.' "

He was speaking to himself, she realized—and about himself. But he was also speaking to her. Amidst his own frustration, his fear of what the future held, Ben was trying to give her something.

Her parents were due to arrive, Whitney thought again. But she did not go home.

That evening they sat by the mooring, snacking on cheese and crackers and drinking a bottle of Chianti. Afterwards she lay back in his arms, watching with him as the sunset spread orange-gold across the water.

"This is my favorite time of day," he told her. "The sun casting a glow on the ocean and, on a perfect evening, backlighting a thin layer of clouds. This island gives us that rarest of things—a western exposure on the Atlantic, so you can see the sun rising from the water in the morning, and slipping into it at night. Since I was a kid, I've sat on the promontory behind the Barkleys, watching sunsets just like this."

He spoke with reverence, so close to tenderness that it surprised her. She realized how little she knew about him yet, how fraught and fleeting the days would be until he left. She felt suspended in time, somewhere between a past that had evanesced and a future that lay beyond the horizon of her imaginings. Being with him felt at once ephemeral and intensely real; for a moment she wished, fancifully, that she could stop the setting of the sun and stay cocooned with him in this no longer finite moment. Feeling him kiss the nape of her neck, Whitney closed her eyes.

"Marry me," she heard him say.

Whitney froze, wondering if her thoughts had drawn this from him, even as the reasoning part of her replayed his tone. In a muffled voice, she responded, "Did I hear you correctly?"

"Yes," he answered calmly. "I asked you to marry me."

She put down her wine glass, turning so that she could see him. Ben regarded her with a seriousness so deep that Whitney had trouble speaking. "The wine is lovely," she said, "and so is the sunset."

His face darkened. "Don't condescend to me, Whitney. I can't stand that."

Quickly, she touched his cheek. "I didn't mean to. I'm just so startled. Forty-eight hours ago, more or less, I was engaged to someone else."

"Believe me, I'm well aware of that."

She looked into his face, struggling to understand him. "When did you start thinking about this?"

He considered the question gravely. "When, deep in my subconscious, did I imagine being with you? Some moment when we were on the water, I guess—well before I kissed you, or even thought that we were possible. But marrying you? When I closed your journal, I knew that something had changed." His voice filled with quiet urgency. "For the first time in your life, Whitney, you're free. I'm the person you were born to be with."

She felt a momentary frisson, as if someone had just read her palm and forecast the path of her life. "How can you know that?"

Taking both hands in his, he answered with the patience of a man forced to explain the obvious to a woman blinded by its seeming novelty. "Because you've broken with them. Would you have done that if we'd never met?"

Mind clouded, Whitney searched her heart for an honest answer. "Maybe not," she managed to say amidst the chaos of her thoughts. But this only deepened her confusion between Ben as catalyst and as cause—how could she, the creation of her family, have become the creation of someone else she had met two months before? Desperately, she explained, "So many things have happened so quickly. I can't tell you why they did, or where you and I fit in."

"*I* can," he said with certitude. "You're Mrs. Me. You and I nourish each other. When I came here, I was dead inside. I'm not anymore. I feel this fierce will to live, to seize the future I've always wanted. You're part of that now."

She felt the pressure of reality, a stab of guilt that rightly belonged to her father. "But you're leaving. In three weeks you'll be gone."

"We know who caused that," he replied with an edge in his voice. "So let him have what he deserves—a marriage to me, without his finger-prints all over it." His tone evened out again.

"Your parents will come around. What choice do they have—exiling their own daughter is too embarrassing. But if they do, to hell with them. I've done without my parents just fine. My only regret is not getting rid of them sooner." He took her face in his hands, willing her to act. "We can make our own life, Whitney."

"But how can we if you're gone?"

"People do," he said flatly. "If we're married, maybe we could even get me back to Yale."

From the sea of print in his induction papers she remembered the instruction: "If married, bring proof of your marriage." Shaken, she asked, "What difference would that make?"

"It might lower my draft priority. All I need is to postpone my induction. From there I can put up a real fight." His eyes bore into hers. "I get what you must be thinking, with Peter always looking for an out. But what's been happening since the day we met has nothing to do with the draft— once you were free, it was only a matter of time until we decided on each other. But your father cut our time short, so I have to ask you now or risk losing you forever." He clasped her hands again. "Whatever we do, I'll probably have to go away. But if marriage gives us back what your father stole from me, call it poetic justice."

There must be truth in this, Whitney thought. They had grown toward each other oblivious to her father's maneuverings, both believing she would be married to Peter, rendering impossible the calculation that had dictated her wedding date. But knowing too late how callously her father had changed Ben's life, what was her obligation, and to whom? She leaned her face against his chest, feeling and hearing the strong, steady beat of his heat. "You've asked me to marry you," she told him, "without ever having said you love me."

Softly, Ben laughed. "When was I supposed to fit *that* in? When you were engaged to Peter? All it took was a kiss to send you screaming into the night. Long ago I learned not to love people who can only hurt you. But okay." Cradling her chin, he said, "I love you, Whitney Dane. I guess that's why I asked you to be my wife."

Whitney could not help but smile at this, then saw that he was waiting for her answer. She tried to find the words that would please him, yet be true to the muddle of an honest mind. "I love what I know about you," she said at last. "I feel things with you that I never felt with Peter, pieces of myself falling into place. But I can't know what I'll know in a year—about you, or me."

Ben's lips compressed. "You can guess. Okay, neither one of us would have chosen how things are. But look how far we've come, so quickly." He stopped himself, smiling a little. "Anyhow, you don't need to answer this minute. I count nineteen days before I disappear."

Whether meant to be sad or simply ironic, she was grateful for this reprieve. In hours or days, it might all become clearer—perhaps then she could see a life with him. But there was so much to absorb, including things she could never tell him, that part of her felt leaden.

"My parents still exist," she finally said. "I'm sure they're home by now, and I have to see them."

"Are you going to tell them I proposed?"

"No," she responded firmly. "This decision belongs to us. But I can't run away from them, either."

For an instant she read the answer in his eyes— *You could.* But his only words were, "Then go, Whitney. Just remember what I've said."

"How could I forget?" she asked him softly. Then she gathered herself for the walk back to her parents' home, the remnant of the life she had always known.

Eleven

Her mother and father were in the living room, snifters of brandy in front of them—Anne haggard, Charles looking deflated. Sitting on the couch with their bodies slightly turned from each other, they reminded Whitney for a lacerating moment of mannequins someone had left there.

Looking up, her father marshaled a semblance of command. "Where have you been?"

"With Ben."

"Doing what?" her mother broke in.

"For the last hour or so? Talking." The disdain Whitney heard in her own voice sounded like that of a stranger. "You know—that's when one person speaks, the other listens, and they keep on taking turns. It works best when both of them are trying to tell the truth." Seeing the hurt and confusion in her mother's eyes, she said more evenly, "But never mind Ben and me. How was Janine when you left her?"

Anne stared at her as though Whitney were as alien as she felt. "Bereft," she said, glancing at her husband. "It felt so cruel to leave her in such a place."

Whitney heard the resistance in her mother's voice, her need to recreate Janine pushing stubbornly to the surface. Turning to her father, Whitney said, "You're keeping her there, right?"

Her imperative tone seemed to widen the fissure between her parents. Anne turned to Charles, her expression pleading. But she did not—could not—know the leverage Whitney had to compel her father's decision. "Yes," he told his daughter. "At least until the doctors have spent more time with her."

The last phrase made her uneasy. "Can we talk, Dad?"

Anne shot her an angry look. "Are you dismissing me like some menial?"

"No, I'm not. But right now I need to speak with Dad."

Without waiting for an answer, Whitney quickly walked to Charles's den, leaving the door open behind her. Her father followed, closing the door before he sat across from her.

"Well?" he asked.

Whitney composed herself. "If you don't make her stay there, Janine could fall apart— maybe even die. I'm not protecting your secret because you deserve it."

"Maybe I don't," Charles said with barely repressed anger. "But your mother does."

Oddly, his outrage increased Whitney's sense, still astonishing to her, that she could force him to do what she wanted. "True. But Janine isn't Mom's consolation prize. Don't let her ruin my sister to buy yourself some peace."

"Yes, all right. But you've become quite the hanging judge, Whitney, for a twenty-one-year-old girl who's throwing away her life."

Once again, Whitney felt the hollowness of not knowing who she was. "Let's talk about Clarice. Have you told her yet?"

"Yes." Charles sounded both accusatory and aggrieved. "I'd like to have done the decent thing, tell her in person. But I no longer know what you'll do. So I called her while your mother was with Janine, and explained what you'd seen and what you wanted."

Whitney could imagine Clarice, hearing this on the phone in her bedroom, the place where they had shared so many sleepovers. "How did she take all that?"

"Except for a brief moment, with admirable self-control." Charles's voice lowered. "It will please you to know I found her poise more painful than anger, and that you'll never hear from her again. So now that I've done my part, I expect the same from you."

"What *is* my part, exactly?"

Standing, Charles began to pace, his voice firm. "You've stumbled on the fact that I have feet of clay, and you're bristling with righteous indignation. But I'm still your father, with the right to expect that this family will pick up as before—*all* of us—and that you'll recommence acting as my daughter, not my parole officer." He paused for emphasis, speaking slowly but firmly. "And, more than that, as Peter's fiancé—not his judge. I've spoken with him, and he's willing to look past this infatuation with Ben if you'll forgive his forced complicity in sins he never approved of. You're getting the best of *that* bargain by a long shot."

"Isn't that up to me?"

"Three days ago, I'd have trusted your judgment about almost anything. Now I'm asking you to stop and think. There's been enough disruption in this family, and in your life. It would be best for you to have the wedding, and to resume living as you were always meant to." Gazing down at her, he continued with the confidence that once had brooked no argument. "This importunate young man you're involved with will never give you the security you've always needed, far more than I think you know. Peter will."

Angry, Whitney stood. "It's you who's assured my future. Including the security of knowing I may never see Ben again."

"I shouldn't have done that, Whitney. But Benjamin Blaine gives me a feeling so dire I can't begin to describe it." Her father's manner became imploring. "When I sense something this strongly, I'm very seldom wrong. All Ben truly cares about is what he wants and needs. Please understand I was trying to protect you from immeasurable heartache."

"So now I should protect myself by marrying Peter."

"You're forgetting all his virtues," her father protested, "including that he loves you and is devastated by what happened. But if you want to put it that way, yes. You've received a jolt for which I've asked forgiveness, more than once. But your judgment is impaired, and mine—about this—is not. If you have any doubts about what to do, please consider your mother's feelings."

Suddenly Whitney felt less anger than a deep and abiding sadness. It was a moment before she found the will and the words to answer. "I have considered her, Father. Not just how she feels, but who she's become. Her example is one reason, among many, that I broke off my engagement." Her tone softened. "Poor Peter. He must feel as lost as I do, still wanting to marry a girl who's in love with someone else."

Before he could respond, she walked past him, out of the room and through the rear door of the house, desperate to breathe the cool night air.

Walking toward the ocean, she sat on a ledge above the water. In search of calm, she gazed up at the stars glinting in the night sky, undimmed by city lights. Since her first glimmerings of comprehension, she had pondered them each summer. As a child, holding her father's hand, she had marveled at how close they seemed; as a schoolgirl, she had struggled to grasp that they were light years away, their illumination far older than she was. Now she absorbed their permanence, an unchanging feature of a life that had changed so much.

She watched them for an hour, weighing her future, irresolute in the face of such confident men, so certain of who she was and what she needed. Whitney would have to face them, knowing all that she might lose or gain while understanding no more than she did now. It was terrible that what she felt for Ben, so immediate and so strong, could be freighted with such apprehension.

"Sleep which knits the raveled sleeve of care," Shakespeare had written somewhere. She wished that she could fall into its spell and awaken as a different woman, strong and calm and certain. But even if she managed to sleep, the most she could hope for was to feel less depleted, a little more able to sort through the men and choices tearing her apart, the fears of a young woman, still barely an adult, who seemed to know so much less about herself than she had three months before.

That she was somehow changed was all she knew, uncertainty her only certainty. With that scant consolation, she went back to the house and climbed the stairs to her bedroom, twisting the sheets in a fractured sleep interrupted by her dread of dawn.

It still brightened her window early, though the light came at an angle that augured the coming of fall. Before her parents could hear her, Whitney dressed and went to find the man who had asked her to marry him, wondering if he, like she, had been unable to find peace.

He was sitting at the end of the mooring, a cup of coffee in his hand, a metal thermos beside him. When he looked over his shoulder at the sound of her footsteps, his eyes were bleary, his hair disheveled. "Didn't sleep much," he said. "Did you?"

"No."

She sat beside him, uncertain of what she would say. "Made any decisions?" he asked.

Perhaps her answer was spurred by the impatience she heard beneath his worry—an echo of her father, though softened by the fact that she might hold his future in her hands, creating a vulnerability that must torment him. She tried to smile but could not. "I can't marry you, Ben."

He searched her eyes so intently that she wanted to look away. "Now—or ever?"

"Now," she answered softly. "Or ten days from now." Fearful of losing him, she clutched his hand. "I'm not talking about the future. I love you as much as I can. But I can't run from one man to another—from two men, actually, not knowing who I am or what I want from life." She looked into his face, imploring him to understand. "Ever since I can remember, there was always someone to take care of me—my mom and dad; our housekeeper, Billie; the teachers at my schools and counselors at summer camp. Even in college, I still came home to the parents who supported me.

"Peter would have been next. And after that I'd have a family of my own, emulating my mother, with our future underwritten by my father." She grasped his hand tighter. "Maybe I want something more—to *be* something more than what other people think I should be. Even you."

"Be whatever you like," he retorted swiftly. "All I want is a life with you."

Whitney felt a stab of fear—that by refusing Ben she was placing him on the dangerous path her father had ordained. "I so hate saying this," she said fiercely. "I'd die inside if anything happened to you, and I value you so much. You make me think, and you make me feel. I need that, much more than I ever knew." She paused, her throat tightening. "But I just can't go from being the future Mrs. Peter Brooks to Mrs. Benjamin Blaine. If you weren't the one who was asking, you'd say I was selling myself too short."

Hurt caused him to look away, and then he tried to cover this with a smile. "It's obvious I talk too much. But you worry too much. I don't see you in an apron, unless that's all you're wearing."

Heartsick, Whitney touched his face. "Whatever happens—even if you have to go away—I won't be married when you come back. That's one thing I'm sure of." She paused again, trying to put words to feelings. "There's so much I have to learn about myself, and about you. For all that's happened, in so many ways I still don't know you."

A glint of anger surfaced in his eyes. "You know enough. Our minds meet, and we're good in bed. Most people never have that."

Whitney drew a breath, then spoke in a more level voice. "I thought I knew my father, and Peter. I didn't. You're a complicated person, Ben, and you take up a lot of space. Sometimes you scare me a little. But even without that, I have to find my way before I can imagine a life with you."

Ben's face hardened in a cast she had never seen, an obdurate mask. "I don't think so," he said harshly. "This feels like our moment, Whitney. In a year or two, I may be dead. You know that, and you've chosen to treat what we have like a summer romance and nothing more. If I get through this, who can say you won't be married? That's an empty promise, a pathetic consolation prize." He stood abruptly. "I'll spare you the awkward days and nights of pretending we're not finished by ignoring where I'm going, and why. Maybe I'll get lucky. But if I wind up getting shot at in some stinking Vietnamese jungle, I'll remember why I'm there—not just by your father's choice, but yours. Even if I survive, I don't think we could get past that."

Shaken, Whitney rose to face him. "You're forcing me to make an impossible choice . . ."

"Am I? Maybe so. But life is choices—at least for you. You're still the daughter of privilege, free to walk away and seek whatever future you can find, no matter what mine turns out to be. So I'm walking away first." He looked at her hard, then said firmly, "Goodbye, Whitney. It's better for me this way."

Gazing into his eyes, Whitney felt guilt, loss, resentment and, beyond that, all the wounds his life had dealt him, too deep for her to salve. He started down the catwalk, then turned to look at her again. "I'll remember you," he said. "You're the one I couldn't have." He stood there for a moment, then finished, "Maybe you'll even remember me. I'm the one who kept you from drowning."

Before she could answer, he turned again, walking swiftly away without a backward glance. A stubborn pride of her own kept Whitney where she was.

Twelve

On the beach at Dogfish Bar, Whitney wept from exhaustion, an aching sense of loneliness and loss. Finally, the shudders wracking her body subsided, and the tears dried on her face. She was all cried out.

What was she now, Whitney wondered, but a strung out girl with an empty feeling in the pit of her stomach, her resources too paltry to navigate the nothingness she faced. Then she recalled her journal.

Writers write, Ben had quoted his professor. *It's like breathing—it's what they do.*

Whitney opened it, staring at the next blank page. Then, haltingly at first, she began to write her future.

Her parents sat on the porch in what struck Whitney as a tableau of their former life, Charles reading the *Wall Street Journal,* with Anne beside him working a crossword puzzle. Regarding them in silence, Whitney felt less anger than sadness, an odd feeling of compassion that she wished seemed more like love than the desire not to jar their fragile hold on this pose of a calm, contented couple. From beneath their veneer, both parents eyed her warily, as though a volatile new element had been added to the play, an ingénue who improvised her lines. With what struck her as exaggerated care, Charles folded the paper in front of him, and Anne placed the crossword puzzle on the coffee table beside her glass of orange juice.

"I'm leaving," Whitney told them. "This afternoon, I think."

Fear stole into her mother's fixed expression. "With him?"

"No. I'm going to Manhattan to look for a job. In publishing, if I'm lucky, but I'll take whatever will support me."

"When did you decide all this?" Charles asked peremptorily.

"A few hours ago. But it's the only thing that feels right to me."

"I assume you'll be moving into the apartment."

Whitney shook her head. "That was for Peter and me, so I'd feel much better if you sold it. I want to make it on my own."

Anne struggled to comprehend this. "But how will you live, and where?"

"I saved up money from all those summers as a camp counselor and what Grandfather Padgett gave me. I'll have to make that last to my first paycheck. As for where, I can sleep on friends' sofas until I find a place."

Anne gazed up at her in dismay, eyes suddenly moist. "This is so very different than what I imagined for you."

"Me, too," Whitney said, then smiled a little. "But it's not like I'm moving to Nairobi—lots of girls do this. In a week or so, I'll call to tell you how I am."

Charles studied her closely, as though discerning something he had not seen before. "Please do," he said firmly. "You're not an orphan, Whitney."

"I know," Whitney answered softly. "Believe me, I know."

Her mother looked perplexed, as though searching for her role in Whitney's new life. "Let me help you pack," she said at last. "Hopefully we can pick out some clothes suitable for the city."

• • •

Before leaving, Whitney took the path toward Ben's house.

She did this without knowing her reasons, or what she would say, but that it would feel cowardly just to vanish. Only when she neared his place did she acknowledge the unpredictable part of her that still craved him, and that might impel her to change course.

On the bluff overlooking the guesthouse, Whitney stopped.

Clarice Barkley stood at Ben's door, her blond hair skimmed back to accent her perfect features. After a moment, he opened it. From a distance he looked surprised—or so Whitney tried to imagine. Then he nodded, and let Clarice inside.

Shoulders slumping, Whitney closed her eyes. Perhaps this was nothing. But she sensed a new dynamic that felt somehow inevitable; she had taken her father from Clarice, herself from Ben, and now their anger at her might feed the attraction between this young man and woman to whom, so recently, Whitney had felt close. Like Whitney herself, Clarice symbolized what Ben must want in spite of his professed loathing —the life of privilege he had never known, the freedom to cross the boundaries that divided a girl like Clarice from the boy who waited on her table. "Poor Scott Fitzgerald," Ben had once remarked, "forever admiring the rich, like a boy with his face pressed against the window of a debutante's mansion." Perhaps Ben understood Fitzgerald all too well. And though Clarice might never tell him of her affair with Charles Dane, through Ben she could exact her quiet revenge on both Charles and his daughter.

Before this moment, Whitney thought, she might have weakened. If so, Clarice had kept her from ever becoming Ben's wife. Then Whitney had one more intuition: that whoever he married —and she suddenly knew that it might be Clarice—the woman would suffer many hours of regret.

Standing there, Whitney fought back tears. Perhaps she was wrong; perhaps she only imagined all this. But whatever the truth might be, she had cried enough.

Beyond the guesthouse, the water glistened in the sun. It had been a long, golden summer, one that might have ended with her wedding. Now her present had parted from her past. There was no mending the rift; all she could do is move into the future armed with nothing but her own heart and mind.

Turning, Whitney walked blindly away, putting one foot in front of the other, each step taking her towards another life. This was all that she could do, or knew to do, until, in some unknown place and time, she met the woman she would become.

EPILOGUE

The End of Summer

Martha's Vineyard

September, 2011

Whitney Dane flicked back a tendril of gray hair. "You must know the oh-so-ironic coda," she told Carla Pacelli. "Ben went to Vietnam and was decorated for bravery. Two years after that he'd written *Body Count*, the first great memoir of the war, paving the way for all the novels that followed. My father had helped make him Benjamin Blaine, the most celebrated writer of our time—chronicler of wars and famine, friend of presidents and prizefighters, and I hardly need tell you, magnet for women."

"No," Carla agreed with the trace of a smile, "you hardly need tell me. But you've made me curious to know how *you* got from there to here. You are a storyteller, after all."

Pensive, Whitney looked around her—at the water, the woods, her parents' white-frame house, the guesthouse where she had once made love with Peter. "Manhattan was right for me," she began at last. "After a few months of temping I found a job as an editor's assistant, then enrolled in a writing class at night. For a couple of years I lived in a walk-up and ate canned soup for dinner. But after some rejections, I placed a story in a magazine. Three years later I had enough good stories that Scribner published a collection.

"By then I'd pretty much worn out my therapist. But I had to work through what had happened— I was too angry and confused, and I didn't trust anyone, really. Especially men."

Carla glanced at the wedding ring on Whitney's hand. "I guess that changed."

"Over time. When Ben came back from Vietnam, I was still single. I'd never heard from him, of course. Instead I had a series of relationships that never quite worked out." She paused, her tone becoming fond. "One night I was in a bookstore, signing my story collection for the occasional discerning customer. I became aware of a guy loitering nearby, with a sensitive face and these amazing deep-brown eyes. When I was getting up to leave he asked me out for a drink.

"He'd already read my stories and wanted to meet the woman who wrote them. He was a painter, he told me, an instructor at NYU. By the end of the night I somehow knew Aaron Ravinsky and I would be together."

Carla nodded. "You dedicated *A Summer in Eden* to him, yes?"

"The least I could do, considering he'd read every page at least three times. Aaron's my most honest critic, and he knows what it means to create. Plus he's wonderful company. We make each other laugh, work through what we need to, and generally reach agreement on the most essential things." Whitney smiled wryly. "The first big one was our wedding—a ceremony at City Hall, followed by a party in the Village where friends supplied the food and drink. Perfect for us."

"And you still hadn't heard from Ben?"

"No. By then he was married to Clarice— thanks to *Body Count*, Ben had the prominence and money to qualify as her husband. Pretty soon Ben was gracing the same social circles as my parents." Whitney's tone held a trace of humor. "The first time I saw him was when, by some terrible accident, all of us were thrown together at a cocktail party in Chilmark—Ben, Clarice, Aaron, me, and my parents. Pretending to be far drunker than he was, Ben draped his arm over my father's shoulder with that pirate's smile of his, eyes dancing. Then he announced to all those assembled that his friend Charles Dane had made him who he was, by encouraging him to volunteer for military service. If it weren't for my father, he'd be a wage slave at a newspaper in some provincial town, and could never have married Clarice Barkley. When Clarice smiled sweetly at my father, Dad's face was a study. At that moment, at least instinctively, I felt sorry for him."

Carla found herself caught between a smile and

a wince. "I'm not sure I'd have liked Ben then. That's pretty diabolical."

"Oh, you have no idea. By this time my father was a very disappointed man. He'd never gotten his cabinet position. He was still hoping for something from Nixon—a plum ambassadorship, perhaps—when Watergate put an end to that for good." Whitney paused, her eyes becoming somber. "But worst of all was Janine. Certainly for my mother, and perhaps for him as well."

Carla felt a sense of foreboding; she had become invested in Whitney's memories, and wanted them to end well. "I was hoping to hear that rehab had taken, like it did for me."

"Unfortunately, it didn't—Janine lacked your strength of character. She became an alcoholic and, perhaps worse, a fantasist. She could only see life through the distorted prism of her own needs, and my mother accelerated her downfall with denial so ferocious that she 'protected' them both as long as she could. Janine married badly, twice, and suffered recurring bouts of bulimia between trips to the plastic surgeon. She died two years ago at sixty-five, looking ten years older."

Carla felt a momentary frisson: for most of her life, she had been valued for her appearance, and—through acting—she had probed every identity but her own. "And Peter?"

"Married a woman from Bryn Mawr, the sister of a guy he'd known in school. After a couple of years, my dad helped him find another job in finance, and eventually they settled in Greenwich and had a couple of kids. My sense is that their marriage is okay, and his career was good enough without being terribly notable." A shadow crossed Whitney's face. "I'd like to know how he feels about his life. But there's really no graceful way to find out."

Carla hesitated. "What about your parents? I don't mean to pry, but you made me feel as if I knew them once, but have no idea what happened later."

Whitney nodded her understanding. "They stayed together, which was no surprise. As far as I know, my father never gave my mother another reason to worry, so I suppose that was a comfort to her." Whitney took a sip of tea, gazing into the cup as if at her own thoughts. "She never knew about Clarice, of course. But after that summer I never saw beneath the surface of their lives. Instead, our family visits took on the quality of Kabuki theatre.

"Still, they got along with Aaron well enough. In Dad's eyes, he was no substitute for Peter, even more so because he was Jewish. But they could hardly fault him as a father, and they absolutely adored our children. I suppose that gave my parents something of a second chance."

"Are they still alive?"

"No. My mom died seven years ago, a few

months after Dad. For a long time before that he had Alzheimer's. When he could no longer live at home, or even remember her, she still visited every day. She seemed happy enough to be there—she was his wife, after all, and there was nothing he could do now to disrupt her world. So perhaps there was something in their marriage after all." Whitney paused, sipping her tea. "Though not by my lights," she added. "As a mother, I was determined to be everything they weren't. So I decided that my children weren't going to be about me, but themselves, and then proceeded to realize my ambitions with a vengeance. David is my father's revenge—he ran screaming from all the creativity around him and became an investment banker."

"The horror," Carla interposed with a smile.

"I still can't quite believe it. As for Rachel, she's the family drama queen, a high-strung beauty who resembles Janine, though darker and with a touch of Jewish exoticism. In her teens, Rachel's highs and lows could be truly harrowing—including, ironically enough, a considerable crush on Adam Blaine. But she's become a gifted writer—her short stories have appeared in the *New Yorker*, and now she's working on a novel . . ."

"So she also takes after you."

"*She* doesn't think so," Whitney amended tartly. "In fact, it rather surprises her that some fairly well-regarded novels were written by a WASP with such a limited emotional range. In *my* view, Rachel still could use a thermostat—as you may soon learn, given that she'll shortly be taking refuge in the main house to complete her novel. Nonetheless, as with David, I take considerable maternal pride in her. Overall, we're a fairly contented bunch, and David's wife is pregnant with our first grandchild." She gave Carla a wry look. "So despite the odds, all of us are living happily ever after. At least for now."

Carla considered how much more to ask. "But not Ben's family," she said at length. "I know what he told me, of course—about Clarice, and about his sons. But I'm still not sure what really happened."

Whitney sat back, teacup in her hand, looking off into the distance. "Ben had this insatiable hunger," she said in a reflective tone. "For all the things he'd never had, and more. When George Barkley's finances went south, Ben swallowed up the Barkleys' life—the house, the boat, the manner of living. Then he swallowed up Clarice." Facing Carla, she said gently, "I know you experienced him differently. But after Adam was born, it seemed clear Ben no longer cared to be faithful. Rumor had him with one woman after another, each more glamorous than the last. It was as though they served as mirrors for the man he'd always wanted to become."

"Did you ever see him then?"

"Only on occasion, and by accident. He always treated me with this curious respect, and never threw what had happened between us back at me. Perhaps because I'd drawn a line with him, as you seem to have." Whitney's expression turned cool. "But Clarice had no image of a life but the one she'd always had. In that life, Ben seized all the power.

"Perhaps he cast too large a shadow, but his relationship with both his sons went bad, as well. With Teddy because they're nothing alike; perhaps with Adam because they're too much alike—father and son, but also competitors, merciless when they sailed against each other. That started with Ben, I'm sure. He'd never really had a father, and perhaps didn't know how to be one."

Pensive, Carla chose not to reveal all that she knew. "That's what seemed so tragic to me," she contented herself with saying. "Ben was filled with regret—for staying with Clarice and for losing his sons. Despite all his success, I think he saw his personal life as a terrible failure.

"Whatever it was, with me he was nothing like his reputation. He stopped drinking when we were together, urged me to keep on going to AA. As he did with your writing all those years ago, Ben had the power to encourage me. We spent hours talking about my future—my plans to give up acting, go to graduate school in psychology after our son is born. He kept saying I could do it, that I'd already shown the willpower. Then, to my surprise, he left me more than enough to accomplish that, and educate our child. For which his wife despises me even more."

Whitney shrugged. "She can hardly claim you disrupted a happy marriage. By choosing Ben to secure her gilded life, Clarice harvested the misery she had coming to her. Perhaps your relationship to Ben was different because you're different."

Quiet, Carla studied the older woman. "Do you wonder what might have happened if you'd married him?"

Whitney looked down. "On occasion," she admitted. "But I had another life, a real one. And there was always the cautionary example of Clarice."

For a long moment, Carla weighed whether to say more. "Perhaps I shouldn't tell you this. But as Ben's death drew nearer, he became much more reflective, willing to share his sadness and regrets. Before he married Clarice, he'd asked another girl to marry him—a woman he respected as well as loved. But she wasn't ready, and he'd walked away out of pride. If he'd been more patient, he thought, his life would have been different." Carla paused, looking into Whitney's face. "He never told me who it was. But now I know the woman was you."

Whitney appeared stunned. Then she shook her head, as if to clear it. "I never imagined," she said in a thicker voice. "But thank you for telling me that." She turned away, looking out at the water. "After all this time, I find it still means something to me. But memories can be more seductive than real, and there's no point regretting the past." Composed again, she turned to face Carla. "I tend to think that character is fate. Perhaps what was fated, in the end, is that you met Ben when he was ready to be different. Whatever the case, it seems to have helped you both."

"It did," Carla assured her. "I think for Ben, and certainly for me." She hesitated. "I only hope this baby will be all right. My mother had way too many miscarriages. Lately, I've rediscovered the need for prayer."

Whitney considered that. "And now there's Adam," she said at last. "But if there's anyone who believes in new beginnings, it's me. I wish you the same good luck I had with mine." She leaned forward, her gaze intent but kind. "In the meanwhile, please stay here in the guesthouse, at least until your son is born. Then you can figure out what's right to do."

In her surprise, Carla found herself inexpressively grateful. "That's more helpful than you can know. Beyond that, I hardly know what to say."

"Nothing will do nicely. After all, it's not as if

I'm obliged to coddle Clarice Blaine's sensibilities." Smiling a little, Whitney added, "It's just something I'd like to do for you—and, I suppose, for Ben. After all, he's the one who kept me from drowning."

Afterword and Acknowledgments

Nineteen sixty-eight, the time of my graduation from college, was the most consequential year of my life, and I would argue, in the recent history of our country. For three decades I've mulled the idea of writing about this time; much more recently, I've focused on the coming-of-age of an imagined young woman of my age and, more broadly, on 1968 as a tipping point for American women. Hence *Loss of Innocence*. While it stands on its own, this novel is also a prequel to *Fall from Grace*, my last novel: it, too, is set on Martha's Vineyard and is part of a trilogy that involves members of the Blaine family, and which will conclude with *Eden in Winter*.

As *Loss of Innocence* required me to imagine the Vineyard forty-three years ago, this required more than a little research. So I am deeply grateful to Carol Brush for her memories of that time, and, especially, to my friend Peter Simon, who lent me his evocative recollections and diary entries. As to the sailing scenes, I would have been literally at sea without advice of Brock Cullen, and my multifaceted friend, Dr. Bill Glazer. And the *Vineyard Gazette* helped fill in the blanks.

Depicting an historic person is never easy, especially one as complex, and as deeply admired, as Robert Kennedy. Critical to this effort was the input of my friend Jeff Greenfield, a close advisor and speechwriter for RFK throughout his campaign. Also important were two books by other friends—*Politics Lost* by Joe Klein, and *Robert Kennedy, A Memoir*, by the late Jack Newfield—as well as *The Last Campaign* by Thurston Clarke. My evocation of the Kennedy campaign and the Chicago convention was also derived from—among other sources—*Miami and the Siege of Chicago*, by Norman Mailer; reports from *Time*, *Life*, and the *New York Times*, and the recollections of Jay Goodman, a delegate to the convention in 1968, whom I thank more fully below.

It's not easy for a sixty-four-year-old man to create a twenty-two-year-old woman as she emerges into adulthood over four decades ago, or to reconstruct the experiences and perceptions of a graduate of a private women's college of that time. So I'm particularly grateful to Betsy Athey, Carol Steiner, and Jill Finkelstein, 1968 alumni of Wheaton College. One of the really fun experiences came when Jill allowed me to crash part of her annual reunion with several classmates who shared their fascinating memories: Kathy Bouckley, Aline Coffey, Jackie Hatch, Nan McConnell, Mardie Prentke, Suzanne Ruch, and

Jill Stewart. It was they who urged me to interview Dr. Jay Goodman, a beloved professor of political science who taught at Wheaton from the sixties until now, and who, I am told, has taught over half the students to graduate from the college in its long and distinguished history. My visit with Jay also gave me a chance to walk around Wheaton itself, which I'd recommend to anyone who enjoys seeing a pristine and beautiful New England campus. Thanks, too, to the alumni relations office at Wheaton, which helped all this happen.

Thanks, too, to my wife, Dr. Nancy Clair, my most faithful reader; my terrific agents at Janklow & Nesbit, Mort Janklow, Anne Sibbald, and Cullen Stanley; my dear friend Philip Rotner, and my wonderful assistant, Alison Thomas. Deepest thanks as well to my publisher and longtime friend, David North of Quercus, and my editor, Jo Dickinson, for their encouragement and advice. On behalf of all those who helped, much of whatever merit exists in this novel belongs to them; the mistakes are all mine.

Finally, there are the dear friends to whom I've dedicated this book. I need not reprise all that the indomitable Ted Kennedy did for our country, and how irreplaceable he is in our civic life; what I want to record here is that it would be hard to find a more generous spirit and considerate friend. And anyone who values a truly public spirit in the public arena knows Eli Segal, founder of AmeriCorps and a central actor in the politics and policy of our time. But equally important to the many young people who followed Eli's example were the power of his ideals, and his gifts as a mentor.

In particular, this book concerns women. The two women who share this dedication with their late husbands are among the most inspiring leaders I know. Not only did Vicki Kennedy share in every particular Ted's protean life in politics, but she continues her own discerning and compelling advocacy on a host of issues from health care to protecting Americans against violence to promoting a more expansive sense of our obligations to each other. Phyllis Segal—aside from being as effective a chair of a non-profit as I've ever seen, and an equally strong advocate for women's rights—is continuing her lifetime commitment to volunteerism by finding new and enriching roles for those of our generation who now wish to use their skills for the public good. Never has a dedication given me more pleasure.